MISADVENTURES & MERFOLK

KELLY RENO

DEDICATED TO
FRANCIS MICHAEL O'ROURKE

Although you couldn't stay here on Earth to read the finished manuscript, your spirit lives on in my heart and your portrait hangs above my desk, reminding me that 'books don't write themselves, you have to sit down and write them.'

There are some special people that I wish to thank who have stood beside me as I wrote this novel. To my husband Fred, a wonderful man who has graciously given me the time and encouragement to follow my dreams - and who never stops encouraging me to make them come true. To Thom Shouse, a kind and generous man who I am fortunate to call my friend, I remain grateful for your expertise, your sense of humor and for your genuine love and true understanding of this old fish tale. And finally, to my Laura Christine Bellerue, a dear friend who has given me a lifetime of friendship and the first spark of inspiration for the character Christine Hamilton. As for the others like the studio executive who said, 'great story, but can we lose the mermaid?" and to the people who raised a brow or two when I set out to write this novel, thank you for your doubt and skepticism, for it fueled me to achieve the impossible.

MISADVENTURES & MERFOLK

©Kelly Reno/2004

ISBN 1-891437-01-1

First Printing: November 2004

Cover design by
Vintage Glory Graphics
with grateful acknowledgment to
The Royal Academy of Arts, London
for permission to reproduce
A Mermaid,
by
John William Waterhouse

REEDS PRESS
(Victorian Essence Press)
P.O. Box 701, Montrose, CA 91021
www.Mer-Folk.com

PRINTED IN THE UNITED STATES OF AMERCIA
10 9 8 7 6 5 4 3 2 1

PROLOGUE

"I soon discovered that there was little else than sheep and senior citizens inhabiting the remote and rugged British Isles, and was undecided on which was the worse of the two.

It was the end of a tiresome and fruitless journey and still, I hadn't delivered a single page of the new manuscript to the publisher who was undoubtedly burning the book contracts at this very moment.

After traveling counter-clockwise from the Orkney Islands through the Outer and Inner Hebrides on sporadic ferries and unreliable public transportation, I was looking forward to the end of the miserable adventure, and at the same time, dreading the moment I arrived back in a province where my cell phone would get reception again. I'd been to sparsely populated islands with names like Rhum, Eigg and Muck, some of them having no automobiles, only tractors to slog their few inhabitants in and out of town – if there even was a town.

Eventually I found myself wandering along the rocky coast of Isle of Skye, my second to last island on the tour. Though it was nearly the middle of summer, relentless, sand-specked winds stung my cheeks and freezing sea spume dampened my hiking boots, seeping into the marrow of my aching bones.

I was miserable. And to make matters worse, I'd lost something invaluable somewhere along the journey. I'd checked every lost-and-found in the grimy bus depots, searched beneath every rock and in every strange face and still, I couldn't locate it, hadn't a clue where I'd lost it, or if I'd ever be in possession of it again.

I'd lost my ability to write

This was far more than just a bout of typical writer's

block. It wasn't that I couldn't write, I just couldn't write anything worth reading. And the worst part of it was – I was under the gun to invent three-hundred pages of witty and profound observations.

I tilted my head skyward, as if searching for answers. Perhaps, I thought, my golden satirical pen had been absorbed like ether into the suffocating blanket of dull thunderclouds I'd trudged beneath for the last month, or perhaps, God himself had snatched it away after I'd written that nasty little number on the Bible Belt last year.

Whatever it had been, whatever I had done to receive this fate, I was willing to repent if I could just get this manuscript written. I was ready to change my ways.

I was ready to make a deal.

Baring my breast to the elements, I began hurling potato shaped rocks into the heavens, attempting to provoke the unseen force that was behind all of this.

Minutes passed and stones flew, just how many I lost count of, and then, as if the breath of the beast itself, a film of hazy fog began to roll in from the sea, the eerie white gloom enveloping my body and everything around me, a terrifying moment that I will never forget.

Oops.

I gulped, willing myself to remain defiant and brave, standing my ground as the vapor thickened and swirled, then thinned again - and there, beyond the gossamer veil of mist, it appeared...

He was a slight, bent character with a walking stick and a threadbare cap of tweed pulled down over a set of ruddy, protruding ears. Spry for his age, he moved toward me at a brisk pace, waving his gnarled wooden cane with a sense of urgency.

Unable to utter a word, I knew that this was what I had been waiting for – this was the moment of truth...

"Av'ya coomapoona weedooglad?"

Perhaps not.

"Pardon me?" I replied incredulously, brushing the sand out of my ears.

He repeated the phrase louder and slower this time with a hint of annoyance rising in his voice. "Av'ya coomapoona weedooglad?!" his eyes alternating between the tumbling surf and the stupefied expression on my face.

"Oh, right, right," I nodded dumbly, hoping that the old bugger would get on his way and leave me alone. But he didn't move. Rather, he stood there tapping the worn leather of his shoe on the slushy sand, his small, cobalt eyes steadily fixed upon mine, telling me that I wasn't going to get out of this conversation with a glib acknowledgment. "Er, I'm not from around here," I explained uncomfortably. "I didn't quite understand what you just..."

He cut me off with a savage grunt, pricked up a finger on each side of his hat, barring a set of tea-stained dentures, "Grrrrrr!"

I instinctively sprung away, alarm bells going off in my head, vaguely recalling something in one of the brochures about werewolf curses in the province.

"AV'YA COOMAPOONA WEE-FOOKINGDOOG!"

"I – I think I have to go now," I stammered, slowly and carefully backing away.

He shook his head in frustration with a ceremonious, "OCH!", then turned and sloshed through the sand muttering to himself, "fookin'shite-mootdoog. Ah'shoodda staadoot-ooom."

Moments later, a sand-encrusted terrier tore across the spewing surf. The old man swung his stick and hobbled after it, leaving me standing there - the proverbial American asshole.

Tripping over my feet, I stumbled off toward a tangled field of heather making my way to a clearing of grass to catch my ragged breath and collect my scrambled brains.

In the distance, the emerald sea continued to churn, its rhythmic waves pummeling on, as they always had, and always would, forever more, no matter what I wrote or thought about this place. And beneath those dull clouds, my life had no meaning – my books had no purpose and I was lost, utterly and overwhelmingly lost.

As I lay there flat on my back, watching the turbulent heavens above, a smattering of black, matted sheep worked their way up the hillside, intruding into my little green plot. Unable to move, I stayed there deathly still, invisible to the dusty, stinking livestock that were inching their way toward the nest of tangled grass beneath my head and I wondered who would miss me if they were to eat me alive. When no one in particular came to mind, I squeezed my eyes shut, waiting for the end.

"Oi," one sheep whispered to the other. "Look at that a-a-a-a-a-rsehole over there pretending to be a rock."

The other stole a slight glance in my direction, bobbing his big woolly head, "Aye. They say he used to be some kind of a famous tr-a-a-a-a-vel writer - 'ad a book on the New York Times best-seller list, he did. Bloody p-a-a-a-a-thetic!"

As I said, sheep or senior citizens. It was a toss-up.

CHAPTER ONE

Things were not going well at all.

Holed up in a gloomy Victorian hotel, and still green with nausea after catching the early morning ferry to Isle of Man, Brendan James slammed the side of the laptop with his hand after rereading the ludicrous e-mail he'd sent off to his editor the night before from a dingy youth hostel.

The first book had topped the New York Times bestseller list within a month of being released by the publisher, surpassing all expectations and instigating a three-book deal.

Three years ago, things were different, things weren't complicated, back when he was an unknown writer traveling Route sixty-six, commenting on the things he saw and quoting the colorful characters he'd met along the ten week journey from California to Chicago. There had been no expectations, no editors riding his ass for another best seller, just an ordinary guy with a coffee-stained notebook and a beat-up Jeep with a full tank of gas.

But things were different now.

This was the last shot. The next book had to be a masterpiece. But there were no words to describe the mundane landscapes and ruined castles and sheep, sheep, sheep that made every island from the Outer Hebrides to the Isle of Skye look and feel exactly the same. There was nothing to joke about, no endearing natives to quote, no seedy ghettos, no deserted factories cluttering up the shoreline to complain about, only vast expanses of gray, dismal nothingness.

Gray.

He never imagined that there could be so many shades of gray in one place. There were at least twenty-five variations of the color, he calculated, ranging from the deep, almost black tones of cigar-ash and old-tire-gray, to the lighter side of the scale where you had your belly-button-lint meets old-sock-gray.

Staring blankly at the empty screen of his laptop, he contemplated how he was going to explain to his editor that his star travel writer not only couldn't write, but was sitting stagnant on his ass, ceasing to write or to travel.

Gazing at his reflection in the monitor glass, he stared back at a mess of disheveled dark hair and a face that hadn't been shaved in three days, mentally adding 'circle-under-the-eyes-gray' to his list.

The critics had once called him a grand travel companion, astonishingly rude, even deliciously witty at times, and always unapologetic. What would they call him now? he wondered as a stream of unpleasant phrases came to mind...

The tiny table in the hotel kitchenette was cluttered with crumpled expense account receipts, miniature size toiletries and a last ditch effort to save his career, a paperback book on overcoming writer's block. Brendan carelessly swiped his belongings off a map of the British Isles and found himself staring down at tiny villages dotting the paper with names like East Butlick and Shagshire Bog, unable to jot down even the most juvenile wisecracks. There was no way to avoid making the dreaded phone call any longer, he knew, picking up his cell and hesitantly dialing the number in New York.

Adventure Books, an experimental imprint of the publishing giant, Reed Press, had been in existence just under four years, specializing in foreign and domestic travel guides with a peppering of humor and adventure essays within the subsidiary's thin catalog - and still hadn't turned a profit. Jake Hogan sat behind his desk, glowering at the life-size cardboard cutout of his most prestigious writer, Brendan James. The piece had been the latest promotional brainstorm from advertising and pictured James standing in a green pasture, dotted with sheep, touting readers to; *Travel the British Isles with Brendan James.* He groaned miserably, feeling far older than his twenty-nine years. Jake was now Editor, having been promoted from an assistant in acquisitions after he'd come across an unsolicited manuscript by a writer named Brendan James. He'd read it over a weekend and recommended it to his Editor-in-chief, who in turn liked it and decided to take it on. The book, eventually released under the title, *Screwed, Blued and Tattooed* had climbed the bestseller charts in record time, putting the small, struggling imprint on the map. The success of Screwed had been the driving force behind a three-book deal with James, whose second book still hadn't sold enough copies to cover the advance money they'd shelled out from Adventure's shoestring budget.

He trembled, recalling the bags of hate mail spurred by that embarrassing blemish titled, *Scorpions in My Jockstrap*, a book so vile that all of the major bookstore chains from Phoenix to El Paso had refused to carry it. In its first week of release, there had been so many complaints and vile reviews, the executives at Reed Press were anticipating the possibility of their first officially 'banned book' the holy grail of forbidden literature. But after the initial hype had fizzled out, the title was largely ignored, rather than officially labeled taboo. Crates of books, still in shrink-wrap were returned to the Reed Press warehouse followed by a flurry of formal complaints from Weight Watchers and The Dixie Chicks to Dr. Laura and the Mayor of Tumbleweed, New Mexico.

It might not have been such a disaster, Jake thought, had Brendan James not portrayed every woman in the Southwest as a truck-stop prostitute and perhaps, if he'd been a little more respectful of the Native American burial grounds on that Indian reservation in Arizona – oh, yeah, and that incident where he landed himself in jail after attempting to ram a 'borrowed' eighteen wheeler through the barriers of Area 51. Sure, he mused, it might have stood a chance. All he could figure was that a screw had come loose somewhere out in that desert heat between Brendan's first and second book, *the major screw that was hinging his head to his neck.*

Unfortunately, Jake's entire future was hanging on the third book. There was talk of discontinuing the Adventure imprint due to weak sales figures on the 'traveling for dimwit's' line combined with, thanks to Brendan James, the astronomical bills from the PR damage control department. But if Brendan somehow came up with another bestseller, something brilliant that crossed beyond the boundaries of travel, as his first book had, the imprint would survive and Jake would still have a job. But if it were to sink like the last abomination – he shuddered at the thought, raking his hands through thinning, blonde hair.

He'd been calling Brendan's cell phone on the

hour for three days now and hadn't received any word back. Bad reception in the remote, British Isles was to be expected, but the deadline had come and gone a week ago and Jake still didn't have a manuscript in his hands. What if he's dead? he fantasized, hoping that the insane writer had at least bothered to drop a finished manuscript in a mailbox somewhere before the natives he'd undoubtedly offended tore him to bits.

A young assistant poked her head through the door. "Brendan James on line two."

Jake's heart thudded in his chest as he snatched up the phone. "Brendan! Where the hell have you been? Where's my god dammed manuscript!"

The long distance connection crackled with static. "Look, I hate to have to ask you this, but…"

Jake rose, smacked the side of the cordless phone and began pacing across the floor. "What! I can't hear you!"

"I need you to extend the deadline on the book for a few more days," Brendan repeated.

"No! No way!" Jake blurted, blood pulsing within his skull. "They've already sent the covers to print and I don't even have the first chapter!"

Brendan leaned against the windowsill, staring mindlessly at the drizzle outside. "Look, I'm working on it. Didn't you get my e-mail from Isle of Skye?"

This had gone too far, Jake glowered, gripping the cordless phone with white knuckles. "What? That crap you sent in on the sheep? What is going on with you, man? Black sheep, fat sheep, talking sheep and sheep – SHIT! Sheep don't talk Brendan! No more diatribes on sheep! I need an in-depth travel essay about the British Isles, not some sick fantasy about the cud-chewing mammal population! We need another Screwed!"

"There's nothing out here!" Brendan growled in exasperation. "How am I supposed to write about *nothing*!"

Jake slugged the grinning, cardboard cutout, toppling it over face-first on the floor. *"Make something up asshole,"* he muttered under his breath. Closing his eyes for a second he managed to restrain his anger for he knew how temperamental James could be. "Look, You're a world-class travel essayist and I need the real stuff that only you can write," he began, attempting to stroke the writer's fragile ego, "the honest, candid interviews with unsuspecting locals, the dirty, gritty details, the same stuff that landed your first book on the best-seller charts. Send me *that* manuscript and I'll put you back on top again."

Brendan gritted his teeth at the words 'best-seller.' "Not on my side, as usual."

"Not on your - !" Jake blurted. "Who do you think got you the three book deal! Your fairy-freaking godmother? No, Brendan! It was me! It was *me* putting my ass on the line for *you*! Me promising the Editor-in-chief two more blockbusters! And this is the thanks I get? A missing manuscript that's about to go to print?!"

"It's just that..." Brendan strained, trying to put it into words, "I can't seem to get the ink flowing through my veins over here. The pressure I'm under, it's making me crazy."

Jake had an idea. It was one born out of desperation, but it just might work. "Hang on a second," he grunted. From a pile of overstocked dimwit guides on his desk, he pawed through the one on Great Britain. "You're on the Isle of Man, right? Okay. It says here they've got Peel castle, motorcycle racing and – here we go. They're having a mermaid festival in a place called Heather Bay. That's a start."

"Come on," Brendan protested. "You know I don't cover *tourist attractions*."

"Right. I almost forgot. You're a serious travel writer – about to blow a serious book deal!" he spat, deciding that there was too much at stake to be respectful any longer. "Look, I'm gonna be honest with you James. In this business, writers don't recover after two bombs in a row and this imprint will be discontinued if you don't come through for us on this one. And no publisher is ever gonna touch you again of you screw this up. Ever. Feast on that."

CHAPTER TWO

Isle of Man was the largest of the micro-islands, nestled directly between Liverpool and Dublin in the middle of the Irish Sea, a place famous for tailless Manx cats and native home to the Bee Gees, although most people assumed they were from Australia – the Bee Gees that is.

From two miles out at sea, the little village of Heather Bay was a picturesque locale with a classic fishing pier surrounded by impossibly high cliffs and a quaint lighthouse with the bold red stripes of a giant's peppermint stick. Wild heather and fields of lavender brushed the tops of the rolling green hills and fairy tale cottages with thatched roofs and grazing black sheep dotted the peaceful landscape beneath a perpetual cover of dark, unsettled skies.

The taxi sped off in the persistent drizzle after depositing Brendan and his soggy luggage before a deserted ferry station where a hand-painted sign hung crookedly from a rusty chain, advertising crossings from Heather Bay to Dublin, twice daily.

He'd spent the afternoon bitterly touring Isle of Man while peering through the rain-streaked windows of a cab that reeked of stagnant cigarette smoke and a greasy pork pie that the driver had eaten for lunch. And the ride had been as dull as the landscape of winding roads, ruined castles, tiny patchwork farms and fields of bluebells, buttercups and primroses, all drooping from the day's downpour. The best idea he'd managed to come up with was to catch a ferry to Dublin, get boozed up on some potent Irish whiskey and deal with the unwritten manuscript in a decent hotel with room service.

He approached the window of the ferry ticket booth and rapped on the glass. "Hello? Anyone there?"

An apathetic man with a yellowed beard in a grimy knit cap tottered over.

"Yeah, hi," Brendan rushed. "What time is the next ferry to Dublin leaving?"

The man blinked at the fast talking American through red-rimmed eyes. "She sunk, lad."

"No, no, no." he shook his head, slowing his words and pronouncing each syllable. "I don't think you understand." He pointed at his wristwatch, then to the water. "What-time-is-the-next-boat-leaving?"

"T'were no casualties," he moaned, stopping to wipe his bulbous nose on the sleeve of his lumpy sweater. "Aye, we're really in the shite over this one. Don't know when they'll send another to replace her. Could be days, weeks maybe."

"You've got to be kidding me," Brendan laughed as a trace of the man's alcohol-laced breath wafted beneath the glass of the window. "You're kidding me - right?"

He shook his jowls despondently, jerking the red and white gingham curtains shut.

Brendan stood alone in the drizzle, his cynical laughter coming to an abrupt halt. Then he remembered the taxi that had dropped him off moments earlier.

"Shit!" he cursed as the taillights disappeared down a street in the village, leaving him stranded. Teeth gritted, he scooped up his belongings and trudged through the blue haze toward the seaside village, smacking his head on the edge of a sagging plastic banner as he passed beneath it, WELCOME TO HEATHER BAY – HOME OF THE WORLD

FAMOUS MERMAID FESTIVAL

The fog horn of a lone fishing boat blared out across the sleepy port to alert the boys in the nearly bankrupt fish smoking factory that another meager load of herring were about to be dumped on her shores. A knot of grisly sea dogs gutted the day's catch into white plastic buckets with sharp knives, grumbling mindlessly to each other about the weather. Curious eyes glanced sideways at Brendan as his heavy hiking boots thudded against the docks, slippery with pungent fish entrails.

The light drizzle began spitting, then evolved into stinging sheets of rain within minutes. Tourists strolling down the pier took cover beneath brightly colored umbrellas and the striped awnings of shops peddling cheap plastic beach goods and postcards of sun bathing fat ladies.

Brendan continued toward the village with his lips fixed into a sneer, undeterred by the video game slot machines, chip shops and other seaside distractions. He'd seen the same scenery in all of the other British holiday resorts and found it all maddeningly dull, even sickening at times. Especially the pasty, dumpling flesh of the British tourists as they exposed themselves to the elements in bikini tops and Bermuda shorts, ignoring ruddy cheeks and gritted teeth as they trudged through gale force winds along the pier. They were a hungry, determined breed, flocking in like vultures for a summer holiday and by God, they would get one even if it meant catching pneumonia in the freezing rain.

Brendan slogged into town, shrouded in his soaking leather jacket. He slung the heavy bag and laptop case over his aching shoulder, noting sourly that the sunny tea houses and feminine boutiques were overflowing with middle-aged women, most of them outfitted in tacky and typical resort garb. Glossy brochures, highlighting the events of the upcoming Mermaid Festival and Midsummer Eve Soul Mate Search were being passed out by a smiling woman with a tight bun of grey hair in front of the tourism office, a small shop front with a single telephone and stacks of promotional leaflets littering its one desk. Brendan accepted a sheet from the drab woman who grinned at him, almost hopefully, "best of luck finding your soul mate, luv."

"Yeah, thanks," he grunted, crumpling the paper in his coat pocket, determined to find shelter.

Further down the block, an overwhelming mist of fruity smelling hair spray hit him unexpectedly as he passed an old fashioned beauty parlor with high ceilings and outdated posters of glamorous hair models hanging on faded pink and white striped wallpaper. Inside, a long row of heated hair-dryer chairs were filled to capacity as the patrons had their rain-flattened locks washed, rolled and set, presumably for the occasion of man-hunting and mischief on the island. A gaggle of spinsters in gaudy, sequined mermaid sweatshirts piled out of the salon, protecting their twenty-pound coifs from the downpour with plastic shopping bags tied around their heads. With vigor and determination, they shoved their way onto the narrow, street, one after another, all in search of a good time. As the mob swept past Brendan, one of the women pinched him on the ass, the wicked laughter cackling from the group like a flock of noisy crows as they swarmed onto the next block, disappearing out of sight.

Lost, a bit shaken and ravenously hungry, he

followed the cobblestone road through the center of the village in search of food and shelter.

On High Street a local shepherd followed a flock of black Manx sheep down the middle of the road, seemingly unaware that the tourists were becoming mingled with his livestock. The gagging odor of steaming, wet farm animals rose to meet Brendan's nostrils as the filthy creatures blindly bumped into his legs, serving as an unpleasant reminder of the conversation he'd had with his editor a few hours earlier, inducing a light sweat to break out on his forehead.

Spotting an inn up the block, he pushed his way toward it, passing fairy-tale Tudor style buildings that housed such proprietors as 'Merfolk Books', 'Fish Out of Water Café' and 'Splash Beachwear.'

A long line of women snaked out the front door of The Mermaid Inn, spilling onto the front brick walk. Hanging before the arched entrance was a large wooden masthead of a smiling mermaid, shamelessly baring her breasts to passers by.

Brendan growled inwardly, noticing the NO VACANCY sign posted prominently in the front window behind a frilly Irish lace curtain. He glanced down the block, searching for an alternative, but wasn't able to spot another inn or hostel anywhere in sight. Just then a clap of thunder exploded across the sky and the rain fell considerably harder, driving the chattering women into the inn and beneath the eaves of the old structure.

Normally he wouldn't have done it. Normally he wouldn't have dreamed of impersonating a reporter from Conde Nast Traveler Magazine, but the situation was anything but normal and called for drastic action. Brendan unzipped his duffel bag and removed a rolled up copy of the slick magazine, knowing that any inn owner would gladly maim and possibly kill to have a favorable write-up in such a prestigious publication. At the very least, it would guarantee him a room for the night, despite the little sign in the window. Ducking to avoid hitting his head on the breasts of the mermaid, he shouldered his way through the crowd.

The inn was warm and dry, crammed with eclectic, antique furniture upholstered in rich velvets and thick brocades. Old oil portraits and landscapes hung on the creamy white walls and the pleasant aroma of beeswax furniture polish, mingled with warm apple tarts wafted through the packed entryway.

Claire Westing was a slender, attractive woman in her mid-sixties with a mane of long silver hair that was swept up in a tidy French twist. A string of hand-blown glass beads hung around her neck and she wore a black cardigan and a pair of simple slacks with her flat working shoes. She'd worked all of her life to make the Mermaid Inn what it was and she was proud of her accomplishments, but she was getting too old for this hotel nonsense. Perhaps in a few years she'd be able to retire.

DING! DING! DING!

She felt the pressure in her temples every time some dammed jackass standing before the counter touched her bloody courtesy bell, reminding herself to mash the thing with a hammer at day's end.

Ignoring the bell, Claire stashed a pencil behind her ear and checked the list on the clipboard in her hand.

Brendan dinged the brass bell again.

Claire smoothed a few stray hairs from her

17

forehead, forcing a pleasant smile. "May I help you?" she asked sweetly through gritted teeth.

He hefted his bag and the magazine onto the counter. "Yeah. I'm checking in. The magazine should have called in my reservation. Brendan James."

She gave the tall stranger a once over, her eyes shifting slightly to the glossy copy of Conde Nast. "Oh my," she breathed, containing her excitement. "And you're here to write about the village in...?" she pointed at the magazine with a slightly trembling finger.

"Right," he smiled, tilting his chin toward an open cupboard of brass keys on the wall behind her. "So, how about that room?"

"Yes, certainly. Just one moment please." Claire frantically sifted through a pile of paperwork behind the counter, trying to figure out how she could have possibly misplaced such an important reservation. No one had called from a magazine that she recalled. She would have remembered something like that. After a moment she stopped sifting and frowned, wondering if it had, in fact, somehow slipped her mind... "Oh, dear. I'm so terribly sorry Mr. James."

"Sorry?" he asked innocently.

Claire apologized again, "It's been bloody batty around here and I've got this group in from London to get situated as well." Her eyes shifted nervously, "I'm afraid we're full to the rafters, but..."

"But what?" He leaned over the counter and whispered, allowing a hint of intimidation to surface in his voice, "what about my reservation?"

"Look," she soothed. "I've got a little place down by the water, reserved only for our very special

18

guests. It's right in the center of the festivities and not a pence more than a room." With a wink she added, "and it's got a really super view of the ocean."

"Great," he nodded. "Let's go."

လ၀ၡ

Claire hobbled down the dock with Brendan's bags in her arms, pointing out a row of boats on the water. "There she is. The one in the middle."

Brendan followed her proud gaze to a sagging houseboat with great flakes of paint peeling off the side. "I don't usually let her out, but I've made a special allowance for you," she continued. "She's all yours Mr. James."

Too exhausted to argue, he accepted the key with a grim smile. "Fine. I'll take—it, her, whatever."

Claire pressed a ticket in his hand. "I'm truly sorry about your reservation. Here, take this. Compliments of the house. The Mermaid Showcase tonight. You won't want to miss it."

He despondently shook her hand. "Right. I can hardly wait."

လ၀ၡ

Inside the musty houseboat the dank air was impregnated with the sickening aroma of mothballs and industrial-strength rat poison. Brendan collapsed on the lumpy mattress as he looked around distastefully at the interior. A trickle of water leaked from one side of the ceiling to the other, forming a large brownish-yellow stain directly over the bed. A pair of gaudy gold lamps sat on a floor of dirty, sea-foam green carpet and frilly, sun-faded curtains completed the nauseating décor - that might have actually matched thirty years ago. Wrenching open the built-in drawers beneath the tiny bed, he removed a dusty wool blanket. As he shook it out, the boat groaned uneasily and rocked to one side sending his laptop and duffel bag sliding across the chipped linoleum table in the kitchenette. He sprang up to catch his belongings and was hit on the nose by another drop of rusty water from a newly sprung leak above the table. On the shelf between a few crusty volumes of poetry, he located a plastic ashtray and slammed it down to catch the spatters. Honestly concerned that the roof might cave on itself, he stood up on the bed, grimly poking at the rotten ceiling with his fingers, wondering what he'd done to deserve this. Several thoughts came to mind…

"Oi!"

The angry voice made Brendan lunge to the floor in a panic as the walls began to shudder from frantic, maniacal pounding that pummeled the flimsy door of his lodgings. The slurring man hollered again from outside.

"Oi! I know you're in there arsehole!"

He yanked back the edge of the tattered curtain and groaned contemptibly. On the dock, a lanky man of forty-five in a straw hat and a pair of sagging Bermuda shorts was poised in front of the houseboat with his bony fists raised for a scuffle. The man bellowed again, his patience waning. "Come out and fight me like a man you slimy bastard!"

Brendan flung open the wobbly door and ducked down as the man swung a weak punch in the air and stumbled backwards, nearly toppling over into the water. Brendan stepped forward and growled, "back off, man! I think you've got the wrong boat."

It took a moment to register with the man that this was not the fellow he'd come to kill. He squinted at Brendan, then let down his guard, his nature instantly shifting from homicidal to friendly as he grinned goofily through a set of big white teeth. "Oh, cheers. So sorry. I thought you were someone else. Name's Julian Wesley."

Without an invitation Julian stepped up on the deck, unaware of Brendan's scowling eyes that were burning into the back of his head. He leaned over the rusted rail and hollered cheerfully at the houseboat in the next slip. "Sarah luv! Bring the zinnie and the cheese next door! We've ourselves a new neighbor!" Julian thoughtfully rubbed a hand across his chin and winked. "American, eh. Sure, I could tell by yer funny accent. Went to Florida once meself on holiday. Bloody hated it." He cocked his head when Brendan didn't respond, "Come on then, speak up man! You've got a name, 'aven't you?"

"*What?*"

Julian took off his hat and settled his lanky body into one of the cracked plastic deck chairs still wet with rain, staring at Brendan with big, protruding eyes. "A name, mate. What do they call you?"

"Brendan," he answered flatly. "And do you always threaten to kill your neighbors?"

The shrill voice of a banshee rang out from the boat next door, "WHERE'S THE *BLOODY* CHEESE KNIFE!"

Brendan shuddered. Julian winked again and hollered back, "In me pocket luv! I was going to drive it through the bastard's heart!"

A moment later the door of Julian's boat creaked open and a leathery woman with a rat's nest of badly streaked hair in an obscenely small bikini top appeared with a cigarette dangling from her lips. She carried a tray of sliced Swiss cheese that had hardened around the edges and had a half-empty bottle of zinfandel tucked under her armpit. She squinted curiously at the stranger beneath the fading sun and smiled.

"Oh, hello luv," Julian smiled. "This is Brendan. Where'd you say you're from again?"

"I didn't."

Julian tugged on the woman's arm to help her aboard. "I'm Mrs. Wesley. But you can call me Sarah." She offered Brendan her hand and one of her press-on fingernails fell off into the platter of cheese. Inspecting the nail briefly, she flicked it onto the deck. "Don't mind him," she warned, shooting Julian a killer look, "Jealous old fool!"

Brendan sat down on a wet, lopsided chair, raking a hand through his hair. "No problem. What's a little death threat between friends anyway?"

Sarah made a sound halfway between a cackle and a cough and tossed her cigarette butt into the water. She divided the remaining wine into three, water-spotted juice glasses and passed one to Brendan, who was imagining what else she might toss into the bay within the next few minutes.

"He thought you was Charlie the Tuna," she brayed. "You know, because that old spinster Claire lets him sleep in her boat sometimes." Narrowing her eyes she inquired, "Say, you're not a friend of his, are you?"

An array of sickening deeds that a man would

have to commit to earn a nickname like 'Charlie the Tuna' flashed through his head as he wondered when the bedding had last been changed. He took a gulp of the unpalatable pink wine that had started to turn. "Charlie - the Tuna?"

Julian's eyes had become seething little slits. "Aye, Charlie the Tuna!" he growled. "The beastly creature that shagged me wife and just about every other female on the island!"

Sarah whacked the side of Julian's head, pleading her case to Brendan. "Jeeee-sus! It was years ago and he acts like it happened last bloody Saturday night!" She pried the cheese knife out of Julian's fingers, "give me that," she hissed.

Still infuriated by the talk of Charlie, Julian shook a warning finger at Brendan. "Keep your women locked up around that Charlie character, I always say! Hell! Use a bloody chastity belt if you have to!" With that he shoved the tray in Brendan's face and smiled pleasantly. "Cheese?"

Brendan waved the pungent offering away, feeling the cheap wine sloshing uneasily in his stomach. "No-thanks."

CHAPTER THREE

The merciless rain had finally let up.

Tourists jammed the pier once again, browsing through the unusual little shops and galleries before closing time, most of them searching for one-of-kind mementos of the island.

The corner of the Mermaid Theater building was the location of The Siren Shop, one of the island's most frequented souvenir boutiques. A pair of top-less mannequins posed in the front window, their slender legs concealed within glitter-dusted mermaid tails. Topping their heads were flaming red wigs with headdresses made of rough fishnet and accented with pearls and bits of colored sea glass. Generous yards of filmy, blue taffeta was draped artfully above the sisters of the sea, and the floor beneath their tails was carpeted with faux seaweed and white sand, a window display that promised unimaginable treasures within the establishment.

No visitor was disappointed as the string of bells on the front door jingled and they found themselves inside the charming boutique, for it was undoubtedly a mermaid collector's paradise. Delicate porcelain mermaid figurines and elaborate mirror and comb sets of sterling silver gleamed beneath the crystal chandelier overhead. In a glass display case beside the cash register was an array of lustrous pearl necklaces, the glory of the pieces enhanced by the folds of black velvet they rested upon. A sign in gold lettering above the case read: GENUINE MANX PEARLS. Upon the shelves and within the narrow aisles of the boutique, shoppers could find jeweled tiaras, dainty seashell wind chimes, handmade blouses in dazzling hues of teal, emerald and salmon, and bangles dripping with coral beads and pewter mermaid charms, all hand-crafted by local artisans.

Christine Hamilton, the shop proprietor was a stunning young woman with a pale, freckle-dusted complexion and the delicate features of the subjects painted in Victorian fairy art. Waves of impossibly long auburn hair tumbled well beyond her slender waist, the fiery color offsetting the pale green dress of translucent fabric that clung to her narrow frame. Perched behind the counter stringing a necklace, she hummed a forgotten Celtic melody to herself. She knew her work well and beaded with steady hands, flawlessly knotting the string between each glistening pearl. Finishing a twisted double strand, she brushed a long tress over her shoulder and held the necklace beneath the bright glow of an antique banker's lamp. Her eyes, flecked green like blades of wild grass, inspected the creation with careful attention to detail. Satisfied, she tied a tiny tag with a generous asking price onto the gold clasp and arranged it in the display case among the other Manx Pearl pieces. She looked up as the brass bell on the shop door jingled cheerfully. Claire Westing let herself inside, peeling off a soggy black raincoat.

Christine smiled, watching Claire going through her usual routine, patting away droplets of rain from her silver hair and efficiently hanging the slicker on the rack beside the door before turning around. Everything about Claire was organized and planned down to the last minute detail, unlike Christine who did what she fancied – when she fancied. The contrast between the two women was perhaps what had drawn them together – that and a history longer and stranger than either of them cared to reminisce about. "Hello Claire. Come to do some shopping, have you?"

Gently shaking her umbrella, she eyed Christine's outfit with a cocked eyebrow. It was breathtaking beyond words. "Beautiful," she breathed.

Christine's wide mouth turned upwards into a bright smile and she stood, modeling the delicate dress made of clinging silk that had been hand-beaded with glittering rhinestones sewn in a fish scale pattern around the plunging neckline. Her thick-soled leather clogs clicked against the polished wooden floor, the filmy fabric fluttering weightlessly as she spun around and around in a pixie dance. "Well? What do you think? I just got these dresses in. Aren't they fabulous? Margaret Howler over in Douglas brought them in just yesterday for the festival. I'll hold one in your size if you like," she offered, indicating three similar dresses on the rack in the center of the shop.

Claire laughed inwardly at the thought of herself squeezed into such a youthful style. "Yes girl. I can just see myself now. A mutton in lambs clothing. No thank you. But they are lovely. You're sure to sell them all."

A trio of awed tourists entered the shop. Christine waved a friendly hello, then turned back to Claire. "So what brings you down here?" she whispered. "The Inn overflowing with estrogen?"

"Aye. It is," she replied, lowering her voice. "But I'm here with a bit of news about the other side of the gender divide."

Christine looked at her warily, "news?"

Although the lines on Claire's face were deep,

26

the sparkle in her cloudless eyes unmistakably gleamed when she was up to mischief. "I let the houseboat to a handsome stranger this afternoon," she chirped in a sing-song voice.

It was annoying, she thought, how Claire was endlessly trying to find her a proper match. She'd have thought her best friend would have had more important things to think about with the festival week just beginning. Christine shooed her away with a grin, "oh no you don't. No more matchmaking."

"I'm not 'matchmaking' as you call it," she defended, adding with a wink, "I invited him to your show tonight and I thought you'd like to know."

Christine looked away disinterested and began rubbing at an imaginary spot on the glass countertop. "Is that so?" she scowled. "Why is it that you are endlessly trying to fix me up with a man? I've told you time after time..."

"He's a writer from a big American travel magazine," she interrupted, "and he's come here to cover the festival. By the looks of him, I don't think he's got love on his mind, so you've nothing to worry about."

"Oh," she blushed.

Wanting to giggle, she took Christine's smooth hands in her own. "Imagine our village featured in an important magazine. Why! Think of what it could do for tourism here, especially in the off season."

She allowed the thought to cross her mind. True, such an article could generate more revenue for the village during the other eleven months of the year, a standing wish that the local shop owners had talked about countless times over tea – but there was more at stake should anyone ever really discover... She gazed dully out the window at the evening purple mists that were fading fast into solid blue. "I don't know."

Claire patted her hand, "so, we'll see you after the show then. It's all settled." She slipped back into her coat and opened the door a crack. "You can save your thank-you's for later," she called over her shoulder, feeling that her efforts had gone slightly unappreciated. "Just thought you'd want to be prepared." She glanced at the leather clogs on Christine's feet with a grin. "Nice shoes you old ninny."

Looking down at her feet, she opened her mouth to say something, but Claire had already disappeared onto the street outside. "You're a pain in the arse. You know that?" she mumbled under her breath.

The bells on the front door of the Siren Shop jangled as the door shut itself. Flipping over the CLOSED sign, she walked across the floor to help her final customers of the day.

ço‑ɔ

A blanket of fog had rolled in from the North where the restless Irish Sea merged with the twinkling, fairy lights of Heather Bay Village.

The houseboat rocked, then settled as Brendan snapped his cell phone into the charger, giving up on arranging transportation off of the island until the following morning. He figured he could catch a taxi back to Douglas and hop on a one-hour flight to Dublin where he'd deal with the unwritten manuscript in more comfortable surroundings. Glancing up dismally at the sagging ceiling of his lodgings, he suddenly found himself growing desperate for some fresh air. Remembering the theater ticket the old woman had given him, he pulled on a bulky wool sweater and put on his damp coat, preparing for the ten-minute jaunt from the docks to the pier.

Antiquated fishing boats seemed to creak and groan to each other about the hard day's work and the shrill cry of a lone seagull still hovering around the chip shops, rang out in the night. With sensible hiking shoes on his feet, Brendan made his way down the ancient cobblestones of High Street. An open carriage driven by a weathered character in a battered leather hat and grubby corduroys was pulled along by a stout workhorse. A pair of loud American tourists in the back of the coach were yapping on and on about the 'quaint little shops' and arguing over what to bring home for mother as they soaked in the evening ride through the magical, timeless village. The tourists rolled past Brendan, their curious eyes still peering into shop windows that would have to wait until morning to be investigated.

There was an air of old in Heather Bay, steeped in rich history like a bitter cup of black tea, that seeped beneath the skin of the hard-nosed writer as he walked through her twisting alleyways and mists of bluish fog that seemed to hang around in patches. Once a pirate's smuggling cove and later, the center of the Manx fishing industry, every brick, stone and wooden beam in the village smelled of centuries old chimney smoke and salt-encrustation, evidence of its intimate connection with the sea. The people of this place, much like its structures were hearty and warm, and a little bit hardened around the edges, Brendan thought, likening them to the Swiss cheese the Wesley's had offered him. Like every other seaside port, the inhabitants prided themselves on endurance and welcomed the outsiders with open arms, but they always could be counted on to watch with one wary eye.

An hour earlier, Brendan had come across an elderly man as he hand-wove fishing nets across the dock from the houseboat. After inquiring about his craft, he'd learned that although the fishing industry in Heather Bay still existed, it was not what it once was. A nostalgic sadness could be seen in the eyes of the old man as he spoke of the ways of his generation, the old language and the culture and how it had all slowly eroded away 'beneath me Wellington boots.' International freighters now imported the bulk of Britain's fish and nylon mesh had replaced the intricate hand-woven traps and colorful blown-glass balls used to float them, trades from days forgotten. Most of the fisheries had long since closed their doors for business and only a handful remained on the island. The most abundant fish, the Manx herring, better known as kippers, were no longer a staple in the native diet. The small fish, cured in smokehouses until reddish in color, was merely an interesting local food for curious tourists to sample. With her silver mines purged and her dwindling fishing fleets, it was evident that time and technology had slowly encroached upon the old ways of the island, reducing the proud industries of the village to little more than a pleasant weekend break. But the locals were strong sea people and had managed to adapt.

It was depressing, he thought, an entire village reduced to putting on a flashy festival for tourists to generate enough revenue to scrape through the remaining months of the year when the place turned into a literal ghost town.

The once glamorous Mermaid Theater stood prominently at the end of the pier, looking like an aged showgirl whose better years had long since passed. The art deco architecture awkwardly set the structure apart from her ill-fitting surroundings of ramshackle card shops and stalls that sold fishing bait and pints of hot tea in jumbo sized Styrofoam take away containers.

Consume and take away, he thought, glancing at a line of eager tourists wrapped around the building, its façade of cracked stucco painted in faded, pistachio green.

A large column at the front of the theater shot skyward, topped with a neon trident that flashed on and off, illuminating an eerie green glow through the haze in the nighttime sky and the bold black letters on the marquee read; LIVE MERMAID UNDERWATER FANTASY SHOW TONIGHT.

Brendan stood before the theater, rubbing the ticket between his fingers, wondering why he'd bothered to come. He shook his head miserably, turning to leave, and restlessly considered returning to the dank houseboat. It was remotely possible, he thought, that he could scrape together a chapter or two from the sporadic notes he'd taken during the earlier leg of the tour. Something had to be sent in to Jake in New York and he had to get himself inspired. Perhaps a drink would do the trick.

Claire spotted Brendan pacing outside the theater and rushed his way. Smoothing down her simple wool dress, she touched him lightly on the shoulder. "There you are," she sang gaily. "Come inside where I've got a nice seat waiting."

Glancing over his shoulder, he acknowledged his apple-cheeked hostess with a nod. The notes could wait for an hour, he decided. After all, he'd shamelessly lied to the woman about being an important magazine reporter and inwardly felt he owed her at least one opportunity to impress the hell out of him with a rinky-dink mermaid show designed for eight-year-old girls. What the hell, he could find a pub later.

Claire whisked her guest past the line of tourists and through the front doors of the theater. She whispered something into the usher's ear, a skinny youth dressed in a shabby uniform with gold braid embellishing the cuffs and brim of his pillbox hat, who nodded, letting them pass through the red velvet rope.

The interior was the size of a small movie theater, outfitted with crushed velvet seats in pale blue and a high arched ceiling with moldings of giant sea horses and shells, all painted in a blinding shade of aquamarine with gold leafing. A moth-eaten burgundy curtain concealed the stage and a sleepy band of old men provided pre-show entertainment, playing nostalgic seaside favorites from an era or two gone by. Claire escorted Brendan to the front row. "Here you go Mr. James."

Leaning back in the overstuffed seat, he turned to his hostess who was gleaming with enthusiasm. "You didn't have to go to all this trouble on my account."

"'Twas no trouble at all," she chirped.

Brendan stretched his neck. "I mean, just because I'm writing about the village and you happen to own a hotel that's seen better days..." he began, letting the concept hang in the air.

Claire clearly understood where the cocky American was going with this. He was testing her, probably wanted free lodgings. "Can I ask you a personal question?" she smiled.

"Fire away," he yawned, disinterested in whatever she wanted to know. He didn't care. He'd be drunk in an hour and gone in the morning.

"Are you always such a wanker?"

The seriousness with which she asked the question made him feel like laughing. But there was genuine concern in the old woman's eyes as she waited for him to reply.

"Yeah. Pretty much," he admitted. "You've got me pegged Claire. And you know what? I think I like you — even though you screwed up my reservation."

Her eyes bore into him slightly, "I may have made a mistake, but I'm certainly not going to go on kissing your arse over it if that's what you're after."

"What?"

Claire patted his hand with a fresh smile she'd managed to generate on behalf of the local businesses that were in dire need of some decent publicity. "Well, I hope you enjoy the show and your stay here because we can use all the good press we can get on the island. I mean, after the festival, things certainly quiet down around here." She furrowed her brow. "Is it the houseboat dear? Does it not suit you?"

"Oh, no, no. It's great," he waved, recalling the floating derelict where his luggage was stashed. "A little seasickness, homicidal neighbors and a thousand mermaid freaks within stones throw? It makes the whole experience very - colorful."

"You've met the Wesley's I take it," she sighed with great annoyance. "I should have warned you about those - people."

"Warned me?" he laughed cynically. "You should have armed me, lady."

Her smile was apologetic. "I can only imagine what they've already said to you. You've got to understand, the Wesley's are not an accurate portrayal of people living in the village, you see. God knows we put up with them, but with his drinking and her loud abrasive manner..." Claire lowered her voice to a hoarse whisper, "houseboat rubbish is what they are."

"What," he snorted. "Is that like trailer trash or something?"

"Listen," she suggested. "I've got a couple checking out of the Inn tomorrow and I should be able to get you into a proper room by mid-afternoon."

"I think I can handle the Wesley's. But thanks," he grinned, making a mental note to talk with the obnoxious couple before he left town, especially after learning that the other villagers were ashamed of them.

Claire was uneasy about all of this. What if he were to write about Julian and Sarah? It would be a bloody disaster. She'd have to figure something out, maybe go and have a chat with them.

The theater lights dimmed overhead, a cue to the band of old men to end off with the antiquated tunes. Brendan yawned, keeping his eyes on the stage out of sheer politeness as the curtains parted

But behind the wall of velvet was not a stage as he'd expected, rather a twenty-foot tank of water rivaling any standard movie screen in size. A very old woman with a hunched back sat on a chair at the front and plucked out a sweeping, dramatic Celtic melody on a massive golden harp. As the music filtered through the theater, pink lights and clouds of tiny bubbles began to rise from the bottom of the tank. Claire was watching Brendan to gauge his reaction.

"Ambitious," he muttered unimpressed. "Shouldn't we be wearing plastic ponchos, being up in the front row and all?"

"You're a long way from Sea World lad," Claire quipped.

And then she appeared, a flash of woman and shimmering silvery scales with a wild tangle of flowing red hair descending into a froth of effervescent bubbles in the tank before him. With one eyebrow permanently cocked, Brendan tugged at the neck of his sweater as the temperature of his body rose, watching Christine Hamilton glide through the water, looking like something out of a big-budget fantasy film. The hardened audience of ordinary people let out a collective "oooh", despite themselves, as the mermaid in the tank spun in dizzying spirals. Long fingers of auburn tresses trailed behind her like dancing flames and her skin glowed translucent under the pink lights, illuminating the pair of cupped seashells on her breasts that had been fashioned into a scanty bikini top. As she twisted downward, light danced off the glimmering, platinum scales of the fish tail that concealed her narrow hips and long legs, leaving him unsure where the woman ended and the costume began. She was fascinating, he thought, from her unruly red hair to the large tattoo on her back of a Celtic mermaid, and he found himself unable to remove his eyes from her.

"Isn't she something to look at..." Claire breathed.

He had to admit, he'd never seen anything quite like the mermaid in the giant fish tank before him. "Who is she?" he whispered to Claire, unable to completely avert his eyes from the silly show. He'd already made up his mind to get an interview with the local siren, if for no other reason than to get a closer look at the costume she was wearing.

"You'll meet her later," Claire smiled smugly. "If you behave yourself."

Behind Brendan's back, Claire waved to Christine, doing her best to draw the mermaid's attention to the guest of honor. She swam to the front of the tank, her filmy and very realistic tail propelling along with skilled shimmies. From the floor, she picked up a lacy fan of salmon colored seaweed and hid shyly behind it, her hair rising upward in a spray of bubbles.

Christine saw Claire through the glass pointing a finger at the American behind his back. "That's him! That's him!" Claire mouthed silently.

From the corner of his eye, Brendan saw what the old woman was doing and began wondering what sort of plans these two had in mind for him. This night might actually turn out to be interesting, he mused. *Perhaps an encore performance in a hot tub...*

Peering out from behind the faux seaweed, Christine looked directly at him for a moment, then rose to the top of the tank.

As faint applause echoed backstage, Christine surfaced, grabbing onto a metal bar mounted on the wall. With ease she pulled herself over the edge and onto an old hotel luggage cart with its base covered in green astro-turf. Checking to be sure the long shimmering tail was securely on the cart, she pushed herself down a corridor toward the dressing room.

CHAPTER FOUR

Claire led Brendan through the crowd in the Mermaid Theater lobby, occasionally pointing out photographs and oil paintings on the lofty walls. She nodded toward and old black and white picture of a handsome young dandy. "And this was Christine's grandfather. He built this theater for Athena, the last mermaid."

"I'm a writer, not a tourist," he muttered, his mind numb with the dull chatter about the theater and its history.

Yapping on, Claire was oblivious to the fact that he wasn't listening to her. "Oh yes. Jack was a poor fisherman until he met Athena – and they say he fell in love with her." She leaned close to Brendan's ear and whispered, "Soon after, he discovered a horde of oysters right here in the bay. Made his fortune in pearls."

"Yeah, send me the brochures," he waved.

She glanced at him sideways, now aware that he was brushing her off. "So anyway," she continued, "after Athena died, Christine's mother took over the theater and now Christine runs things. Even after all these years, the show hasn't changed much. She likes to keep it authentic."

Authentic what, he wondered.

"I'm a mermaid mummy! Look mummy! Look at me! Wheeeeeee!" A little girl in pigtails and a frilly white dress had broken away from her mother and was running wildly through the lobby in circles. She bumped into Brendan's leg with a thud and kept going. Giving him an apologetic look, the woman lunged and snatched her child firmly by the arm. She whispered sternly to the little girl, "Now dear. That is not the way we behave when we're out. You know that mermaids aren't real."

The girl's bottom lip trembled, "but they are real mummy! We just saw one! The most beautiful one of all..."

Claire smiled at the child's mother and knelt down next to the girl. "I believed in mermaids once, a long, long time ago." Claire tilted the child's chin upward and whispered in her ear, "and she is the most beautiful mermaid. But it's a secret – some grownups don't believe."

With a polite smile, the woman hauled the spinning child off, unaware of what the old woman had said to her. The little girl looked back over her shoulder at Claire with a jack 'o lantern grin on her face.

Brendan shoved his hands in his pockets. "Nice job. You've just warped the poor kid for life."

"There is absolutely nothing wrong with encouraging a child's imagination," Claire countered. "Besides, it's all true."

"Right," he nodded, checking his watch and wondering what time the pubs in this town closed.

Claire studied him, cocking her head as if measuring him up in some way. "Ever been married yourself?"

He looked at her suspiciously, unable to avoid a bit of sarcasm, "Why? You asking me?"

"Oooh," Claire grunted. "You are absolutely impossible."

She pointed out a winding staircase that led to the upper level of the theater. "There, second door on the right. That's where you'll find Christine's dressing room." She shook a finger at him. "And your manners! She's a very sensitive girl."

The murky black waters of the Irish Sea twisted and churned beneath tumbling rain clouds and bulky fog. Beyond the crashing waves, a lone voice howled above the whistling wind that propelled the craft toward the hazy coastline of Heather Bay.

"Awoooooooooo!"

The billowing clouds above parted, revealing a slice of ethereal green radiance in the nighttime sky. The Northern Lights were dancing in the heavens like ghostly spirits, dropping shadows of dazzling light across the powerful swells.

A teak vessel from the 1930's with its unfurled sails billowing, skipped across the rising emerald waves, manned by a single soul. Charlie Hamilton stood at the deck of the craft as the wind swept through his longish black mane, contrasting drastically against his ashen complexion. He was a tall, gruesomely handsome lad in only a pair of faded jeans and a white fisherman's sweater, despite the nearly freezing temperatures. The illumination above streaked mistily down in shafts on his boyish, chiseled features as his wide eyes tilted up at the heavens and he basked beneath the greenish glow, his smooth skin beginning to prickle with desire. He gazed toward the blurry lights outlining the rocky coast, nearly able to taste the human misery upon his tongue, the salty tears, the unanswered cravings, the longing of aching souls as they secretly called out for him to come to them in the pitch black of midnight...

But above all, he was going to her, to stand beside his beloved, for he knew that she must be protected and carefully watched over, especially during the season when the lights above the atmosphere overcame her every cell with the same, unquenchable desires that were filling his right now. The need to taste them, to love them, the insatiable desire that was gravitating and navigating his course toward the island. He inhaled the sharp ocean spray that crashed against the head of the craft as it plummeted down another large swell. He was close to them, he was nearly there now. His full, youthful lips curled into a devilish grin, his eyes glittering against the blackness of the sea.

৩৯৫৫

From the top of the staircase, Brendan peered down the long dark hall, stopping before a door with a starfish affixed to it with the name *CHRISTINE* spelled out on the dried creature in pink rhinestones. A trail of water streaked across the wide corridor, ending next to the luggage cart that was still dripping. He stood for a moment re-evaluating his reason for being there, and reminded himself that he was supposed to be there from the magazine. The entire area reeked of chlorine and lavender he noticed as he knocked on the door.

A sultry, female voice with a heavy Manx accent rang out, "come on in Claire. He was sort of handsome, although it's so hard to tell through all the muck on the glass. Would you help me with this strap?"

Creeping into the dressing room, he watched her with unexpected amusement.

Oblivious to his presence, Christine towel dried her long hair in front of an art deco vanity where a large vase of lavender sat before her. The silvery

mermaid tail, still encasing her legs glistened beneath the orange light of a crystal chandelier outfitted with a dozen tiny flicker bulbs.

He squinted to get a better view, the tail looked
so realistic...

With a step forward, his tall frame appeared in
the mirror as she struggled to untie her top.

The strap snapped, sending the shells clatter-
ing to the floor. Catching his reflection in the mirror, she turned around slowly to face him with only
a wisp of red hair covering her breasts. She quickly
sized him up, not a bad looking man, she thought,
taking in his tall build and the city smirk on his unshaven face. Taking a step backwards, his mouth
slightly gaping, he was unable to avert his eyes from
her perfection. Her gaze was clear and intruding as
if she could see right through him. She sat still,
watching him fumble with his hands as he tried to
politely avert his eyes. "What?" she asked with a
cool, half smile. "Haven't you ever seen a mermaid
before?"

This woman was not flustered by her state of
near nakedness, rather embraced it, used it to get
what she wanted, he guessed. A bemused smile
flicked across his face, a mere reaction to being so
near to this perplexing female with the upper body
of a Victoria's Secret model and the lower half of a
rainbow trout. She stared him down with intense,
piercing eyes as he cleared his throat. "Me seen a
mermaid? No, actually. I haven't," he rushed. "But
it's been my utmost pleasure." Stepping a little
closer, his mind raced with thoughts of what might
occur in the next few moments. "Look, Claire said
that you'd be up here and I wanted to get an interview with you. You know, up close and personal?

But I suppose we've just taken care of that part." He offered her his hand. "Brendan James."

Reporters, she thought distastefully, intentionally ignoring his gesture, they flocked in year after year, summing up the village and its inhabitants in a few fluffy paragraphs. Disinterested, she went back to brushing her hair, sweeping the fiery strands over her shoulder. "Christine Hamilton," she responded lazily between strokes. "So, you're the writer. A big magazine is it?"

He found it difficult to concentrate as she sat there so immodestly. For a moment he wondered if she'd recognized his name as the author of 'astonishingly rude' travel essays. Unavoidably, his eyes swept over her delicate skin, dusted with flecks of cinnamon freckles. Her small, rounded breasts, now in full view, rose and fell with her every breath she drew and he felt himself stiffen. She watched him watching her, making him feel exceedingly uncomfortable, just the way she intended it, he supposed.

Bending over, he picked up her top from the floor to keep his fidgeting hands busy. "Yeah. Maybe I should come back tomorrow," he suggested, setting the shells on the counter.

"Tomorrow?" she blinked with childish innocence.

"Er, for the interview?"

A sigh escaped from her lips as she removed a glittering gemstone ring from her long, slender finger. "You assume much Mr. James," she said to the reflection in the vanity. "I'll have to think about it."

He was taken aback – baffled really. Who was she to play games with him? For God's sake, he was impersonating a reporter from Conde Nast Traveler! "*You* want to think about it?"

Aggravated by his presumption that she would automatically leap at the opportunity for a little publicity, she snapped the lid of her cherry wood jewelry box shut and turned around with a cool expression masking her delicate features. "Not everyone longs to be written about in glossy magazines. Some prefer a quieter existence."

Brendan eyed the flamboyant costumes and sparkling baubles that filled every inch of space in her dressing room. Two convincing, mermaid tails like the one she wore now, one in pink and the other in blue hung from a brass rack on heavy duty coat hangers. Quiet. Right, he thought. "Like you?" he asked, sarcasm straining in his voice.

"I'll let you know," she mused, fixing her eyes upon his, deciding on a sudden whim to give him a little more than he'd bargained for. As he searched for a clever reply, she seemed to be taking him in, holding him helplessly in a hungry stare. Her eyes closed, then slowly opened and she was gazing at him again, this time, her eyes smoldering. Whatever it was she was doing to him... He breathed in again deeper...

The erotic perfume that trailed around his head like a veil of invisible smoke was becoming unbearable. He stood, almost paralyzed as an impossible, magical essence of the swelling ocean, mingled with notes of deep, heady musk seeped into his nostrils, saturated his skin and entered his bloodstream, promising undreamed of pleasures... Tiny droplets of sweat began to form on his brow and his heart thudded wildly within the wool oatmeal sweater that covered his clammy skin, now tingling and sweltering with sensation.His legs trembled with weakness, his vision blurred slightly. Unflinching, she sat before him like a dangerous spider in the center of her intricately woven web, waiting - daring him to move a muscle. He tensed, fighting off the painful instinct that begged him to take her right then and there, to taste her skin of fresh cream, to bury himself in her tangle of supple, radiant tresses, to utterly explore every inch of the exquisite, precarious creature before him...

"Oidhche mhath..."

How long he had been standing there in a dazed stupor, he didn't know. Her sultry mouth had just whispered something incomprehensible in what sounded vaguely like Gaelic. "What?" he rasped groggily, shaking his head.

Her lips curled, "Oidhche mhath. It means good night."

Opening his mouth to speak, no words came from his dry throat. He couldn't understand it, the overwhelming attraction he was feeling toward her. Thoroughly baffled, he glanced at her sideways before rushing out the door.

Christine allowed herself a snigger as his footsteps thudded heavily down the corridor. She'd enjoyed toying with him immensely. *Perhaps a little too much*. This one had been stronger than the others, she thought, her curiosity about the American aroused. He'd be back, she assured herself. They always came back for more.

By the time Brendan had reached the staircase above the arched lobby, his head was beginning to clear and the hazy feeling had subsided a little, but he was still reeling within from the encounter. Taking a deep breath, he collected himself before the descent down.

.Claire spotted the American as he reached the bottom of the flight. He appeared stunned, as she figured he might be after spending time in a closed room with Christine.

She rushed to his side. "You're leaving already? How did the interview go?"

"It was very — revealing," he managed. "Do you know where a guy can get a drink around here?"

"That'd be the Siren's Whale you're looking for," she offered sympathetically as if she understood his sudden yearning for alcohol. "Unfortunately, she does have that effect on men sometimes." Watching him for a moment, she noticed that he was swaying slightly. With a hint of concern in her eyes, she dug through her alligator skin handbag and shoved a small metal tin beneath his nose. "Would you fancy the smelling salts, then?"

"Auugh!" he snorted, swiping the tangy stench from his nostrils and shaking his head incredulously, "You - you carry smelling salts in your purse?"

"Always," she nodded emphatically. "Never know when they might come in handy around here."

Brendan waved contemptuously, "I don't know what you people are up to around here, but…"

"Really, I can explain…," she offered, realizing she'd just made a terrible mistake.

He held up a hand and exhaled, "please, don't bother."

Before she could elaborate, he'd stalked off toward the exit. Watching helplessly, he passed through the velvet corridor and vanished into the ghostly fog beyond the great panes of curved glass. "Sod it!" she steamed under her breath, glancing antagonistically at the second floor landing where Christine was undoubtedly still perched before the mirror in her dressing room, just chuffed to bits that she'd managed to transform the most important reporter in the village into a bloody blob of gelatin!

But she'd deal with that later.

Grumbling to herself, Claire pushed through the thinning crowd, ducked into an arched alcove and frantically punched a number into her cell phone.

ഗ൧

Glowing golden light flickered through the diamond shaped windowpanes of the ancient Tudor style pub, situated in the middle of the village. From the quiet cobblestone street outside, the sounds of rough, local voices coated with heavy Manx accents rose and fell, mingled amongst a backdrop of lively Celtic music. Brendan shivered in the fog and passed beneath a warped wooden sign depicting a mermaid riding on a whale's back that hung over the front entrance. As he reached for the gleaming brass handle of the thick wooden door, he imagined the Siren's Whale was the kind of place where the local sea dogs gathered after a day's work at the kipper factory to share the latest wise cracks and pass along remnants of village gossip. Local pubs were not among the kind of establishments he made a habit of frequenting, but he really felt like a drink after his stunning encounter with the girl, whose essence was still lingering in his clothing like an overpowering perfume

Brendan took a seat at a barstool upholstered in red vinyl, well aware of the suspicious local eyes upon him. He peeled off his leather jacket and soaked in the native atmosphere. A crackling, fire blazed and popped in the wide stone fireplace and he inched his back toward the flames attempting to melt off the chill that he hadn't been able to shake since he'd arrived in the village five hours ago. As the glowing embers began to warm his back, he noticed a mummified creature looking something like a half-pig, half-porpoise that was perched behind the bar above an assortment of mismatched bar glasses. Framed tabloid magazine articles and faded, local newspaper clippings about the hideous thing were hung on the walls of the establishment with sensational headlines such as CREATURE APPREHENDED and MERMAID CANNED.

Gazing around the unusual pub, he noticed that the floor of splintery wooden planks was in need of a good sweeping. The aroma of greasy pork pies wafted through the bluish air, dense with cigarette and pipe smoke, giving him the odd feeling that he'd stepped backwards into another century. A trio of local musicians played a rollicking seafaring melody with effortless coordination on a tiny corner platform. Brendan found his toes tapping along with the rhythm of a hollow drum, pounding out the steady cadence of a jaunty, Celtic melody in a surprisingly superb display of skill and musicianship. Sweet, lively notes from the violin flowed with the joyful trilling of the tin flute, the complete effect of the song twinkling through the room like flitting fairies. He felt fortunate to have happened upon this rich and genuine music that was played from the heart, evident by the empty tip box on the edge of the stage. Despite the occasional, sideways glances from the local fishermen, he felt the tension in his neck and shoulders easing up for the first time in weeks.

A large man in his late thirties with a shock of unruly black hair appeared behind the bar through a pair of swinging double doors. Brendan swiveled in his chair to place an order, noticing that the man wore a red vest and an apron stained with splotches of beer and flour that was wrapped snugly around his barrel-like physique. The bar man curiously eyed Brendan and nodded, "What'll it be mate?"

"Yeah. What have you got on draft?"

"Guinness."

Brendan waited for him to spout off the rest of the selection, but he didn't. The burly bartender stared at him blankly.

"And bottled?" he finally prompted.

The bartender hocked his chin toward some bottles behind the counter with odd-looking labels, lined up in a neat row. His big chest puffed up with pride, or possibly flatulence as Brendan noticed that a button or two had popped off the man's wool vest. "Aye. We've got the finest selection of local micro-brews on the island. Mermaid's Milk Lager, Codsucker Ale, Poop Deck Pilsner and Thar' She Blows Dark."

He shuddered with a ripple of repulsion. "Thar' She Blows Dark?"

"Wicked bitter shite, that one. Rip the hair right off your arse," he warned with a grin.

"Uh, better make it a Guinness."

The man grabbed a glass, released the tap, tilting it sideways and slid a thick-headed pint across the counter. Wiping his hands on his apron, he suddenly remembered something, putting a finger to his nose. "Ah, sure. You're that American in town to write about the Mermaid Festival. I shoulda known!"

Swallowing a gulp of the dark brew, Brendan squinted suspiciously. Claire again, he frowned, the busybody who had elected herself his own personal cruise director.

The bartender's soppy brown eyes were fixed on Brendan as he nodded his big head up and down. "Sure. Claire Westing rang, said you'd be heading down here, told me to look after you." Letting out a low whistle, he smiled enthusiastically. "Conde Nast Traveler, is it? Pretty glamorous shite for these parts."

Forcing a smile, Brendan wondered about the legalities, should he decide to actually write anything about these people in his book after intentionally misleading them. He had to get out of this place. Just after this drink, he promised himself.

The bar man nodded at his pint glass and snatched a packet of potato crisps from a rack against the wall. "That's on the house, man, and these too. I'm Michael Blake," he grinned, offering a meaty, flour dusted hand. "Welcome to Heather Bay."

"Er, Brendan."

Michael inquisitively glanced at the American with a twinkle in his soft, sable eyes. This could be the big break he'd been waiting for, he thought, imagining stretch limousines depositing famous movie stars and sleek super models at the doorstep of his pub. Leaning over the counter, he whispered, "say, in that article you'll be writing? Do you think there might be one of those most eligible bachelor's columns?" He grinned expectantly, bobbing his large head back and forth again, occasioning the mop of loose curls to fall across his bushy eyebrows.

"Uh, I don't think so."

With a sheepish smile, Michael went back to

work wiping the counter. "Right, then. Can't hurt to ask, I always say. Just let me know if you need me for anything."

"Right." Brendan's stomach was rumbling now as a framed menu posted on the wall caught his eye. Judging by the price list, 1/2 DOZEN GENUINE MANX OYSTERS - 3 pence, he figured that the yellowed card was at least eighty or ninety years old. "Got any of those genuine Manx oysters?" he asked hopefully.

"No, man. 'Aven't had any genuine anything around here for a hundred years – except kippers of course, but those are drying up too now," Michael professed. "Bloody merfolk scarfed down the whole damn supply." Reaching behind the counter, he passed Brendan a greasy laminated menu. "But have a look at this. Whatever you want – no charge."

Taking the menu with a nod, he scanned over the limited selection; toad in the hole, fish and chips, a soup called cock-a-leeky and the house special, pork pie. "Thanks. I'll try one of your…" Brendan started, just as the front door of the pub creaked open and Michael's attention shifted away. The band stopped playing as if the plug had been pulled and an eerie silence settled upon the room.

Standing silhouetted in a narrow shaft of smoky light that streaked in through the cracked doorway of the pub, was a large dark figure. He appeared to be a bulky man carrying some sort of a weapon. Brendan squinted while instinctively shrinking back toward the wall in his seat.The sea dogs in the corner whispered and cursed amongst themselves while peering through the dim atmosphere, trying to determine if the new arrival was friend or foe. Keeping a wary eye fixed on the situation, Michael uneasily washed a glass in the bar sink, as the door closed behind a hefty man with a salt and pepper beard. He stepped forward, cloaked in a white smock stained with fish intestines and shook off a pair of grubby gloves. With gritted teeth, he held up a gleaming harpoon for all to see, trailing his fingers along the razor point of the spear. "Destiny boys!" he announced with danger glittering in his black eyes. "Destined for his *fooking arse!*"

The suggestion caused a wave of howling laughter among the patrons of the pub, and to finalize his point, the filthy fisherman aimed the harpoon at the ceiling and released the trigger.

SWOOSH! THUNG!

The spear sunk into a thick beam on the high ceiling and quivered with a humming sound for a good five seconds, inducing another eruption of hysterical laughter among the rough characters.

Trembling slightly, Michael turned his eyes away.

The fisherman settled into a chair, joining the others at the table where they raised shot glasses of whiskey in a toast. "To 'is arse!" they cheered, sloshing more spirits across the floor than into their mouths. The band started up again and things went back to what Brendan guessed was normal around the Siren's Whale.

He raised an eyebrow at Michael. "What was that all about?"

"Aw, nothing but a bit 'o shite," he waved, nodding polite salutations in the direction of the fishermen. He leaned across the counter, lowering his voice to a whisper, "word is, Charlie the Tuna's coming to town and the boys have got their pitchforks poised and ready for him this time."

Glancing at the harpoon, he remembered that he hadn't placed his order yet. "I'll have one of your pork pies."

"Aye, good choice. I'll be right back, mate," he told him, disappearing through the swinging doors and returning a moment later, sliding another pint and a fresh-baked pork pie on a chipped white plate across the counter. "This here is a local delicacy. Bake 'em me-self daily. It was me grandfather's recipe."

"Thanks," Brendan nodded, his mouth already watering from the delicious aroma of tender pork and grilled onions swimming in a shell of bubbling gravy. Taking a hungry bite of the buttery pastry top, he peered over his shoulder again at the fishermen. "So, that was the second time today I've heard the name 'Charlie the Tuna' around here. What's the deal?" he asked between mouthfuls.

Michael stared wistfully out the rain-streaked window. "Aw, good ol' Charlie," he grinned. "Drifts in and out of town every year or so like some kind of a ghost. Says 'tis just his nature, you know, to please the women." Stealing a glance at the fisherman in the smock, he whispered, "and by the looks of things, he's pleased of few of their women. Aye, they say he's got some sort of magical powers over the females, so the boys have voted to annihilate him this time."

"You're shitting me," he uttered, vastly enjoying the hot meal and the direction the ludicrous conversation was taking.

"I shite you not," Michael clarified. "He's shagged more ladies than we can count, he has. Three, sometimes four in a night! Thousands, I tell you. It's like they can't bloody resist him. Sure, he's a handsome lad and all, but there's something else.

Something in his eyes and before you know it, WHAM! In their knickers. Just like that."

The look of dead seriousness in the bartender's defiant expression induced a slight smile across Brendan's face. "Right. Remind me not to come here on my honeymoon, unless of course they've harpooned the village sex fiend by then."

A weathered fisherman in a knit cap spattered with seagull shit growled something inaudible to his grisly and intoxicated companions, obviously eavesdropping on the conversation at the bar. Unfazed, Brendan shifted in his seat, absently reaching for a pen.

Leaning forward on his elbows, Michael knitted his bristly brow. "Make fun of it all you want. Won't change the fact that Charlie's a living legend 'round here."

Taking another gulp of Guinness, Brendan scribbled down some notes on a cocktail napkin. "Is that so?"

"Tis fact!" he grunted emphatically. "Do you think the boys over there are just fooling about? Think again. This is serious business you're looking at."

"They're really going to harpoon some poor bastard?" he sniggered with sarcasm. "Whatever happened to tar and feathers?"

"Tried that five years ago," he whispered, indicating a wild-eyed man across the room with a large shiny scar replacing a missing patch of hair above his right ear. "Seems they ran across some trouble though, preparing the resin."

Brendan squinted at the disfigured man as as Michael went on, "sure, I'd give my right nut to find out what it is old Charlie does. Huh! I can't even get a piece of skirt in me own pub."

The old sea dog with the crap-spattered hat unsteadily teetered up to the bar. Holding onto the edge to keep his balance, he glared at Brendan through a set of bloodshot eyes. "The curse ish what it ish!" he hissed in a gravely slur. "That boy ain't one of ush! Ain't human! The spawn of the unspeakable!"

Brendan shielded the meat pie with his hand to protect it from spittle droplets spraying from the man's whisky drenched mouth. "Excuse me, but did you just say – *the curse*?"

Michael shooed the fisherman off. "Go home old man. You're drunk again."

The spawn of the unspeakable, Brendan thought with mild amusement. The line had potential…

Spitting on the floor, the sea dog stumbled across the room mumbling something incomprehensible.

"There's more to this place than meets the eye," Michael offered, eager to steer the conversation back to his own pub.

"Yeah? So how come I didn't read about this curse business in the brochures?"

"Some things are better left unspoken," he scowled, glaring at the old fisherman with annoyance as he stumbled out the door.

"Yeah, I can see that."

Michael pointed out the mummified creature behind the bar. "Bet you've never seen one of these," he grinned.

"I must admit, it's a first."

Swinging around with a proud grin, he picked the thing up in his arms, meticulously pointing out the row of razor sharp teeth and claws of the brown leathery beast. "Caught it myself back in '84. It put up a mighty fight too! Had to stab it five times before it died. The bastard nearly took me watch clean off!" He shoved his hairy wrist in Brendan's face, showing off a beaten Timex with a few scratches and dents in the metal band. "There. See that? Eh? Those are *teeth marks,* my friend. Now there's a bit of proof for you," he nodded convincingly.

"Right. That would explain the stitches between the head and the body?" Brendan challenged, waving a finger at the creature.

Running his fingers along the neck of the mummified fish-boy, Michael set it down on the bar in exasperation. "Aw, for Christ's sake. It's called TAXIDERMY. You didn't think I'd leave the guts in it, did you? It'd stench up the place something terrible."

"No, no, wouldn't want to stink the place up," Brendan waved, rolling his eyes in the direction of a fisherman puffing away on a corncob pipe and his companion who was scraping something from the bottom of his boot with a table knife.

By the look on the American's face, Michael knew he wasn't going to buy the tale. "Look," he confessed, "twixt you and me, that's just a story I've been known to tell the ladies occasionally. But this here, this is an authentic wee Dinny Mara."

"A what?" he asked, shifting his gaze to the leathery hide of the creature that seemed to be grinning at him.

"A Dinny Mara," he repeated. "You know? A merman? They exist, you know. Oh yes, we've got plenty of these suckers trolling the coves 'round here. You've just got to know where to look."

"Sure," he sighed, rising to leave. "I'll keep my eyes open."

With a goofy grin, Michael picked up the creature and perched it on his broad shoulders, speaking for it in the high, squeaky voice of a mad ventriloquist. "Would you like to take me picture for your magazine? It'd make a lovely human interest piece..."

Brendan turned and scooped up his jacket, now toasty warm from the fire. Nestling into it, he absorbed the searing heat on his back. "Er, no thanks."

Thinking fast, Michael tapped his fingers across the counter. "Say, do you play golf?"

"A bit. Why?"

"Meet me here after the parade tomorrow morning. We'll be off to a real man's course. None of that American airy-fairy shite, eh?" he challenged.

"Sorry buddy, but I'm leaving in the morning," Brendan nodded. "Maybe next time."

"Why, the first hole alone would make your Tiger Woods curl up in the fetal position and whimper," he teased.

This was by far the best offer he'd had on the trip, and Brendan wasn't the kind of man to turn down a game of golf, even when the deadline for his unwritten book was overdue and he hadn't produced a single presentable page.

"You can't go without having a round of Manx golf," Michael persisted. "Besides, you won't be able to get a ride out of town until well after the streets have been cleared from the parade. Stay on until tomorrow afternoon. Have a closer look around here. You won't find another village like this one, that I promise you."

Considering the suggestion, he admitted to himself that this place was starting to get interesting. "Fine," he nodded in agreement, shaking Michael's hand. "You 're on."

"We're on," he growled enthusiastically.

Walking across the pub, Brendan caught a glimpse of his reflection in the time-scarred mirror behind the bar, startling himself momentarily. It wasn't his dark, unruly hair or the circles beneath his eyes that caught his attention. It was the fact that he looked – transparent, an invisible spectator, naked against a circus of the foolish and grotesque creatures of this village he'd stumbled upon. He grinned inwardly. He was beginning to feel like himself again. *Perhaps staying on for another day wasn't such a bad idea.*

CHAPTER FIVE

Gentle waves washed against the barnacle-encrusted columns of the pier and a thick blanket of swirling mist had rolled in. The suffocating silence was interrupted only by the ghostly blare of a solemn foghorn from a far off ship, the lonely sound echoing across the moorlands of tangled grass above the seaside village.

Pale moonlight cast a silvery glow upon the wet rooftops and streets, and on the third story of the Mermaid Theater beneath a dome of arched glass, faint, dancing flames shone through the large skylight.

In the apartment atop the old building, Claire Westing sat primly with her legs crossed properly on an olive colored fainting couch. Christine clopped through the living room in her favorite pair of worn leather clogs, placing a silver tea service on the coffee table. The walls were painted a brilliant shade of aqua and glimmered like sea water as the mismatched collection of half-burned vanilla and lavender scented candles on the entry table flickered and danced. The maritime trinkets and souvenirs, filling every inch of wall space was eclectic, even strange, but Christine Hamilton wasn't one to care what other people thought about her life, let alone her taste in interior decoration. A large portrait of a mermaid, so old that the oil paint had cracked, hung prominently in the cozy room and the smoky, sensual saxophone from a 1930's jazz record wafted through the room from the end of a wind-up phonograph machine. A pair of curious, yellow eyes belonging to an African gray parrot peered through the bars of an ornate birdcage carved of warm rosewood, set before a wide window in the corner of the room overlooking the pier. The parrot had spied the pile of shortbread on the platter and tapped the bars with its beak impatiently, "Ahem! Room service please! I'm starving in here!"

The old bird always brought a smile to Christine's face. "Sorry Pearl, darling." She poured a third cup of tea as the bird flapped its wings in anticipation. Opening the latch, Christine set the teacup and a square of shortbread on the floor of the cage, then returned to the couch.

Rolling her eyes as Pearl dipped her beak into the tea, Claire turned her attention back to Christine. She had to handle the reporter situation with some degree of delicacy. "So," she began carefully. "Tell me about your meeting with the American writer this evening. How did it go?"

Christine spooned several heaping globs of honey from a ceramic jar into her tea, then licked the spoon. "I don't trust him," she managed after swallowing a gulp of the sweet, sticky substance. "And I don't like him either."

Claire crossed her arms over her lap, a slight gesture indicating the mood of annoyance that Christine's aloof attitude had intensified. Couldn't she see that they were sitting on a golden opportunity? "Why would you say a thing like that?" she asked gently. "He's with a very prestigious magazine. Just imagine it. No more slow seasons."

Frowning, Christine recalled the brazen attitude that he'd sauntered into her life with. "This village is nothing but an ant hill to a man like that. He's come here to kick it down and watch us all scatter about, then he'll be on his way. I've seen it before

Claire."

"I think you're mistaken," she argued.

"Think about it," Christine sighed. "Why would such a glamorous publication send a reporter here? We've no proper lodgings for influential and famous people. How do we really know he's even from a magazine?"

"Because I saw it with my own eyes," Claire defended, her temples beginning to pulse. "And don't pretend to be so detached from it all," she added, anger surfacing in her voice. "I saw the aftermath, had to give him me salts."

Glancing up from the tea, Christine challenged her to continue with a raised brow.

Claire squeezed her eyes shut for a moment. Direct confrontation was always uncomfortable, but something had to be done about this. "I saw the condition he was in after you - you finished with him! The poor bloke could hardly stand up!"

"Well, he had it coming," Christine retorted childishly.

"He is *writing* about the village in a magazine that could very well put this rundown dump on the mainstream map!" she spat. "Do you realize what a positive article could do for tourism on the island – or that a negative portrayal could destroy us? Did you even think about what this might mean to the other business owners – or were you just amusing yourself at our expense?"

Christine hadn't been thinking of the others, in fact, she hadn't been thinking at all, just reacting when she'd made herself so painfully alluring to the obnoxious reporter. Something about him had agitated her beyond words. But she hadn't intended to cause such a powerful effect upon him. Until now, she hadn't been aware that he'd physically stumbled out of the building. She'd overdone it, especially if it were bad enough that Claire noticed his condition. The old woman's foot tapped on the hardwood floor, waiting for an explanation.

"He came in there expecting me to jump into his lap over some stupid magazine," Christine finally defended. As she recalled the helpless look on his face, her eyes glimmered with a twinge of mischief, "I only thought about having him just long enough to release the scent, to get his head spinning. It was only done to put him in his place." Taking another sip of tea, she set the china cup on the table. "No harm done."

"No harm?" Claire repeated incredulously. "Now he'll be after you like a bloody hound dog," she reminded her. "I hope you're ready for that and the consequences of your reckless actions. He'll be clawing his eyes out just to get close to you again," she warned, shaking her head in despair. "This is bad. This is very, very bad."

"I can take care of myself – and of him," Christine decided aloud. "Besides," she mused, "he's sure to write flattering things about the village under the circumstances. Let's just try to think of it as quality control."

Glancing uneasily at her young companion, Claire mulled it over, eventually nodding in agreement. What's done is done, she told herself. It was a cruel plan, but perhaps it might work in their favor. But still, she didn't like being part and parcel of it, not one bit, as she was well aware of the misadventures that certainly awaited the American should he not come to his senses and leave this place before Christine really got under his skin.

The uncomfortable silence between the two women intensified when a set of knuckles rapped on the door. "Who could that be at this hour?" Christine asked, casting a suspicious glare in Claire's direction. "You didn't invite him over for tea, did you?"

"I did no such thing," she snapped, insulted by the accusation. "Perhaps he caught your *scent* and sniffed his way here," she smirked.

Cautiously, Christine approached the door wondering how she would react should she actually find the reporter standing on her doorstep. She glanced through the peephole, then turned back to Claire with excitement, "It's Charlie!"

Claire hastily smoothed down her hair. "Oh my goodness. Oh my goodness gracious."

Christine fumbled with the locks as a velvety voice seeped through the door, speaking words in Manx Gaelic, words that only Christine could understand, "Ah, ben aeg chleaynoil bwaagh, cimar a tha thu?"

Giggling, she flung the door open. "I'm well, thank you. Oh my God! Come in! Come in!"

Stepping inside, Charlie swept her into his arms, then grasped her hands and spun her around in circles as his laughter filled the room.

Catching her breath, she stumbled back from the vertigo, staring in wonder at the elegant man who'd breezed into the flat after nearly a year. "Where have you been?"

Charlie's intense eyes swept over her. "The question is not where I've been and with whom…"

With unspoken understanding, Christine kissed him on the cheek. "Claire let the houseboat out this week, but you're welcome to sleep on the sofa."

"Thanks," he replied with a devilish grin, "but I've got the boat and besides, I don't anticipate any trouble finding accommodating sleeping arrangements around this town." His cobalt eyes traveled around the familiar room, then stopped dead on Claire Westing. the sight of her sweet, elderly face jolting him a little. He instantly regretted speaking of sleeping around and quickly changed his tone. "And what - have we here?" he growled hungrily.

A little lump formed in Claire's throat and her voice squeaked. "Oh no you don't!"

With his stare locked onto her, he prowled across the room like a jungle cat.

"You stop that right now Charlie Hamilton!" Claire warned, shaking a finger at him, blood pressure rising with every graceful step he took in her direction. "Charlie! I mean it this time you shameless bastard!" Ignoring her idle threats, Charlie growled again and leapt on top of her, playfully biting the white flesh of her neck. "You good for nothing bastard!" she screamed, attempting to swat him off.

"How about it Claire ol' girl? What do you say we have a go!" Unable to resist teasing her, Charlie lifted the edge of her dress, exposing a pair of industrial strength knickers. "Oh girl," he whispered seductively, "have I got something for you."

"Get off of me you bloody maniac!" she screeched, kicking her skinny limbs like an overturned tortoise.

"Stop it Charlie!" Christine shouted trying to pull him away from Claire. He reached out, tickling Christine until she fell away, then zeroed in on Claire again. "Grrrr!" Mounting her fragile frame, his lips fused onto hers with unbridled passion. Her flail-

64

ing legs straightened as his firm body stiffened against the wool dress she wore. And as quickly as he'd overtaken her, he unlocked his mouth from hers, staring at her for a long moment. That spark in her eyes was still there, the same eyes he'd stared into so long ago. How much time had passed, he pondered dreamily. As his face brushed against her neck he caught a trace of the powdery cologne that she still dabbed behind her ears. He closed his eyes, inhaling her scent in a rush of pure nostalgia…

Angrily, Claire wiped off her mouth and spat, "Jesus! Have you no respect for ripened women!"

SQUACK!

The parrot in the cage flapped her wings as she watched the humans scuffling on the sofa. Charlie tumbled onto the floor, laughing now, the careless laugh of a young man who knew nothing of old age and woe, Claire thought bitterly. Looking up at her from the carpet with a mischievous gaze, he ran his tongue across supple lips. "The more mature the tree, the more *succulent* the fruit."

Claire twittered uncomfortably in her seat, unable to do anything but drink in the closeness of him. It was surreal to see him like this, for him to treat her with such casual and utter disrespect. Licking her lips, she could taste the traces of sea salt from his mouth, could feel the dampness in his clothes, still moist with the spray of the ocean. She guessed he'd come in by sea as he usually did. Forcing herself to turn away from his glossy black hair that curled around the neck of his wool sweater, she halfheartedly cursed, "you and your honey coated tongue. May the cat eat you and may the devil eat the cat!" That said, she crossed her legs, managing to collect what was left of her composure.

With a firm, warning look, Christine clasped Charlie's cool hand, pulling him up from the floor. Pearl pecked at the empty teacup in her cage, ruffled her feathers and squawked again.

Like an easily distracted child, he looked over at the parrot, forgetting all about Claire and the repercussions he'd just imprinted upon her life with a single kiss and a few casual words that had carelessly fallen from his lips. "I don't believe it!" he gawked. "The old bird's still alive and kicking? She must be ninety years old!"

"Ninety-two," Christine corrected uneasily, glancing sideways at Claire who was busy digging around in her handbag for the tin of smelling salts.

Pearl belched. "Uh-oh. Better swab the poop deck matie."

Cringing at the blob on the newspaper lining the bottom of the cage, Charlie quivered with disgust. "Wicked!"

"Welcome home" Christine smiled.

An acrid whiff from the tin jolted Claire back to her sensible self. "Yes," she added. "Welcome home – you dirty rotten scoundrel."

Embracing the two women, Charlie stroked Christine's flaming tresses with one hand and Claire's strands of spun silver with the other.

ജ∽

Head swimming with Guinness, Brendan walked solemnly through the quiet village. The streets and buildings glimmered with droplets of rain that had fallen and dissipated again within minutes. Peering overhead, he reminded himself to buy an umbrella in the morning. But his gaze remained fixed on the swirling clouds above that were flowing in odd-shaped, black patches and seemed to be dancing with flashes of color. Eerie shapes in the mist tumbled like ghosts waltzing in a ballroom to a long forgotten tune. Pausing to stare at the magical phenomenon of the Northern Lights, he felt something musing from within. Beneath the flashing glow, the slurred warnings and curses of the old drunk in the pub surfaced now, repeating themselves in his head. The corners of Brendan's lips turned up and he found himself scrounging in his pockets and sifting through crumpled cocktail napkins on which he'd written down the exact quotes. Yes, he thought, it was beginning to take form - a story unlike any other he'd ever written. And these people, these lunatics, were practically begging for it.

Overwhelmed with inspiration, he jogged off toward the houseboat with a flood of ideas running through his head.

Perhaps fate had stranded him here, he mused, winking secretly to the heavens above.

By midnight, Brendan was anchored down at the kitchen table before the screen of his laptop. He breath was ragged as his fingers danced just out of reach above the keyboard. *This is it, write something,* he willed himself, eyes squeezed shut. *Just write – write…* He touched the keys, gingerly at first, managing to peck out the heading of the first chapter – THE SPAWN OF THE UNSPEAKABLE. He stopped, reread the line and allowed himself a laugh. It was funny.

No - it was brilliant.

'I soon discovered that the village I'd stumbled across

was far more than a typical tacky seaside resort. To my utter delight, this deranged province was inhabited by whole-hog lunatics.

Moments after settling into my lodgings, a derelict, rotten houseboat, my intoxicated neighbor, referred to by another islander as "houseboat rubbish," proceeded to gallantly gouge me with a cheese knife after mistaking me for the town hooligan, Charlie the Tuna, a man whose claim to fame is 'shamelessly shagging every female on the island.'

After polishing off a bottle of strawberry wine with my would-be gouger and his raisin of a wife, I ventured into the village where I had the great pleasure of being excruciatingly blue-balled by a topless mermaid after her underwater fantasy show, an ambitious production that would put the seediest of Vegas strip shows to shame...'

Hours later, Brendan slumbered restlessly on the lumpy mattress within the moldering confines of the houseboat.

Fog, dense as clam chowder had rolled in over the small boats and only blurry patches of yellow light from the tall dockside lamps remained to outline the narrow wooden plank path. A bulky figure wove between vessels and piles of dried fishing nets. She was a plump woman in her late forties with a round nose and a pair of small, dull eyes that were set too closely together, giving her face an orangutanian quality. She helped herself to the last swig from a bottle of ale, tossing the empty into the black water that lapped tirelessly against the boats. Dim light from an overhead lamppost illuminated a cluster of green sequins adorning her mermaid sweatshirt and she swayed unsteadily from the alcohol, tossing a mat of stringy, sea-dampened hair over her shoulder.

Staring out at the water, erotic fantasies began to swim through her mind again. She'd heard things about this place – incredible stories and impossible miracles that sometimes happened here to women like her beneath the Northern Lights on nights like this. Of course she didn't believe a bloody word of it, but who the hell cared. She had nothing but a white cat and a basket of knitting waiting by the hearth of her cold stone fireplace back at the cottage. Music of the cove made by settling groans of vintage vessels and the stretching of tethered ropes melded with the steady rhythm of her frosty breath. It was dead quiet out here among the boats, she thought with a shiver. *Just a few more minutes,* she decided, flopping down on a pile of rough fishing nets. Minutes ticked by on her gold plated wristwatch, the woman growing increasingly impatient, and eventually discouraged. Heaving her heavy bottom from the nets, she rose to her feet, ready to retreat toward her meager cottage in the hills.

SPLISH!

Something stirred in the water beneath the wide planks. A twinge of excitement, mingled with fear shot up her spine. The woman perked up hopefully, not quite sure what to expect, then slumped her shoulders a moment later. *It was only the water you old cow,* she silently cursed herself. Cupping her hands around thin, painted lips, she exhaled in an attempt to breathe some warmth into her frigid fingers before sneaking back into town. Feeling ashamed and foolish that she'd carried the ridiculous fantasy this far, she prayed that no one would notice her slinking through the village at such an hour. The locals would certainly know what she'd been after and they'd all have a good laugh about it behind her back at the market while she bought vegetables and at the post when…

SPLASH!

"It can't be," she breathed, eyes madly scanning the isolated boat slip to her right. A little lump formed in her throat as she gravitated toward the edge, despite the nagging, inner voice protesting that such an occurrence was *impossible*. A phrase she'd lived by all her life ran through her head now in the sugary voice of her mother, *if you don't expect anything, you'll never be disappointed, dear*. Well, she'd never expected anything and just look at the lot it had gotten her. Fat, forty and frumpy. *Sod it*, she decided. After all, she'd been milling around in the soggy weather for nearly three hours freezing her crumpets off.

Might as well have a peek just to be sure…

Ripples danced across the black water beneath the planks.

Ripples large enough to be made by a…

Her wide silhouette was all that she saw in the inky blackness below, yet the water still spread out from the vicinity of the splash. Heart fluttering, she stooped over further, scanning the area with narrowed eyes. She sprang back like a cat, emitting a high-pitched squeak the moment she saw it.

A pale, masculine hand emerged from the murk, clawing onto the rough edge of the dock with slender, widespread fingers, followed by a crest of raven hair and a set of broad shoulders that rose beneath the pallid moonlight. And then she saw it, *sweet Jesus*, the glorious face of an angel, his colorless, chiseled features glowing brilliantly with the wetness of the sea. And as she stared down upon this creature, she was sure now that he had somehow heard seven, lonely years of tears and silent prayers whispered in the darkness of her bedroom.

4:03 A.M.

Rolling over in a tangle of dusty blankets, Brendan squinted at the numbers on the alarm clock while attempting to rest his aching neck on the mealy pillow that had come with the accommodations. His temples were pulsing now from the pints consumed at the pub and three intense hours spent banging out the first two chapters of the new manuscript.

The manuscript.

He glanced at the printer on the table, sighing with relief that it hadn't been a dream. Yes, he'd actually written something – something good, evidenced by the thick pile of pages with the ink barely dry that had spit out with a soft whirring sound while he'd drifted off.

He bit his bottom lip, well aware that there was still a hell of a deadline to meet, but he was off to a good start. Figuring if he could manage to get a few hours of sleep, he'd be able to snoop around the village in the morning and dredge up some more material to fill the unwritten chapters of his book. Rubbing his unshaven face with a sense of contentment, he congratulated himself for stumbling across Heather Bay, the quirky little village that had infuriated him – and its inhabitants who had unknowingly provided enough absurd material to fill forty double-spaced pages. It almost didn't seem fair, he thought, how easy it had been to write it all down, every last quote and impression that the locals had practically handed him. It had been too easy.

He flinched as an image of the ludicrous, topless mermaid flooded his mind again, not particularly enjoying the fact that she'd crept into his head for the fourth or fifth time tonight. In fact, he resented her for making him feel like a pimply teenager when he'd happened upon her in that dark lair that she called a dressing room. He'd always thought of himself as the kind of man who took what he wanted, when he wanted – but she'd somehow managed to leave him wanting – wanting her. He groaned in frustration, willing himself to fall back asleep again.

Minutes passed silently until a dull noise from outside began to percolate in his ears. Craning his neck, he strained to hear, unable to decipher if the sounds were human or animal. Low, muffled voices rose and fell on the docks, just loud enough to send stabs of annoyance through his exhausted limbs.

The same voices that probably woke me up in the first place, he thought sourly.

Provoked by the untimely disturbance, he bolted upright, fought off the scratchy blanket and stomped over to the small round window.

On a mound of fishing nets, Charlie Hamilton was nude, glistening wet and straddled on top of the homely woman, she giggling incessantly as he thrust his powerful hips into hers. The large black tattoo of a Celtic mermaid on his muscular chest danced rhythmically with every motion of his finely tuned musculature, his glittering, dark eyes dancing with mischief as the wave of robust pleasure welled up inside of him.

"I don't even know your name, lad," the woman moaned between braying bursts of laughter. "Why! I'm old enough to be your mum."

In response, he slowed his thrusts and kissed her feverishly, his smooth fingers trailing beneath her frumpish sweatshirt. His satiny voice whispered a vaporous passage from the Birth of Venus into her ear, "her silky ringlets float about her breast, veiling its fairy loveliness. While her eye is soft and deep as the blue heaven high, the beautiful is born..."

Nearing climax and almost mad with laughter, the woman clung onto Charlie's shoulders, riding along with his extraordinary force, each thrust delivering a rhapsody of pleasure through her mounds of quivering flesh.

The outside temperature was shocking as Brendan's bare feet touched the landing just beyond the door of his houseboat, making him wish that he'd packed a pair of slippers. Squinting through the fog to make out the shadowy figures that writhed and moaned on the nets like a pair of beached sea lions, he stepped forward, aghast at the wallowing mass of marshmallow flesh before his eyes. "Excuse me," he growled irritably. "What do you think you're doing out here? It's four-o'clock in the morning!"

Hopelessly enveloped in the woman's huge thighs, Charlie whirled his neck around like a trapped animal, his eyes dangerously flashing with pure, seething hatred.

Muscles tightening, Brendan backed off cautiously. He hadn't given a second thought to the repercussions of his actions – until now. Perhaps interrupting the moonlight interlude hadn't been such a good idea after all...

The woman yanked her shirt down over an enormous breast and shouted back brazenly, "what in the bloody hell does it look like we're doing!"

Just as Brendan was sketching a quick getaway in his mind, Charlie suddenly sprang to his feet, sending a jolt of adrenaline screaming through his gut. The youth's eerily, white flesh gleamed beneath a sharp shaft of lamplight and Brendan caught a flash of the unusual tattoo inked across his torso, identical to Christine's. The young man, stark naked and obviously still in a painful state of arousal, stared menacingly at the intruder, and towered a good six inches above him. Brendan instantly knew who he was, the town ruffian he'd heard so much talk about – Charlie the Tuna.

Oh – shit, shit, shit!, he panicked, nerves unraveling beneath his skin.

Brendan shuffled back another pace. But to his surprise, Charlie didn't lunge forward as anticipated, to the contrary, he faced the sea, pivoted in a single fluid movement and dove into the briny depths, his velvety white essence vanishing into the blackness. The only evidence that he'd even been standing there at all was the small splash that had followed his descent.

In wide-eyed disbelief, Brendan gawked at the bizarre scene, trying to make some sense of it in his groggy state. But all he could manage to do was stand there reeling. *The unclad nut had just jumped naked into the freezing Irish Sea!*

The woman stared achingly at the water, then slowly turned around to glower at the bastard who'd just spooked off the shag of a lifetime. She angrily wrenched her pants back up, shaking a meaty fist at Brendan. Tensing again, he now noticed the formidable storm brewing in her eyes. She was far more frightening than the black-haired youth who'd just

74

moments ago, been spouting off poetry while screwing the holy daylights out of her.

He backed toward the open door of the boat with extreme caution. She was an extraordinarily big woman and, to make matters worse, she was furious – no - livid.

Hot breath steamed out from her flared nostrils. "Thanks a lot! You went and scared the bleedin' fish away!" she screeched on the edge of tears.

"I – er…," he managed to blubber before instinctively bolting into the houseboat. In a wild panic, he jammed the frail lock down behind himself.

Standing with his back against the door, heart thudding in his heaving chest, the unnatural encounter replayed itself in his head, transforming his ragged breath into bellows of hysterical laughter.

He stumbled to his laptop and began writing.

ᮣᮧᮧᮣ

It was well after lunch by the time Jake Hogan had finished reading the e-mail from Brendan. Engrossed in the pages, he'd ordered out Thai food and had mindlessly munched down a dozen egg rolls while consuming the first two chapters of the manuscript. He found himself laughing out loud again as he finished reading the latest attachment that had just come in from Brendan James.

'As I stumbled upon the couple, entwined on the rough wooden docks, his firm, lean body lost between the pickled thighs of a giggling woman old enough to be his mother, I couldn't help but think that the poor old lass was going to be picking splinters out of her ass for a month.'

"Yeah, baby," Jake grinned. "He's back."

CHAPTER SIX

By mid-morning the streets of Heather Bay were bustling with tourists who had gathered along the narrow route for the village's annual Mermaid Parade. A twenty-man bagpipe band marched down the middle of the road playing <u>Scotland the Brave</u>, kicking off the festivities as excited onlookers waved red Manx flags and colorful balloons. The pipers were followed by an old fishing boat situated atop a flat bed trailer, a pitiful effort sponsored by the Manx Fishing Council. On the deck of the boat a pair of fishermen stood by a woven net with a girl in a mermaid tail, tangled within the ropes and knots. The mermaid feigned terror as a troop of dancing teenage girls, dressed in Manx cat costumes with brass bells around their necks, meowed and chased after the captured siren. Hand-painted lettering on the side of the boat read; THERE'S NOTHING LIKE MANX FISH.

The locals had exerted months of hard work to pull off the various attractions that paraded before his bleary eyes, Brendan determined, standing on the sidelines while jockeying his position on a rubbish bin to get a good look at the approaching Mer-Dog competition. Small children and their mothers trotted two-dozen dogs down High Street, every creature dressed in some sort of ludicrous mermaid or sea organism costume. The tiny furry feet of crabs, lobsters and fish clicked along the route, melting hearts and inducing waves of 'ooohs' and 'ahhhhs' from the crowd. Heading the pageant was a fluffy Pomeranian with fur dyed green for the festivities and a long blond wig that appeared to have been affixed to its head with hot glue. The spunky animal wore a turquoise, spandex mermaid tail, squeezed over its hind quarters with great, fanned fins trailing behind on the asphalt. At the back of the group, a black Scottie with one lopsided ear wore a plastic crown and gripped a tiny trident in his mouth. The scruffy black furball began sniffing and whimpering, ignoring the stern hissing from its master, a thin woman dressed in brown tweed. In a flash, the Scottie broke away from his lead and before anyone could react, had rushed toward the head of the group and mounted the Pomeranian from behind. The Pomeranian's owner screamed at the spectacle as the children giggled and gawked, the startling disturbance resulting in the entire parade screeching to a halt while the two Mer-Dogs shamelessly went at it in the middle of the road. Two women tried to pull the dogs apart to no avail. The Scottie snarled and snapped viciously at its owner. "They're bloody stuck together!" the tweed lady hollered. "Somebody fetch me a garden hose!"

Growing hysterical with laughter, the crowd of onlookers hooted and cheered for the canines.

The next attraction was rapidly approaching behind the Merdogs, which had thoroughly blocked the parade route, a giant paper mache merman riding a chariot of golden sea horses, towed along by a battered pick-up truck. Three local beauty queens in mermaid costumes stood on the moving platform waving at the crowd and Julian Wesley, decked out in a powder blue tuxedo made an announcement into his microphone. "And joining me today are this year's winners of the Something's Fishy Pageant, sponsored in full, by Wesley's World Famous Fish and Chips.

As the creaking float closed in on the humping dogs, the truck driver suddenly slammed on the brakes, bringing the contraption to a jolting stop, tossing the Fishy girls and Julian off the platform into a writhing pile in the gutter. Amidst the commotion of howling beauty queens, a baffled shopkeeper managed to locate a hose and tossed it to one of the Mer-dog mothers who wasted no time blasting the animals apart with a stream of cold water.

Charlie popped out of the crowd and grinned to himself at the unfolding fiasco. He casually picked up the Scotty dog's discarded crown and placed it upon his own head. With trouble brewing in his glittering eyes, and unable to resist pissing off the locals, he climbed onto the back of the Wesley's float, quickly locating the sound system beneath the platform. Removing a CD from his pocket, he slipped it inside with a devious grin as the soggy Mer-dogs were yanked mercilessly down the street allowing the parade to move again. Charlie leaned over the edge of the float and signaled to the truck driver, who from his vantage point, couldn't see that its rightful inhabitants were still floundering on the street.

"We're good to go man!" Charlie hollered to the driver. "Step on it!"

With a groan, the float lurched forward, leaving Julian and the mermaids bewildered in its dust.

Fiona Cross, the icy queen of British morning television was positioned on the sidelines of the route with her young cameraman, who signaled to her silently with the gesture of a hand. Tossing her bobbed blonde tresses, the slick reporter hastily smoothed her pink cashmere suit before stepping in front of the camera with a fixed and glassy smile. "Good Morning Britain. This is Fiona Cross for Wakey Wakey, Britain's number-one morning program. Today I'm reporting live from an adorable little village on the Isle of Man called Heather Bay, home of the world-famous mermaid celebration. Festivities are high and as you can see, this morning's mermaid parade has attracted quite an enthusiastic crowd."

Scanning the masses for local faces, she pulled two, sweet-looking elderly women forward, both wearing mermaid sweatshirts and straw sun bonnets. She shoved the microphone in their faces. "And here we have two lovely mermaid fans. Hello ladies. Would you like to tell the viewers of Wakey Wakey why you've come to the Mermaid Festival this year?"

One of the old ladies grinned through dentures and sheepishly stepped up before the polished hostess. "Aye. We've come to get us a piece of arse, we have."

The other old woman nodded enthusiastically.

The cameraman groaned audibly in the background.

Without flinching, Fiona snatched the microphone back and stepped in front of the camera, filling the lens with her dazzling, capped teeth. "So, there we have it. Plenty of excitement for all, here in Heather Bay. Back to you in the studio."

The cameraman signaled to Fiona.

"CUT!!!" she shouted. "Bloody old bats!" she hissed at the women, stamping her high heels in frustration. The elderly ladies scuffled out of her way, unsure of what they'd done wrong.

"Fuck all! Have you ever heard of LIVE television?" Fiona growled at them. She shook her head, mussing the perfect hair style and sighed angrily, lighting a quick cigarette between takes.

This bloody place, she thought furiously. It was *her* god damned show, *her* bubbling personality that had made the program number one, yet here she stood, *Fiona fucking Cross* on the sidelines of an idiotic parade in some nowhere village. She seethed inwardly, recalling how her executive producers had unanimously decided to ship her off to the island in an attempt to 'reach out' to even the most remote stretches of the British Isles; a dim-witted brainstorm to boost Wakey Wakey's skyrocketing ratings even higher than they already were. Ooh! I'm ready to 'reach out' all right, she thought, *Reach out and strangle somebody*!

"We're back in five minutes Fiona!" the cameraman hollered. "What do you want to do next?"

Crushing out the cigarette, Fiona glanced at the Mer-Dog competition that was back underway.

The tweed woman yanked the Pomeranian's leash unmercifully and scowled at the dog's disheveled wig and sodden ripped costume, "bloody waste of time this was!" she hissed. The Scottie, now crownless, and waterlogged, skulked along the sidelines resembling a large, black rat on a lead.

The hijacked float forged down the street. Charlie waved to the crowd and now straddled the back of a giant sea horse. The first notes from the song, <u>Desperate, But Not Serious</u>, by Adam Ant blared out of the speakers, drowning out the leading band of bagpipers. Bewildered, the kilted musicians looked at each other, then one started jamming with Charlie's song alongside the float. The other pipers followed, supplying a local flavor to the eighties pop song. Charlie opened his loose white shirt, baring rippling muscles at the ladies, a gesture welcomed with a cacophony of squealing.

Fiona smiled wickedly at the delicious young creature with skin of white velvet. "Mmmmmm. What have we here?" she smiled.

The cameraman began to panic. "Fiona! We're back in thirty seconds!"

"That!" she frantically pointed at Charlie. "Get a shot of that one!"

Following orders, the cameraman focused in on Charlie as the hijacked float inched toward their position on the curb. As the camera setup caught his eye, the youthful rogue winked at the sexy female reporter while proclaiming to the unruly crowd, "beware ye lonely ladies! Men! Lock up ye daughters, ye wenches and ye wives! For the king of the Merfolk has arrived and it's mating season!"

The pair of stuffy town officials perched in a wooden booth above the bleachers stared at the production in astonishment, throwing their parade schedules into the air out of frustration as a sea of female bodies along the route danced to the unplanned music.

Women in the street shrieked and cheered, every one of them ogling Charlie, who was now dancing and singing.

Loving it, he devilishly scanned the crowd, his dark eyes fixing mischievously on Fiona Cross as he continued to sing. The shameless hooligan thrust his hips back and forth at the reporter as his float approached her setup on the sidelines.

The cameraman remained steady on Charlie, "Fiona! This is obscene!" he hissed. "We can't show this on morning television!"

Fiona grinned maliciously, after all, this is what the executives were after, right? It would be her utmost pleasure to give them a taste of 'local life' on the islands. "Stay on him!" she growled through capped teeth, positioning herself just to the side of the frame to avoid blocking out a single, friendly thrust of Charlie's groin from her millions of live viewers.

Tossing her hair, she exhaled innocently into the camera, "Well, as you can clearly see, things are heating up here at the Heather Bay Mermaid Parade."

"Let's get the bastard!"

Fiona spun around the moment she heard the scuffle erupting from behind. Julian and three of the sea dogs from the pub were in hot pursuit of the float now, screaming out streams of obscenities, followed by the infuriated beauty queens who cursed and stumbled along in their fabric mermaid tails.

Fiona continued narrating, "Where the town elders seem to be having a problem with the...entertainment."

From his roost on the float, Charlie craned his neck around, surveying the noisy commotion encroaching upon him. He stopped singing mid-song and swallowed hard. "Bollocks! The mid-life crisis squad!" In a swell of panic, he scaled up the giant merman effigy and leapt into the air, grasping onto an overhead banner that stretched across the street between the crests of two Tudors. Hanging on with white knuckles, he smiled victoriously as the float rolled beneath his dangling feet, and only then realized that he didn't have anywhere to go – but down. The edge of the banner started to unravel under his weight.

"Oh, shite!"

As the banner ripped, Charlie dramatically swung across the road and over the heads of the crowd with his wild eyes locked on Fiona.

"And where mermaids and mermen don't just swim – they soar…" she commented listlessly to the camera.

As he swooshed toward her, she hissed through a clenched smile to the cameraman, "You bloody well better be getting this on tape!"

He nodded limply, "aye," panning the lens, following the hooligan's Tarzan-like descent. Charlie thudded to his feet next to Fiona, swept her into his arms and delivered a searing kiss to her glossy lips.

"Arrrrr!" he growled with a devilish smirk.

Wilted by the kiss, she swooned against his firm, lean body, forgetting her television show, and her own name for a moment.

Sharp obscenities from the angry men and livid mermaids spiked in volume as the mob closed in. Charlie had no choice but to drop Fiona's entranced body. She collapsed in the street and was trampled over by the livid throng of men as they stampeded down the parade route after the hooligan who had done unspeakable things to their women. The cameraman, unsure what to do, panned down to Fiona, still dazed and listless, her lipstick smeared and pastel suit smudged with grime. Swooning from the kiss, she shook her head dizzily, "And that's all for today's live coverage here at the Heather Bay Mermaid Festival. Wakey - wakey…"

The crowd was beginning to thin. Brendan hopped off the rubbish bin just as the last and gaudiest attraction in the parade approached the bend.

Two weary horses pulled a puny, flat cart with a vulgar, life-size paper mache mermaid on it with her siren tail wrapped around an enormous bottle of Codsucker Ale. A hand-painted banner on the side of the rattling wagon read, 'AVE AN ALE AT THE WHALE.

Michael Blake, wearing his finest tartan kilt rode a rusty, sputtering motorcycle alongside and pulled over next to Brendan. "What do you think of her?" he shouted, pointing at the float. "Designed her meself!"

Puffs of choking smoke farted into Brendan's face from the tailpipe. "Very - ambitious," he coughed.

Michael beamed proudly as his obscene creation lurched down the route. "She ought to bring in a bit of business, eh? I'm thinking about hanging her from the ceiling of the pub after we're done with her."

"Sure," Brendan mused. "You could fill her belly with candy and let the drunks take turns busting her apart with boat oars."

Placing a finger on the side of his big nose, He considered the suggestion. "Eh," he nodded, "you just might be onto to something there."

"Uh, yeah."

Michael pointed to the bag of golf clubs slung over his shoulder. "You coming or what?"

Eyes traveling from the decrepit motorcycle to the barkeep's stubby, hairy legs jutting out from beneath the kilt, Brendan wavered with mild concern. "Er, what about your skirt? Is that thing gonna fly up once we pick up speed?"

"Aw, piss off, man!" he defended. "I'll have you know, this kilt is a mighty hit with the ladies."

Reluctantly, Brendan raised his hands in surrender and climbed on the back of the bike. The sharp odor of gasoline burned his nostrils as he wondered how serious the leak was.

"Want to see some real excitement?" Michael challenged.

"Uh, I think you're leaking..." he protested.

Before Brendan could say 'gas', the bike heaved forward with a terrible clatter.

"Watch this!" Michael whooped. The vibrating motorcycle shot off down the parade route with Brendan clinging to the big man's back. As they picked up speed, the wind lifted the edges of the kilt up to Michael's shoulders, flapping up madly in the breeze. And to Brendan's horror, Michael wasn't wearing any underwear. He cringed, squeezing his eyes shut while trying to determine which was more frightening; a thrill ride on a sputtering, wobbling bike or the gruesome display that lurked beneath the Blake family tartans.

Women on the street pointed, screwing up their faces at the exhibition roaring by. With a devious grin, Michael cranked the gas to keep his kilt air born.

"Aw, God!" Brendan howled. "You're a sick man Michael!"

The golf course was situated above the cliffs on a high grassy knoll, dotted with granite boulders and treacherous potholes. Beyond the amethyst heather moorlands a breathtaking view of the Heather Bay lighthouse was exposed far below. A flock of black sheep milled around on the neatly trimmed grass, gnawing mindlessly until nothing remained but patches of dirt.

Brendan shook his neck and shoulders in an attempt to forget about the terrifying ride up the hill as they'd raced around hairpin turns on Michael's rattling means of transportation. He glanced thanklessly at his jolly host who had just handed him a club. As he stood there gripping the handle, the thought crossed his mind to whack the lunatic over the skull with it.

Michael held his hands up to the clear sky, inhaling an exaggerated breath of air through flared nostrils. "Look at this scenery. It's enough to make even the grimmest score bearable."

In response, Brendan skillfully swung, his ball landing just a few yards from the flag by the edge of the cliffs.

Michael hadn't realized that the American was a half-decent golfer and swallowed hard. "Not bad," he eeked.

The two men picked up the clubs and headed toward the flag. "So, last night, you said there's more to this place than meets the eye," Brendan inquired casually, determined not to let the big oaf know how churned his insides had become from the nauseating ride.

"Aw," Michael winked, "what meets the eye is simple enough: one big fish story to generate tourism. Ever since some lovelorn sailor discovered that he could reel in the quid by telling tales of mermaids to tourists, this place has never been the same. And of course, there's the single ladies word-of-mouth circuit. It's all the talk this time of year in the hairdresser shops from Brighton Beach to Edinburgh," he said. "Come one! Come all and find your soul mate during Midsummer Eve! What a load of shite that is," he waved bitterly. "And then there's the part that might be for real." Michael motioned for

Brendan to follow as they approached the edge of the cliff.

Brendan uneasily peered over the edge at the dizzying view, immediately overcome with vertigo as he glanced down a hundred feet at violent emerald waves crashing on the jagged rocks below.

Michael pointed. "They say that's where Athena died. You know? The last mermaid. Right down there."

Light-headed, he backed away from the staggering drop-off, welcoming the crisp gust of ocean breeze that stung his cheeks. "And I'm supposed to believe this because...?"

Kicking a pebble over the edge, Michael watched it disappear in the frothing foam. "They say that Athena gave up her immortal powers when she fell in love with a human. But she couldn't let go of her lust for the sea. Legend has it that she was headed out to the briny depths one night – when there came a mighty swell. The storm of 1929. And she drowned."

Brendan was dulled by the fairy tales and folklore. "A mermaid drowning?"

Michael shrugged, retrieved his ball and set it on the tee. A woolly black sheep had wandered up to the hole and was gnawing violently on the flag. "Get out of my way you hairy-arsed bugger!" he hollered at it. "Go on! Shoo!" But the sheep was oblivious to the pair of golfers. Michael stamped his foot in frustration, swinging anyway. His ball sailed through the air and landed in a sand trap, infuriating the Scotsman. "Bugger me! Bloody sheep! They're a real nuisance around here, you know."

Brendan patted Michael on the back, consoling, "ah, the pitfalls of a real man's golf course. But this incredible scenery makes even the grimmest score bearable. Am I right?"

He shook off the American's arm, muttering through clenched teeth, "wanker."

Brendan set up his shot. "So, what do you know about Christine Hamilton?"

"Och! No man's land!" Michael warned. "Christine's a bit like the moon or the stars. You can gaze at her from afar, but you don't want to get close enough to touch her."

"Yeah? Is that so?"

Michael cast a wary eye toward the American, "You want to know a thing or two about curses? Ask the boys in the cemetery about her."

Squinting inquisitively, Brendan shielded his eyes from the glaring sun.

"Dead," he continued, "every last one of them. Seems her men don't last very long. Even the summer flings. All disappeared or six feet under."

"Really?" Brendan asked, scoffing off the nonsense. "What about Charlie then?"

"Charlie!" he gawked.

"Yeah, I figured they were a hot item, you know, with those matching tattoos and all."

"Bloody hell!" Michael sputtered. "We ain't that small of a village! Charlie's her brother! Get your mind out of the gutter, man!"

Brendan's heart lifted a little, feeling a sudden surge of energy. Then it dawned on him that he really shouldn't – and didn't care whether Christine was single or not. But thoughts of her returned, the spell she'd cast upon him briefly, that scent... Forcing himself to concentrate on his game, he sliced the club. His ball streaked across the course and descended toward the sheep. Down, down, down...

SMACK!

The animal let out an earsplitting, BLAAAAAAAAA!, zigzagging wildly across the grass.

Squinting. Brendan scanned the green. "Where'd it go? Where's my ball?"

Overcome with a convulsing fit of mad cackling, Michael fell to the ground, managing to point at the sheep that had tottered crookedly halfway across the course. "Hole in one my friend!" he gasped. "You got a bloody hole in one! Wait 'til the boys hear about this! Now that's what I call golfing!"

Brendan stared incredulously at the twittering sheep.

Michael licked his finger, hoisting it into the air, *"Touché!"* He propped himself up, shaking a victorious fist at the animal. "Serves you right! Ha ha!"

∞∞∞

The weather had taken a turn for the better, nearly developing into a decent summer afternoon. Warm rays of sunlight graciously spilled down upon the perpetually soggy wood of the promenade, drawing out record numbers of ruddy-faced tourists. Like an army of ants, they buzzed and swarmed through the shops and food stalls, consuming everything in their path.

After Michael had dropped him on the post-parade route, Brendan began wandering in the general direction of the Mermaid Theater and Siren Shop, thirsting to discover more about the woman who had succeeded in capturing his imagination.

Among the shivering tourists clutching

candyfloss and jugs of hot tea, Brendan stopped mid-pace, the idea dawning upon him suddenly. He stood motionless in the crowd, astonished by his own brilliance. What if he was to document this peculiar, semi-obsession with the mysterious Manxwoman in the book, twisting it into a sort of romantic adventure? Of course it would have to be a sideline that was cleverly woven through the story, he rationalized, but it could be great; an honest tell-all from the unadulterated viewpoint of a man who had brushed off all relationships with the opposite sex (save the occasional one-night stand), since the night in nineteen-eighty-something when he'd found his high school sweetheart banging his best friend beneath the bleachers at the Winter formal dance. After all, Adventure Books *was* hounding him for another manuscript that would cross the narrow boundaries of travel/humor into the realm of best-selling non-fiction. He sniggered gleefully, recalling the way the extravagantly costumed vixen had held him helplessly in her cool gaze, then crumpled him like a tin can. Oh, yeah, he mused. This could be hilarious. It was a mission bound for disaster – the hopeless bachelor in hot pursuit of a Manx mermaid impersonator - and to top it all off, she hated his guts. A devilish grin spread across his face and he began walking again with a little hop in his step. Ooh, the things he would write…

At the end of the pier, an outdoor stage had mushroomed up where an amateur theater group was performing an original play called, ATHENA'S LAST MOMENTS. Although Brendan had already decided to go with the surprising new turn the un-written book had taken, he paused beside the stage to watch the trivial production that was laughably supposed to be the tale of Christine's grandparents. He slumped down against the edge of the platform. This was the perfect opportunity to collect his thoughts before he approached her again. It would have to be carefully maneuvered, he determined, allowing himself a moment to watch the tiresome play that was already underway.

Two stagehands moved painted plywood waves in the background, creating the vertigo effect of the rolling sea and an old man, positioned off to the side was bent over an ancient Wurlitzer organ, churning out classic seaside tunes while keeping a hopeful eye on his tip jar.

In the role of Athena was a middle-aged actress wearing heavy, theatrical stage makeup reminiscent of the silent films of the 1920's. Her glittery bikini top and fishtail costume were adorned with jumbo-sized sequins that sparkled in the mid-afternoon sun. She crossed the stage and stumbled over the fans of her fabric tail, sending a trickle of muffled chuckles through the crowd. Undaunted, she untangled the fin and delivered her lines. "I have returned from my world beneath the surface and have said my fare-wells to the ocean. I come to the shore, and to you my mortal lover!"

An actor in a thick, wool sweater and captain's hat stood center stage behind a perch of foam rocks. He watched the actress through a spyglass and shouted, "Athena! Athena! You've come back!"

As if searching for the voice of her lover, the mermaid scanned the audience, finally turning to him. "If you truly love a creature of the sea, throw it back! And if it returns, it surely was a love meant to be!"

Brendan groaned at the asinine rendition of the old saying, shoving his hands in his pockets miserably.

The booming voice of the actress commanded his attention back to the stage. "Jack! I'm yours for all of eternity!"

Dramatic background music poured out of the Wurlitzer and colored spotlights struck pink beams upon the actress. She closed her eyes and with a crash of organ keys, shimmied out of her tail, revealing a pair of skinny, bare legs. "The transformation has been made," she announced. "I am human now!"

"Take my hand my love!" Jack called to her as the stagehands began to lift a giant wave of blue fabric behind the unsuspecting ex-mermaid. Upon seeing the danger looming behind his lover, Jack panicked, "Athena! No!" But the wave continued to rise in the backdrop behind Athena as she reached out toward the fingertips of the distraught fisherman. Just as their hands touched, the wave made of rumpled, blue bed sheets engulfed her, prompting the actor to scream out his final wooden line, "Nooo! Athena! Come back! Come back!"

The curtain fell and the crowd groaned unanimously.

Brendan awarded the effort with a round of mindless applause as the cast reappeared and took a bow for the thinning audience. Leaning up against the stage, he set out to plot his next move. The Siren Shop was visible from his position across the pier, but he wasn't able to determine whether or not the fiery-haired, man-eater was inside or not. In a worn notebook, he scratched down some ideas.

Fiona Cross struck a match, touching it to the end of her cigarette while the cameraman broke down equipment after taping the droll, live performance. Reveling in triumph, she thought about the phone call she'd taken an hour ago from her executive producer back at the studio. Apparently, the tape of the unplanned fiasco at the parade this morning had aired in full – resulting in a flood of phone calls from Wakey Wakey viewers, demanding a replay of the un-scripted segment. In fact, the piece had caused such a buzz that it had already been sold to the evening newscasts and was scheduled to rebroadcast at six and again at eleven. Evidently, the comical mishap had captured the interest of everybody in the nation; Fiona Cross, Britain's most sought-after single, swept off her feet by an unknown playboy at a soul mate festival. According to her producer, the party invitations and phone calls had been pouring in all morning, inundating the assistants. But more importantly, the fans of the popular program were dying for more. So when he'd suggested that Fiona graciously consider staying on through the weekend to participate personally in her very own, prime-time soul mate search, she'd immediately agreed. Of course a new set of contracts would have to be drafted and the ludicrous sum of money she'd demanded would have to be sorted out…

Her cell phone rang. "We're on? Wicked," she grinned. "Bloody wicked."

She took a drag of her cigarette and glanced around at the backward little village, amusing herself with the absurd idea that she, Fiona Cross, should be here seeking true love on this dismal island. For God's sake, she thought, eyeing the unsavory bodies cluttering the pier. If this were the lot she'd have to sort through, she'd be earning every pence of the outrageous sum she'd negotiated. Perhaps, she sniffed, her soul mate was a greasy fisherman who could open a beer bottle with his teeth, or maybe he was a balding, middle-aged divorcee with a belly the size of New Zealand - or could he be that tall, dark-haired man over there in the leather jacket – the one who kind of reminded her of that asshole Brendan James...?

Her head cocked awkwardly to the side.

Brendan James?

"Oh my God," she inhaled sharply, her eyes fixed upon the lanky American who sat brooding on the other side of the stage.

What in the bloody hell is he doing here?

Not letting the dark-haired Yank out of her sight, Fiona crushed out her cigarette, barging through the crowd. She approached from the side, took a deep breath and tapped him on the back. "Brendan James? I don't believe it," she purred coolly.

Brendan looked up from his notebook, startled by her sudden and unexpected presence. His eyes unavoidably raked over the tall, icy blonde – and she looked good, he thought. *Really good.* "Fiona? God, you look - outstanding. It's been years since we, I mean, er, you know. Uh, yeah, so - what are you doing here?"

Fiona rolled her frosty blue eyes, impatiently tossing her lustrous coif. "Wakey Wakey? My morning show?"

"Oh, right. Right," he responded, flashing a smile. "How's it going?"

"Super," she chirped. "Just super. Number one in the ratings."

"That's great. No one deserves it more than you," he nodded, growing increasingly uncomfortable with the awkward small talk. "So..." he uttered, running out of things to say.

A sinister grin flicked across her lips as she trailed a set of French-manicured fingernails across his cheek, sending a tingling chill down his spine. "You know, I've never forgotten those nights we spent together in London," she breathed intimately.

"We had some good times," he managed, snapping his notebook shut.

"There's nothing quite like interviewing and shagging a best selling author," she sniggered sarcastically. "Is there?"

Her voice was grating at his nerves and a forgotten vision the two of them, entwined on the floor of her posh, Mayfair flat came flooding back in full color. "I wouldn't know, would I?" He tucked the notes into his jacket with a yawn.

She retained her composure, but was having some difficulty bottling her temper. He was still an arrogant asshole, she determined. The urge to gouge him with another bitter insult was irresistible as he glowered at her through sullen blue eyes. "Wait a minute," she sniffed, gazing around at the gaieties of the festival. "You're not actually here to write a book about this *tourist attraction* are you?"

Brendan wished that she would just go away. He wasn't in the mood to discuss the sour, short-lived relationship that he'd backed out of after two weeks when she'd suggested that he move to London. His shoulders tensed and he lowered his voice. "Look, I'm sort of working undercover."

"Oh! Right! Your specialty, working undercover!" she gasped dramatically. Placing her hands on narrow hips, she leaned into his face with a smug grin. "Tell me Brendan, how did it feel to fall from grace?"

"And - what exactly is it you're talking about?" he sighed impatiently.

"I want you to tell me how it *felt* to see your second book being sold as firewood on the bargain tables in the bowels of discount book shops," she growled.

He flinched, her vicious words leaving him utterly speechless.

"It hurts, doesn't it?" she whispered adding a saccharine sweet, "poor baby."

His stare was hard, and he hated her for rubbing salt into his unhealed wounds. He blinked, attempting to mask the anguish and the rage flashing just behind his eyes. "I – can't believe you just said that to me."

"And I can't believe that I fell for you!" she spat. "How many other women did you charm into bed with your big, best-selling book?"

He raised a hand in an attempt to end the derailed conversation that was headed for disaster, but she wasn't finished with him. She went on, swiping a lock of hair from his ashen, unshaven face. "Just look at you now, the washed up writer and - man you've become. It's pathetic!"

"It wasn't like that," he snapped back angrily, "what happened between us…"

Fiona stopped herself. People were watching. She took a breath, unable to determine if the welling tears she now fought back were for the way he'd injured her, or because of the cruel, cutting words she'd just spoken to the man who'd dumped her like last week's rubbish. "I have to go now," she choked. "I have a television show to host." With that, she turned on her spiked heels and stalked off. It took him a moment to react. "You always were a sentimental old cow, weren't you Fiona!" he hollered childishly.

He watched her disappear into the crowd, the encounter leaving him naked and shaken. He slammed a fist into his palm. Being insulted by a woman was nothing new to him, but the scene that had just unfolded with Fiona was downright offensive and had left his blood simmering. So what if the fling hadn't worked out, he scowled. That didn't give her any special privileges to stomp on his failures as a writer. That was below the belt. But what really gnawed at him was the fact that she'd managed to magnify his own self-doubts and had aired them out in the open, leaving him gorged with an uneasy concern about his ability to actually pull off the new book. He rose to his feet, urgent with the need to leave the spot where his newly-found confidence had just been pitilessly unraveled.

CHAPTER SEVEN

It was determination alone that drove Brendan toward the dazzling Siren Shop; determination to carry on with the project and, above all else, to prove Fiona and the critics of his last book wrong. As he stood before the window display of the mermaid boutique, recalling key phrases from the outrageously funny chapters he'd produced just last night, a slight grin crossed his lips and his ego began to re-inflate. He peered through the glass, his calculating eyes searching for a glimpse of her beyond the flamboyant window dressing. A pair of jabbering women exited the shop wearing headdresses woven of fishnet and strands of dried seaweed, twinkling with fragments of sea glass in the afternoon sun. He grasped the door, holding it open for the two ladies, then silently slunk into the shop.

An awkward feeling crept over him as he stepped into the cozy, feminine boutique, determining immediately that this was no place for a man. The shop reeked of home-made lavender bath splashes, perfumed sea salts and an assortment of other scented potions, all neatly packaged in cobalt blue glass bottles and jars displayed on the shelf next to him. Peering beyond the slats on the rack of concoctions, he spotted Christine and found her looking sexier than should've been legal at eleven-o'clock in the morning, a vision that made his throat tighten. Nymph-like auburn tresses spilled across her shoulders beneath a sheer, silvery halter top. The clothing was artful, no sinful, he thought, taking a step back to watch her in full view and noticing the black, embroidered shawl that she'd knotted into a skirt around her hourglass waist. She was mid-conversation with a very old woman in a moth-eaten dress, who was busy poking through the racks of glittery clothes with a black, hardwood cane. She hobbled over to the counter, dragging several, paper shopping bags behind the frayed hem of her coat and hefted them before Christine with a wheezing "humph" sound.

"Oh yes," the old woman tattled. "It happened just this morning. That American, he hit the ball and it went POP! Straight up his bum, it did!"

Christine covered her mouth to avoid giggling. "No, he didn't…" she whispered dreadfully.

"He did!" she cried. "And something has to be done about it. I say we ban those Yanks from the island before they destroy our bloody livestock! First they burn our tea - and now this!"

"The – Boston Tea Party?"

The old woman nodded emphatically. "Old man Gibb said the animal's gone absolutely mad. Even attacked his Australian shepherd 'fore it ran off into the wood. Said he'll to have to put it down – can't have a mad sheep roaming the countryside like that." Her eyes narrowed into constricted slits, "and that's one less skein of wool on me plate as well."

Biting her tongue, Christine uneasily focused her attention on the lumpy paper bags the woman had dragged in. "Right. So, uh, what have you brought me today?" she pointed with an apprehensive smile.

Brendan ducked back behind the shelf and bumped the display of bottles, nearly dumping over an entire tester jar of ocean essence dusting powder. Cursing under his breath, he patted spots of fine white silt off of the adjacent rack of long dresses it had spattered on.

The feathers of an ancient, African gray parrot ruffled with excitement as it eyed him suspiciously from a perch on the curtain rod. With head bobbing, it opened its beak to squawk.

Brendan pointed a deadly finger at the bird, cursing in a barely audible hiss, *"I'm gonna pluck every feather from your mangy body and rotisserize your egg-laying ass if you utter so much as a peep!"*

The parrot's yellow eyes went wide and it hissed back at him before scuttling off to the other side of the curtain.

Using more force than necessary, he replaced the powder puff back inside its wide round box, sending another whiff of the stuff swirling up his nostrils. He held his breath, trying to suppress a sneeze that was building with great intensity within his sinuses.

The dusty old woman poked at her grisly bags. "Nearly knit me fingers to the bone to have these finished before the festival week," she griped, disgorging a pile of black wool sweaters onto the counter. She pointed a gnarled finger, indicating the clothing racks within the shop. "I see you already sold the entire lot I brought in last month. I ought to raise me prices seeing that you're making a bloody fortune from me handiwork."

Forcing a smile in return, Christine hesitantly removed a few crisp bills from the register. She slid them toward the woman, which the old lady first held up to the light, then counted through squinted, miserly eyes.

"Yeah – thanks again Dotty," Christine sighed. "It's been lovely seeing you."

Something in her words confounde the woman.

She dropped the cash, suddenly grasping Christine's hands in her own. Her blue eyes, clouded with cataracts, grew watery and sentimental as she gazed unmoving into the face of the youthful redhead. "That's the name she used to call me - *Dotty*. We were the very best of mates, your grandmother and I," she breathed, pausing to study the familiar characteristics of Christine's face. "Looking at you takes me back. You remind me of her so. The spitting image." The old woman blinked away tears, shaking her head nostalgically. "Why do all of the good ones have to go and kick the bucket?"

Christine's lip trembled slightly, tightening her grip on the woman's age-spotted hands. "Why don't you pop by for tea one afternoon? I'd love to hear all about - the good old days."

Dotty sniffled, crushing the money into her battered purse. "Tea. I'd like that. That is, if the Americans don't burn it all by then."

Something rustled within the racks, followed by an earsplitting "AH-AH-ACHOO!"

The parrot let loose, squawking bloody murder and fluttering her wings. She dove from her perch, flapping wildly around Brendan's head.

"Aaaaaah!" he screeched, swiping at the attacking bird as it sunk its claws into his scalp and pecked at the fleshy part of his earlobe.

"Pearl! Stop that!" Christine hollered, peering beyond the dresses as Brendan stumbled out of the place he'd been hiding, his leather jacket speckled with a flurry of dusting powder. He ducked down, covering his head as the bird's wings rustled across the shop. "Ow!" he cursed, rubbing his bitten ear. From her mixed expression of surprise and annoyance, he wasn't sure if she was startled by his presence or angry that he'd been concealed behind her garments eavesdropping. Probably both, he decided.

Dotty shuffled over to the door and took Brendan by the shoulders, steering his tall frame toward Christine. With a wink and a shove, she heaved him forward with an awkward stumble. "Now here's a nice customer for you dear. Go on," she prodded, "show him me sweaters. Don't be shy."

Brendan opened his mouth, feeling the pulse of his blood unexpectedly quicken. Finding himself face-to-face with Christine, he couldn't quite remember the reason for his visit. She was stunning, in the literal sense of the word. The jumble of merchandise around him seemed to disappear and he felt himself slipping away from reality. In the background, he vaguely heard the shop bell jingle as the old woman tottered out, leaving him alone with the creature he'd been drawn to.

With an arched brow, Christine shoved the sweaters back into the paper bags they'd arrived in. "Congratulations on the sheep. You're the talk of the village," she sniffed, glancing sideways at her cowering pet parrot. "I can see that you really have a way with animals."

"Yeah, about the sheep. It was an accident," he explained with a laugh. "A very strange accident."

Her eyes shone vibrant green, grazing over his physique. Not bad, she thought, sizing him up in proper light. He was handsome and well-built, a man who liked to roam, she determined by his profession and his lack of a gold wedding band on his ring finger. She shrugged casually, "Doesn't matter. The boys at the golf course are liable to name you a bloody saint for it." Shoving the bags aside, she raised her intense eyes to meet his again. "So, what brings you down to the shop?" she nodded, indicating the white spots on his clothing with a slight smirk. "Shopping for a special lady friend?"

Brendan looked down at his coat and hastily dusted himself off. Once again, he felt like a teenager even though she was at least ten years younger than he. "I – no. No. I was just browsing," he stumbled, noticing the ethereal glow of her skin illuminated by the sparkling sunshine that slanted through the windows. "Well, maybe just a little something for my mother, I think," he lied.

"I still haven't made up my mind about you yet, you know," she scrutinized, straightening a stack of paper receipts by the register. "On the other hand, a man who goes out of his way to pick up trinkets for his mother can't be all that sinister."

Shifting from one foot to the other, he inhaled a sharp whiff of the lavender water that she'd trailed along her sleek, graceful neck. "Actually, I just came down here to apologize for barging in on you last night like I did." With his head spinning slightly now, he willed his brain and mouth to work together before he made an even bigger fool out of himself

"I didn't mind," she responded lazily, tossing a wavy tress behind her pale shoulder.

He wondered incredulously what part of it she didn't mind, startled by her relatively warm reception. Unavoidably, he watched her move with a thrill of fascination and desire as she shifted slightly on long, strong limbs. She was delicate and stoic, he noticed, and there was something almost fairy-like about her as her wide emerald eyes observed him gazing at her. Brendan indicated her smooth, toned

calves, visible beneath the fringed edges of the embroidered shawl she wore. "I see that you're wearing your leg costume today. Very realistic."

"Hmmm," she considered, the corners of her lips
curling with a small hint of amusement. "I never
thought of it that way." She reached for a feather
duster and brushed the tip across a wind chime
crafted of tiny seashells, sending a weightless sym-
phony of tinkling music through the boutique.

He surveyed her breathlessly, this stranger, this
woman. It was impossible to predict what she would
say next, he mused, but decided he'd figure her out,
in this life or the next. "Well they suit you just fine.
The legs."

She'd expected him to come back hungry for her
after the little spell she'd cast on him, but hadn't expected him to be charming. She looked away from
the underlying expression of longing in his cobalt
eyes, beginning to wish that she hadn't amused herself with him. Something about him had intrigued
her from the first moment he'd brazenly waltzed into
the dressing room, but now she'd have to wait until
the charm wore off before she could determine what
was genuine - and what she'd done to him. It would
be hours yet until the effect entirely dissipated and
he was back to normal, a thought that sent a thrill-
ing shiver down her spine. "So," she asked coolly,
"will there be anything else then?"

"I...," he breathed, beginning a sentence that
trailed into the ether. The magical smell of the sea,
the salt spray, the sand, the deep, fathomless secrets
that seemed to ooze from her being, began to envelope his head, casting all reason and intellect aside.
His vision began to blur, his limbs becoming light.
Skirting on the edges of blissful confusion, he began

to see this woman for what she was; a phenomenon that could inspire painters and writers to madness attempting to capture the intangible essence that exuded from every pore of her body like gossamer...

"Everything," he confessed, drawn closer to her by magnetic intensity. "I want – everything..." He reached out to touch the flesh of her forearm with the haunted emptiness of a man who had never known enchantment...

Cat-like, she sprung back before he could make physical contact, quickly sliding open a drawer beneath the counter.

Damn! Where is it! she panicked, fumbling through the jumble of contents amongst the scissors and the tape and the letter opener. *There!* She curled her fingers around a tiny, crystal perfume atomizer filled with sparkling golden liquid, something that she'd been cornered into using on the rare occasion that a lovelorn man got out of line with her. It was a last resort, but she had to do it as much as it repelled her. This had gone dangerously far enough.

Standing motionless, staring at her full lips, he was unaware that moments had passed - and that she was aiming a bottle at him. All he could think about was pressing his mouth against hers, tasting her – discovering her every...

PFFFFFFFT!

Christine squeezed the bulb of the atomizer with unsteady hands, spraying a mist of acrid solution directly into his face.

A sharp tang jolted him back a pace, his head buzzing with a humming sound as if he'd been hit like a gong. Blinded for a moment, he could hazily hear her echoing voice chattering at a rapid pace somewhere in the vicinity. "It's a new perfume I created. What do you think of it? Do you think it will sell or do you fancy the scent's too strong for most women? Really, be honest," she jabbered on, setting the bottle next to the register, "Do you like it?"

Shaking his head fretfully, he attempted to escape the putrefying stench of rotten eggs, mingled with ammonia that had startled him back to reality. "What - what in the hell is the matter with you?" he gagged. Still pawing at his face, the veil of swirling confusion seemed to evaporate, and with complete and sudden clarity, he knew exactly why he'd come here and what he'd come after. The book, he remembered, I've come to write about – *her*.

He squinted at Christine through watering eyeballs, finding himself relieved of the overwhelming desire to kiss her that he'd been overcome with just moments ago. How dare she arouse me to the edge of ecstasy, then spray that horrible, repelling scent, he thought caustically, smirking to himself, knowing secretly that he'd give her what she had coming in the in end. He picked up a twinge of apprehension in her expression as she waited for him to respond to her bizarre behavior. He'd be dammed if he'd let her get under his skin again.

Remaining very still, she held her breath while looking him over carefully. Yes, she decided with uneasiness, he was definitely coming to. The cocky, arrogant manner had returned, the color in his face was resurfacing and he began to look just as he had the night before. The preparation of distilled, black cat urine had done its work well.

He narrowed his eyes, first at her, then at the potion.

Startled, she shrunk back a step.

Without warning, he stretched a long arm across the counter, swiping the bottle out from under her nose.

"No, please don't – touch that…" she protested, attempting to pry it from his fingers.

Shooting her a warning look, he held it away at arm's length. His calculating mind scrutinized the unmarked, glittering container of crystal as he sniffed the surrounding air with repugnance. With eyes locked on hers he announced grimly, "I'll take it," dangerously shaking the bottle of volatile yellow liquid. He wrenched the wallet loose from the pocket of his jeans with his free hand. "How much do you want for it?"

Struck speechless, she stood gawking for a moment. "You - you'll - *what*?"

"The perfume," he repeated, gripping the bottle before her with a grimace. "I want to buy it. I-want-to-buy-it!"

"I'm sorry," she informed him sternly, grasping for the atomizer that he dangled just out of reach. "I'm afraid that is not for sale!"

He peered around the shop at the merchandise, then back at her, enjoying the taunting that was making her perfect features screw up so unattractively. He hid the bottle behind his back, watching her expression turn from concern to near anxiety. "This is a boutique isn't it? You sell things here, do you not?"

"*Not - that*," she hissed, swiping at the concoction with desperation.

He clutched it in his hand a second longer, not allowing a grin to crack across his face. After an intense stare down, he placed the crystal bottle on the counter. "Too bad," he sniggered bitterly, his thoughts turning to Fiona Cross. "I know a woman it would suit."

She hastily snatched the potion up, tucking it well out of reach, them spoke, her sultry voice an octave higher than usual. "You see, the formula, it obviously hasn't been perfected at this time. But I'll let you know if I ever start bottling it for retail consumption," she rambled.

"I don't believe you," he challenged. "I think you're lying to me."

Cheeks flushing now, she busied herself with the feather duster again, swiping at imaginary particles of dust on the glass display case. "I don't know what you're talking about and I don't like your tone Mr. James," she defended without looking up.

Brendan planted his hand on the counter, plucking the duster from her white-knuckled grip. He flicked it across the tip of her nose and she blinked back in surprise. "Fair enough. But, if you ever decide to market that, *eau de stench*, of yours, I'll take the biggest, gift-wrapped bottle you can muster up."

"Right, then," she nodded, her pulse quickening from the way he stared at her with such amusement. Her eyes flicked upward and caught his grin. Something dangerously weakened inside her being, an omen of peril to come, should she explore this man any further. Before she could make any sense her own confusion, the shop bell clanged, followed by a group of cackling tourists that had barged into the boutique. She snapped to attention, glanced at the customers, then back at Brendan, "I've got to get back to work now."

An obese American held up a green mini dress, yelping across the shop, "you got one of these little numbers in a full figure size?"

"I'll be right with you," Christine responded, wrenching her duster away from him. "I've got to help them. You have to go."

He didn't feel like going anywhere. "Maybe we should talk over dinner," he suggested, putting forth his most dazzling smile. "I still want to get some comments from you for the article. Besides," he added with a grin, "I never got the opportunity to ask you why your friend Claire insists that your grandmother was a mermaid. Pretty interesting family tree."

His voice was mocking now, she thought. "I don't think there's anything more to say. Claire is a silly old woman and why she's telling you these fairy tales – I'll never know. Anyway, you really should go now," she persisted.

With his feet planted firmly on the ground, he nodded, indicating the pile of sweaters on the counter. "All right then. I'll be a customer and you can help me. After all, I was here first. Weren't you supposed to sell me one of those?"

Christine picked up a sweater in exasperation, "one of these you say?" Shoving one at him she added, "be my guest."

Unraveling the garment, he squinted at the lumpy mass of wool. The neck was ridiculously long and the arms were six inches too short. She plucked out another from the pile with unusually thin arms and crooked zigzag stitching down the front, holding it before his eyes. "Perhaps one of these will suit you then?"

His brow wrinkled as he scrutinized the odd garments trying to make heads or tails of them. "You've got to be kidding me."

"Oh, no. I've got a stockpile of genuine Manx, mutant wool sweaters in the back store room," she sighed, softening a little at the thought of the old woman who'd made them. "The poor thing's blind as a bat. But it's the only way she can make a little extra pocket money these days…"

In response, he removed his jacket, plucked up a lopsided sweater and struggled to pull it over his head.

Christine covered her mouth to avoid giggling at him as he pushed his skull through the narrow neck. "Really, you don't have to…," she told him.

"Well? What do you think?" he asked expectantly, modeling the peculiar turtleneck before her.

She shook her head and grinned, her eyes flicking to meet his, "I think - that was sweet."

Straight-faced, Brendan dropped a twenty-pound note on the counter and walked toward the door, ignoring the tourists in the shop who were gawking at his purchase. He slipped his coat back on, shooting a dirty look at the parrot on his way out.

"Wanker," the bird mumbled, as the shop bell jangled.

Leaning against the door outside, he replayed every moment of the scene through his head. He was overcome with words, describing the enchanting, bizarre encounter and found himself longing to write down every last detail of it. But first, he decided, a good, long walk was in order to replenish his energy and more importantly - to rid his clothing of the dusting powder and rancid perfume he was now drenched in.

The stroll along the colorless beach beneath the pier did the trick and he was eager to sit down before the computer to bang out another chapter. Although his face was sand-stung and his teeth permanently clenched from the relentless blasts of sea spew, his head was clear and he was hungry. His stomach rumbled from the aroma of deep-fried cod, wafting through the crisp air. Deciding to grab a quick bite to eat before settling in for the evening, he headed back up the steep, cement staircase toward the Wesley's fish and chip shack on the pier.

The promenade crowd was thinner now, consisting mainly of locals toting wicker baskets, taking advantage of the mild weather to purchase their weekly rations of fresh seafood from the grumbling fisherman displaying the day's catch in buckets of ice along the shop fronts.

Sarah Wesley was working behind the counter of the fish and chip shack, the third Brendan had seen in the village with a sign boasting the 'world's greatest.' With his notebook open, he jotted down some observations before approaching the ramshackle shop.

Sarah spotted him and ripped off her hair net. "Would you stop writing me bloody life story already!" she bellowed.

Taking a seat on a vinyl stool at the counter, he poked his head through the sliding glass window to watch her work. "And what exactly are you cooking back there?"

Removing a wire basket from the deep fryer, she flipped some oily, breaded balls onto a draining rack. "House special," she explained over her shoulder, patting the food with a paper towel. "Neptune's Nards. Julian's idea of revenge I suppose," she muttered bitterly. "He started selling them right after that whole Charlie theTuna fiasco." She flipped the balls over,violently stabbing them onto a wooden skewer. "But honestly! Who could blame me? The man hasn't pitched a bloody tent since 1989!" With that, she shoved a plate across the counter with a clenched smile. "They're right tasty with a wee dab of mustard and a splash of vinegar."

Brendan flinched, "Right."

Sarah forced a tighter smile. "We sell these balls by the ton around here. Oh, yes. Very popular with the holidaymakers. They're quite gourmet, you know. It's really a shame you're not writing for Food and Wine Magazine," she wished aloud.

"Yeah, a shame…"

She squinted in the mid-afternoon sun. "So, have you found her yet?"

Brendan poked at the greasy food. "Found who?"

With a wistful sigh, she handed him a plastic fork . "Your soul mate. That's why all these people gather here every year under the Northern Lights."

"I thought they came to get laid."

"That too," she informed him, her dark, brown eyes becoming soft like melted milk chocolate. "But they say that if you see a silhouette against the moonlight on the Midsummer Eve, it'll belong to your one true love. I was just reading in the paper the other day that we've made over eighty successful matches at the festival. There's gotta be something to it. Right?"

"I'm here to observe, not to participate," he reminded her.

Sarah shrugged her shoulders and went on, "we've all got our reasons. But don't you think it a trifle odd that you somehow showed up in this place at this time?" Her narrowed eyes swept over his dark demeanor. "What? Don't you believe in love?"

"You don't want to know what I think about love," he waved, "trust me."

Sarah's eyes were fixed on him now, filled with a look that demanded he give her some sort of an explanation.

With a sigh, he picked up the plate of nards and scowled. "You really wanna know what I think? Okay. Love is like – is like this delicacy here for example," he analogized. "See, you're walking along the pier, minding your own business and then you catch this delicate aroma wafting through the air. Before you know it, your mouth is watering so badly that you follow it all the way back to the shack and then before you can think twice..." He took a vicious bite of the battered merman balls to make his point, "you consume it all in one bite! But wait! Wait! It gets better! Then, ho, ho, ho, then you're left with this queasy feeling in the pit of your stomach and wish you'd just kept on walking *because you really weren't even hungry in the first place!*" He slammed his fist down directly into the plate of greasy balls, squashing them flat.

"Jesus man. You're really screwed up! Do you wanna talk about it?" she brayed sympathetically, passing him a pile of napkins. "They say it's good to talk about it."

Brendan wiped off his hands, picked up the notebook and handed her a five-pound note. "No. I don't want to talk about it. I'm off to the boat."

"What? And miss the beauty pageant?" she questioned. "Julian's the master of ceremonies this year you know."

Brendan was pretty sure that his head was about to implode. "Another beauty pageant?"

Sarah nodded, "Oh yes, We have two in the village every year. But this one is a very important cultural event around here."

৵৵

The rickety outdoor stage that had been used for the amateur theatrical production of *Athena's Last Moments* had been taken over by Heather Bay's campiest attraction. A large banner stretched across the platform touting; UGLIEST MERMAID COMPETITION.

Brendan stood off to the side of the stage taking notes as ten male contestants in wigs, makeup and mermaid costumes tried to win over the unruly, beer-sloshing crowd that had gathered.

A burly man with a five-o'clock shadow was stuffed into a skin-tight, spandex mermaid tail as he sang the old holiday favorite, *I Do Love To Be Beside the Seaside.*

At the end of the number, Julian appeared, still wearing his rumpled, powder blue tuxedo and staggering as though he'd had a drink or two. He walked on center stage and took the microphone from the contestant. "Let's hear a round of applause for our last contestant!" The audience howled with laughter as the hairy-chested mermaid grabbed Julian's bony ass. "Mortals beware!" Julian shouted at the crowd. "Don't fall in love! For these sexy sea beasties must return to the ocean by midnight. Don't let the song and the beauty of the sirens tempt you! Be strong!"

The audience howled as the contestants threw strings of plastic beads into a sea of grabbing hands below. Julian expertly dodged a beer bottle that whizzed by his head and went on with the show, pointing to the line up of gruesome mermaids. "And now it's time to select the winner of the competition who shall be crowned this year's ugliest mermaid!" He walked the line-up, singling out each of the hopeful contestants as the rowdy audience booed and laughed at the choices. Julian reached the end of the line and spotted Brendan on the side of the stage. Before he could react, Julian had grabbed him by the arm, thrown a blonde wig on his head and shoved him out to the center of the platform. "Hey man! What are you doing?" he choked.

Grabbing the microphone, he nudged the bewildered writer toward the edge of the stage. "Ladies and gentlemen! We've just added another last-minute contestant!" he announced. "May I present to you, all the way from the land of stars and stripes, the home of apple pie, Miss Big Apples! Let's give her a hand!"

The crowd booed and Brendan looked helplessly at Julian who was frantically motioning with his hands for the American to do something. "It's a bloody talent show!" Julian hissed. "Do something – or God help you! The bastards will eat you alive!"

Brendan shot a desperate look at the old geezer behind the Wurlitzer. With a knowing wink, he began playing "I'm Too Sexy" on his organ. Forced into the spirit of things by the mob of booing drunks, Brendan lifted the leg of his pants, showing the onlookers a hairy calf. To his surprise, they began to applaud and whistle. Certain that he'd already made a complete fool out of himself and with nothing else to lose, he stripped off his sweater before the masses, cutting loose with the cheesy song that ground out from the wheezing organ.

"I thought you said he 'ad big apples!" someone jeered, sending the crowd into a wave of uproarious laughter.

As Brendan danced around the stage, the other contestants had huddled together, suddenly swarming him like angry bees, just as he tossed his mangled Manx sweater into the groping hands of the audience.

"Aaaaaaaugh!" Brendan hollered as the mermaids picked him up, promptly tossing his half-naked body into the howling mob below.

Peering over the edge of the stage, Julian shrugged his shoulders and went on with the show. "Around here we've gotta throw the small ones back! Eh folks?"

Among the crowd, Brendan scrambled to his feet, not bothering to search for his sweater and t-shirt among the spectator's feet. He stood and found himself facing a large drunken man with piggish eyes who blocked his way with an enormous gut. "Oi sunshine! What's the matter? Ain't getting any?" he leered.

Brendan grunted nonchalantly, attempting to step around the man, but the pissed giant blocked his path making a kissing sound. "Come on luv! Wanna have a go?"

The crowd backed up in a circle around the two men, anticipating a brawl. The drunken man dropped his plastic cup of beer and raised a set of swollen fists. Brendan flipped a strand of golden wig hair from his eyes, then punched the jeering stranger in the stomach. He crumpled in half and dropped like a fallen tree. The rambunctious onlookers cheered as Brendan stalked away, shirtless, with only the gleaming blonde wig protecting his goose pimpled flesh from the elements.

Brendan trudged along the rocky, overcast beach, lost in an overwhelming jumble of thoughts and phrases that he planned to write down as soon as he got back to the houseboat. Massive rain clouds rumbled with thunder over the sea as he reflected with gleeful exhaustion, that the day had been too good to be true. The usual exaggerations and embellishments of the details wouldn't be necessary to depict the madness that enveloped this place.

It was a writer's dream.

In his contemplation of where to begin, he'd forgotten his own appearance. A pair of hopeful women, attempting to sunbathe on the lackluster beach, wrapped in wool cardigans over floral-print bikini tops, giggled through chattering teeth as Brendan passed by. He nodded politely, then remembered the ludicrous wig that crowned his head. He snatched off the tangled nest of golden hair, flinging it into the icy sea froth, where he watched the surf carry it off like a jellyfish. "Wasn't my color," he smiled at the ladies who were suddenly clutching their plastic beach bags, ready to make a run for it.

Further up the lonely stretch of beach, a little girl of five played in the cold gray sand with a mermaid Barbie and a battered Ken doll with matted hair. The child was chattering to her dolls in a heavy Manx accent as Brendan approached. He stopped, observing the game in silence as Barbie sailed through the air, landing in Ken's outstretched arms.

"So," he inquired, "what's in the future for these lovebirds? Do they shack up in a two-bit houseboat and live happily ever after on Ken's measly salary as a fry cook?"

Crinkling her ruddy nose, the girl stared up at him with innocence and curiosity. "Everybody knows what happens to them, tra-la-la-la la," she sang.

He crouched down beside her, trailing his fingers through the sand. "Everybody but me, apparently."

She looked away from the setting sun and gazed at him again, slightly annoyed that she had to explain such things to grown-ups. "When she falls in love with him, the magic in the sky takes her tail away and she turns into a real girl."

"Ah, now I get it," he nodded with a grin, rising to leave.

"You're a silly man," she giggled, returning to the dolls.

"I've been called worse."

Still shirtless, Brendan shivered in his leather jacket and made his way down High Street, numb to the stares that the tourists and shopkeepers shot his way. Michael Blake was sweeping the steps outside the Siren's Whale and gawked as the writer slogged past the pub. "Jeee-sus! What happened to you, man? Where's your shirt?" he shouted.

"Don't know," Brendan waved.

Laughing heartily, he called out after him, "Come on down to the pub later tonight. I've got a surprise for you and a fresh pallet of Codsucker's just in from the brewery!"

The setting sun cast an eerie, platinum glow

across Heather Bay Cemetery. A moss-covered church loomed in the distance and ancient, leaning gravestones carved from eroded granite, cast lofty shadows along the broken stone path.

Christine's midnight-black cloak dusted the crumbled walk as she opened the twisted, wrought iron gate of the graveyard and slipped inside. In her arms was a large wicker basket filled with fragrant bouquets of purple flowers. Hand-scrolled notes on parchment paper were affixed to each cluster of fresh lavender, and bound with a strand of grainy seaweed. Once she was hidden behind the time-scarred block stones of the chapel, she removed the hood of her cloak, releasing a pile of ginger tresses down her back. Then she went about her business, methodically picking her way through the cemetery, stopping before certain graves and depositing small bunches of flowers before headstones, some so old the epitaphs were unreadable.

Within the stone church, an elderly clergyman moved toward the thick glass windows after noticing a flash of movement in the quiet fenced area outside. Pulling a faded velvet curtain aside, he peered out into the graveyard and spotted the woman, leaving her offerings just as she did on this same day every summer. Seeing the girl, the temptress, flitting about his cemetery, sent a surge of panic through his aching joints. Fumbling in the pockets of his robes, he clasped his fingers around a small, wooden object with some sense of relief. He slid the window coverings shut, turned his gaze away from the woman outside, and quickly clipped a wooden clothespin onto the end of his nose.

In the center of the graveyard stood a striking statuary monument of a beautiful mermaid perched inside of a giant seashell. The inscription on the tomb read: FOR ATHENA – THE LAST MERMAID.

Christine set her largest bouquet of flowers at the base of the statue, kneeling down before it. She reached up, lovingly streaking her fingers across the rough surface of the weather-battered statue and hung her head in silence.

❧

Brendan sat before the laptop within the grimy confines of the houseboat, grinning as he typed at a mad pace.

'Where else can you wake up in the morning and find yourself standing on the sidelines of a parade where the most prominent float on the route is hijacked by an Adam Ant impersonator, complete with the accompaniment of a twenty-man bagpipe ensemble - all preceding a giant bottle of Codsucker Ale?

Perhaps it was the hoopla of the humping Pomeranians, in mermaid garb that got me going, or when I whacked a golf ball up the ass of a sheep, (which incidentally is the sole cause of the current wool famine on the island, according to a local shepherd.) But after seeing how one, loud American can devastate the Manx sweater industry with a single golf ball, I reflected upon my national heritage, and became frightened of it for the first time in my life.

Environmental menace or not, I stumbled into the Siren Shop, blinded by lust for the flaming haired she-devil, whom I'd chatted with the previous night. As I gallantly entered her souvenir boutique on the ground floor of the Mermaid Theater, I succeeded in dumping an entire box of dusting powder on my clothing, spurring her carnivorous parrot to peck my eyeballs out of their

120

sockets. Perhaps it was the 'love me' look that prompted her to douse me in the face with a generous spurt of rancid, eau de toilet. I don't know, but dazed from the reeking concoction, and feeling a little bit guilty about destroying the Manx wool supply, I purchased a sweater from her, hand-knitted by a blind woman, and promptly left the shop.

Cloaked in someone else's crocheted failure, I sauntered off along the pier and gorged myself in an island delicacy of deep-fried merman testicles (quite gourmet, actually with a little Dijon mustard and a splash of vinegar), then was forcefully entered in, and ejected from an ugly mermaid competition. I should have won, but I'll take that matter up with the judging committee later.

At present, I am still attempting to remove the repulsive stench from of my leather jacket, (which now smells curiously of a litter box) by laboriously scrubbing the hide with the can of scouring powder I found beneath the kitchen sink of my decomposing houseboat. Under normal circumstances, I wouldn't go to such lengths to make myself aromatically acceptable to other human beings, but I've been invited out for a night on the town by the Scottish proprietor of the Siren's Whale, who, despite his nasty habit of not wearing underwear beneath his tartans, has promised me a good time and all the Codsucker's I can put away. What can I say? I love this place...'

121

CHAPTER EIGHT

As night fell upon Heather Bay, the only sign of life in the sleepy, seaside village was the Siren's Whale. Loud disco music rattled the panes of the establishment's diamond shaped windows and boisterous female whooping and squealing howled from within. Brendan had hoped for a quiet nightcap, but it looked as if that was not going to happen. After a moment of hesitation, he passed beneath the arched, brick doorway, scowling at the banner that hung across the red wooden door; LOVE BOAT NIGHT.

Shouldering his way through the packed pub, he snagged an empty seat before the bar, noting that the fisherman's harpoon spear was now missing from the ceiling and most of the tables had been pushed aside to make room for a sweaty throng of dancing ladies. The loud, throbbing music, conglomerated with fifty varieties of perfume and the relentless cackling of the women promised a splitting headache. There were over a hundred of them, mostly singles on the dance floor, pumping, gyrating and sloshing mixed drinks all over one another.

Brendan's wandering gaze stopped dead on Christine who stood out dramatically amongst the frumpish female patrons. Beneath rainbow colored lights, her long, tousled hair was piled into a network of tiny braids and knots, framing her statuesque profile, then cascading down her bare back into untamed waves. Then they caught his eye, a pair of whimsical clamshells dangling from her earlobes as she spun around in circles to the pulsing rhythm. His charmed smile became lustful as he soaked in her dress, black and clinging, flecked with obsidian beads and fluttering capriciously just above the knees. Continuing the visual line from head-to-toe along the length of her long, slender legs, he squinted abruptly at the amusing pair of duck-like clogs on her feet. Her ensemble, by far the most magical and curious he'd ever seen a woman dressed in brought a goofy grin to his face.

With Claire at her side, the pair boogied like teenagers to the disco song, It's Raining Men – the tune serving as a battle cry for the mob of drunken women. In the spirit of things, a couple of hags on the floor popped open umbrellas, pumping the colorful nylon shields to the pulse of the music.

Michael looked Brendan over, giving him a complimentary pint and a hearty pat on the back. "Good of you to come. You're just in time, mate."

"Just in time for what?" he asked warily, turning to face the grinning bartender.

"You'll see," he winked. "You'll see."

Exhausted from dancing, Claire and Christine collapsed into a booth, the old woman craning her neck to peek at the bar. "Will you look at that!" she giggled. "I think somebody's caught your scent..."

Christine followed Claire's nod, spotting Brendan hunched over a pint. She quickly ducked back behind the seat. "He has not for Poseidon's sake! He's a writer. They always end up at the pub."

"Aye," she laughed uneasily. "A writer with little hearts dancing in his eyes."

"Oh, sod off," she snorted. "I had to spray him today, for your information. At the shop. He's perfectly normal now."

"You didn't!" she gasped, desperate for every detail. "What did he say? What did he do?"

Leaning across the table, she recounted the tale in a whisper to her wide-eyed friend.

Brendan had nearly finished his ale when Michael appeared before him, gazing at the door with a puppy dog grin on his face. He nudged the American's arm, pointing at a woman who had just walked in. The cool blonde peeled off a tan cashmere coat, steeled her nerves, then glanced around as if looking for someone.

"Bugger me! Isn't that Fiona Cross? You know, from Wakey Wakey?" Michael gawked.

"Probably," Brendan groaned miserably, not bothering to turn his throbbing head.

Michael waved to the female television hostess, motioning frantically to the empty chair beside Brendan. "Miss Cross! Over here! I-I've got a seat for you!"

Brendan's teeth clenched automatically. "NO Michael!" he hissed.

"Wow!" he whispered. "A real celebrity in the Siren's Whale! 'Aven't had a big star in here since Barry Gibb from the Bee Gees came in that time, or was it Andy?"

Fiona spotted Brendan's tousled hair and crossed the floor toward him. With some hesitation, she laid her fingers on his shoulder. "Just like old times. Right?"

Brendan spun around in his chair, greeting her with his nastiest scowl. "You know Fiona, you're getting dangerously close to becoming a character in my latest book," he threatened, downing the remainder of his pint and slamming it on the bar top.

Michael eagerly pointed to the empty seat again. "Right here Miss Cross."

Fiona ignored the bartender, dumping her coat and handbag on the stool. Wrapping her arms around Brendan's neck, she slid into his lap like a large reptile. "Come on, you know my solicitor would eat you alive in court."

"Yeah, I guess he would," he scoffed cynically. "So, what brings you here? Risen from your coffin to feed on the warm blood of the village peasants?"

Fiona laughed, but the sound was hollow and tinny. She knew that this wasn't going to be easy, but the way he was glowering at her at her made it even more difficult than she'd imagined. "Actually, I came here hoping to find you," she blinked hopefully.

"Forget it lady, I'm out of blood." He waved at Michael, gesturing toward his empty glass. "Another," he shouted.

"The thing is," she began uneasily, trailing a finger through his dark hair, then stopping as he swatted her hand away, "I've been regretting what I said to you, ever since those horrible words spilled out of my mouth this afternoon and I came here to... I came here to apologize, you know, in person."

There, I said it, she thought. As much as she loathed Brendan James, he was by far the best match for her on the island, judging by the grisly characters she'd seen bumbling around today. After all, she was being forced to find a 'soul mate' on a national television special and Brendan would be a safer bet than some intoxicated fishermen, if only she could somehow re-kindle the old flame between them for the remainder of the weekend. "I really am sorry," she repeated.

He'd been fully prepared to toss another insult her way, but held his tongue now, carefully studying her heart-shaped face through slanted eyes. "I don't believe you," he nodded suspiciously. "What are you really up to?"

"How dare you accuse me of being up to something," she defended, growing increasingly agitated with his attitude. "I don't think you realize how badly you hurt me and my reaction when I saw you after all those years was perfectly normal."

Brendan looked away from her blood-red lips, "there's nothing normal about you."

She turned his face to meet her eyes and continued, "I agree that what I said today was out of line - but certainly no more out of line than when you packed up your bags in the middle of the night and left! You didn't even write a goddamn note to tell me what I'd done wrong. Nothing. You just walked away. How do you think that made me feel?"

Brendan closed his eyes and sighed, supposing that she had earned the right to spout off ridiculing insults at him - or worse. The brief affair began with a whirlwind of hormones and ended fourteen days later after he was nearly suffocated with endless strings of parties, restaurant openings and dinner engagements with her set of stuffy, intellectual friends. Fiona Cross was a national celebrity, complete with stalking tabloid photographers documenting every fling she had. The woman lived in a soap opera world, a small detail that he'd overlooked until he began to feel like a character that was about to be written out, so he'd gotten rid of himself before they had the chance to do it for him. "Shit," he groaned guiltily. "I was a real ass, wasn't I?"

For the first time, Fiona saw a glimpse of the

man she'd fallen for so many years ago. "Yes," she she nodded. "You were."

"Look…," he began, starting to extrapolate on his reasons.

"Please, don't say anything," she dismissed. "Why don't we just buy each other a drink and forget about the entire thing? To old friends?" she suggested.

Brendan adjusted her weight on his lap. "All right. But let me pay for this one. I insist."

Christine was still jabbering to Claire, the two of them giggling now. "So he said, I-want-to-buy-it!" Christine burst out, imitating Brendan's accent. "He wanted to buy my bloody bottle of perfume!"

"Oh, Jesus," Claire choked, taking a drink of her strawberry margarita, "I hope for your sake that his taste in woman is better than his taste in fragrances." She stole another sideways glance at Brendan whose lap was now occupied by – Fiona Cross? "On second thought…" she motioned to the bar with a slight tilt of her chin.

Jealousy was the last emotion that Christine had expected to feel tonight, but her system began seething with it when she saw him with another woman, and not just any woman, but a successful, wealthy, famous one at that. Her eyes narrowed slightly, fixing upon the cool, frosty blonde that had her long, slender arms wrapped around his neck. "Looks like he's already made a friend," she sniffed, turning away from the pair as they downed shots of something with arms entwined. "Oooh!" she burst out suddenly, surprising herself. "He's driving me insane! What is he up to now?"

"That's Fiona Cross, the big television reporter,"

Claire informed her, secretly gloating at the sight of of Christine's envy toward another woman. She squinted at the couple, rubbing it in, "my goodness. What is she doing in his lap?"

"I know who she is," she growled irritably. "And I don't want to know what they're doing together making a spectacle of themselves in public."

"Looks like he's back to normal. Very humane of you to spray him this afternoon," Claire smirked.

Michael approached, warily eyeing the couple as he tried to conceive what a woman like Fiona Cross was doing writhing around on Brendan's thighs. He nervously handed her a pint, then wiped his hands on his apron. "On the house."

Fiona didn't avert her gaze from Brendan. "Thanks," she mumbled to the dumbfounded bartender.

Brendan peeled her arms from his neck, lifting her into the empty seat next to him. "Here. Have Codsucker," he told her, turning to Michael.

"I beg your pardon?" she coughed.

"Michael Blake – this is Fiona Cross, an old friend of mine."

Michael enthusiastically pumped Fiona's hand across the counter and gushed, "Wow. It's super to meet you Miss Cross. I'm your biggest fan. I watch your program every day. It's a real honor to have your presence gracing me humble..."

But before he could slip in the fact that he was an available man - and the owner of The Siren's Whale, Heather Bay's most prominent hot spot, the ladies in the pub began pounding on the tables chanting, "LOVE BOAT! LOVE BOAT! LOVE BOAT!", their collective voices rising to deafening levels. Michael glanced at the wild crowd, apologizing to Fiona, still gripping her hand. "I - I've got to get back to work now. Can I, I mean, can we, talk a little later perhaps?"

Fiona gazed blankly at the big man crushing her hand in his sweaty grip, then turned back to Brendan, rolling her eyes ever so slightly.

Michael blushed patting her hand, "Right. So sorry," he apologized. "I'll – give you some, uh, space." He fumbled for a microphone from behind the bar and busied himself with the speaker system.

Brendan smiled distastefully at Fiona and teased, "well, I'm glad to see that you're handling the fame thing all right, you know, treating the *little people* with such kindness and respect, now that you're number one in the ratings."

"Oh, for God's sake!" she protested. "Look at him Brendan! The man looks like a shrub in a kilt for crying out loud!"

He squinted at Michael, cracking a grin. One thing about Fiona, he thought, she had an eye for seeing things as they were – and wasn't afraid to say it, which was why, he supposed she was hosting her own television show.

"So, about the ratings..." she began, swallowing a gulp of ale, "there's something that I wanted to talk to you about. I have a sort of - proposition that might be of interest to you."

"What," he joked, "you in the market for a masculine co-host? Because I know this burned-out travel writer who'd love a shot at the gig."

"Not exactly," she hesitated. "It's more along the lines of a PR caper that could make things easier for both of us."

Brendan raised a brow. "You're serious?"

"Always." She leaned close, whispering in his ear, "Let me put it like this, the publicity alone could turn your next book into another best-seller."

He studied the smug grin on her face, the color flushing to his cheeks. "Publicity stunts don't make best sellers," he scoffed, offended by the suggestion that he should need her help to sell his books.

"I didn't mean it like that," she quickly apologized, blinking her eyes at him. "What I meant was that I – we, have a fabulous press opportunity sitting before us. All we have to do is snatch it up."

He exhaled cynically. "Is that what this visit was all about? First you insult me in a public place and nearly blow my cover, then you realized after the fact that you might actually have some use for my mangled carcass that would forward your own selfish purposes?"

"Yes," she answered straight. "That and the fact that I really did want to clear the air between us."

Her blunt honesty surprised him.

Not quite sure how to approach the subject of rekindling their romance on a television special before millions of viewers, she reached for her cigarettes and lit one with book of matches. Her eyes shifted around the crowded bar at the gawking patrons who were undoubtedly beginning to recognize her from the telly. "Look, can we talk about this someplace private? Where are you staying?"

Before he'd made a decision one way or the other, ear-splitting feedback reverberated through the pub as Michael flipped on the Karaoke system.

"Please," she persisted delicately. "I think you'll like what I have to say. If not, we'll just forget about it. It'll be entirely up to you. I promise."

He watched something churning behind her frosty blue eyes, wondering what kind of escapade she had in mind for the two of them. As much as he smelled a rat, he also knew that Fiona Cross was a sharp businesswoman who'd run London's top public relations firm for eight years before transforming herself into the queen of British morning television, an accomplishment that was nothing to scoff at. After careful consideration, he determined that there wouldn't be any harm in hearing her pitch. He could always say no. "In a houseboat," he finally answered over the noise from the sound system. "Second dock, sixth boat on the right."

"Great. I'll stop by later," she nodded with a wink, about to leave.

"Ladies and gentlemen," Michael announced waving his arms. "Please take a seat now. It's time to step aboard the love boat! Our almost famous matchmaking ritual!"

Glancing around in surprise, Fiona wondered why the local pub hadn't been mentioned in the debrief pack on the village's love-related festivities the studio had sent over earlier by courier. If there was any matchmaking going on, she needed to be informed about it so she could have her cameras set up. Heads were going to roll if the research department had overlooked this opportunity. "What's going on?" she whispered with aggravation.

The women in the crowd cheered as Brendan swiveled his seat around, trying to figure out why everyone was scrambling for a chair. As baffled as she was, he shrugged, "I don't have a clue."

The overhead lights dimmed to a flicker as Michael ducked behind the counter, disappearing from sight. The LOVE BOAT television theme song swept through the room and the bartender rose wearing a captain's hat and coat with a pair of heart-shaped sunglasses. A glittering disco ball lowered from the ceiling, filling the pub with a whirl of twinkling, colored light. Michael jumped up on the bar top and began dancing while holding some sort of a control box in his hands.

Brendan noticed that there was a small light bulb before every seat in the pub and they were blinking on and off to the beat of the music. The entire place was now singing along with the sappy seventies television song at the top of their lungs.

Michael pressed a button on his control box and the bulb in front of Brendan at the counter was the only light illuminated in the entire place. The ladies cheered in a collective roar. "Oh, shit, not him," Fiona thought grimly, furious that it was too late to pull in her cameras.

Michael reached across the bar, yanking Brendan onto the bar top where he stood up, his head nearly skimming the ceiling. "Our first passenger!" he announced grandly. "And what a catch he is ladies! A big shot reporter from Conde Nast Traveler Magazine - who just might be persuaded to write favorable things about the village if we can pour enough alcohol down his gullet and get him shagged within an inch of his life!"

Fiona rolled her eyes at Brendan who stood towering above her. "Conde Nast?" she murmured rolling her eyes.

He shot her a warning look and turned to Michael. "You did that on purpose!"

The ladies in the crowd were buzzing with excitement while Brendan was busy praying that the ugly mermaid incident wasn't about to repeat itself.

With the flick of a switch, the lights in the pub were blinking again. Brendan grimaced as the homely, grinning faces of the women were lit up, one by one. Watching the pattern with a skillful eye, Michael pressed the button on the box again, lighting up the bulb on the wall behind Claire.

"Ahhhh! Claire! Go get him you man-eater!" Christine howled.

Fiona laughed inwardly as the blushing old woman across the pub rose shakily in her seat. The pub's matchmaking 'ritual' she determined, was nothing more than an unofficial stunt that the human hedge had invented to drum up a little business. She relaxed, looking forward to moment that she and Brendan would leave this dump.

"Some things are just not meant to be. And some things are!" Claire growled, shoving Christine off the edge of the booth and onto the floor.

"Ouch! Claire!" she snapped, clumsily stumbling to her feet.

Michael spotted Christine and pointed as the crowd inexorably guided her toward the bar. "It wasn't my light!" she protested.

Immensely enjoying Brendan's misfortune, Fiona turned to watch the proceedings. But to her dismay, the old woman remained seated and a young, ethereal beauty with a tangle of fiery red hair was being pushed forward across the floor.

"Thanks a lot pal," Brendan hissed at Michael. "Weren't you the one who told me that all of her boyfriends are dead? Are you trying to kill me or something?"

Michael winked at him, shouting into the microphone, "And here we have the other half of our happy couple! Come on up! Drink your love potion!"

Michael took Christine's arm, helping her up next to Brendan where he handed each of his victims a syrupy rum drink garnished with orange slices and paper umbrellas.

The crowd chanted, "DRINK! DRINK! DRINK!"

Brendan and Christine drank and she began laughing as another disco song blared from the sound system.

"And now! The couple must dance!" Michael shouted, turning to the crowd, "Do you believe in love?"

The ladies screamed a collective, "YES!"

Christine wrapped her sleek arms around Brendan, her touch making his temperature rise. In response, he gritted his teeth, pulling her hips close to his. She waved her arms in the air, leading him along the counter as the crowd hooted and hollered. She shouted over the blaring music, "Don't look so surprised!"

"I think we've been set up," he said, shooting a sideways glance at Michael.

"Well, Mr. Big City Reporter, didn't you know that these small town contests are always rigged for the benefit of the locals?" she joked, making her way to the spot on the bar directly above Fiona.

"So what happens when the dance is over?" he shouted. "Is there any more to this matchmaking ritual that I should know about?"

Crinkling her nose, she informed him, "oh, nothing much really. We'll just go back to your place, I'll shag you within an inch of your life and then persuade you to write favorable things about the village. Weren't you listening?"

Brendan choked on his drink as Christine

sniggered to herself. Overhearing the comment, Fiona shot her darkest glare at the beautiful young girl.

As the song came to an end, Michael turned the lights back on in the pub.

Not willing to lose him to the female reporter, Christine took Brendan's face in her grasp and brushed her lips across his in a single, fluid movement that melted his brain. "Thanks for the dance. I have to go." She hopped down off the counter, purposely kicking Fiona's glass with one of her thick-soled clogs, dumping half a pint of sticky brew down the front of the television maven's designer silk blouse.

"Bloody hell!" Fiona screeched, standing up to gawk at her dripping, ruined garment.

"I'm so sorry," Christine apologized, rushing to her side. "Look, come by my shop tomorrow if you want and I'll replace it for you. The Siren Shop, down on the pier."

Fiona growled, baring a set of gleaming capped teeth.

"Okay then, perhaps not," Christine whispered, disappearing into the crowd.

Brendan blinked, his system electrified by the small kiss she'd treated him to. He saw Fiona glowering below, then searched the crowd for Christine.

Seizing the opportunity, Michael rushed over to Fiona with a damp bar rag and began clumsily dabbing at her chest.

Flinging the rag across the counter, Fiona grabbed her coat from the back of the chair and whirled out of the Siren's Whale.

Standing on the counter in a daze, Brendan was unaware that Fiona had left to go change her clothes.

He touched his lips, still tingling with enchantment where the temptress had kissed him.

Michael nudged him in the leg. "Come on slobberchops. Off me bar. Captain's orders." With a hearty laugh, he wiggled his heart shaped glasses up and down at the dazed writer. "Sorry we couldn't get you laid and all. You can lead an 'arse to water, but you can't make it drink." With a sad laugh he added, "Welcome to my world."

CHAPTER NINE

Fiona trudged alone along the damp sand as the chill of night numbed her limbs and her mind. Traces of muddy sea water soaked the edges of her Versace trousers as she rethought her plan to entice Brendan to go along with the matchmaking caper. Now that the local girl had entered the picture, it could complicate things. After all, the beautiful young woman had made her intentions with him clear when she'd kissed him in the pub. *"He's such an asshole,"* she grumbled to herself, determining that one hell of a shag was in order to get things back on track. She took a long swig of gin from a flask concealed in the lining of her coat. A gust of wind swept across the beach, snarling her precision cut locks and carrying with it a faint melody. Someone else was near. Someone was whistling. Tucking the bottle away, she scanned the rocky coast.

The sea was calm and solemn as Charlie crept down the isolated cove beneath a bath of pale moonlight. He whistled an old, Celtic melody, anticipating the thrill of the hunt, as he liked to think of it. Instinct told him that someone was waiting for him as he moved like a predator along the edge of the jagged coastline. The feverish desires welled up within him as he climbed up the side of a mossy boulder just below the lighthouse.

Fiona zeroed in on the beautiful stranger who'd kissed her mercilessly during the commotion at the parade, the one who had single-handedly created a frothing-mouthed frenzy amongst the viewers of her morning program. His lean, muscular body effortlessly moved along the slippery rocks like a spider, slipping in and out of looming shadows. He stopped for a moment, plucking up a handful of seagull eggs from a nest high on the cliff, then dropped them into his pocket and continued on. Silently, she brushed the hair from her face, ducking into the darkness to observe. *No, he certainly wasn't rock climbing.* The hardened eyes of the television anchor widened as she watched him remove every stitch of his clothing. Within the mist of the frothing sea, his pale, velvety skin was illuminated by a shaft of moonlight that broke through the restless clouds. Letting out a small gasp, Fiona squinted in vain, searching the craggy formations for a better look of the gorgeous rogue. *Forget about Brendan James,* she sniffed, her attention now focused on the whereabouts of the disrobed hunk on the beach. A small splash in the ocean confirmed that he had indeed plunged into the icy water of the Irish Sea. "Jesus," she whispered, rubbing her hands together with a grin, *perhaps she'd get more out of the deal than was bargained for...*

Concealed beneath the black murk of the cove, a shapeless entity swam silently just inches beneath the surface, gliding past a row of docked vessels, nestled securely in their slips. The figure, detectable only by its streaky shadow and a few soundless ripples, hovered in the vicinity of Brendan's houseboat, gazing toward the porthole window on the craft, then squinting upwards to peer inside. And in a flash, it descended into the shadows beneath the dock, watching and waiting patiently, until the right moment arose.

Brendan settled into the wooden chair before his laptop, reflecting back on the kiss that Christine had bestowed upon his lips. How to describe it, he mused, throwing adjectives around in his head; simmering, luscious - *primal*. He managed to scratch a few words down in his worn notebook before the cell phone rang.

"Hey Jake. No, actually, it's going fine," Brendan assured his editor, balancing the chair on two rear legs as he leaned back with feet propped up on the table. "Yeah. Glad you like the new direction it's taking. It's fucking weird around here." He eased the chair back to the floor, turned on the computer and rubbed his eyes. "Yeah, the next chapter. I was just sitting down to bang it out now."

There was static on the line, then Jake's voice came through clear again. "What I've read so far, it's amazing, your best yet Brendan." He cleared his throat and continued, "only problem is..."

"Problem," he scowled.

"The book, its been promoted as covering the British Isles - and you've only written about this one little village on one island, not that it isn't fabulous shit, mind you, it's just that it creates somewhat of a - situation. I haven't shown it to my Editor-In-Chief yet and..."

The houseboat was suddenly rammed from beneath, tilting craft to one side with an unsettling groan. Rising unsteadily, Brendan grabbed the laptop that was sliding toward the edge of the table while balancing the phone between his ear and shoulder. "Whoa!" he exclaimed, trying to get his bearings back as the boat was jolted a second time.

"Look, I've gotta go," he rushed. "I'll send you something later." Brendan turned off the phone, parted the curtains and peered outside with penetrating eyes, wondering dourly what sort of mischief the locals were up to now. Sliding into his coat, he stepped outside into the harsh cold.

Inspecting the perimeters of the vessel, the ebony waters appeared calm. His lone reflection waggled back at him. "Who's out there!" He ducked as a pair of wings rustled above and a seagull cried out in response. Startled by the sudden motion, he watched as the bird sailed downward and perched on the mast of a sailboat a few slips away.

Shivering, he shrunk into his jacket and walked to the end of the dock, facing the cove of steep rocks beneath the lighthouse.

The clear moon illuminated the restless water of the bay and the Northern Lights glimmered neon turquoise against the inky black heavens above. Drawing a deep breath, he came to the conclusion that the boat had been bumped by a wayward porpoise, or it was just preparing to collapse in on itself, neither possibility doing much to put his mind or his stomach at ease. Crouching down on the end of the landing, he looked up and began soaking in the nighttime magic of the island. The breathtaking view seemed to instill a sense of calm as he sat back, enthralled with the simple lullaby of creaking boats and the dull, clanging of bells as they rocked sleepily with the gentle current of the sea. Staring out at the dancing reflections of the lights on the ocean, he caught a glimpse of unmistakable movement out in the center of the cove. He squinted to hone in on the figure that had disappeared again in a blanket of blackness.

Rising to the surface, Christine allowed the gentle, emerald swells to carry her body further from the refuge of the harbor.

"My god," he inhaled, not quite believing what the spectacle before his eyes, entirely unable to turn away from it. Heart pounding in his chest, he rose to his feet.

Her vanilla skin was illuminated beneath shafts of glowing, colored light and she was gazing toward the vast openness, unaware that another human being was watching. Long tresses floated in a tangle of sea lather, her eyes clear and childlike as she approached the unfathomable depths.

Faint, tinkling laughter rang out eerily across the cove, entering Brendan's ears like a shot of honeyed velvet. Then, in an elegant, fluid movement, her body disappeared beneath the surface once again. Breathless, he squinted at the water while instinctively removing his coat and shoes. "Come on! Where'd you go?" he whispered, eyes still searching madly for another glimpse of her. But she was no where in sight. Pacing along the dock edge in his socks, he attempted to catch his breath while trying to determine what in the hell he was supposed to do now. Okay, he thought, stay calm. You're a mediocre swimmer and might be able to make it out that far if your life depended on it, but the temperature of the water has to be freezing - or close to it.

Shit!

Calming the panic rising from within, he reminded himself that just last night he'd witnessed her brother plunging into the briny depths at some ungodly hour of the night. They're insane, he assured himself. Insane, not suicidal...

SPLASH!

The water erupted directly beneath his feet. Stunned, he leaned over the edge, peering down at the ripples made seconds earlier.

Huh?

Before he could conceive what was happening or even react, a pair of hands covered in seaweed shot out of the glassy water, grabbing his ankles and yanking him headfirst into the freezing sea.

"Aaaaaaugh!" The icy water shot through his body like tiny spears of lightening, degrees of cold so shocking he was unable to think. Plunging into the icy depths, he struggled to strike his attacker, a figure concealed behind a mass of murky water and entangled fishing nets.

Don't panic!

Disoriented and tumbling downward in the darkness, he made a feeble attempt to fight back. Kicking with all his strength, he lashed out against the veil of seaweed and rope to grasp the thing that was pulling him down like a lead weight. The beam of the lighthouse swung by twenty feet above, illuminating a horrifying glimpse of a face, manlike with a piggish nose and pair of black, soulless eyes that flashed back at him. Brendan screamed, emitting the last bubbles of oxygen from his lungs, managing to clench a death grip fist around something that appeared to be a red piece of cloth. And suddenly, the thing released him and he began kicking furiously toward the surface through a veil of effervescent bubbles and knotted ropes tangled with sea foliage. Every muscle in his body shot with fiery pain as he clawed for the surface. Dim moonlight rippled above fifteen, ten five feet above...

Crashing through, Brendan gasped, inhaling

gulp after gulp of cold night air. Thrashing and buried beneath a mass of fishing nets, he screamed out for help as the horrifying notion entered his head - the thing was still lurking beneath his feet somewhere in the blackness - and might not have finished with him yet. "Help me somebody!" he gurgled, trying to orient his location to the docks. "Help!"

A tiny wooden dinghy bobbed up and down on the bottle green swells of the bay. Liam O'Leary, a shrunken man of eighty with a yellowed beard and a black cat perched upon his shoulder, set down his binoculars after spotting the man floundering around in the water. In response, he took a slow puff of his pipe, fired up the outboard motor and maneuvered the craft toward him. "Fucking tourists," he grumbled to the cat.

"Help!" he choked again, his frozen muscles beginning to fail him as he spit out a mouthful of water.

Liam pulled alongside Brendan, dangling a lantern over the water where he squinted at the stranger.

"Please!" he gasped.

The old man cut the motor, setting the cat down on the wooden bench by his side and lifted the heavy nets off of Brendan with one of the wooden oars. "Take me hand lad. Quickly!"

Gripping the man's hand, he scrambled over the edge of the boat, shuddering from the cold. "There's – something down there! It pulled me in and was dragging me under!"

The cat shrunk away from the dripping newcomer, observing it all through a set of wide yellow eyes. "Course it did." Liam calmly removed the red cloth from Brendan's clenched fist and went to work inspecting it carefully by the flickering glow of his rusty oil lantern. The object was a small cap, adorned with red feathers and sparkling ruby-like jewels. Hundreds of pink lights reflected off the facets and glittered magically around the rough interior of the boat beneath the lantern flame. "Name's Liam O'Leary," he offered without looking up. "Hmmmm. Northern Merfolk," he mumbled, his attention intensely focused on the object.

Brendan shivered violently, convinced that the old man was certifiably deranged. "Did you hear what I just said! I was almost killed out there!"

With a glint in his eye, Liam handed the soggy cap back to him. "The Dinny-Mara. Come down from Northern waters. You're lucky to be alive lad. If you hadn't of nicked his cap, you'd have been a dead man for sure!"

Propping himself up on unsteady elbows, Brendan glared at his rescuer furiously. "Look! I don't know what kind of crazy, screwed-up stunt this town is trying to pull, but whoever did this crossed the line! I could have been killed!"

"'Twas no stunt," he nodded, knitting his brows together. "I've been on these seas for sixty-five years and seen them beasties with me own eyes. 'Twas the Dinny-Mara for sure. If it's the truth you're looking for lad, look beneath the surface."

"Excuse me!" he sputtered, "but some psychopath just tried to murder me! I'm calling the police is what I'm doing!"

The cat crawled up on the old man's shoulder, perching itself into a tight ball on his hairless scalp like a bad toupee. Liam chuckled, only infuriating the American further. "You go and do that, lad.

Sure, go and tell em' you've been seeing *the Merfolk.* 'Bout time someone filed a proper complaint with the authorities."

By now, the cold water that soaked into every fiber of his clothing seemed to be seeping into his bones. And to make matters worse, the old lunatic and his pet were staring at him as if he were the crazy one. *For Christ's sake,* he thought, *the guy's wearing a cat on his head!* "Great! This is just great! What kind of a con is this town running anyway!"

"You know nothing!" the old fisherman growled.

Brendan was livid now. "Look Liam," he snarled. "Would you just take me back to the goddamned dock already so I can find *somebody* around here who isn't drunk or doesn't have their head shoved up their ass – or both!"

Taking a puff from his corncob pipe, Liam scowled. "Paag my hoyn!" he spat. "Means kiss me arse 'round here! he translated.

Brendan shivered again, gasping through blue lips, "F-freezing out here…"

Liam shoved the pair of boat oars at him, turning his back, "Well then. Guess you'd better start rowing then, hadn't you."

༄

Fiona followed a trail of wide footsteps in the wet sand to the base of the cliff where the young man had left his clothing strewn along the rocks. For ten minutes, she'd scanned the water in the bay, but couldn't find any trace of the enchanting creature.

As she climbed higher to get a better view of

the beach, she tried to imagine what he was doing swimming in the freezing ocean at midnight, and more importantly, what she might say if she were to find him.

Her thoughts were interrupted by the far off sound of a woman crying. Straining to hear against the tumbling surf, she determined that the voice was coming from the other side of the steep cliff. Fiona dug her foot into a crevice to climb higher, but halfway up the steep, slippery grade, the heel snapped off her leather pump, cascading thirty feet into the frothy water below. "Bugger," she cursed under her breath. Then she thought of him again. Suddenly undeterred by the perilous hike, she managed to claw her way to the top where the surface was smooth and even - and where she heard that bloody woman sobbing even louder.

Peering down, she spotted an isolated cove, strewn with great ragged rocks and a small sandy beach. Barely visible beneath the glowing heavens, was a worn trail of loose granite stones that wound behind the mouth of a dark cave, leading up to a steep grassy bank.

Fiona's eyes landed on a plump woman in her late thirties who sat on a boulder beneath the last granite step and she was blubbering to herself, her soggy teardrops falling into the ebb of the swirling surf. The woman's dull brown hair whipped in the crisp wind and she cursed herself, "oh, why did I ever come here! So stupid! You stupid, stupid old cow!"

Because you're a stupid old cow, Fiona thought, annoyed by the distraction that sat wailing between herself and possibly the hottest piece of ass she'd ever laid her eyes on. Then, something stirred in the shadows on the beach. The crying woman became very still and silent. Swearing under her breath, Fiona ducked down from her perch atop the cliff to avoid being spotted.

Squinting into the dark, the woman turned her head from side to side, her meek voice trembling with anxiety. "W-who's there?"

Fiona peered out from behind a rock. The vision on the beach inexorably caused her jaw to drop, it was Charlie in all his naked glory. *"Jesus Christ…"*

He emerged from the tumultuous tide, and stood glistening wet just a few yards before the cowed and drab woman. In response, the frump gasped, Charlie's dark eyes flashing back at her with boyish mischief. "Born was I from the salty tears of a maiden fair, lost in thy foam of the sea."

Scuttling to her feet, the woman slipped clumsily on the smooth slick stone. "Oh-my-god…"

Fiona grinned, muttering under her breath, "Oh my god is right sister…"

Charlie stared calmly at the woman and slowly approached while reciting The Mermaid by Tennyson. "I would be a mermaid fair. I would sing to myself the whole of the day, with a comb of pearl, I would comb my hair."

Within a few syllables of his melodic, musical voice, the woman seemed to fall hopelessly under his spell, her muscles loosening with every word that dripped from his full, luscious lips. The very essence of the sea and the indescribable musk that emitted from his flesh seemed to swirl everywhere, enveloping her entire being with lust.

Charlie continued, slowly stepping closer. "And still as I combed I would sing and say, who is it loves me? Who loves not me? I would comb my hair till my ringlets would fall. Low adown, low adown from under my starry sea-bud crown, Low adown and around." He reached out, his cool fingers gently streaking across the woman's face. Hot tears streamed down her cheeks as she felt herself becoming powerless before him, enchanted by the magic words he uttered. "And I shall look like a fountain of gold, springing alone, with a shrill inner sound, till that great sea snake under the sea from his coiled sleeps in central deeps would slowly trail himself sevenfold and look up at the gate with his large, calm eyes for the love of me."

Watching with sweeping amazement, Fiona had chewed her manicured nails to bits as the woman allowed him to pull the bulky sweatshirt over her head.

Charlie gazed into her dull gray eyes as if she were the most beautiful creature in existence, "and all of the mermen under the sea would feel their immortality die in their hearts for the love of me." He leaned forward and tenderly kissed her parched mouth, a weakened moan emitting from her throat. The pair parted speechlessly, she staring at him with wonderment. He whispered seductively to her in the old language, "Yn taitnys smoo anys bea te anys jannoo shen ta'n sleih gra nagh vod mayd jannoo," a Manx Gaelic phrase that meant, *the greatest pleasure in life lies in doing that which people say we can not do.*

"I can't – believe this," she stammered incredulously, not comprehending the words he'd just uttered, but understanding that he meant to make love to her.

Pressing a finger to her trembling lips, he whispered softly, "Shhhhh. Believe."

The woman's frozen expression melted into a slight smile and she allowed him to take her by the hand.

In a peculiar, jealous sort of way, Fiona found herself rooting for the old scarecrow. She craned her neck to watch as Charlie removed the rest of the woman's clothing, then led her into the low, wide mouth of a dusky cave, concealed beyond a veil of sea mist and shadows.

Taking another swig from her flask, Fiona listened intently as shrieks of joyous laughter arose from the dark, mingled with the lull of crashing waves.

"Lucky old cow..."

৩⊷৶

Feeling as if his body had iced over, Brendan shuddered in waterlogged jeans, throwing on his jacket and shoes where he'd shed them earlier on the dock. He kicked at the air, cursing out vehemently at the water, "Bunch of freaking LUNA-TICS!"

With the cat still clamoring to his head, Liam shoved the scanty fishing boat away with an oar and scowled. "Piss off!"

The door of the houseboat slammed shut behind Brendan, nearly falling off its hinges. Numb with cold, he stumbled across the cabin and collapsed into the tiny cubicle of a shower, not bothering to remove his drenched sweater and pants. He cranked the corroded brass handle marked 'hot' that dribbled out little more than a weak stream of lukewarm water over his shuddering body. After a few miserable moments, the meager source of heat began to thaw his frostbitten flesh and he peeled off the soggy garments. As the blood started flowing again and he was able to think of things other than *imminent survival* and *heat*, he reflected upon the night's events with bitter resentment toward whatever had happened out there.

The more he thought about it, the ethereal beauty of the girl and the sinister glare of the one who had tried to drag him to his death, the less it made any sense. He banged his fist against the frosted vinyl door of the shower enclosure, determined to do *something* about it. But what?, he mused, what... He didn't even know what had occurred. The only thing he could be sure of at that moment, huddled in a shivering lump on the tile, was that reporting the incident to the local authorities would surely land him in the nut house for a night or two of observation.

"Arrrrgh!"

Half an hour later, small puddles dotted the shag carpet from the soggy, dripping clothing that now hung upon a makeshift clothesline of twine strung across the length of the vessel. After changing into a pair of dry sweatpants and warming his fingers before a small space heater that sputtered out more dust than warmth, Brendan had decided upon his next course of action. He was going to write about it in his new book, every last detail of it, figuring when he eventually discovered who was behind the attack, and he had a pretty good idea already, he'd make a fool out of her – and her cohorts forever and eternally in print.

While the laptop was booting up, he scoured

the cabinet in the kitchenette, unearthing a small, half-empty bottle of vintage Jamaican rum. Uncorking it with a thunk, he sniffed the fumes, finding it surprisingly aromatic and helped himself to a generous portion, the dark, potent spirits of fermented sugar searing his gullet and placating his rattled nerves. He leaned back in the stiff wooden chair, staring blankly out the porthole window, trying to determine where to start.

Fuzzy. The edges of everything in the night were velvety like chinchilla or mink, Fiona thought cloudily as she staggered down the dock in search of Brendan's houseboat. Resembling a demented ballerina, she stumbled and skipped along on the broken heel of her shoe while fluttering around the boats like a moth, peering into every illuminated porthole. Vivid images of the erotic scene on the beach ran wild through her mind and the contents of her gin flask flowed through her bloodstream. She knew she was intoxicated – downright pissed, but didn't care. She needed to see Brendan James. He'd understand... Mumbling giddily, she recited remnants of the poetry that the creature had seduced the frumpy woman with. "I would comb my hair – and all of the mermen under the sea – would – would fucking be in love with me!" she slurred. Nearly mad with desire, she wriggled out of her twelve-hundred-dollar coat and blouse, hopelessly stained with Codsucker, and flung the clothing carelessly behind her on the dock. Her frosty eyes half-mast, she counted off the houseboats with a wavering finger, then rapped on the door of the sixth.

Alarmed by the knock, Brendan jumped to his feet, shutting the laptop closed. "Who's there!"

"Open up James!" she whined, shivering from the cold. "I'm freezing out here!"

Having forgotten that she was going to drop in for a talk, he sighed with relief that it was only Fiona and reluctantly opened the door.

His mouth hung agape at what stood before his eyes, Fiona, in nothing but a lacy black bra and a pair of sand-spattered slacks. She staggered inside with an inebriated grin on her face.

"Jesus Fiona! Are you insane!" he hissed, slamming the door behind her. "What do you think you're doing!"

Paying no attention to him, she ducked beneath the line of dripping garments that sagged across the houseboat and rolled onto the small, rumpled bed. "I am a maiden born of the salt of thy sea...," she sang breathlessly.

"You're drunk," he scowled, tossing a balled-up sweater at her from his open suitcase. "Cover yourself up for Christ's sake." He glanced out the window, then turned to face her. "Did anyone see you out there?"

She rolled her eyes and shoved the sweater aside, attempting to have a serious conversation. "You've got to listen to me. I was down at the beach and there was someone out there – a man," she began, her eyes growing wild.

"Oh my god!" he hissed, rushing to her side.

She'd been raped.

Gingerly, he touched her hand and blinked. "Did he – did he violate you?"

Fiona tossed her head back, overcome with a mad fit of giggles, her reaction throwing Brendan completely off base. "I wish!" she snorted, suddenly bolting upright with her gaze fixed on his bare chest, hunger growing in her eyes. "I saw him crawl out of the sea and seduce a woman into his cave and – oh god James! Fuck me already!"

Lightheaded from the island rum that was seeping into his system, he stood before her at the edge of the bed in complete shock. Her petal soft hands ran across his bare skin, feverishly grasping his face, pulling him so close that her hot, gin-laced breath stung his bulging eyes.

"Fiona, I don't think this is a good idea…, "he groaned, the man in him painfully tempted by her unexpected proposition.

Sweeping a piece of disheveled hair away from her eyes, she stared into his. "There's something I have to tell you. It's what I wanted to see you about," she confessed lazily. "I was thinking that – what if you and I are here on this island at the same place at the same time - *because we're supposed to be.* Did that thought cross your mind too?"

It had, in fact crossed his mind and he'd swatted it away like a poisonous insect. He steeled himself, arching a suspicious eyebrow at her. "Is that why you came here?"

"Mmmmm," she purred, running her hot tongue along the trail of hair on his chest. "That and other things…"

"Fiona. Stop it," he warned, the blood dangerously rushing to his groin. He gently pushed her back, waiting patiently until her cockeyed gaze traveled north to his eyes. "What did you want to talk to me about?" he asked slowly. "In the pub? Do you remember?"

Annoyed that he needed an explanation at a moment like this, she exhaled in frustration. "The network is having me stay on the island to search for my 'soul mate' as part of a special program. All we'd have to do is suffer through a few of the matchmaking festivities, make an announcement, get a few shots and then we can go our separate ways."

"What?" Brendan blurted out. "No way." He paced across the floor, looking back at her incredulously. Besides setting up the entire scheme for her own benefit, asking him to play along with such a ludicrous plan could be dangerous, both professionally - and personally. "It would destroy my whole book. Did that even cross your mind?"

"What are you talking about?" she brayed. "This nowhere village is going to be like, ONE paragraph in your roaming adventures around Europe or whatever you're writing about this time." With a wave of her finger she added, "I'll cover your entire stay on the island on my expense account. Now, is that so bad?"

"You'll – you'll cover my expenses?" he gawked.

"Of course I will, darling," she growled, beckoning him closer with an index finger.

"Jesus! This village and the people in it," he snarled, *are my entire book*! And I have my own expense account thank you very much!"

Unfazed by his outburst, she cattily stretched her long limbs across the bed, leaning back on her elbows and blinking back at him through dusky eyes. "Look, if you don't want to accept everything I'm offering, and I do mean everything..." she proposed, slowly sliding the straps of her bra over delicate shoulders, "no strings attached..."

Unavoidably, he grazed over the luscious curves of her bare skin and down the length of her slender legs, wondering how such a physically attractive woman could house such a cunning, dangerous mind. In one day she'd managed to infuriate him, embarrass him in public - and she'd just insulted him for the second time in eight hours, he reminded himself. Now she wanted to sleep with him? It would be a mistake he would regret should he avail himself of the immediate opportunity that lay before him like an all-you-can-eat buffet. But damn it, she looked really good, he thought. "I can't Fiona," he managed.

"Oh, yes - you can," she teased, twisting a lock of tousled platinum hair temptingly between her fingers. Reaching for the drawstring of his sweatpants, she untied it with a gentle tug. He stiffened, knowing that he'd better do something fast before his trembling body gave in to her demands.

"The thing is – I've got feelings for someone else," he stammered, a statement that sounded alien to his own ears - but he'd meant it, he realized, grinning inwardly. Christine Hamilton had another thing coming if she thought she'd seen the last of him.

Fiona's heavy lids widened, "You? Having feelings?" she parroted, a drunken fit of giggles bubbling up in her throat. "Oh please, don't make me laugh!" she gasped, his proclamation by far, the most humorous utterance that had crossed her ears in weeks. She leaned forward with a grin, waggling a finger at him. "Wait, don't tell me! With the – with the elfin creature at the pub?" she burst, "the one with the – *clamshell earrings*?"

"They were oysters!" he growled, his comment sending her into a howling fit of hysterics. The fact that she was doubled over now in his bed laughing at his confession – and at Christine, served only to infuriate him further. What did she know about his personal life - and why was the idea so amusing that he might actually have genuine feelings for someone? So what if they were just feelings of lust, he glowered. They were feelings. Weren't they? He swiped away her delicate hand, still clawing at the edge his waistband. "That's it Fiona! I want you to leave!"

His anger sobered her a little. She shrunk back with a slightly wounded look, his unexpected rejection cutting more deeply than she would have imagined. Pressure and pain mounted up behind her eyeballs as he stared her down with bitter contempt.

"Leave," he repeated menacingly.

The emotion she struggled to hold back swelled into an unattractive sob. "Oh God! Why do you hate me!" she snuffled as the tears spilled out.

Hesitating for a moment, he watched the mascara stream down her cheeks. He hadn't meant to make her cry, he just wanted her to go away. "Don't," he started with a wince, attempting to settle her down. "Come on."

She looked into his eyes for a moment, then threw herself back on the bed in a dramatic flop, moaning even louder.

Perching on the edge of the lumpy mattress, he reluctantly took her bejeweled hand in his. "Look, I don't hate you," he assured her with a comforting pat, smoothing the hair from her face.

"You do too!" she blubbered. "You bloody hate me!"

"Come on. You've got the number one rated morning show,'" he reminded her. "Right? What's to hate?"

"No!" she howled. "You don't understand! I LOATHE my bloody job! You don't know what it's like to be me James. You don't know what it's like!" Her wild eyes stared at him with desperation.

"Fiona," he consoled gently, "You've got a great life."

Slowly, she thought about it and calmed down a little. A trace of a grin cracked across her lips. "Really?"

"Really," he smiled. "Any woman would kill to be you. Do you know that?"

"Yes. I suppose they would." His look was so kind, so affectionate, she thought. Grasping his hands, she stared back at him through haunted, lonely eyes. "Brendan. Did you ever love me?"

He flinched as he felt the grip of her fingers tighten around his. It wasn't the question itself that frightened him to near speechlessness, it was the sad emptiness of another human being who was craving affection as desperately as he. In her eyes, he saw a female version of himself. But before he could answer the simple, yet extremely complicated question, he weakened in her piercing stare, allowing her to pull him down on the bed. And before he found the will to stop it, his body was stretched across hers, his lips a fraction away from a great mistake.

"No..."

With a flurry of hands, the remaining clothing was shed and cast aside, her hungry mouth all over his.

Just testing the water, he told himself as he returned the reckless and barren kiss. Skin upon skin, he slid across her belly, his groin aching with necessity, striving to fill the emptiness within him that he knew she could never fulfill. He kissed her again, her body warm and groping, but lacking any real desire. It was numb and she was emotionless. And he felt nothing but the mechanical movements of two people hardened by too many one-night-stands - could only think of Christine, could only go on if he were to close his eyes and imagine her face... He pulled away suddenly, restraining the urgent craving to finish off what they'd started, and rolled over to her side with eyes squeezed shut.

Fiona turned her head slightly to face him with a weak, dejected smile.

"I'm sorry," he breathed, staring up at the stain on the ceiling.

Eyelids fluttering, her limbs wilted like a week-old vase of flowers. With a final dizzied moan, she snuggled back into the pillow, barely conscious now as the alcohol caught up with her.

Relieved and unsettled, he stroked the champagne colored hair away from her smooth forehead. "I – might have loved you," he whispered gently, kissing her moist cheek. "For a little while..."

And she was out cold.

Rising to his feet, Brendan felt surprisingly contented with the decision he'd made. Emitting a barely audible sigh, he reached for the scratchy wool blanket and quietly arranged it over her. He squinted, catching a glimpse of the alarming hour on the digital clock, and resumed his seat at the kitchen table before the computer. A little work is just what I need, he told himself. Taking a swig from the bottle of rum, he began typing.

Jake. Something quite magical, yet deeply disturbing, occurred tonight after our earlier conversation…

One of many quaint boutiques on High Street

The Black Cat, a shop catering to local superstions and curious tourists

Catch of the day in the village fish market

The fishing fleet may be dwiindling, but it hasn't lost its sense of humor

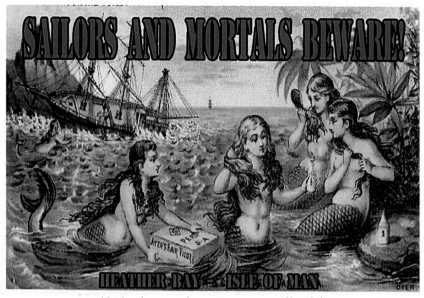

An old island postcard warning visitors of local dangers

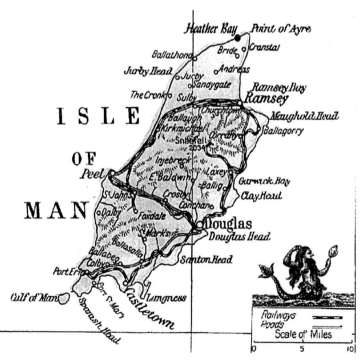

Heather Bay is located at the northern tip of the island

Heather Bay, home to the annual Mer-dog Competition

A mermaid's tomb in Heather Bay cemetery

Midsummer in the seafaring village

A breathtaking view of the Northern Lights on the harbor

O'Leary cottage in Heather Bay

A poster advertising the annual Mermaid Festival

The mysterious sea caves were once a haven for pirates and outlaws

The Siren's Whale Pub shows off its mummified merman

A vintage advertisement from the Mermaid Theater 1935

A worker on break at the kipper smokehouse, the village's main export

CHAPTER TEN

Jake Hogan entered his office early and shoved aside the usual pile of unread manuscripts on his desk. Right now there was only one project on his mind. He logged online before taking his first sip of Starbucks, eagerly anticipating the new chapters from Brendan James. He'd already checked his e-mail late last night before going to bed and again when he woke up this morning in hopes of finding the latest pages of the manuscript waiting in his inbox. But there had been nothing but the usual smattering of Spam and a couple of polite query letters from unpublished travel writers. A wave of relief rushed through him as he scrolled through the new e-mail and spotted a fresh message from the writer with an attachment. Taking a gulp of coffee, he began to read.

'You're probably worried about delirium caused by the bacterial overload from warm British beer. So I won't ask you to believe what you read in the following chapter, just take a look and consider this as the new title for my book: 'MISADVENTURES & MERFOLK.'

"Oh, Shit."
With a twinge of apprehension, Jake opened the file.

'I had the distinct feeling that all the hard work scrubbing the urine smell from my leather jacket had paid off, for my evening out on the town proved to be one of the most interesting and baffling nights of my life.
Not only did my lack of repulsive stench attract

Christine, the woman of my dreams in the bar top matchmaking festivities, but I succeeded in nearly getting myself murdered and received an offer of no-strings-attached sex from an ex-lover whose name we will not mention, and who happens to have serendipitously shown up on the island during the soul mate festival, as have I, a thought that frightens me more than I will openly admit.

Anyway, after participating in the pub's LOVE BOAT NIGHT, an unofficial ceremony in which two 'lovers' are chosen by the bar's bushy proprietor, I staggered toward the houseboat in a dazed stupor after five heated minutes of close dancing with Christine on the top of the bar. Badly in need of a cold shower, I ignored my body's urgent needs and forced myself to sit down at the computer to jot down the thoughts and impressions I'd collected throughout the day, but instead found the houseboat being rammed from beneath by some unseen force.

Venturing out into the rolling fog to investigate, I spotted a young woman skinny dipping beneath the Northern Lights in the middle of the tumultuous bay. As I squinted for a better look, I realized that it was Christine, who was not drowning, rather basking beneath the pale moonlight. I don't recall just how many Codsucker's I'd put away, but I watched her for what seemed like forever, her perfectly formed limbs glistening beneath the fairy Northern lights in the inky black waters, a woman as deep and mysterious as the Irish Sea itself...

It must run in the family, I rationalized, as I discovered earlier that she is the sibling of the notorious village sex fiend, Charlie the Tuna, who too enjoys swimming in sub-degree temperature waters. As I watched her glide effortlessly amongst the crashing emerald swells, I began concocting an unnecessary, but nevertheless, gallant plan to rescue her. I began to wonder if she were of the same

162

breeding as her brother, the spawn of the unspeakable, those shameless creatures that were into violating elder members of the opposite sex of which I was one, being at least ten years older than she.

Perhaps, I thought - I might stand a chance.

But before my fantasies could be realized, I was yanked into the water and plunging to my early death by a stranger cloaked in seaweed, a porky-pig mask and a sequined bathing cap, an obvious attempt to persuade me into writing kind and endearing things about the village.

I narrowly escaped my attacker and was fished out of the freezing bay by a withered geezer named Liam O'Leary who called me 'lad' and professed that the 'Merfolk' were responsible for the attack. Maybe I should have listened to what he had to say, but since he didn't even bother to offer a freezing man his hat, (fashioned out of a mangy black cat,) that didn't say much for the kind of person he was. So I in turn, insulted him, slogged back to the rotten houseboat and took a lukewarm shower.

Back to the sex, my ex-girlfriend arrived an hour later at the doorstep of my boat wearing only designer underwear and begging me to take her, where I don't know. Then she passed out cold after I declined her offer and professed my love for the young local who had charmed the pants off of me the moment I saw that pair of oyster shells dangling from her earlobes in the pub.

I think I'm finally starting to figure this place out. From what I can tell, the village is a unique province where the following lewd and illegal acts are perfectly acceptable:

1. trotting around naked in the wee hours of the night while shouting phrases like "fuck me already!"
2. operating a motorboat when one is intoxicated, senile, demented, or any combination of the above.

3. *shooting one's harpoon off in public places and up the 'arses' of one's enemies.*
4. *wearing slinky evening dresses paired with foot attire such as Birkenstock clogs or Wellington boots.*
5. *challenging a foe to a cheese knife duel. And my favorite,*
6. *It is perfectly acceptable for an old maid to have a casual shag with an ethereal creature that apparently gets off on cellulite, dentures and the fresh, wintergreen scent of Ben Gay.*

Tomorrow I plan to purchase my own tube of arthritis cream and will try my luck again.'

Jake slammed his fist on the desk victoriously. "Yes! Oh yes! He's doing it! Jesus Christ! He's gonna do it!"

Mr. Pinkerton, the formidable Editor-in-Chief entered the cluttered office with one arched eyebrow. "Everything all right Hogan?" he inquired with deep concern rising in his voice.

Jake jumped. "Mr. Pinkerton. Yes. Yes! Everything's great. In fact, I was just reading an e-mail from Brendan James." He tapped at the glass of the monitor. "You've got to see this stuff. It's fantastic!"

Mildly interested, Pinkerton surveyed the screen with owlish eyes. "Really. It's that good?"

Clicking the print icon, Jake turned to the Editor-in-Chief. "I think we've got another best seller on our hands." He grabbed the first page off the printer, nearly knocking the coffee over in his eagerness. "Here, listen to this…"

Morning sunlight sparkled across the water of the bay, the orange glow searing Brendan's bloodshot eyes. He sat on the edge of the dock with legs dangling over the edge, too weary to pay any attention to the footsteps padding toward him from behind. He'd been up all night working on the manuscript and had staggered outside just before sunrise to avoid contact with Fiona when she stirred from her drunken slumber.

Julian wore a faded cotton bathrobe and kicked the empty bottle of Jamaican rum into the water with a bony bare foot. "Morning mate!" he grinned, picking up Fiona's crinkled blouse and coat from the dock and depositing the garments in a heap next to Brendan. "Nasty hangover, eh? Hope she wasn't too scaly."

Brendan groaned, "she passed out."

"Really?" he prodded, rubbing his hands together in anticipation of the details. "Nothing less than a mermaid will do for you then?"

Shielding his eyes from the sun, he squinted up at his neighbor. "Yeah. But that's the least of my problems," he sighed. "But since you brought up the subject…"

"What! Mermaids?" he cackled. "Right disgusting creatures they are. And not a good subject before breakfast I might add." His eyes grazed across the water as he positioned his finger and thumb into a gun. "Carry a harpoon, I always say! Why? You seen one of them slimy sons of bitches?" he laughed.

Brendan peered into the murky depths below the dock. "Don't know what happened," he managed, the mere utterance of words intensifying his

165

splitting headache. "Oh, my brain…"

Julian watched for a moment with interest percolating behind slightly narrowed eyes. Grasping the American's shoulders, he promptly helped him to his feet. "There we go, easy now," he said, guiding Brendan's unsteady stride toward his own houseboat. "Come inside and have a cuppa char and some toast," he suggested, lowering his voice to a hushed whisper, "I've got something you might be interested in having a look at. A little bit of local history."

From the interior of Brendan's boat, the horrifying howl of a woman shrieked out across the quiet bay.

"Ah," Julian nodded knowingly. "You've still got yer' company. I won't keep you then."

"No, keep me!" he whispered on the verge of panic, ducking behind Julian. The two men disappeared inside the relatively safe haven of the neighboring houseboat.

ঔৎ

In the flat atop the Mermaid Theater, Christine lay awake in her nest, a bed crafted out of an old fishing boat that was suspended off the floor with thick ropes attached to the high ceiling. The wooden seats in the vessel had been removed and replaced with a double mattress, a down comforter and a few plump pillows covered in thick, silver velvet. She reached up, trailing her fingers across the ends of long, hanging strands of fishnet and seaweed, adorned with sea glass and pearls that ornamented the glass dome above. The stings twinkled and chimed as the mass of a hundred or more of them

166

shifted in a waving motion like sea foliage in an upside-down garden.

Wearing a floor-length robe of ebony silk, tied loosely at the waist, Charlie crept into the bedroom carrying a sterling sliver tea service and a plate of scrambled eggs. He stopped for a moment to gaze down upon his sister's tousled tresses, bringing to mind vibrant coral he'd once seen when diving in the warm waters of the Caribbean. He smiled and gently rocked the boat bed, setting the tea and food on the bedside table. "Wakey wakey," he whispered, cattily climbing into the boat and snuggling himself beneath the warm covers. "I brought you some gull eggs just like mum used to make," he teased. "Now isn't that worth getting up for?"

Christine turned over slightly and groaned.

"My, don't we look ravishing this morning," he purred.

"We *always* look ravishing," she grinned sleepily, yanking the edge of the comforter across her body. "You were out late last night getting into mischief somewhere. Who was it this time?"

Charlie recalled the full curves of the woman's body as he'd taken her on the beach with the poetry of Tennyson - or was it Shelly? he wondered. "Nobody you know. Just a girl."

"Ah, the lonely woman drawn to the seaside, seeking to fill an indescribable yearning that you no doubt - *filled*," Christine smirked.

"That's right," he defended. "You know, you have a terribly annoying way of removing the beauty and mystique from the ritual. You're no fun at all."

Christine sat up and reached for her cup of tea with a smile, years beyond her age. "You forget who you're talking to."

"It was strange though, last night," he confided. "Different, if you will. I felt as though I were being watched, hunted almost."

"Really Charlie," she sighed. "What did you expect after you no less than sabotaged the parade yesterday? People are talking," she scolded, distastefully glancing at the small portion of scrambled eggs. "You really need to be more - respectful."

"Yes," he smiled devilishly recalling the mayhem he'd created at the festival. "Now those bastards will really have something to talk about around here. It was classic. You should have been there."

"I was working." Setting down her teacup, she shot a sharp glance in his direction. "I have to live here," she reminded him quietly. "You can't just go around antagonizing the villagers."

Charlie pressed a finger against her youthful lips and stared into her troubled eyes. "What's on your mind, luv?"

Her gaze was fixed on the seaweed strands above for a moment, then she turned slightly to face her brother. "Do you ever think about mum and dad?" she asked, hopelessly, searching his dark eyes for answers. "Do you think that they were truly happy – was it worth it?"

He stroked a lock of hair from her face, kissing her cheek. "They're dead," he whispered resentfully. "Now would you stop worrying about things like that and enjoy life for once?"

But she couldn't stop worrying, couldn't stop thinking. "What about us? What's going to become of us?"

"Love is everywhere, Christine," Charlie told her, stroking her hand with his fingertips. "It's a wonderful, intangible element that can't be bottled or harnessed – or made to last." He added with a bitter laugh, "I fall in love most every night."

"And out again the next morning," she reminded him, growing tired of his hollow dissertations on the subject, and weary of the way he carelessly breezed into the village once a year, spending the remainder of his time roaming the globe and indulging himself in pointless affairs and one night stands, that is, when he wasn't amusing himself with his treasure diving. He certainly wasn't here because he actually wanted to make a home, she thought resentfully.

Charlie groaned, flopping back on the pillows. "We're not built to love, you and I. Have a fling if you must, get it out of your system, but you must never let them get under your skin."

"A fling," she repeated flatly. "Is that all she was to you?"

A faded memory in black and white welled up as he remembered making love to the delicate young woman for the first time, in what now felt like a thousand summers ago. "I nearly lost everything," he managed, blinking the pictures away. "I made the mistake for the both of us. I sacrificed one life for another."

"And what of the sacrifice she made for you? Don't tell me that wasn't love."

"It wasn't love," he answered icily, turning to face her, his churning eyes becoming cold and steely gray like those of a shark. "Is there something going on? Something that you want to tell me?"

She sat up in bed, tucking her legs beneath the covers. "Of course there isn't," she sighed, his prodding stare beginning to annoy her. She yanked the edge of the blanket away, exposing him to the morning chill. He glowered at her slightly.

"What?" she spat. "It is my bed after all."

The siblings stared at each other for a tense moment, the profiles of their straight noses and sharp cheekbones mirrored face to face.

"Brendan," a deep American voice echoed from the living room. Christine jumped up at the sound of it, blood flushing to her cheeks.

What in the hell was he doing here!

Charlie narrowed his eyes, then turned to the voice outside the bedroom door.

"Everything. I want – everything," Brendan continued.

It took a second for her to realize that Brendan wasn't in her living room and that she wasn't hearing things.

It was that damn bird again.

"Pearl!" she hollered, "knock it off!"

"Oh, bloody hell! Not the American!" Charlie exploded with sweeping arms.

"His name is Brendan James – and that was completely out of context!" she defended, still gawking in horror. "What? Are you going to believe that senile bird over your own flesh and blood?"

Barely able to contain his vile temper and still livid about the encounter with the writer on the docks, Charlie rose to his feet, shaking a menacing finger at her. "He – for your information is a very, very dangerous man. And I forbid you to speak to him again! Are we clear?"

"I – am aware of what he is," she snarled back, "and you have no authority to forbid anything. Are we clear?"

Controlling his emotions was an art that Charlie had mastered long ago, yet as he stared at Christine and the outrage flashing in her eyes, his only companion on this earth, his blood boiled at the thought of losing her.

If she were ever to leave him...

Raking a hand through his raven hair, he slumped down in the corner of the room, burying his face in the black silk robe attempting to conceal the forming tears. "I'm sorry."

As much as she wanted to hate her brother for what he was, she found herself moving toward his curled up body, wrapping her arms around his shoulders. He was growing weak and he'd become weary from wandering. He was alone.

"Charlie."

Closing his eyes, he swallowed hard, taking her delicate hand in his and squeezing it with desperation. "You must be cautious. Promise me that you will."

"You're tired," she whispered soothingly. "Why don't you rest for a while."

His watery eyes tilted upwards, his smile fragile. "Come and travel with me. There's a Spanish galleon off the coast of Hawaii that I want to search for. Say you'll do it with me. Just the two of us."

She peered through the window at the village below that was beginning to stir. "I can't leave this place Charlie. Not now. This is my home and I've made a life here for myself. A good life. Unlike you, I can't just jump from one lover to the next like there's no tomorrow."

"There's always a tomorrow," he blinked, his words sending a shiver down her back. "And because there is, you've got to go away for awhile."

"I don't have to go anywhere," she sniffed defiantly.

"Far too much time has passed. The locals – they're starting to whisper about it - about you. I've heard the hushed voices, murmuring beyond their proper flower boxes, voices uttering the old wives tales while snug in their beds in the cloak of night," he told her, his eyes serious and dark.

She turned away, not wanting to hear another word of it.

"Christine," he continued, "they've not forgotten *the curse...*"

The ugly word made her flinch, dredging up years of dark, unspoken secrets that she'd worked so hard to bury. She'd known that the villagers were wary of her beyond their friendly smiles, that they still wondered about her dead lovers, but she'd survived, nevertheless, by scoffing at the occasional rumor that cropped up. The pressure behind her eyes increased. She would be strong, wouldn't cry in front of him. But he was right, there was no denying it. After a moment, she nodded her head in agreement. She would leave Heather Bay with Charlie and not return again for twenty years.

"Shhhh," he told her, cradling her head against his chest while humming a forgotten lullaby.

The Wesley's houseboat was even tackier than Brendan's, undoubtedly decorated by Sarah. The floors were covered with inch-high shag carpet in bright orange and the furniture was upholstered in some kind of fabric that might have once been a zebra or tiger print. It was impossible to tell beneath the tobacco stains that had discolored everything from the couches to the drapes with a yellowish-brown tinge.

At the kitchen table, Julian dug through a worn shoe box, stuffed with photographs and newspaper clippings while Brendan nursed a bitter cup of coffee and tried to remember if he'd closed the Word document on his laptop before stumbling out this morning.

Delivering a pile of buttered toast to the two men, Sarah smiled sympathetically at Brendan.

"Take a look at these mate," Julian said, sliding some photos of Christine across the table. One was a creased newspaper article advertisement for the theater, another an old black and white promotional photo from the 1950's of the Mermaid theater and the third, a recent color photograph of Christine.

Brendan swallowed another sip of coffee. "I've already seen the mermaid show."

"But did you really look? Same girl?" Julian challenged, pointing to the old piece of paper. "Look again. Look at the date on this newspaper clipping."

"Nineteen thirty-five," he read wearily. "So? She looks a lot like her mother and grandmother."

Sarah quietly hovered by the counter to gauge Brendan's reaction to her husband's conspiracy theory while pouring equal amounts of blackberry brandy and tomato juice into a glass measuring cup of boiling chicken broth.

"No," Julian corrected. "She's *identical* to her mother and grandmother. I've been studying these photographs at great length." He paused for effect, eyes darting back and forth with excitement, "*It's the same girl.*"

"Please, my head already hurts enough," Brendan groaned.

Sarah squeezed a lemon wedge into the steaming concoction and slid it across the table to Brendan. "Here. Made you a Rooster's Bloody Revenge. Handles a hangover before you can say cock-a-doodle-doo."

Brendan sniffed at the thick, reddish liquid, raised it to his lips and shrugged, swallowing the unpalatable potion as fast as possible. "Cheers," he gagged, setting the empty glass down.

Pointing at the pictures again, Julian strained to get his viewpoint duplicated. "Yeah Mr. Conde Nast Traveler? Do you think everything has to have a logical explanation?"

Sarah stepped in and smiled apologetically. "Julian, please. I don't think you need to get nasty with our guest."

He ignored her and continued ranting, "Tell me then Brendan, how do you explain what happened to you last night?"

He squirmed uncomfortably as Julian's bulging eyes bored into him. "I don't know," he finally responded, raising his hands defensively. "Maybe this village is just dying for a little publicity and some moron down at the tourism office is hoping that I'll write about it. Who knows? We could be sitting on the next Loch Ness monster here!"

"Some reporter you turned out to be," Julian grumbled, cramming the papers back into the shoe box. "Huh! And I thought you fellows were supposed to investigate matters like this."

The men stared at each other in silence.

"No souls," Sarah interrupted.

"Please pet," Julian growled sideways at his wife who was flitting over the coffeepot. "Can't you see that we're busy right now?"

Sarah refilled Brendan's cup and placed her

hand on his shoulder, determined to get a word in. "They say that mermaids don't have souls. One would think that all you gotta do is look her right straight in the eye and have a look for yourself. Simple as that."

Julian smacked Sarah's bottom and laughed, "very insightful, luv! Perhaps he should throw her into the ocean as well and see if she turns into a bloody salmon!"

She angrily snatched Julian's plate away and Brendan decided that it was about time he left before the Wesley's killed each other. But before he could excuse himself from the table, a disturbing howl rang out from the vicinity of the docks outside. *"You fucking bastard James!"*

The shrieked curse sent a chill down his spine and he knew that the creature had risen, probably trying to figure out what in the hell had happened last night.

Rushing to the porthole window, Sarah peered through the yellowed curtain, covering her gaping mouth. Outside, Fiona had scooped up her cashmere coat from the dock and was furiously kicking the side of Brendan's boat.

"I'll be fucked!" Sarah gawked. "It's that woman from the telly and she's gone absolutely batty! Come and have a look at this boys!"

Julian punched Brendan's arm and rubbed his hands together, "So, you've been holding out on us, eh big man?"

Brendan yanked the curtain shut to avoid being spotted. "Er – no. She's just an old - friend of mine."

A wave of laughter rose from Julian's gut as he peered outside again, watching the disheveled blonde limping down the dock on her broken heel while spitting out venomous curses beneath her breath. "Look at her go, man! Grrrrrrrr! Bet that one's a real tiger in bed!"

Sarah whacked him on the side of the head, "Julian!" she scolded.

Upon witnessing Fiona's crass exit, Brendan considered himself fortunate that he hadn't been present when she'd finally come to. He hastily turned to the Wesley's, "I've got to go now. And Sarah, thanks for the bloody whatever it was. Did the trick."

Julian shook his head. "What? Was it something I said?"

"It's always something you bloody said!" Sarah blurted out. "No wonder we ain't got no friends Julian!"

His cheeks flushed and he sheepishly handed Brendan his shoe box. "Sorry for raising me voice and all. Take a look through the rest of these. I'll cut you a deal if you want to use any of them in your magazine article."

"Thanks," Brendan nodded as he ducked out the door and made a run for it.

CHAPTER ELEVEN

Charmed by the unusual country market, Brendan tossed a couple of disposable razors, a bottle of drinking water and a locally made bar of goat's milk soap into the wicker arm basket that the quaint village grocery had provided for the convenience of its customers. He gawked in wonder, strolling through the narrow aisles of the peculiar, rustic emporium where consumers could still purchase carcasses of skinned rabbits and whole legs of mutton that hung from the ceiling above a tidy display of rat traps and bottles of HP Sauce. Nowhere to be found were the instant mashed potatoes or the frozen microwave-ready meals that he'd grown so accustomed to in the States, in fact, the market didn't even appear to have a freezer. Sweet milk in thick glass bottles and ceramic crocks of farm-fresh butter lined the shelves of the cooler and the shop proprietor had set out a generous platter of homemade shortbread and tiny plastic cups of elderberry wine for shoppers to sample. Perhaps it was the friendly welcoming from the plump shopkeeper when she'd greeted him with an endearing "cheerio," - or maybe it was because he'd just had his first real taste of a simpler way of life. Whatever it was, the unexpected find had brought a smile to his face.

Brendan paid for the goods with his nearly maxed-out credit card and stepped onto the uneven pavement outside, lowering a pair of black sunglasses over his eyes. With his brown paper bag in hand, he grinned to himself in anticipation of his next stop, the Siren Shop.

177

❧

The storeroom of the boutique was piled high with empty cardboard cartons and Styrofoam peanuts as it always was during the busy season. Sitting at the worktable, Christine opened a shipment of her most popular item that had just arrived from the silversmith in Peel. She removed the delicate jewelry from plastic bags and counted out four dozen pairs of earrings. Beneath each dazzling opal bead and silver Celtic knot, dangled a slender mermaid charm of gleaming sterling with a little hinge cleverly connecting the torso and tail that allowed for a swishing effect whenever the pieces moved. Still amused by the whimsical design, she held an earring up under the florescent light and flicked the end of its tail. Glancing at the wall clock, she scooped up the order and decided to make space for the merchandise in her main display case by the cash register, hoping to sell them all before the festival week was over.

Christine nearly dropped the armload of jewelry when she spotted Brendan James casually leaning against her display counter, his eyes concealed by a pair of sunglasses, making it impossible to tell what was going on within his shifty mind.

Mischief, she figured. What else would a man like that be up to?

Setting down the goods, she cocked her head curiously at him. "What are you doing here?"

His pulse quickened when he saw her again, nearly forgetting how incredibly stunning she was since he'd seen her just last night swimming in the ocean. Her long, vibrant hair was pulled back into a thick ponytail and her slender body was wrapped in a sexy halter top of pale gold, sparsely dotted with pink sequins that dipped down to her lower back. The effect was nearly staggering.

"Cat got your tongue?" she grinned.

Fascinated, he studied every curve of her full lips that were swept with a light iridescent gloss, suddenly aching to taste them. But that would come later, he reminded himself. "Actually, no," he answered, helping himself to a drink from the bottle of water he'd purchased earlier. "I came to talk to you about last night."

"Oh? And what about it?"

He set the water aside and lifted his glasses, shooting a smoldering look in her direction. She flinched as he leaned closer. "I just thought I'd stop by and see if you were in the mood to shag me within an inch of my life," he purred.

"Are you mad, man!" she hollered, blood flushing her cheeks.

"I'm joking," he laughed. "Come on, where's your sense of humor?"

Before she could respond, he let his elbow slip on the counter, resulting in the entire bottle of water spattering across the front of her shirt. Gasping from the cold shock, she glared back at the American. Her hands trembled and he realized she was on the verge of tears. About to apologize, he stopped as a tortured moan escaped from her throat, her frail body suddenly collapsing with a dull thud behind the counter.

He stared blankly at the empty space she'd occupied a moment earlier.

"Oh! My legs! My legs!" she gasped.

"Oh-my-god...," he uttered, unable to move

for a moment.

Shifting forward, he willed himself to lean over the counter, "Christine?" he gulped, "are you all right?"

"Owwwwww…"

Suddenly, she sprung up next to the register, her beautiful face transformed into the monstrous head of a hag with pallid, sagging skin, hissing fiercely and sending a pang of stark terror through his brain. In a wild flash he scrambled back, tumbling head over foot across a rack of dresses. Losing his balance, he fell over and flattened the mermaid mannequins positioned in the front window with a crash. Unfortunately it was halfway there as he was plowing through the merchandise, that he realized she'd only been wearing a rubber mask. But by then it had been too late to stop the course of his stumbling body. With a final flailing of arms, he came to an abrupt stop, amongst a sea of wigs, tails and yards of filmy blue fabric - and the sound of trilling laughter ringing in his ears.

Pulling off the mask, Christine's howling subsided a little as her eyes scanned over the damage. "Jesus man! I was just having you on!"

Ten degrees beyond embarrassment, he encompassed the jumble of clutter he'd made out of her boutique. He silently willed his knees to stop trembling and glared at her incredulously. "Do – do you always do that to your customers?" he managed to stammer, flinging a wisp of fabric away from his face.

"No," she smirked, offering him a hand, "I save that one for cocky magazine writers."

Not sure if the nervous laugh that came from his mouth was one of relief or terror, he waved her outstretched hand away.

She insisted, offering her hand again. He took it in his, her touch sparkling with electricity. His eyes cast downward, then flicked up to meet hers. Helping himself to his feet, he up-righted the tangled rack of dresses for her. "Look, I'm sorry about that."

She sighed, stifling a giggle, "you don't have to apologize. You just got swept up in the spirit of things. I can understand. And you know what?"

"What?"

Her voice was soft, almost melodic, "It's okay to believe. In fact, I find it sort of attractive when a grown man can still be boyish and a little bit gullible."

For a brief second, he did, in fact feel like a boy again. A naughty boy. "Actually," he grinned, "I just wanted to see you in a wet shirt."

"What!!!"

Clasping his hands around hers, he pulled her close. Her clear, green eyes were darting with confusion attempting to make sense of this man. "*You're crazy!*" she managed to whisper, turning her head away.

"There's something that I need to know" he told her, pulling her face just inches to his, welding his lips upon hers. She rigidly pushed him back, then despite herself, felt her shoulders relaxing, lost in the taste of him. As they parted, she smiled dreamily. "Wow."

Brendan flipped the closed sign over on the front door and moved toward her again.

"What do you think you're doing?" she demanded, blocking his way with arms suddenly akimbo.

"You're closed for remodeling," he told her with

a firm grin.

Flustered, she pushed past him and turned the sign back over. "Might I remind you that this is my shop and you have no right to come in here and tell me how to run my business. I want you to leave!"

Brendan's lips curled into a dangerous smile and he stepped forward. "Not until I've finished with you."

Furious about being pushed around and insulted on her own property, she grabbed the wooden push broom in the corner and shook it at him threateningly. "I want you to go! NOW!" she demanded, the gesture only making him burst out in laughter.

"What are you gonna do? Sweep me to death?" he challenged.

Exasperated, she hurled the broom to the floor.

The wild spark in her eyes was irresistible and before he knew it, his searing lips had unavoidably locked onto hers again. She tried to fight it, the force that was drawing them together, but weakened as the whole world fell away from her feet in a blur of color. Nothing else mattered and she kissed him, breathless, weightless, timeless…. The potent pheromones began releasing from every pore of her body, so powerful that both of them began to grow intoxicated with it. Hands traveled boundlessly over new territory, desire increasing to unimaginable heights. Feeling extremely lightheaded, Brendan willed himself to keep the upper hand with her, knowing that he had to leave before things got out of control. He pushed her back, looked her over, "Yeah," he panted, "you've got soul all right."

Anger pulsed through her temples. "Bloody hell! Is that all you kissed me for?"

"I've gotta go now," he grinned, stumbling for

the door. "Gotta get back to work, looks like you do too," he teased, glancing at the mess on the floor. "Maybe I'll see you later?"

"Ooooh!" she growled, banging her fist against the wall as he jogged out of the shop. "Wanker!"

Colorful stalls had sprung up like mushrooms down High Street where merchants were peddling everything from farm fresh produce and hand-crafted artwork to woolen sweaters and raspberry jam. The tourists buzzed along the road sampling homemade mustard and gushing over meticulously tatted lace doilies.

Brendan's vision was hazy as he rambled through the lively marketplace, inwardly reflecting upon his visit to the shop. He'd set out to confuse her, but had resulted in confusing himself. He hadn't planned on kissing her, but the improvisation had worked out well, much to his liking – and hers too as far as he could tell. The woman was a phenomenon. But the lingering buzzing in his head was driving him mad. He stopped walking for a moment, and found himself standing across from a stall where a sprightly little man in a polyester suit was demonstrating a new cleaning product called WHAM! Trying to focus his cloudy eyes, he stepped closer.

"Only five pounds for an entire three month's supply!" the man called out to the onlookers. He sprayed a stream of the green cleaning solution onto a grimy sample window while shouting, "WHAM!" and then again on a tarnished silver tea pot, "WHAM!" both of which instantly came clean.

Brendan staggered to the head of the small crowd that had gathered to watch. "Sir, may I demonstrate...," the salesman began, but Brendan had already snatched the bottle out of his hand. Sniffing at the nozzle, he aimed the trigger at his own face and sprayed a cloud of the solution. The crowd backed away from Brendan with a collective gasp as he inhaled the mist, shook his head vigorously and stalked off.

"Thanks," he croaked over his shoulder.

Wide-eyed, the little man scuttled over to where Brendan had dropped the bottle, picking it up with a baffled expression. Turning back to the bewildered crowd, he continued his sales pitch. "There we go then. So, as you just witnessed, WHAM! has many uses…"

In the near distance, an unusually large man lurked in an abandoned storefront, looming among the shadows of the tattered green awning. The black hooded sweatshirt shrouded his features in darkness, unlike the jolly holidaymakers bumbling along with ice cream cones and candyfloss. He was observing, waiting and watching for the perfect moment to strike. This was what he'd been waiting for. Calculating eyes focused in on the one he'd been tailing for hours, the one that could deliver what was rightfully his… His piggish nose twitched, inhaling the sharp smells of the lively street market, overloading his senses with possibilities. Sweat beaded on his clammy skin as he prepared himself to mingle, to blend in with the others. Lowering a pair of cheap, violet-tinted sunglasses over his dark eyes, he disappeared into the crowd, trailing at a safe distance behind the American through the open-air market.

Impressive was the selection of books on

mermaids and water spirits displayed in the front window of The Merfolk Book Shop, situated behind a row of cramped stalls.

For the first time in months, Brendan felt at home among books as he spun around in the musty shop, wondering what treasures he might find in a store located in such an awkward village. Worn, Persian runners lay on the floor beneath tall shelves stretching to the ceiling, reminding him of his neglected apartment back in Los Angeles where the walls were stacked with piles of books ranging from cheap paperback novels to rare volumes he'd collected over the years. There was something comforting about books, he thought, the smell of the ink and cracked leather bindings. He took a deep breath, reminding himself that he had research to do and a manuscript of his own to write.

From the window display, he picked up a large volume with an old woodcut illustration of a mermaid on the cover. He opened it, leafing through the pages, deciding to treat himself to a quick look around the rest of the shop before paying for the book that might come in useful in his work.

A small matted dog with cloudy eyes followed at his heels as he walked down the aisles. Colliding snout-first into the leg of a table, the blind dog collapsed with a wheezy grunt.

A handwritten card positioned before a pile of books at the back of the shop caught Brendan's eye, ROTTEN POTATOES – 50 pence. The sign was referring to the jumble of close-outs, stacked high on the card table. Rejects graced the heap such as, <u>Feng Shui for the Farm</u>, <u>Doily Tatting for Dummies</u> and a book with instructions on how to weave color coordinated sweaters, booties and tail-warmers for cats distrubingly titled, <u>Knitting for Pussy</u>.

By far the most creative display he'd ever seen to dispose of publisher overstocks, he sniggered at the cute sign - then he saw them. A pile of <u>Scorpions in My Jockstrap</u>, his second book that had nearly sunk the publisher and brought disgrace upon his name. There were seven, maybe eight copies insultingly and crookedly stacked behind some abomination called, <u>Let's Get Fat</u>!

Horrified, he picked up a book, thumbing through the pages. *It had been written in a hurry*, he admitted, *but it wasn't this bad...*

Was it?

The shame and anxiety closed in on him like a dark cloud as the scathing review in Publisher's Weekly swam to the front of his mind, '*Sadly, a disappointing runner up to his first title. After suffering through Scorpions, author Brendan James has proven himself to be nothing more than a shallow and unintelligent tourist.*'

It was ego that had written the book, he knew now, his head so swollen from the success of his first blockbuster, he'd assumed that every sentence he wrote was pure, unadulterated genius - and no one could tell him otherwise. The first book had gone to his head - but the second had gone to his heart.

The heavyset proprietor in a pair of thick glasses and a bun of hair held in place with a pencil was heading toward Brendan. In a panic, he buried his books at the bottom of the pile, spinning around with a guilty grin plastered across his face.

She'd seen the man carrying around her priciest mermaid book and had hoped he might splash out on an additional copy of the local mermaid lore book she gripped in her hand. But something was off about him, she observed, unable to put her finger on it. Her crookedly waxed eyebrow rose slightly as she attempted to peer behind the table that he was obviously striving to block with his body. She cleared her throat uneasily.

The fixed, bloodless grin was starting to make his cheek muscles twitch.

"Can I help you find something?" she asked.

"Er – no, no, just browsing," he managed through a clenched jaw.

"Suit yourself," she sighed, glancing down at the expensive mermaid book in his hand and offering him the small paperback. "If it's local mermaid lore you're looking for, you ought to try this one as well. It was written by an author from Heather Bay. It's one of the best I've read on the subject."

"Right," he nodded, inching away from the card table and tripping over the visually impaired dog that had managed to curl itself around his foot. She snatched up the mutt, frowning disapprovingly as he caught his balance.

"Thanks" he said, inspecting the book she'd given him, reading the author's name across the cover. "This guy lives around here? Kieran McVee?"

The woman's glasses slid down her narrow nose and she pushed them back again. "Oh yes. In the cottage up past the lighthouse. He's a real horse's arse though. I wouldn't go knocking on his door if I were you. Doesn't fancy tourists, that one. Doesn't fancy much of anyone."

"Thanks. I'll take it," he told her, setting the larger mermaid volume back on the counter.

She sighed with annoyance, realizing that she'd just talked him out of buying the more expensive book.

As soon as the peculiar American exited the shop and disappeared out of sight, the woman rushed over to the discount book table and began rooting through the pile. "Hmmmm," she pondered suspiciously, "now what exactly were you trying to hide over here?" She picked up a copy of <u>Scorpions</u> and flipped it over in her hand, then opened the front cover, inhaling in shock. Instantly, she recognized the black and white photo of the man who'd just been standing in her shop, *the man responsible for writing what was possibly the worst book she'd ever read.*

The woman squinted at his picture, then glanced out the window at the cheerful marketplace they'd all worked so hard to pull off. Her eyes narrowed into little slits, now taking his presence personally. *If he were planning to write about the village,* as she suspected he might – *oh dear.*

In a bustle, she waddled across the store with his book gripped in hand. The woman picked up the telephone, frantically dialing the village's tourism office. They'd know what to do.

No answer.

She hung up the phone, glaring down at the grinning photograph of Brendan James. "Come here to write things about us, have you? Bastard."

Brendan departed Merfolk Books with mixed emotions. On one hand, he was horrified to discover his book being dishonored in a village as remote and as backward as this one. On the other, he was elated with his little find, an absurd text on the subject of mermaids, *that he'd grudgingly paid full price for.* But, nevertheless, written by a local author who apparently believed that the creatures were real from what he could tell by flipping through the pages - a writer he could go and visit to add a little color to his manuscript. The first chapter alone; Mermen - Masters of Seduction, was enough material for a good ten-page rant he estimated. *These people don't know the meaning of rotten potatoes*, he sniggered, brushing off the insulting manner in which his books had been displayed. He made the undaunted decision to show them all just how *'shallow and unintelligent'* he could be when he really put his mind to it. Crossing the street, he reentered the crowded market while scanning over the pages of the ridiculous paperback.

The figure in the hooded sweatshirt had been waiting across the street. He spotted the American exiting the book shop and resumed trailing him.

An Irish woman with wild red hair stood within her stall arranging jars of honey while admiring the attractive, gold-edged labels she'd personally designed. The gold had cost a bit more, but had been worth it based on the brisk sales so far today and she'd already turned nice a profit.

Working his way past a booth selling bangers and beer, Brendan tucked the mermaid book inside his coat as he strolled past the honey stall.

The man in the hood trudged behind the American, trying to stay focused on the dangerous job at hand. Willing his subject to stay on track, his bulbous nose twitched as the sweet, unmistakable aroma of honey swept into his nostrils. He squinted behind the tinted sunglasses and allowed his hands to begin shaking. *The time had come*, he decided, beginning his descent toward the roadside stall where the vendor hummed to herself standing back to look at the neat display of bottles and jars, glistening so cheerfully in the sunlight.

The man's breathing was heavy and labored now as he kept the American in sight. Another waft of honey invaded his nostrils and he whimpered audibly, "oieeeeeee!" attracting the attention of a few tourists.

Now!

His attention shifted from the American, then back to the honey stall, just meters away now as his large body barreled toward it, grunting and squealing with excitement.

The red-head handed a customer a paper bag and tucked the cash in her apron, deciding to sign up for a stall at next year's festivities. Then something odd caught her eye. A strange and very large man across the road was knocking tourists out of his path and - heading her way. The freckle-faced woman hadn't thought much of it with all the beer-toting youths bumbling about – until she saw the disfigured face shrouded beneath the hood and the strange, dark eyes, eerily fixed on her wares. He charged directly toward her with great velocity and force, knocking terrified tourists out of his way. A horrified whisper crossed her lips, "Jesus, Joseph and Mary!"

Screaming and spilling paper bags, the shoppers scattered in the opposite direction of the grunting lunatic.

Brendan whirled around hearing the commotion. Stopping dead in his tracks, he gawked as a man clad in black tore through the peaceful marketplace raising hell.

As the figure closed in on the Bees Knees, the woman froze in terror, unable to move until the last instant when she managed to cross herself and dive out of his way. He smashed into the stall head first, overturning the fold-out card tables with the ear-splitting shatter of broken glass and flying honey pots. His large body slid into the booth, stopping just inches before the nose of cowering woman. With a single glance into his ruddy, piggish nose and small dark eyes, her eyelids fluttered and she collapsed in a heap.

With clumsy, rough hands, he snatched up several jars from the ground, allowing his tongue to dart in and out of the containers, greedily licking droplets of the sticky substance from his fingers and sides of the broken glass.

The thing in the water, Brendan suddenly cognited, catching a glimpse of the assailant's face.

Before the frenzied crowd had settled, the man rose and scuttled through the curtains at the back of the booth, vanishing into an alley off of High Street, his eerie squeal echoing off the cobblestones and plaster walls, "Oieeeeeeeeeee!"

This is too good to be true, Brendan grimaced, pushing his way forward through the panicked circus of excited shoppers.

He barged into the stall, scanning over the wreckage, the toppled wooden crates, the broken glass, and the frightened eyes of the woman who was coming to. He knelt down at her side and helped her sit up, "Are you all right? How much money did he get?" he questioned rapidly.

Shaking her head fearfully, she tightened her fingers around the large wad of cash, still safely tucked in her apron. "No – no luv, I'm all right, and he didn't take me money," she stammered, peering around in disbelief at the smashed, sticky mess. "But I think he was after – me goods…"

They stared at each other with identical expressions of bafflement, neither able to understand the motive behind the bizarre attack. *Unless it was done for my amusement*, he thought.

"Stay here," he ordered, dashing through the back curtains, now chasing after a man who'd just astonishingly ripped off, and destroyed – *a display of honey?*

Running through the dark and narrow alley between buildings, Brendan followed the one-way path until he wound his way to an arched alcove on a quiet residential street. Bits of gravel crunched beneath his boots on the unpaved road, yet his eyes found nothing suspicious as he peered beyond the low hedges and vegetable gardens of the cheerful sixteenth-century cottages.

Come on you bastard. Where'd you go?

Spinning around on his heels, he attempted to locate the moron who'd nearly drowned him last night. As he stepped forward onto the boulevard, the sole of his boot scraped against something. He bent and picked it up, holding the object out before his eyes in the fading remnants of daylight. It was the broken base of a glass jar, still glutinous with the sweet substance. He dipped his finger in it, tasted it to be sure, and then noticed another sticky glob on the street a few yards away. The idea of finding an actual trail was ludicrous, he knew, but the fool who'd squealed away with the honey in tow had left him with the general idea that he'd scuffled off in the direction of the old cemetery a few blocks up the winding avenue.

As Brendan jogged up the complacent street in the seafaring village, he noticed subtle changes in the architecture, most likely the neighborhood that the wealthy merchants had built for themselves in the 1800's when the town was the center of the island's fishing industry. Numerous chimneys sprouted from a row of narrow, three-story brick houses with flat roofs, some of the flues trailing with fragrant wood smoke. One building in particular caught his eye as he hiked up the hill, a well kept home with a burst of pink roses climbing up white-washed lattice beside the front door. Hand-carved Celtic symbols were permanently etched into the old wood and an inconspicuous sign with bold black lettering hung just below the brass door knocker; KITTENS FOR SALE, ORANGE TABBIES & MULTICOLOURED – EIGHT POUNDS, BLACK - THIRTY-FIVE POUNDS. INQUIRE WITHIN.

Assuming that the people in this town were really into bad luck, or that black cats were in great demand for some reason, he shrugged, trudging a little slower toward the iron gates ahead.

Brendan stopped before the cemetery to catch his breath and rethink his next plan of action. Having serious second thoughts about chasing some buffoon through an isolated graveyard, he hesitated for a moment, peering across the grounds at a formidable granite church tower that loomed on the hillside like a ghost of stone. *What if it was some kind of trap to finish off the drowning business from the other night?* he thought grimly, reminding himself that people around here *were known* to spear each other with harpoons if the occasion called for it. And after all, galloping off alone into a crumbling cemetery after dark in a strange country was never a good idea, no matter how you looked at it. But the warm glow of candlelight flickering through the window of the ancient church instilled just enough confidence that he creaked open the black iron gates and gingerly crossed the threshold of the dead, his skin prickling with goosebumps. *For god's sake, you're a travel adventure writer, damn it! And travel adventure writers do stupid shit like this so they'll have something to write about!*

Knowing that he'd never forgive himself if he whimped out before seeing it through, he fished the cell phone from his pocket, dialed Jake Hogan's voice mail in Manhattan, leaving a message in a hoarse whisper. "Jake, Brendan here. Remember that pig creature that tried to kill me last night? Well, I'm about to follow it into a cemetery. So if you don't hear back from me by tomorrow morning, uh, call the police and plan a really kick-ass funeral for me. Thanks buddy. Bye."

With the flimsy insurance policy in place, he crept cautiously down the twisted path. The deep orange sunset cast an eerie glow over snarled patches of bluebells and protruding granite crosses and headstones that jutted out at odd angles like a mouthful of crooked teeth. Keeping a watchful eye on the premises, he moved in the direction of the crumbling church, its walls cloaked in patches of moss. As he prowled onward, fresh flower bouquets caught his eye, fifty or more, that were scattered before some of the decaying headstones. An oddity, he thought, in a cemetery of such utter neglect. He glanced around, picking up a cluster of lavender and inspected the hand-written note bound to it with a strand of dried seaweed;

Tra ta'n ghrian ersooyl, cha vod ooilley ny cainleynayns y siehll jannoo soilshey yn laa.

Impossible to translate the Gaelic sentiment,

he removed the paper, shoved it in his pocket and replaced the lavender before a marble headstone, dedicated to a young man named Ned who had *"drifted off and was carried away by seagulls"* in 1959. Brendan squinted uneasily at the epitaph, noting that a guy could get himself swooped up by a flock of birds for falling asleep around here if he wasn't careful. With that in mind, he proceeded with extreme caution across the boggy grounds.

Cold was the only word he could think of to describe the interior of the ancient church built of solid blocks of speckled granite. The wooden door with iron hardware had been open a crack when he stepped inside. He gravitated toward a small table below a stained glass window where a dozen beeswax votive candles were set out and flickering in the drafty stone chapel.

The hardwood floor creaked uneasily as he crossed the room, taking care to move as quietly as possible. Holding his frigid fingers above the dancing flames, he rubbed them briskly together while pondering what he was supposed to do now. The lunatic he'd been in hot pursuit of had seemingly vanished and he certainly wasn't in the mood to pray. With a sigh, he determined that he'd generated more than enough interesting material to work with for the day. Time to take off.

Then he heard it, felt it, the breath behind his back and he knew that he wasn't alone.

Oh shit...

Brendan whirled around with such speed that the tail of his coat swiped half of the burning candles to the floor with a nerve-wracking crash that echoed sharply off the stone walls. But it wasn't the creature standing there that he faced, rather an elderly clergyman, with a shiny pink head and a wooden clothespin pinched on the end of his unusually long nose. Still reeling from shock, Brendan stood frozen as the clergyman dove for the burning candles on the floor. Using the hem of his black robes, he patted out the tiny flames while mumbling something about *God's work never being done.*

Awkwardly, Brendan stooped down beside him, attempting to help with the waxy mess that was now seeping into the hardwood. "Oh – jeez, I mean, forgive me," he apologized. "Look, I thought that you were someone else…"

With twitching eyes, he looked at the American with mild annoyance. "I'll leave the forgiving to God," he said quietly.

Brendan shifted uneasily, his attention consumed by the clothespin squeezing the ball of the man's nose into a purplish bulb. "You've got a – uh – you know, on your…" he winked uncertainly, brushing a finger across his own nose.

Ignoring the comment, the clergyman rose to his feet, carefully cradling the smashed votives, still dripping with hot wax. "If you've come to see the church, you've seen all there is to see," he waved, indicating the chapel room. Staring icily down the bridge of his nose, he added, "We're accepting organ donations - if you care to help the cause."

"Organ donations?"

The man hocked his head toward a sagging pipe organ on the lurching balcony above. "The collection box is by the door," he gestured curtly, indicating that the tour was over. *"You'll find it on your way out."*

Feeling guilty about creating extra work for the

old guy, Brendan nodded politely, removing a few pound notes and the paperback mermaid book from the inner pocket of his coat.

Blinking rapidly, the clergyman's eyes grazed across the cover of the book. "Come here looking for the Mer-people, have you?" he inhaled.

"Actually, I'm here researching the subject," he squinted, craning his neck to peer out the tall window facing the cemetery. He turned back to the man, "did you just happen to see anything - strange going on out there?"

"I see strange things most every day," he sputtered impatiently. "Stranger than you'll ever know."

"Maybe then, I mean if its not too much trouble," Brendan began, unrolling the small piece of parchment, "you could tell me what this says."

Without touching the paper, the clergyman stiffened, apprehensively readjusting his clothespin. "The work of the nymph..." he scowled.

"What?"

"I can't help you," he snapped. "That's written in the old language. Hasn't been spoken in these parts since my grandfather's day."

"Then what was it doing out there in the graveyard? Obviously somebody around here still speaks it," he persisted, vaguely remembering the words Christine had said to him on the night he'd met her.

Odiche mthath.

"You said something about a – nymph?" he prodded curiously, the conversation growing surprisingly more interesting.

The clergyman ran a hand across his bald head, deeply disturbed by the fact that the stranger had brought a piece of the temptress's sorcery into this sacred place. As he glowered at the American, a hazy ray from the setting sun broke through the trees outside, sending a single shaft of light streaming through the stained glass. Brendan shielded his eyes as the man thought it over for a moment, scratching his chin.

Everything happened for a reason, did it not? Perhaps this was a sign from God himself. Perhaps if he knew what sort of spells she were casting, he could do something about it.

"I suppose," he hesitated, indicating a row of dusty volumes on a bookshelf, "that you could have a look through the dictionaries if you wanted to..."

By the dim light of the remaining altar candles, Brendan pored over an ancient Manx to English dictionary he'd located on the top shelf, painstakingly translating the words on the paper. Adding to his aggravation, the clergyman was continuously shuffling in and out of the room while peering over his shoulder. When the man wasn't scrubbing at the spilt wax on the floor or carting cleaning supplies and dustpans back and forth, he seemed to be stealing suspicious glances in his direction with every pass.

After nearly half an hour, Brendan managed to decipher the phrase. Halfheartedly, he waved at the curious little man who eagerly rushed to his side with perked ears. "It says, when the sun is gone, all the candles in the world cannot make daylight," he frowned, expecting more of a revelation after all that drudgery. "What's that supposed to mean?" he snorted.

The clergyman scuffed his shoes against the floor. He too was disappointed, not because it had just been an old island proverb, and a common one at that, but because the translation had shed absolutely no light on the wicked work of her dealings within his cemetery. "Better get the broom and dustpan put away then," he mumbled before disappearing again into one of the shadowy passages.

Sighing, he shut the cover of the heavy book with a cloud of dust. He'd completely wasted the opportunity to find the idiot he'd come here chasing in the first place. And worse than that, he realized that he'd been hiding from any real or imagined danger in the safe confines of a church with a musty dictionary under the guise of 'research,' all of which had been thoroughly unnecessary. Hefting the book into his arms, he climbed back up the stepladder and shoved it into its slot on the high shelf with a grunt. He shoved again harder, but wasn't able to make it fit back in.

In exasperation, he pawed at the grimy shelf above his head, jostling the other volumes with his hand to make enough space for the dictionary, resulting in the entire row of books toppling over sideways. He stepped to the top tier of the ladder and lifted a few books out so he could see what he was doing. Peering into the shelf, he located the bulky object that was blocking the way. Irked, he yanked on the moldering clump of black velvet with a bit too much force, causing the delicate fabric to tear and expose the shiny edge of something concealed within.

Forgetting about the jumble of books, Brendan removed the heavy object he'd discovered and set it down on the table. As he carefully peeled away crumbling layers of velvet, he found himself staring at an unusual and very old pair of silver scissors that looked like something used to prune rosebushes with. Mesmerized by the age of the object alone, sixteenth-century he guessed, he carefully ran his fingers along patterns of waves and more Celtic symbols engraved into the silver handle, wondering how many years this exquisite antiquity had been stashed away in the walls of the church. In his excitement, he was about to call out for the clergyman, but spotted something else buried within the cloth, forcing himself to shut up until he'd had a chance to check it out.

The yellowed scroll was rolled up in a tight tube and bound with a piece of twine, so deteriorated that it snapped open when he touched it. Expecting to discover little more than gardening tips, he gently unrolled the parchment beneath the soft candlelight. But what he found was,

Oh-my-god...

Disturbing illustrations glared back at him from the strange paper, ghostly pen and ink drawings of infants with webs connecting tiny fingers and toes into miniature flippers. His eyes traveled down to an ancient surgeon's chart in the corner of the diagram, depicting a tiny webbed foot with dotted lines drawn on it, presumably where one should slice.

Eerie - and obviously phony, he attempted to convince himself, all the while painstakingly inspecting the scroll before the light, checking for authenticity. But he could find no evidence that it had, in fact been fabricated.

Footsteps shuffled from the corridor.

The clergyman.

Needing more time to investigate, he tucked the document inside his coat, intending to return it after he'd had a closer look.

"What's this!" the old man croaked, rushing

200

across the floor with a push broom in hand.

"I – found these," Brendan grinned sheepishly, holding up the heavy scissors.

Horrified, the clergyman confiscated the sterling shears and scolded the American with an unsteady finger, "Don't you know that's official church business you're looking at!" he accused, "you can't just come in here and help yourself like a public library!"

"Sorry," he waved, wondering what he'd done that was so offensive. He pointed at the bookshelf innocently, "they were out in plain sight. So, what are they for anyway?"

Livid now, the clothespin pinching his nostrils quivered as he threateningly jabbed at Brendan with the end of the broom. *"There are some things that are best forgotten,"* he hissed, threatening to pop a vessel, *"things like the curse!"*

Brendan had just about had his fill of these simpletons and their absurd superstitions – *and being threatened with push brooms.* At first glance it was kind of cute, almost charming, but now it was grating at his nerves. "What curse are you talking about exactly?" he prodded caustically. *The one that's got you wearing a clothespin on the end of your freaking nose!?*

"Out!!!"

"What about my organ donation?"

Seething and disgruntled, Brendan found himself ejected onto the muddy steps in front of the church. He could still hear the wheezing of the clergyman inside as he frantically fumbled with the heavy hardware of the doors, presumably locking him out.

❧

As night fell upon the village, fierce drums of the natives pounded and notes of trilling tin flutes drifted through the atmosphere where the Junior Step Dance competition was in full swing down on High Street.

But Brendan James wasn't interested in watching any more contests or partaking in the senseless festival activities. Instead, he'd settled in for a quiet night of serious writing, a nearly impossible feat, he soon discovered.

"Don't you people ever stop!" he growled scathingly out the porthole window, stuffing wads of toilet paper into his ears and pulling the red, jeweled cap snugly down to his jaws in a desperate attempt to drown out the noise of their relentless merry-making. With a thin pair of reading glasses on the bridge of his nose and a red feather from the ludicrous beanie dangling above his right eyebrow, he faced the laptop, forcing himself to concentrate on the manuscript. His mood was beyond vile, not improved by the fact that Jake Hogan had just called demanding a synopsis of the half-written book for a five o'clock sales meeting that very afternoon. Taking the six-hour time difference into consideration, that left Brendan with little more than thirty-minutes to put something together.

Under normal circumstances, Jake had explained, the PR department would have cranked something out by now, *but being that they didn't have a manuscript to work with...*

It was entirely up to Brendan to condense his own tale into a colorful, one-page description that the boys in sales could mesmerize the book buyers with. Setting aside his notes and ideas for his evening rant, he furiously pecked at the keyboard, attempting to satisfy his publishers at Adventure Books.

MISADVENTURES AND MERFOLK

SYNOPSIS:

When Brendan James arrived in the British Isles to write an honest and vivid profile of the craggy landscape and mysterious network of micro-islands, he found little more than sheep and senile inhabitants, too toothless to chat up. But after a serendipitous ferry sinking, James found himself stranded in a remote and peculiar village on Isle of Man where the locals were celebrating their annual mermaid carnival.

At first glance, the festivities appeared innocent enough, but as James dug deeper, the famed travel essayist found himself ill-equipped to deal with the lunacy of the locals who would stop at nothing to convince him that mermaids were, in fact – real.

High above Manhattan, four sales reps in dark business suits sat around the polished conference table in the publishing house meeting room, chuckling over their coffee as Jake Hogan continued reading the e-mail in his hand:

"After personally being enchanted by a local mermaid impersonator and nearly killed after interrupting the moonlight mating ritual of a hog-faced, honey-sucking merman, James vowed to expose the slimy underbelly of the seemingly innocent festivities in the alien world he'd discovered. A place where it's considered 'fashionable' to wear your house cat as a hat, where aging rock

stars like Adam Ant still rule the day and where the neigh-
borhood church solicits for, and accepts organ donations
from tourists. In summary, "Misadventures and Merfolk"
is the tale of a seaside village gone mad."

Still cloaked in the red cap, Brendan yawned before the computer screen. It was two-thirty in the morning and he'd been writing about the day's events, leaving out the part about discovering his own books on the bargain table of Merfolk Books. No need to remind anyone about that, he decided, keeping the shameful details of the incident to himself.

He reread the new chapter, checking it for typos before sending the second attachment off into the ether.

I awoke on the docks this morning with a severe hang-
over. But luckily my body was discovered by my toothy
neighbor, Mr. Wesley, who plucked me up by the scruff of
the neck and instructed his wife to pour a concoction of
fruit juice, chicken soup, and what tasted like mule piss
down my parched throat. Still staggering from the rem-
edy within his shagadelic houseboat, he proceeded to ex-
plain his theory to me that 'all is not what it appears,'
specifically, that Christine Hamilton is really an eighty-
year-old woman. I know, I know, it sounds crazy, but old
Julian's got all the hard evidence stuffed into a sagging
shoe box which he gave to me as a peace offering after our
heated argument on the subject of 'do the Merfolk really
exist among us?" Thank goodness the cheese knife was in
the dishwasher.

But just to be thorough about it, I went to check out
this Christine business myself and succeeded in demol-

ishing her gift shop after she frightened me with a rubber sea-hag mask that she keeps cleverly hidden behind the shop counter to discourage rambunctious holiday-makers and love-starved writers from stalking her. But me? Put off by a little scaly green latex? Hah! The entire incident was a turn-on. And I had to have her. Overcome with emotion, I gave her my finest French kiss, checking her gums for dentures, mind you, and finding her clean of Polident, threw Julian's theory right out the window, just as she tossed my ass out the door of her boutique.

Before I forget, I must mention a fabulous new product that I came across today, an ingenious British invention called WHAM! that has absolutely nothing to do with the pop singer, George Michaels. One squirt of the stuff'll clean your copper kettles, dissolve the black off a crow and disintegrate dog shit before it ever hits the carpet. Besides its many household uses, WHAM! is also quite an effective tool for curbing one's carnal appetite, as I discovered after stumbling away from Christine in a terrible state of, well, never mind.

So what if the British have let their shipbuilding and fishing industries go to shit. They've got WHAM!

Feeling invigorated and looking for some action, I attempted to nab the pig-faced menace, who not only tried to drown me the other night, but robbed an Irish street vendor of her honey in broad daylight. He ran off to the cemetery, presumably to lick his fingers of the evidence and I, being very brave, or very stupid, chased after him. Losing the creature somewhere along the winding back roads of the village, I found myself drawn to the old church atop the hill where inside, I was confronted by a frightened looking clergyman with a wooden clothespin pinched on the end of his nose. In his nasally voice, he wasted no time hitting me up for an organ donation while mumbling something about a curse. Never being much of a *church man myself, I was promptly shooed out of the chapel with a push broom after I discovered a set of instructions on how to perform plastic surgery on infants born with fins and gills. Go figure.*

In closing, the charming customs, the endearing natives of Heather Bay, the lingering aroma of WHAM!, was all so overwhelming that I crawled back to the houseboat and spent the latter part of the evening retching my guts out over the toilet.

Bleary-eyed and fatigued, Brendan hit the 'send' icon on the e-mail program, then slumped over the keyboard in exhaustion.

৩৯৫

Christine was restless and filled with the uneasy longing to prowl. She'd spent the afternoon straightening up the shop after Brendan had plowed through it like a scalded cat, then kissed her, not once, but twice.

Agitated, she cracked open another oyster with a rock, removing a single gleaming pearl from the center. Eating the raw meat from the shell, she hurled the remains into the water. As she sat camouflaged on a barnacle-encrusted beam beneath the docks, wearing nothing but a small leather belt and pouch full of pearls secured around her slender waist, she found her gaze fixed upon the bobbing boats as the bright northern lights reflected a sprinkle of colored glitter upon the water.

Gathering pearls in the dark of night had become part of her routine, for doing such work in daylight would be a fool's errand, with all the tourists and nosy fisherman that might spot her or discover the secret oyster cache in the center of the bay. Normally the work was calming, even satisfying, but collecting in the shallow waters tonight had done nothing to ease her nerves nor clear her head of Brendan James.

As much as she hated everything about him, his brash arrogant attitude, his stormy calculating eyes and the way he made her react in general, she found herself drawn to him, despite the stern warnings from Charlie – and despite her own common sense.

Silently, she slid back into the water, making her way to the edge of her friend's houseboat that Brendan was temporarily inhabiting. "Temporary," she whispered, longingly drawn to the light of the porthole window. Everything about this little infatuation was like gossamer, she thought, threatening to disintegrate at the slightest breath. It was fragile, delicate, not made to last, she knew - and that scared her. As she drew closer, treading water just outside the craft now, sweet, teenage recollections of summer boys, lips laced with elderberry wine and innocent, moonlit kisses flooded her mind. She allowed her torso to surface and she grasped onto the side of the vessel. She knew that he would leave the village when the festival came to an end - and wondered if he would remember her when he went back to his home. California, she guessed by his laid back manner and the way he pronounced certain words. But as she sat on the edge of the dock with only a thin piece of glass separating her from what she wanted, no – needed, she wondered why she was so dangerously attracted to him and out here prowling in the night like her brother. The compulsion to have him had grown from a mere desire to taste, to a ravenous hunger that took every ounce of will-power to control with the pheromones running perilously out of control after he'd devoured her lips and some unseen force had made their world's collide. She needed to discover the man who had breezed into her life and turned her inside out. Stopping her hand from rapping on the window, from giving into the instinctive cravings that had led her body here, she reminded herself what was at stake.

Everything, eternity perhaps…

Turning away from the vessel, she peered down into the black water of the sea, her youthful reflection and glistening hair mirroring back for examination, wondering what would become of her if…

Before finishing the thought, she turned back to the boat, wedging her body between the side of the craft and the splintery wooden dock. With curious eyes, she pressed her face against the glass of the tiny porthole window where she saw him within the cramped cabin, slumped before a computer – *and wearing the unmistakable cap of a Dinny Mara on his head.* Sure that her eyes were playing tricks on her, she squinted, but the glittering gemstones winked back at her through the window. She clamped a hand over her mouth to avoid gasping audibly. The sight had sent her mind racing with possible explanations as she tried to comprehend what he was doing with such an article of clothing.

Perhaps he has ancestry on the islands… Blood ties to the clans…

Sarah Wesley stepped out on the deck and struck a wooden match. Shrieking, she dropped the unlit cigarette that had been dangling between her lips. "Oh bloody hell!" she gawked, urgently rapping on the glass. "Come and have a look at this!"

Oh no!

Certain she'd been spotted, Christine ducked out of sight between the two boats and the dock, vanishing beneath the surface without a sound.

Inside the houseboat, the movement of the water created just enough force to rock it sideways, gently rousing Brendan to his feet. He yawned groggily, about to cross the cramped cabin and crawl into bed, then he heard the Wesley's yapping outside. He tied the belt on his bathrobe, deciding to see what all the noise was about.

Julian was already at Sarah's side by the time Brendan had slipped into his shoes and grabbed a blanket. Poking his head out the door, he saw Sarah standing awestruck in her bare feet, pointing to the sky. He climbed onto the deck of his own boat and followed her upward gaze.

"Oh my," she whispered to Julian, "Just look at it. I've never seen it so bright." She turned to Brendan for a moment, "do you see?"

The aurora borealis was brilliant. Streaks of gleaming fire opals, burning and twisting with incandescence against a tremendous backdrop of inky black velvet lit up the night. Allowing himself to become mesmerized by the phenomenon, Brendan slumped into a plastic deck chair on the bow, watching the jeweled heavens in silence as a twinge of guilt began surfacing from somewhere in the back of his mind. This harbor, as it gleamed with magic, was perhaps the most enchanting place he'd ever seen, yet there he'd been, not more than thirty minutes ago writing tarnishing, scandalous things that would forever change the beauty, the mystique, the very soul of the village...

Nah, they have it coming, he decided with a yawn, snuggling up beneath the coarse wool blanket that was draped over his shoulders. Glancing seaward, a thick blue haze was rolling in and he knew that the phenomenon would be soon be completely obscured from view. Resting his neck rest upon the back of the chair, he gazed skyward through heavy-lidded eyes. Five minutes later he drifted off.

A brass bell clanked dully from the derelict lobster boat to Christine's right. Realizing that she hadn't been seen after all, she began breathing again. She'd swam beneath Brendan's boat to the other side where she wedged herself in the narrow space between the houseboat and the fishing rig in the next slip, waiting silently for the Wesley's to retreat into the confines of their vessel. After their door clicked shut, she lifted herself up to the dock and peered over the railing of the houseboat where she discovered Brendan asleep in a deck chair. The fog continued to roll in great tufts of white, blotting out the lights above, providing the perfect camouflage.

Dripping with sea water, she slicked the icy droplets from her smooth skin and crept up onto the deck, cautiously moving closer until she hovered just inches away from the warmth radiating from his body. Silently, she stood above him for several minutes, entranced by the swirl of his breath evaporating into the night air, listening with sensitive ears to the constant pulse of his blood. With lips slightly parted she exhaled slightly into his ear as the pheromones began releasing. Her salty skin tingled with sensation, warmth flushing through the very core of her being.

Brendan groaned in his sleep, every sense captivated by the magical smell of the sea within the intoxicating dream in which she had come to him.

A perfectly formed silhouette of ivory skin with shell pink breasts exuded a vaporous mist that rendered him powerless against the creature of unearthly beauty. Fiery masses of sea dampened hair cascaded across her shoulders and down her back as small, gentle hands reached forward. She removed the blanket from his body and unwrapped the thick bathrobe that he wore, exposing his flesh to the chill of night. Words of the forgotten language seeped beneath his skin and a pair of warm, strong thighs were pressed against his, promising to release the painful throbbing of his groin...

Christine stood straddled over his sleeping body, her tangle of hair scattering droplets of water upon his bare chest. He shifted with hips pushing upward as an urgent moan emitted from his throat, begging her to fulfill the unspoken promise.

Prickled with heat, she could no longer endure the instinctive and dangerous temptation to take him inside her. She closed her eyes and began to descend upon him.

Voices.

She blinked, listening intently with keen eyes darting around the dock through the dense fog. Heavy footsteps clad in work boots thudded down the planks toward a fishing rig and coarse, boisterous voices rose and fell.

Beginning to stir, Brendan mumbled something inaudible and desperate in his drowsy state.

Unable to risk being seen by the locals, she sprang up and disappeared into the mist.

As he awoke from the dream, a small splash at

the bay side of the boat caused the craft to rock gently, jostling him awake. A split second later, he jumped up as the freezing night air embraced his bare flesh. Trickles of sweat streamed down his face and discovering his mysterious disrobing, he became aware of the torturous state of arousal that the fantasy had left him in. He yanked the terry bathrobe around himself and found the wool blanket in a ball on the deck.

What the...?

Baffled by the circumstances and weary from the late hour, Brendan didn't notice the trail of wet, webbed footprints on the deck, nor the streaky, dark figure in the bay that was gliding away just inches beneath the surface. He snatched up the fog-dampened blanket and quickly descended into the warmth of the cabin below.

❧

The proper little cottage sat alone at the end of a narrow cobblestone path facing the tumbling sea. A wisp of silver smoke trailed from the chimney and the whitewashed walls gleamed pink in the brilliant light of dawn. Hazy orange rays crept beyond the lace curtains, spilling through diamond shaped panes of leaded glass on the perfectly spotless dwelling - except for a small pile of honey cake crumbs dotting the edge of the windowsill just outside the bedroom.

Charlie rolled over in a tangle of blankets on the four poster bed belonging to the bespectacled proprietor of Merfolk Books. He shielded his face from the brilliance of morning and turned slightly to the wide-eyed woman by his side, squeezing her enormous thigh with a grin, "Of his bones are coral made, those are pearls that were his eyes. Nothing of him that doth fade, but doth suffer a sea-change into something *rich and strange*."

"William Shakespeare!" she panted, exhausted, yet invigorated from hours of lovemaking with the fine young lad who had done impossible and wondrous things to her. "I don't know if you're rich, luv, but strange," she giggled, "you've got that one down pat."

"Right you are, you naughty girl," he growled seductively, nuzzling up against the hollow of her neck. "And you know your literature."

"I do own the book shop," she smiled, lifting her large body out of bed, still not quite believing how she'd come across him.

The old honey cake recipe she'd discovered in an antique book on Manx superstitions had arrived to the shop the other day from an estate sale - and had miraculously and impossibly lured this scoundrel into her bed. Just last night she'd followed the curious instructions, carefully adding each ingredient in proper order from the flour and the sugar to the human teardrops which had been, by far, the easiest element to come by.

She glanced over her shoulder at the black-haired youth in her bed who was smiling back at her. Feeling completely and uncharacteristically desirable despite her obvious weight problem, she walked naked across the hardwood floor, stepping directly into a shaft of sunlight that streaked through the curtains, magnifying her every imperfection. But none of that mattered in her lover's gentle and affectionate gaze. *You've still got it old mum*, she thought giddily, feeling sexier than an eighteen-year-old girl.

Cheeks flushing with vitality now, she flipped on the stereo, permeating the fussy room with the smoldering voice of Shania Twain. "This one's for you, kinky boy!" she shouted over the music.

Charlie propped himself up on a mountain of pillows and beheld the silly woman with amusement as she paraded around the bedroom, shaking her hair loose while singing along with, *Man I Feel Like a Woman*. From the bed, he rose to his knees and began dancing along with her. As she belted it out, he tossed his head back in utter delight - this capricious creature had surpassed his every expectation - and had managed to captivate his imagination. They always did, he reflected, his smoldering gaze fixed upon the woman as she jiggled across the floor like a jolly pot of orange marmalade. Gone was the dullness from her eyes, the sadness of her soul and the sweet little honey cake dusted with cinnamon and brown sugar that she'd left out for him on the sill, the sugary bait that had drawn him to the dark and lonely window of this bedroom the night before.

He looked at her now and grinned. It was the quirky little moments like these that made life pure bliss.

An hour later, the clanging of copper pots and wooden spoons sounded from the kitchen as the aroma of fresh coffee and bacon grease drifted through the cottage. The woman had insisted on preparing Charlie a proper breakfast before he departed. Pleased by her kind offer, he'd managed to get a light catnap on the cozy goose down mattress before rising.

As he stood and stretched his taut limbs, he caught a glimpse of the woman through the doorway wearing a white cotton nightgown, embroidered with tiny yellow daisies. She was chirping to herself while bending over the flames of an old-fashioned stove where the leftover cakes were warming within. He thought about creeping up on her from behind and sliding into her again on the cool tile floor beneath the collection of blue willow plates lining the kitchen walls.

Perhaps after breakfast.

Whistling to himself, he slipped into his jeans and picked up the sweater that he'd carelessly shed over the lamp on the bedside table last night when he'd crawled into her bed, rousing her with a kiss, his mouth still sweet with the taste of her cake. He grinned, recalling how she'd tried to beat him with a candlestick at first, then submitted to his dark desires – and her own after he'd whispered two or three sinful suggestions into her ear.

He put on his sweater, surveying the items deposited on the table, a ball of crumpled tissues, a bag of cherry sours and a paperback book. Popping one of her tart candies into his mouth, he glanced at the volume, curious to know more about the private life of the woman who ran her own successful business and was a fan of American country music. Why she didn't have a man of her own, he'd never understand. Perhaps things would change for her now, he smiled, listening to her singing in the background. He shrugged, as something about the book caught his eye again.

Brendan James...?

The blind dog trotted at the heels of the woman as she padded down the hall and stopped, beaming at the magnificent young creature with tousled black hair, standing beside the rumpled patchwork quilt. He sure looked good in that bedroom, she thought, damn good. "Breakfast is ready, luv."

Charlie shook his head incredulously, still staring at the name printed across the front cover of the paperback as reality sunk in.

"Don't bother with that one," she waved with a snort. "It's a real piece of shite. I only brought it home after I found the author nosing around me shop yesterday afternoon. Nearly trampled poor Garth too," she said, reaching down to scratch the blind dog's head. "Isn't that right baby? That mean American man almost squashed my widdle Garth Barks."

Charlie blinked, "Brendan James…"

"That's right," she nodded, "I figure he's probably come here to write nasty things about us and our silly festivals. So to hell with him, right? Let him try to bring us down. How's he going to make fun of a village that's already laughing at itself?"

The revelation about the true identity of Christine's new 'friend' darkened his mood considerably. "Right," he smiled politely, quelling the rage that had already begun surging through his blood. "May I have this?" he asked, gripping the book with white knuckles. "If you don't mind."

"Sure, it'll make great firewood," she chuckled, pulling him by the hand. "Come on you sexy beast. Your eggs are getting cold."

ᦿ᪣

As Christine locked the front door of her upstairs flat, she noticed the brown paper package sitting in the hall. With one eyebrow arched, she picked up the small rectangular box, inspecting the note scrawled in Gaelic that was tucked beneath

216

a knot of twine.

'Not dangerous...?' she read aloud.

"Jesus Charlie," she sighed impatiently, recognizing the sloppy handwriting. "What are you up to now?"

She nearly blanched as she tore away the thick paper and saw the copy of Brendan's paperback book, titled, *Scorpions In My Jockstrap.*

ৎ৽৵৻

Claire stood on a stepladder, humming to herself as she polished the breasts of the wooden mermaid sign with a rag and a jar of beeswax furniture polish.

Christine unlatched the white wooden gate in front of the Mermaid Inn and stomped up the path, cursing in Gaelic while shaking the copy of the book in her hands. *"Bwoid niargan! He can - paag my hoyn! Ooooh!"*

"Watch your tongue girl!" Claire warned, stepping down with a shocked expression on her face. "What are you doing here at this hour – and cursing like a sailor?"

"Actually, I just popped by to borrow a cup of arsenic," she hissed lividly, flinging a streak of hair aside.

"What?"

"As it turns out, Brendan James is some kind of a famous author," she spat, thrusting the book into Claire's hands. "And I think he's here writing about us!"

"But – the magazine..." Claire began, inspecting the pages before her eyes. After flipping through a few sentences and scrutinizing the black and white photo on the inside flap, undeniably the same man letting her houseboat, she looked helplessly at Christine. "Oh, my," she whispered darkly. "What are we going to do?"

"We'll start with a cup of tea," she nodded decisively as a devious plot began to brew behind glittering eyes. With lips curling into a wicked smile, she wrapped an arm around Claire as the two women proceeded up the steps of the inn.

"By the way," Christine asked innocently, "do you happen to have a spare key to the houseboat?"

Claire's eyes went wide, then narrowed cunningly at the preposterous suggestion. "I suppose," she murmured, "that one might have a look in the cupboard behind the front desk. You never know what's lying around in that disorganized mess back there, keys, *misplaced reservations from Conde Nast Traveler magazine reporters that senile old women forget about*, you know, things like that."

They turned to face each other, eyes locked in silent agreement.

CHAPTER TWELVE

Brendan trudged up a narrow dirt path toward a thatched roof cottage that could have been torn right out of the pages of Grimm's Fairy Tales. He still had about a mile of rough steep road to cover before he arrived on the doorstep of the isolated hovel that was inconveniently situated atop the cliffs above the cove. He stopped to catch his breath and sat down in a kaleidoscopic patch of shamrocks and bluebells, deciding to skim through the small mermaid book before approaching the author for an interview. Skipping past the illustrations, he flipped through the pages and stopped at the ludicrous chapter that had enticed him to buy the book in the first place and read:

Mermen – Masters of Seduction.

'Mermen of the British Isles are notorious for their powers of seduction over the human female species. Perhaps this is because un-comely and shy women are often overlooked by the male population of their own kind. Without proper companionship and lacking sexual satisfaction, such women are drawn to the seaside, searching to fill certain urgent desires that life has not provided. It is said that when a vulnerable woman approaches the seaside in the vicinity of a merman's territory and her teardrops fall into the surf or sand, a merman shall appear and will attempt to mate with her. It is well known fact that human teardrops are a potent aphrodisiac to the merman, overcoming him with intense attraction toward the female whose tears he's come in contact with, regardless of the subject's age or physical appearance.

I have heard of, but not seen, an old recipe on the islands for honey cakes, a spell of sorts that is said to lure the Merman into a woman's bed when she leaves the offering out on her windowsill. The small round cakes were made of clover honey, cinnamon and her own teardrops among the other standard ingredients one would find in a cake. These offerings, made by lonely wives while their men were at sea for weeks, sometimes months at a time, were banned from the village many years ago. According to Manx law, baking such a cake was at one time punishable by twenty lashings of the cat o' nine tails. Tis a very loose woman indeed who leaves honey cakes at her window.

So powerful is the spell of a heartbroken woman that the only known way for a merman to reverse his feeling of attraction is to couple with her. If the woman runs away before mating occurs, the merman will often stalk the female, releasing his intoxicating pheromones within her vicinity until she is coaxed into submission and does alleviate his arousal. Once his seed has been sown, he will return shortly thereafter to the sea to bathe. It is not of his nature to return to the female again, nor to stay with one woman for more than a few hours.

Mermen are known to keep secret lairs within familiar territory, most often a secluded location near the water's edge where they will take the female for the sacred union. Although his den is the preferred place, merman have been said to couple in open locations, so long as the place is reasonably near the water.

It is myth that mermen are full creatures of the sea with the upper torso of a man and the lower half of a fish-like creature. Mermen of the last century have been described as seductive young rogues that may mingle among us on land, the offspring of Mer-creatures from earlier times. These hybrids appear human in every way except *for the distinctively webbed feet and the telltale patch of rough, scaly flesh found on the lower abdomen. They are adept swimmers and can stay underwater much longer than humans, but they are warm-blooded mammals and require oxygen, much like a porpoise or the now extinct porgy. The life span of the merman is uncertain, but reports within recent years always describe them of youthful flesh. It is believed that the elders of the species, seemingly un-aged, are the most cunning and active due to years of experience in the arts of seduction.*

Specific rituals of seduction among the different clans of mermen vary, and may include, but are not limited to, song, gentle words of stimulation and general persuasion. Combined with the aphrodisiac effect of his natural pheromones and the youthful appearance of his flesh, no woman is safe from the sensual charms of the merman. Lonely ladies should heed warning when longing for companionship near the sea, for encountering such a creature could be dangerous to her honor and reputation. Mermen are lustful and mischievous beings with only one deed in mind, and will go to great lengths to obtain it.'

"Yeah – don't we all," Brendan sniffed, closing the pages of the book. He stood up and brushed off his pants, looking forward to a chat with the local whack job who wrote this abominable piece of shit. The afternoon promised to be an amusing one.

Crooked. Brendan cocked his head sideways and realized that the windows of the sagging cottage were askew in their frames, presumably from three-hundred-years of wear and tear. A pair of muddy Wellington boots stood upright on the small porch next to a rusty watering can and a worn, woven door mat. He knocked, half expecting to be greeted by the wicked witch or the big bad wolf.

"Hello? Is anybody there?"

A moment later, the heavy door crafted of splintered, wooden planks creaked open. Liam O'Leary poked his head out, scowling distastefully at Brendan. The old man blew a cloud of choking, blue pipe smoke into the American's face and growled, "I thought I told you to piss off!"

"Liam? I – I'm sorry to bother you," Brendan stammered, taking a step back. "I must have gotten the directions mixed up. I'm looking for a man named Kieran McVee."

"Bloody hell!" he spat. "And I thought using a pen name was supposed to give a man a little piece and quiet! What do you want you batty arsehole?"

Brendan made a mental note to be courteous from this day forward to battered fishmongers, local drunks and little old ladies. He wondered if he had it in him to coerce the old guy into an interview. "Look, I apologize for what I said the other night. Can I just ask you a few questions?" Removing the book from his jacket pocket, he smiled goofily at the old man. "Please?"

"No, you may not!" he spat, slamming the door closed with a shudder.

Creeping through the weed-choked vegetable garden, Brendan removed the ancient scroll from his pocket. He rapped on one of the crooked windows, pressing the document up against the glass for the old man to see. "One question! It's important!"

The yellow-eyed cat on the windowsill leapt to the floor as the front door creaked open again. Tripping over tomatoes and pumpkin vines, Brendan made his way back to the entrance where Liam snatched for the document in his fingers.

"Where did you get that?" Liam questioned suspiciously, trying to steal another glance at the paper Brendan held just out of reach.

"I'll tell you where I got it if you just answer a few questions," he bargained.

Without agreeing to anything, Liam stepped aside, motioning for him to cross the humble threshold.

ငှာ&ၣ

Fiona Cross sat on an antique sofa in her room at the Mermaid Inn, making notes for her television special on the laptop computer. Details of the previous night were foggy and she couldn't quite recall what she'd said or done after arriving at Brendan's houseboat. Obviously she hadn't succeeded in getting him to go along with her matchmaking scheme, which infuriated her even more than the fact that he hadn't slept with her.

Now what?

Closing her eyes, she thought about of the encounter she'd witnessed with the beautiful, ethereal creature and the frumpy woman on the beach. It was clear and vivid in her mind – it was what had spawned the brilliant idea.

She'd go after him for herself.

Fiona blew a ring of smoke out her nostrils, toying with the notion. Pursuing the very man who had caused such a stir at the parade would be the perfect solution to her soul mate problem. After all, this whole crock of shit about mermaids and fairies was the heart and soul of rural British life. The viewers would lap it up like a bowl of cream. Of course she'd have to participate in some of the other festivities, but those were minor details. She smiled wickedly, entertaining the idea that she might even get laid in the process.

Fiona rapped on the door adjoining her luxury suite to the cameraman's budget-rate room. The young man attentively poked his head through the door.

"Get the lighting set up in here. We're going to start the piece over there in front of the vanity while I'm putting on my makeup and I'll explain my quest of searching for a soul mate. Then we'll take it out in the field," she told him, adding with a grin, "and wear something warm. We're going to the beach."

ℛ

The air in the cottage was acrid with the piquant stench of cat. Brendan sat uncomfortably on Liam's threadbare couch before a massive stone hearth and was pretty sure he'd just pressed his hand into a wet spot on the upholstery. Shifting forward, he perched on the edge of the reeking sofa and shivered from the cold. A pile of smoldering embers in the wide hearth with coffee and stew pots hanging within, radiated insignificantly through the drafty room. Tufts of peat moss were stuffed into the cracked plaster walls and rafters as insulation, doing little to retain anything but the god-awful stink of that cat.

Liam entered and removed the iron coffeepot from inside the fireplace, pouring some of the lukewarm liquid into a tin cup with chipped enamel. Brendan noticed that he'd reloaded his pipe since returning from the other room, a sign he took to mean that the old man was willing to talk.

"Nice place you've got here," he started in an attempt to break the ice.

"Bollocks," Liam grumbled lighting a match to his tobacco. "You Americans call everything old and worn out, 'antique' and 'quaint.' Reminds me of that pop star, whatshisname, bought a castle on the other side of the island, froze his bony arse off first winter and high-tailed it back to London." He took a long puff, smoke swirling around his head, "see, the problem with most people is they never stay anyplace long enough to understand it. Things get tough or the weather takes a turn for the worse and they leave." He leaned forward narrowing his pale watery eyes, "tell me, are you willing to look - or are you just skimming the surface?"

"I don't plan on going anywhere until I get some answers," he nodded defiantly.

The old man puffed on his pipe and stared as if sizing him up in some way. As Brendan tried to make out where the guy was coming from, the mangy black cat strolled across the room and relieved itself on the knotty woolen rug.

"Ooh! Uh, I think your cat is..."

Trying to be helpful, he automatically reached out to grab the animal and toss it outside, but Liam caught the tail of Brendan's coat, stopping him short with a crazed gleam in his eye. "No, lad! Let him do his business!"

Raising his hands defensively, Brendan stared in disgust as the cat sniffed at the dark blot on the carpet, then slunk off into the kitchen.

"The fumes keep me head clear," Liam cackled, drawing in a deep, exaggerated breath through flared nostrils.

"Really, I don't mind, uh, putting him out for you," Brendan offered, realizing that the elderly fellow was just making excuses for his squalid living conditions.

"You don't know what you've stumbled upon, do you?" Liam winked. "You 'aven't got a bloody clue."

Brendan glanced around the disorderly room and forced a tight smile, supposing he'd somehow won him over - or the old man was completely insane. "I guess not. Care to fill me in?"

ை

The cameraman's back sagged under the weight of the equipment like a broken pack mule as Fiona led him down the slippery trail of granite stepping stones behind the cave she'd spotted the night before. "Hurry up!" she hissed, "we're losing the light."

The late afternoon sun threatened to sink below the horizon within half an hour and they didn't have much time. The pair slid down the remainder of the treacherous terrain, stopping at a rocky perch twenty feet above the mouth of the caves. Fiona pointed downward and instructed him to set up shop. "Now I'll be waiting down there," she whispered. "And if things get H-O-T, turn the camera off. Do you know what I mean by that?"

"Y-yes Fiona," he nodded dumbly.

Concealed within a large green brooch on her blouse was a miniature camera. The cameraman turned on the portable monitor screen for her to see.

Satisfied, she gave him a thumbs up and carefully picked her way down.

The wide, dark mouth of the cave seemed to be smiling at her as she stepped into the cool, dank shelter at the base of the cliff. *How many women had he brought here?* she wondered.

The interior of the hollow was a large, deep cavern and had definitely been occupied recently. An ancient ship anchor hung from the ceiling as a makeshift chandelier with a thick candle of beeswax jammed on either point. Fiona removed a small flashlight from her pocket and shone a shaft of light around the walls. The floor seemed to glow, and on closer inspection she discovered hundreds of gleaming pearls radiating a soft, gleaming luster amongst the carpet of rocks, rough gemstones and sand. Toward the back of the cave her torch illuminated a heap of brown sealskins that had been spread out across the floor. *What kind of a savage occupies this lair?* she mused, a small thrill traveling down her back. As she spun around in wonder flashing the light along the walls, childlike drawings in faded colors came to life, depicting buxom mermaids and wooden sailing ships. Swept away in the romantic, old-world charm, Fiona guessed that this den might have been a pirate's nest in days gone by. Closing her eyes and breathing in the musty ocean air, she could practically hear the accordion grinding out a lively little tune in the background.

Wait a second, there was an accordion grinding!

Fiona snapped off her flashlight and ducked behind a smooth round boulder near the edge of the opening, heart beating furiously in her chest. The music had stopped abruptly and she peered outside the cave, eyes darting along the sand in anticipation.

A voice from behind nearly frightened her out of her skin. "Looking for someone?"

Spinning around toward the back wall of the cavern, she attempted to focus her eyes in the darkness.

Charlie stepped forward, his young firm body fully visible now. A curl of raven hair swept across one glittering eye and a red silk tapestry was draped around his pale shoulders. He held an accordion in his arms and was stark naked. Her unbelieving eyes traveled down the length of his body, stopping dead on his feet. A small squeal emitted from her throat as she stared at the wide, flipper-like webbing that connected his toes to one another.

"I remember you," he whispered seductively.

Fiona was enthralled by his melodic voice. *To hell with his feet - to hell with the show*! she thought. The stranger's smoldering look promised ecstasy, she vividly imagining her limbs entangled with his. Tossing her hair, she growled playfully at the beautiful young man before her.

In response, Charlie squeezed the accordion and began singing a long forgotten sea shanty to her.

My father was the keeper of the Eddystone light
And he slept with a mermaid one fine night
Out of this union there came three
A porpoise and a porgy and the other was me
Yo ho ho, the wind blows free,
Oh for the life on the rolling sea!

One night as I was a-trimming the glim
Singing a verse from the evening hymn
I heard a voice cry out an "Ahoy!"
And there was my mother sitting on a buoy
Yo ho ho, the wind blows free,
Oh for the life of the rolling sea!

Oh what has become of my children three?
My mother then inquired of me
One's on exhibit as a talking fish
The other was served in a chafing dish
Yo ho ho, the wind blows free,
Oh for the life of the rolling sea!

The phosphorous flashed in her seaweed hair
I looked again, and my mother wasn't there
But her voice came angrily out of the night
"To hell with the keeper of the Eddystone Light!"
Yo ho ho, the wind blows free
Oh for the life of the rolling sea!

Although the song had been ridiculously silly, there was something terribly sexy about a naked man playing an accordion. Fiona rose and began unbuttoning her blouse, he licking his lips with a smile.

"Take me," she rasped huskily.

Charlie's eyes glittered with mischief as he took another step forward. "Tell me. Where would you like to go?"

Enthralled by the curves of his full mouth she growled, "anywhere you'll have me you naughty delicious creature."

In response, he set the accordion down on the sandy floor, letting the silk fabric fall from his shoulders atop the bed of sealskins. He sank to his knees, pulling her to the ground with him.

Laughing, tears of pure joy ran down her cheeks and she couldn't believe that she was about to get shagged by this mysterious creature.

As he licked the salt from her skin, his body shuddered with pleasure, each delicious kiss becoming increasingly more passionate. Fiona threw her head back, groaning with feverish anticipation as he caressed and tugged the clothing away. "Oh, yes, yes," she cried, "shiver me timbers baby!"

With her blouse in a clump on the floor, his tongue trailed over the curves of her breasts, sending her slender frame into an electrified delirium. Lips upon lips, her hips arched toward his, allowing the magical perfume exuding from his pores to overcome all senses until she was lost in the ambrosial and erotic scent of fresh earth mingled with budding blossoms and sea salt. Her open mouth tasted the intangible aroma, desperate hands explored the cool touch of lustrous, scaled skin that slicked against her trembling belly. Velvety words of the old language drifted into her ear as he playfully tugged on the diamond stud in her earlobe with nipping teeth, "Onid aalid ben..."

"Ooooh," she groaned between gasps, "I don't know what you just said, but say it to me again and again and again..."

"Let me show you," he whispered, sliding down the small zipper on her slacks.

"Mmmmm -yes..."

"Fiona? You all right in there? I – I lost the feed to the mini-cam. Are you down there?"

The voice of the cameraman echoed through the cavern, sending a pang of fury through Fiona's aching body.

Noooooo!

Charlie leapt to his feet, confronting the young man who poked the bulky lens of a Betacam through the entrance.

"Oh, sorry," Bill said, stumbling into the dimly lit cave. "I was just looking for Fiona Cross. You seen her?"

"What is this!" he demanded.

Fiona hastily threw on her shirt and glared at the cameraman. "What in the bloody hell are you doing down here!" she hissed through clenched teeth.

He blushed, turning away, only then realizing what he'd interrupted.

With fury in his dark eyes, Charlie snatched the brooch from Fiona's blouse taking a button along with it. "Where is the videotape," he glowered, stepping toward her menacingly.

"Give him the tape," Fiona grumbled to the kid.

With shaking hands, he pulled a cassette out of the camera and handed it to him, catching a glimpse of his feet. He inhaled sharply as Charlie snatched the tape, then turned on Fiona with gritted teeth.

"Look," she smiled nervously backing out of the cave. "It's not what it seems. I mean, I came here to check things out for a story and then I was overcome by, by everything and I forgot why I'd come and…"

His eyes had turned dangerous and black. "You have poisoned purity and innocence!" he bellowed, his powerful voice piercing her eardrums.

"Purity? Innocence? Hah!" she spit, poking him in the chest. "Whom was just about to shag whom here! Huh?"

He stepped closer and snatched her hand before she could jab her finger into him again, his presence towering above her, his features contorted with rage. "Never return!"

He was serious Fiona gulped hard and scrambled out of the cavern without looking back.

Charlie's hands trembled with fury as he smashed the videotape against the wall, crushing the splintery shards of shattered plastic into the sand with his deformed, bare foot. Through tear brimmed eyes, he gazed around at the faded paintings on the walls from a childhood gone by. Although she had left with her cameras and her cynicism, this sacred place, he now knew, was no longer safe. *Reporters and television people invading the den, ruffians with harpoons chasing him through the streets in broad daylight, dull and common men writing about his beautiful rituals and the very nature of his being, things that they were never meant to scrutinize or understand…*

Before the hot tears spilled down his cheeks, he turned to face the glowing orange sunset, filling the mouth of the cave with a golden glimmer. He screamed out, a mad and tortured shriek, then raced recklessly through the sand and in a flash, he dove into the crashing waves, vanishing beneath the surface.

CHAPTER THIRTEEN

Undetected by the fisherman unloading nets and crates on the docks, Christine made her way toward the houseboat, cloaked in a navy blue pea coat with her flaming hair tucked up under a yellow rain hat. At Claire's boat slip, she removed the key from her pocket and swiftly disappeared inside.

Where to start?

Christine began by carefully unzipping the black duffel bag at the edge of the bed. Not sure what she was even looking for, she dumped out the contents on the floor and rooted through miniature toiletries and dirty laundry, then stuffed it all back inside in frustration. Crossing the cabin, she hovered over the sleek laptop on the kitchen table. Gingerly, she lifted the cover and uncertainly pecked at the keyboard.

Locked.

Concerned about the time, she shut it closed again and glanced around the space. A pile of face down pages on the printer caught her eye, which she snatched up and sifted through.

Misadventures and Merfolk?

Odd, she thought, determined to find out exactly what Brendan James was up to. *Was this perhaps part of a new book,* she wondered, thumbing through the thick stack, *or was he actually on assignment for the travel magazine as he'd claimed?*

She plucked out a page and began to read, her eyes growing wide as they darted across the black ink on crisp white paper.

"I ventured into the village where I had the great pleasure of being excruciatingly blue-balled by a topless mermaid after her underwater fantasy show, an ambi-

tious *production that would put the seediest of Vegas strip shows to shame…"*

She covered her gaping mouth, blood pulsing in her temples, *"seediest Vegas strip shows?"* she gawked. "You – *bastard!"* She slammed the paper down on the table, hastily skipping ahead through the rest of the pages with unsteady hands.

"As I stumbled upon the couple, entwined on the rough wooden docks, his firm, lean body lost between the pickled thighs of a giggling woman old enough to be his mother, I couldn't help but think that the poor old lass was going to be picking splinters out of her ass for a month."

Despite herself, she giggled, recognizing the 'youth' he described as her brother. "Oh, Charlie, you big idiot, you had that one coming," she nodded in agreement.

Wait a minute, she thought, shaking the manuscript in her hands. *Who in the hell is Brendan James to write about us anyway?* Admittedly, he'd been correct about Charlie - and the prose was hilarious, *but he's making a mockery out of our lives — and to think that just last night on the deck of this very boat I almost…!*

She slammed down another stack of pages and stamped her foot as she skimmed over his words, her fury increasing with every sentence on every page - until she came to the part that took her breath away.

'I watched her for what seemed like forever, her perfectly formed limbs glistening beneath the fairy Northern lights in the inky black water, a woman as deep and mysterious as the Irish Sea itself…'

"Oh my god," she whispered, reading on, absorbed in the words.

'Back to the sex, my ex-girlfriend arrived at the

doorstep of my houseboat, begging me to take her, where I don't know, and passed out cold after I declined her offer and professed my love for the young local who had charmed the pants off of me the moment I saw that pair of oyster shells dangling from her earlobes in the pub.'

Dropping the rest of the manuscript in a flutter of paper, Christine flopped onto the bed and reread the single page aloud three or four times through shallow breath.

"Love," she whispered, the word catching in her throat.

He - loves me...?

Oh no!

The realization that she'd broken into the houseboat dawned upon her suddenly as she lay on the bed like a dreamy teenage girl. Springing to her feet, she hastily gathered up the scattered pages from the floor and put them back in order. Satisfied, she replaced the stack of paper back on the printer, inclined to just take the whole pile with her, but grudgingly resisted the temptation and straightened things up instead. As she rearranged the computer and the dirty laundry exactly as it had been, the dreadful reality of the situation began to sink in. He was definitely writing about the village, she was sure of that now. As comical and accurate - and at times - beautiful as his writing was, something had to be done about it. It would be disastrous if the book were ever to be published. There was only one way to handle the situation, she decided. She had to persuade him to stop. *But how?* she wondered. *How do you stop a writer from writing what he feels and what he observes? How do you tell a mean-spirited American that his humorous words would bring sorrow and woe to good people? How do you make him understand the things that he could never comprehend?* That was the part she needed to figure out. And time was running out.

Christine raised the collar of the coat to disguise her face, slipped out the door and dashed back into town.

ço∿

"So, what's your opinion then?"

In Liam's living room, Brendan set another log on the fire, poking at the embers with a rod of twisted steel as he waited for a response.

"I thought you read my book," Liam mumbled irritably.

Brendan turned his back to the brick fireplace and faced the old man as the log flared up. "I sort of skimmed through it," he admitted sheepishly.

With a heavy sigh, Liam sifted through a pile of creased art prints on the beaten travel trunk he used for a coffee table. He came to an illustration of a pig-faced creature with a fish tail and a bejeweled red cap, pointing at it with a gnarled finger. "*This* is the Dinny-Mara. Come from Northern waters up around Scotland. A different clan of Merfolk. That's what you saw down there in the bay. The males are fierce creatures with piggish features and dark, soulless eyes, and the women? Och!"

The frightening face Brendan had seen in the murky water flashed through his mind. *Of course it hadn't been a real face,* he reminded himself.

Liam sifted through the pile and held up the famous oil painting by J. Waterhouse titled, A Mermaid, a breathtaking turn-of-the-century oil depicting a silver-tailed siren perched on the beach before

236

a treasure chest as she worked a comb of bone through auburn hair. It made Brendan's thoughts wander to Christine.

Liam pored over the details of the painting and went on with his explanation and theories about the 'Merpeople.'

He listened to the dissertation for several minutes, then eventually shook his head wearily, unable to take the mindless chatter any longer.

"...and the Manx Merfolk on the other hand were gentle, beautiful creatures," Liam babbled. "Your classic Merpeople. Long, salmon like tails, singing sirens. That's the clan I believe the girl and her brother descend from."

"Right," he nodded absently. It wasn't the nonsense about the 'Merpeople' that dumbfounded him, but the fact that Liam actually believed all the crap he'd written in his own book. It was beyond his understanding how a grown man could be living in such an absurd fantasy world. Then again, he speculated, Liam O'Leary was a simpleton, spending most of his lifetime in a remote village that was steeped in childish folklore and superstition. With little else to do but tool around on a boat in the wee hours of the night with a bottle of booze and a cat perched on his head, he could almost understand where the guy was coming from. Almost.

But seriously. Merfolk?

Brendan tried to break the news to him gently. "Come on. Her tail's a fake. I've seen the costumes in her dressing room and she does have legs. Very nice legs, I might add."

Liam winked as if to show the American he knew better. "Follow me."

Blinding. As the brilliant orange sun sank below the horizon, Charlie surfaced miles from shore in the vast expanse of golden water.

Eyes red from weeping, he tilted his beautiful, boyish face skyward, raising a tortured fist to the heavens. "What do you want from me!" he screamed, his body exhausted and shuddering from treading water against the large swells. He rose and fell with another. And no answers came in response, no answers ever would. He was left alone with the madness that threatened to swallow his very being. Breaking into wounded sobs, he drifted aimlessly in the glowing nothingness, the sun bathing his perfect form in sparkling pink brilliance. He was cursed, he knew, dammed to an eternity of an aimlessness, a place where there were no goals, no purposes and no ambitions. And his flesh, a mere slave to desire and insatiable greed that could be set off with the tiniest wish of another, or a wounded cry, and he was helpless to ignore those wishes and demands. Lest he deny them, the dark delirium would wait around the next turn to take him as it always did.

The material riches flowed in abundance in the form of treasures and trinkets he collected from the ocean floor, then peddled to men and museums when it suited his needs. Antiquities and coins of gold, priceless objects that men would and had killed for - all meaningless. It was those same men who would look upon his fortune, his flesh, his power and believe that he lived a blessed life, for he had everything that they desired - money, women and a face that could make God himself weep. In their dull and common eyes, he was the blessed one, the fools.

If only they knew. Another sob escaped from his lips as he drifted atop the swells, weeping for the one thing that would make his life bearable. If there was one want within him, it was Christine. If only she would come with him, he thought, his beloved sister. His only true companion. But headstrong and stubborn, she forever and maddeningly refused to accept the wealth he brought to her doorstep and the gifts he laid in her hands. She refused to uproot herself from the dull and small life she'd made among them, entertaining them, peddling souvenirs to them, *pretending to be one of them.*

She had to be persuaded away, somehow…

"Where are you taking me?"

Liam ignored Brendan's question as a chilly current swept across the grassy meadow on the property. A white rabbit scampered away from the cabbage patch in the small vegetable garden behind the cottage as the old man moved at a snail's pace in the fading light, picking his way along an overgrown path with a cane. Brendan reluctantly followed him up the incline, then stopped suddenly at the top to behold the panoramic scene before his eyes. Beyond the rocky coastline and turquoise sea, the colors of the sky faded into a deep indigo where the heavens met the edge of the ocean. Liam stumbled over a rock and cursed, nearly losing his balance.

Attention snapping back to his host, Brendan realized the man's eyesight was failing him.

Great.

Shivering, he breathed on cupped hands to keep his fingers warm. Liam stood before an eroded granite statue, perched on the edge of the cliff. The effigy, a crumbling mermaid, cradled two human-like children to her breast, the little ones sprouting fins from tiny forearms and ankles.

Liam tapped it with the cane. "You see that, lad?"

Brendan checked the time on his watch. "Yeah, That's really cool. Look. I think I've taken up enough of your afternoon already. But thanks for the coffee."

Liam squinted at the statue. "She's a half-breed. Like this. Like the drawings you found at the church."

Not wanting to hurt his feelings, he nodded vaguely, deciding to feign interest for a few more minutes. "Like in the old stories when mermaids would marry mortals and have children," he rushed.

"It has been said to happen. I've been watching her for some time now. Got the Merfolk instinct without the equipment. A shame really," he reflected, shaking his head. "Reminds me of those wolf-hybrid dogs. Half wolf, half dog. Can't live in the wild, can't live with humans…"

"Can't live with them, can't live without them," Brendan finished, his patience waning, "that's mermaids for you."

Liam smacked Brendan's leg hard with the cane.

"Ouch!" he yelped, eyes boring into the old man. "What'd you do that for?"

"Have you been listening to a word I've said?"

"Sure I have."

Liam nodded toward the sea caves, indicating the bitten-out coastline below with a finger. "She's been diving in the cove at night. Right down there."

Brendan sighed, "I know, *I saw*. But since when

does skinny dipping classify one as a mythological creature?"

Liam steadied his walking stick on the ground, narrowing his eyes inquisitively. "Do you recall just how cold that water was out there? Just about the temperature of melting ice - and that's on the warm days. Nobody likes to swim out there – but there's some that have to."

As much as he wanted to shrug it all off, the facts were undeniably bizarre. That water down there in the bay had been, and still was - freezing. Not only had he witnessed Christine's little moonlight swim, but her brother Charlie as well, both of them carelessly basking among turbulent swells in the middle of the god dammed night. With a perplexed crease on his brow, he found himself unable to spit out the logical explanation - whatever it was. His gaze shifted from the churning sea to the twinkling eyes of the old man.

"Haven't got a cocky comeback for that one, have you lad?"

"All right. You've got a valid point."

"Damn right I do," Liam winked.

ॐ

"Ooooh! You should read this rubbish!" Christine snorted, her nose buried in Brendan's paperback book as Claire helped her shimmy into one of the silvery mermaid tails in the theater dressing room. "I can't believe I kissed him and then nearly..." she stopped mid-sentence and grew very quiet.

Claire stopped fussing over the costume and cocked an eyebrow, studying Christine's reflection in the vanity mirror. "Nearly what?" she inhaled, her eyes widening. "Are you telling me that you almost had - *carnal relations with him?*"

"No," she sighed impatiently, clarifying the blunder, "I said that I *kissed him.*" She straightened up in the chair and busied herself applying a coat of glitter gloss to her lips.

Interest perked, Claire leaned over her shoulder with a grin. "Really. How was it?"

Annoyed, she puckered her sparkling mouth and spun around. "What do you mean 'how was it?' We're talking about the enemy here! The man that's out to destroy the village! He betrayed me Claire."

"Right. So how was the kiss?" she persisted.

Recalling the touch of his lips, the rough stubble on his chin brushing against her cheek, sent a warm and uninvited thrill down her back. "It was unbelievably magical," she admitted reluctantly. "So staggering I nearly swooned." In her mind, she re-read the beautiful - and offensive words he'd written on the pages she'd stolen a preview of, her tone suddenly shifting. "There are you happy?" she blinked. "He's happy I'm sure. He only did it just so he could go off and write all about it in one of his stupid books!" She shook the paperback before Claire's nose, pages fluttering. "Brendan James is the most pompous, arrogant man I've ever had the rotten luck to..."

"Fall in love with," Claire finished.

Christine slammed the book on the counter with wild eyes. "Did you say love!? Are you out of your mind? I'm never going to fall for some – *man* and you're a fool if you think otherwise!" She turned to Claire now, directing a misguided attack on the lovelorn old woman who wore an absurd necklace of jangling glass hearts around her neck. She flicked her finger at a cobalt heart in the center. "You and your silly notions about love, love, love and the relentless matchmaking! There isn't anyone in this world for me – and there never will be! When are you going to understand that?"

Claire's voice was quiet, her body very still, "you're beginning to sound like your brother."

"And you," she spat bitterly, "are beginning to sound like my mother, which you are not!"

Claire's eyes instantly cast downward. She focused on the rubbery mermaid tail, yanking on the side zipper a little too roughly. "Well, there we are," she eeked, forcing a taut smile over trembling lips. "I must be on my way. Things are so very, very busy at the Inn." She turned to leave, to hide the wounded expression that filled her eyes. She snatched her black coat off the hook on the wall and reached for the doorknob, her heart necklace tinkling hollowly.

"Claire, wait," Christine began. "I didn't mean to hurt your feelings."

Claire stopped mid-step and whirled around on her wide chunky heels, cheeks flushed like cherries. "Feelings! You don't know the first thing about real feelings because you're terrified to let anyone into your little world!" With a quivering finger she added icily, "You're a coward Christine. *It runs in your family.*"

"That's not fair!" she fired back, eyes glittering. "You don't understand what it's like! How could you?" she asked, tossing a flaming lock of hair over her shoulder. "You're nothing but a – a lonely old spinster with nothing to lose!"

At that moment, Christine looked anything but

beautiful to Claire. Her own conceit, her deep streak of vainglory had contorted her flawless features into a repulsive mask of ugliness. "There is more to existence than beauty and youth. Do you see the lines on my face?Do you?" she pointed,trailing a finger along her sagging, powdered skin. "Deep as they may run, these creases and wrinkles and are evidence of a life that's been *lived*." She looked at Christine now, not with anger, but with pity. "Just look at yourself, thinking that you're the fortunate one because your tresses still glisten in the moonlight. You've learned nothing in your lifetime Christine. You're an even bigger fool than I."

"Claire," she whispered, the burning shameful tears building behind her eyes now.

The old woman stood over her, staring beyond the ethereal illusion in the vanity glass. "What I once had, a taste of true love, however brief it might have been, was somehow enough to last me until the end of my days. And you know something?" she asked as a tortured laugh escaped from her throat, "I wouldn't trade it for an eternity in your shoes, pardon me, *your clogs*."

"Stop it!" Christine cried, struggling to rise in the heavy costume she feared might suffocate her, "just stop it!"

"And the next time you talk of spinsters, perhaps you should have a long look in the mirror," Claire accused, her quavering voice stabbing like a sharp blade. She grasped the handle of a silver hand mirror, thrusting it into Christine's face. "What a pity. You've only your lovely reflection to keep you company now. *Oidhche mhath!*"

Claire stalked away, slamming the dressing room door shut.

Ears ringing from the vicious quarrel, Christine exploded and hurled the mirror at the wall, shattering it into a thousand sparkling shards. *Damn him!*, she thought angrily, slamming her fist down, the impact jostling over bottles and tubes of spark-ling makeup.

Why did he ever come to this place?

❧

"See how they're shining?" Liam asked, squinting up through the cloud cover at the aurora borealis, bursting with color as the velvet blue of night settled upon the horizon. The two men sat perched in the boggy meadow behind the cottage. "The lights are calling out to what's left of their kind," he continued, lifting his cane to a greenish swirl that twisted slowly like a ghostly flame. "They say those are the elders up there, the sea nymphs, forever swimming in the heavens until the time comes that they can return. Some believe they're up there waiting, waiting for the half-breeds to mate successfully, to produce a full-fledged child of the sea so that they may once again flourish." He glanced skyward anew, "like the chiming of an ancient clock, the spirits are telling them it's time to gather."

Brendan rolled his eyes in the dark. "And you're actually suggesting that I was nearly drowned the other night because I interrupted some sort of a mermaid mating ritual out there?"

He took a thoughtful puff on the pipe, exhaling a thin trail of bluish smoke. "It may be why the Dinny-Mara attacked, though I've never heard of the clans mixing like this. But there are many things we don't know. A hundred years ago, we had a large population of Merfolk," he stated. "Oh yes, there's been scores of documented sightings from very credible people all around the British Isles."

Right, Brendan thought, *back in the days when the world was flat with ghastly creatures lurking in the depths that swallowed entire boats for kicks.*

"Perhaps he's the last of his kind and has come down from Scottish waters to claim the girl. That's my theory," Liam contended.

"Or perhaps he was the lousiest bagpipe player in the clan and the rest of the Dinny-Maras ousted him, or MAYBE he's just some loser in a mask trying to get a little free publicity at the expense of my neck! Did that *theory* ever cross your mind?" Brendan rose to his feet, realizing that this conversation, while greatly amusing, was going nowhere. "I really should be getting on my way now."

As Brendan walked away, Liam called out after him, "Tell me! Have you seen her feet?"

He sighed, attempting to make his way back to the dim light of the cottage without tripping over a stone or a pumpkin or a goat. "Yes, I've seen her feet!" he shouted back irritably.

"No, you haven't because she's always hiding them in clogs!"

"Yeah," he mumbled to himself, continuing to walk. "Clogs and clamshell earrings."

Wheezing, the old man caught up with Brendan, leaping out in front of him, the look in his eyes frantic. "You feel dizzy, almost intoxicated whenever you're close to her, don't you?"

Brendan backed up a step. Liam's gaze was desperate. "Who wouldn't? She's a knock-out."

"*Enneghtyn haitnys,*" he whispered hoarsely. "That's what they call it. Sense of pleasure, a sense beyond mere smell and touch, the pheromones their kind put out when they become aroused, one of the charms of seduction. Makes them utterly irresistible to us."

Brendan thought about it, the vertigo, the strange perfume.

Yeah, sure.

The old man was a raving lunatic.

"Why do you think I let the cat piddle all over me house!" he suddenly croaked, his bushy eyebrows rising up and down as if he'd just posed a perfectly rational point. "Hmmm?"

Brendan stepped away slowly. Liam had gone from being a little on the eccentric side to downright scary. "Look, I'm leaving now," he said calmly.

Liam tittered gleefully, "didn't know that cat urine counteracts the effects of the *enneghtyn haitnys*, did you! Ha! They're never gonna get me!"

"Just take it easy," Brendan warned, considering making a run for it. He glanced at the path just a few yards away, then stopped. *What am I thinking? This guy's not a threat, he's a ridiculous old fool in need of a serious reality adjustment*, he glowered.

"They have the curse, she and her brother!" Liam hissed. "Both of them have the webbed feet of the Merpeople. I've seen them me-self."

"And I thought the church took care of all that," Brendan taunted.

Liam circled him now, talking faster, "the church only knows of the ones that young, frightened mothers brought in after they'd had an illicit affair with one of the creatures. But that wouldn't be the case if their mother was one of them and unregistered herself. Would it?"

Brendan twisted his body, following Liam's dizzy pacing. "Right, I know, and the ones that are still trolling around the coves lose their flippers when they fall in love with a human! I seem to recall hearing a similar story from a *six-year-old girl*."

"You know nothing Mr. James!" he wheezed, the blue veins in his puffed cheeks surfacing.

Brendan waved his hands in frustration and continued hiking through the meadow, feeling as though he was about to wake up from a nightmare.

"I know who you really are and I know about the books you write!" Liam bellowed in a sing-song voice, stamping a foot down on one of his tomato plants. "Picked one up me-self from the rotten potato table for fifty-pence just last week!"

That's it!

Brendan whirled around within a fraction of exploding. Stalking back across the boggy ground and stopping, he now towered above the narrow-eyed little man with cherry tomato seeds splattered all over his slacks. "Congratulations Sherlock. So why are you telling me these ridiculous things that you know I'll go and write about?"

The moment the words spilled from his mouth, the answer hit him like a boomerang; he was writing the very book that Liam had only dreamed about authoring. In Liam's mind, he was scooping the big story out from under him, the old man's follow up to the silly little mermaid paperback published by some back-assward vanity press. "The story," he groaned. "Now I get it. You feel like it belongs to you. Am I right?"

Liam said nothing. Trying to explain it to him the way things worked in the real world, Brendan began, "you – how do I say this? You can't copy-right a story that hasn't been written. Do you understand what I mean by that?"

Liam held his position with both feet planted solidly on the crushed plants. "I'm telling you these things because you're in too deep to walk away," he snarled, an assuming smirk crossing his lips. "And you're not going to write that book."

This was news to Brendan. "Really? Is that so?" he challenged, annoyed by Liam's arrogance. "For your information *Mr. O'Leary*, well over half of my manuscript has already been delivered to the publisher and precisely one-hundred-thousand book covers are spitting off the presses somewhere in a New Jersey printing plant *as we speak*. Now, how is it that I'm not going to write this book?"

"You're too close to the truth now," he uttered quietly, a trace of apathy rising in his ashen eyes.

"Look," Brendan sighed, raking his hands through wind tangled hair. "No promises, but I'll see if I can't work in a mention of your mermaid book somewhere in the manuscript, maybe something in the bibliography. You've really gone all out for me, given me some great inside information. I won't forget that." He shifted uncomfortably, feeling sorry for Liam as he stared blankly out at the sea with a watery gaze.

The old man fumbled through the pockets of his wind breaker and removed a half-empty bear-shaped bottle of honey. With a knowing wink, he thrust it into Brendan's palm. "Here lad, take this weapon."

Brendan held the strange offering up to the light emanating through the window as a smile cracked across his face. "Now, *that's funny*," he chuckled, delivering a light, friendly punch to Liam's shoulder. "Tell me, have you ever thought about writing comedy?"

"Jesus man!" he exploded, the intensity and volume of his voice frightening Brendan backward the tangled pumpkin vines. "You've got his magic cap Don't think he won't come after it!" He leaned in close, eyes glittering with lunacy, "if there's one thing the Dinny-Mara can't resist, its honey. Stops 'em dead in their tracks every time!"

Stifling another grin, he gripped the honey bottle in his fist and carefully stepped over a monstrous pumpkin. "Right. Thanks again Liam. I'll use it - appropriately."

With that, he sprinted through the garden without looking back.

CHAPTER FOURTEEN

Claire trudged along the white shell sand in her bare feet, taking the long route back to the Inn from the theater. She just had to pull herself together before returning to work, before facing the customers. Cheeks moist with bitter tears and her leather loafers tucked beneath her arm, the nasty argument reran through her head as she walked. How could she make Christine understand that she was about to throw away her one chance to be with the very man who was made for her?

From her purse, she fished out a cotton handkerchief and dabbed at her stinging eyes, watching great waves rise and crash down, leaving a long line of thick sea froth. In a last ditch effort, she tossed the tear-stained cloth to the surf, then crossed the buttercup-dotted meadow up to the main road.

The early dinner crowd had cleared out of the Siren's Whale, gobbling down a collective fifty-three pork pies at two pounds, fifty pence apiece, Michael noted cheerfully. He'd already cleared the tables and set his mind to make good use of the down time before closing up early for the night. Standing high on a tall yellow ladder, he made a few final adjustments to the puny mermaid float, now hanging from the rafters of the pub by a set of thick ropes. Stepping down to admire his creation with a proud grin, he folded up the ladder and carried it out a back door.

Julian entered the pub and nodded approvingly

at the new addition to the décor, taking his usual seat on a barstool before the counter. Michael appeared a moment later. Wiping his hands on a bar towel, he indicated the mermaid on the ceiling with the flick of his chin. "What do you think?"

"She's a real beauty," Julian agreed as Michael automatically poured a pint of Poopdeck Pilsner, Wesley's favorite.

At the far end of the bar, a cluster of flickering container candles of green glass and fishnet surrounded a framed publicity shot of Fiona Cross alongside an empty pint glass with blood-red lipstick staining the rim. Julian squinted curiously at the display, unable to make out the photo without his glasses on. "What's all this shite? Somebody kick the bucket?"

"What, that?" Michael waved. "That's my tribute to Fiona Cross. See there?" he pointed enthusiastically, "the very glass she drank out of, mate. She sat there just the other night you know."

Sniggering, Julian took a gulp, "She sat on more than your bar stool the other night, lad."

Michael's expression fell.

"Sure. The woman was out of her head with that Brendan James fellow," he continued. "Out of her clothes too, I might add. Found her blouse and coat on the docks the morning after. Must've been some wild shag."

"Och!" Michael waved in disgust, frowning at Fiona's smiling photo. "Say it isn't true."

"It isn't true," Julian grinned patting the big man's shoulder. "Ah, forget about it. You're not cut out for a woman like that."

"I'm not?"

"Two wise words for you," he whispered with

a raised brow, "high maintenance."

Mindlessly polishing the beer taps, Michael scowled, unable to comprehend what a gorgeous, talented woman like Fiona saw in that American anyway. Then his thoughts turned to Christine, who also appeared to be showing some interest in him. "Just my luck," he grumbled miserably, secretly wishing that she'd finish him off like the others in the cemetery.

Reaching into his pocket, Julian slid a copy of the island's daily newspaper across the counter. "This ought to lift your spirits. Picked it up in Douglas just this afternoon. For your collection," he offered, glancing at the tabloid articles on the wall.

Michael scanned over the headline; HEATHER BAY HONEY BANDIT TERRORIZES HOLIDAYMAKERS.

"Jesus! They're writing about us all the way in Douglas!" he gawked. Flipping open the paper, he grinned at the police sketch of the pig-faced creature, then tacked it up on the wall alongside his mummified merman. "This ought to bring in a bit of business," he speculated hopefully. "Hah! A real Dinny-Mara running roughshod over the local honey stalls!"

"More likely that no good hooligan Charlie the Tuna," Julian stewed, finishing his pint. He placed a few crumpled pound notes on the bar, "So, we still on for later?"

"You bet your arse we are," he growled.

"Right, then. I'll meet you at the docks around seven o'clock," Julian confirmed, placing a small, black box on the counter. "Here. I brought you something else for the occasion. Sarah found it in the beauty parlor today, thought it might, you know, increase the odds?" he suggested.

"No shite? You got me a present?"

As Michael watched, Julian carefully opened the package before him, extracting a small bottle of blue cologne. Holding the box up close to his nose, he read the print on the side aloud. "Let the invisible and silent sexual powers of nature work for you with the potent lure of Wolf Musk."

"Wolf Musk!" Michael panted enthusiastically, grasping for the potion with his big clumsy fingers. "I like the sound of that!"

"No!" Julian warned abruptly, clapping a swift hand over the bottle. "This is mighty powerful stuff we're talking about here! A genuine American Indian *sex serum*. You can't just go spraying it all over the place like a bottle of bloody disinfectant!"

"Why not?" Michael asked curiously, leaning across the counter for a better look at the potion.

"Listen to this," Julian winked knowingly, continuing with the text, "scientifically extracted from the glands of wild wolves in the deserts of New Mexico, Wolf Musk has no detectable fragrance, but exudes loads of sexual undertones, which both *men and women* respond to." He gently replaced the bottle in the box, handing it over to Michael. "Can't have you humping me leg or vice versa," he snorted. *"Wait until I leave."*

"Ah," Michael smiled, bobbing his head up and down. "Gotcha."

Drumming his fingers in anticipation with eyes fixed on the package, Michael waited anxiously for Julian to exit the pub – and the moment the door closed, he ripped into the box, flinging shreds of crumpled cardboard on the floor. Giving the bottle a vigorous shake, he proceeded to douse himself in a great cloud of Wolf Musk.

The Inn was dead quiet Claire observed, sitting in the parlor by the front window, listening to the grandfather clock as the minutes ticked away. Nearly all of the guests were out searching for soul mates and she didn't anticipate seeing them again until the wee hours of the night – if at all.

Although she'd been expecting him, her heart jumped with apprehension as a man in a long dark coat stormed up the path, his pale skin illuminated beneath the flickering gas lamps on the porch.

It was Charlie and his mood was black.

Claire stiffened as he whirled into the sitting room, not bothering to shut the front door behind himself. "We have to talk," she began nervously, beckoning him to join her on the parlor sofa. His eyes were the color of steel, the cold eyes of a predator, she thought as a little lump formed in her throat.

Saying nothing, he stood before her now, his flesh prickling and vulnerable, his gaze vicious. He removed the handkerchief from his pocket, still dripping with sea water and dropped it on the floor at her feet.

"I have my reasons," she shuddered, observing a trickle of sweat running down the side of his chiseled profile as he inwardly struggled to fight off the instincts that were threatening to tear his soul in half. Seeing him like this frightened her, so reckless, so tortured. "It was the only way," she uttered, casting her eyes to the floor.

"I thought we agreed," he whispered, hands beginning to tremble.

"You can't stop her, Charles!" she shouted, startled by the volume of her own voice. "There's nothing you can do now. She's fallen in love with him. Please, let her go. Let her love. Let her live. It's too late to stop it."

His eyes shifted away, concealing a dark and murderous glare. "It's never too late," he winced painfully, turning to face the door.

"No!" she cried, rising to stop him.

As he spun to defy her, she saw what lay beneath his angelic features, finding herself frozen with fear.

"I think you've done quite enough Claire." Tearing himself from her strained clutch, he slipped through the door and bolted into the night.

కాలు

Darkness had fallen upon Heather Bay and the entire village was buzzing with excitement as the much-anticipated Midsummer Eve festivities were finally getting underway, an annual tradition that had been repeated on this night for as long as anyone could remember.

Hundreds of single women pushed and shoved for a prime spot on the crowded docks near the houseboats, most of them carrying small gifts wrapped in pretty paper and fancy curling ribbons. The woman from the tourism office stood at the edge of the dock, addressing the unruly the crowd with a bullhorn. "All right ladies! This is it! The night we've all been waiting for!"

Excited chatter and enthusiastic applause rippled through the crowd of hopeful wallflowers.

Glancing around in puzzlement, Brendan pushed his way through the flock, straining to make out the shadowy figures that were clustered around his houseboat.

Julian and a couple of fisherman from the pub were huddled in murmured conversation on the bow. They nodded in agreement, then proceeded to push Michael's enormous body up the tall mast ladder with lots of heaving and brute strength. Spotting Brendan, Michael shouted down gleefully, "ahoy matie!"

One of the fishermen hopped on the dock and cocked his head sideways at Michael. "A little more to the right lads!" he hollered. Michael swayed to the right, nearly losing his balance. As his big body flailed on the ladder, the entire boat groaned and rocked to one side. The men scrambled onto the opposite side of the deck to balance out the weight.

"Hey!" Brendan hollered up at them. "What do you think you're doing to my boat?!"

Julian hopped onto the dock, rubbing his bony hands together while squinting up at the mast. "Michael's volunteered to be our honorary village virgin for the festivities tonight," he announced, turning to Brendan with a grin. "Hell, he might even be bona fide."

"He's definitely bona fide," Brendan scowled, peering across the deck at the grisly characters standing on his boat. "Forgive me for my ignorance of local customs," he spat, "but isn't there supposed to be a beast that goes along with these village virgin sacrifices?"

With a fearful glance, Julian indicated the unruly throng of women at the end of the dock. "It's out there, lad," he shuddered, "a ten-ton, estrogen fueled, biological ticking time bomb that's just had its fuse lit."

"You know, if you guys damage this boat...," he warned.

"Not to worry," Julian assured him with a hearty pat on the back. "It'll all be over in a blink." He pointed up at Michael, now dangling from the top rung, and explained, "see, it's all about raising his profile between the ladies and the moon. And there's a lifetime supply of pints to the man – or men – who can get the poor sod back in the hay."

"You guys are frigging nuts," Brendan waved in disgust.

"Here, take one of these and relax," Julian offered, handing him a bottle of ale from a paper bag. "And stay out of the moonlight tonight. Mark my words."

Brendan cracked the top off and took a swig. "Thanks, but I think I can handle a third-rate panty raid."

"You just try and square off against a pack of single women over thirty-five at a soul mate festival!" he guffawed. "Not as easy as it sounds. Had me clothes torn off by a mob of them three years ago. I was lucky to get away alive! Just keep a low profile tonight, my friend."

"Thanks for the advice," he groaned, realizing that his chances of getting any work done on the manuscript tonight were looking dismal.

∞∞

Fiona and her cameraman were set up at the front of the mob. Stepping before the camera, she addressed her viewers with a smile, "I'm standing here about to participate in Heather Bay's Mermaid Midsummer Eve soul mate search. As you saw in the earlier clip, my trip to the beach proved to be a fruitless one. But I am still hopeful, as ever, that fate will lead me to find my soul mate."

Fiona motioned to the cameraman to get a shot of the wild crowd of women.

The woman's voice crackled through the bullhorn, "Ladies! These are the rules of the game. You throw your offerings to the mermaids into the water. If your gift sinks, you're in the game, but if it floats back up to the surface, you're out. For those that are in, you'll be looking for a silhouette or a shadow against the full moon tonight. According to the legend, that shadow will belong to your soul mate. Are you ready!"

Explosive cheers came from the crowd as they hurled hundreds of presents into the water as if it were the city dump.

Fiona tossed a large gift box full of rocks over the edge of the railing and whooped victoriously as it sank into the bay. She smiled into the camera, "Wish me luck!'

Atop the deck of the houseboat, Brendan and Julian sat on the pair of sagging lawn chairs. Peering out at the crowd, Brendan spotted Fiona who just happened to be smirking at him. His first instinct was to crawl into the boat and hide, but she'd already seen him and slyly gave him the finger. Turning away from her gesture, he violently ripped open a bag of pretzels and nodded toward the women. "And what exactly are they throwing into the water out there?"

"Gifts for the mermaids," Julian explained. "Combs, mirrors, bottles of lavender perfume, honey cakes, shite like that."

"Wait a second. I thought that baking honey cakes was an offense punishable by law," he snorted.

"It is," Julian nodded, "but being as the original recipe was burned by a mob of riotous fisherman over two-hundred years ago, those are just harmless imitations they've got in their hands. It's a test. See, they believe that if the gift sinks, then the mermaids have accepted it. Sort of like receiving a blessing I suppose."

Reaching into his pocket, Brendan removed the bottle of honey and hurled Liam's 'weapon' over the rail of the boat. "Right," he nodded with a laugh. "A license to screw. Wouldn't it just be easier to set up a registration office in town? You know, where people could just sign in once they step off the ferry?"

"It's nothing to joke about," Julian warned. "Those ladies out there mean business. And may God help you if they catch you tonight."

Ignoring the advice, Brendan watched the honey bottle sink below the surface, turning to Julian with a smirk. "Oh yeah, we're feeling good now. Look at that."

Julian polished off his beer and popped the bottle cap off a second one. "Ah, it may have sunk, but the question is, will the mermaids accept it?"

"Of course they will," he grinned, "it's a Merfolk delicacy."

❧

Like a phantom, Charlie moved around the back of the theater, the tails of his black leather trench coat sweeping along the ancient cobblestones. The back door of the building was open a crack and a NO ADMITTANCE sign posted. With ragged breath, he slipped inside and rushed up the stairs.

The crowd at the Underwater Fantasy Show had been a little thin, Christine observed, presumably because of the Midsummer Eve festivities. She'd peered through the glass of the tank a couple of times during the show, but hadn't recognized any faces in the audience. Despite herself, she wondered what Brendan was doing right now. Faint applause echoed through the theater as she treaded water for a moment at the surface, contemplating whether she should pop in on the beach party tonight or cuddle up on her sofa with a sensible cup of peppermint tea. Drifting to the side of the tank, she grasped onto the ladder bar.

Uncharacteristically, Charlie was waiting by the side of the tank with an agitated scowl on his face. He took her by the hand, tugging her over the edge.

"Thanks," she blinked uncertainly, reaching for a towel. "What are you doing here?"

Setting her costumed body on the floor, he knelt down, glaring into her eyes for a moment. "I know all about the American. Claire told me everything," he accused. "So you can stop the little game of charades right now!"

"Oh, she did, did she?" Christine defended, propping herself up on her elbows. "Well what exactly did she tell you?"

"I won't allow it Christine!" he growled. "She said that you've – fallen in love with him!"

"Believe me Charlie, I may have some emotions for Brendan James, but love is definitely not one of them!" She struggled to lift herself onto the luggage cart, "Now if you'll excuse me…"

"Great!" he laughed madly, clawing his

hands through tousled hair, rising to his feet. "Then you'll have no problem staying away from him tonight and forever more!"

She met his deranged glare with a sarcastic sniff, her large tail fin tapping impatiently. "What? Why you're free to prowl around in the night with perfect strangers! Why is it that you get to have all the fun?"

Enraged, he grabbed her by the wrist, angling his nose against hers. "Because I'm clever enough to know when to move on!" he growled with teeth flashing. "Have you even stopped to think about the consequences?!" he screamed, shaking her arm with a jerk, "have you!"

Charlie released her as she stared back at him silently, tears welling behind her stormy eyes. "I hate you," she whispered, wrenching her arm away from his cool and clammy grip. "You're acting like a wild animal Charlie. Go and finish her off, whoever she is," she uttered, staring at the dark circles beneath his eyes and the light sweat that had broken out upon his forehead, telltale signs that he was in pursuit and hadn't had his way yet. "Go on," she spat, "go and have your woman."

"I – cant!" he cried out in tortured frustration, looking helplessly into his sister's eyes.

Claire.

"Oh, no," she panicked, suddenly understanding his predicament, forgiving his rash behavior and violent outburst. "But how did it...?"

"I'm sorry," he sobbed, his voice cracking, "so sorry." Cradling her face with gentle hands, he kissed her forehead desperately. "We have each other. Now and always. Remember that."

"What are you going to do?" she whispered.

"I have to go now." He kissed her once again before rising. "Go straight upstairs. I'll be back soon. I promise." And he was gone.

Outside the theater, Charlie shuddered with fury. Slumped against the building, he ran his knuckles against the rough mortar between the bricks until the skin scraped off and the blood began to trickle down his fingers. Numb to the throbbing pain, he thought about what he had to do as his entire world was threatening to fall apart. Squeezing his bleeding knuckles with rage, his mind clouded over with thoughts. Violent and dangerous thoughts.

Eyes glittering black, he cloaked himself in the trench coat and swept off into the night to find the one that could destroy everything.

♋∝ℰ

Still dangling from the mast, Michael tittered with anticipation as the thick cloud cover began to part, revealing a tiny slice of the full gleaming moon. "Fire in the hole!" he cried out to Julian and the fisherman below.

Nearly spilling his beer, Julian glanced upward and saw the great white orb coming into view. "Shite on a stick! Here we go boys!" He sprang to his feet barking out orders, "Take cover! Batten down the hatches! Move, move, move!"

As Brendan glanced around with mild amusement, Julian and one of the burly fishermen snatched him up from his chair and dragged him down into the cabin.

A wide grin crossed Michael's face as he listened to the sweet cacophony of female squealing and footsteps that were thundering in his direction. He squeezed his eyes shut. "Thank you God!"

The wooden dock vibrated and bodies pummeled closer. The other fisherman, who went by the name of Salts, was still standing on the deck, contemplating Michael's position and was oblivious to the approaching danger with that 'lifetime supply of pints' clouding his common sense. It was only when the squealing had reached a deafening level that he spun and saw them, the mob of spinsters stampeding forward with outstretched arms.

Huh?

Too stunned to move, the women swarmed the deck of the houseboat like a hive of killer bees, grabbing at the bewildered fisherman. The man was knocked off balance and dragged from the boat as they stung him with sloppy kisses, fighting over him like a bridal bouquet. He put up a good fight with arms and legs flailing in all directions, but there were just too many of them. The swarm carried him off into the night.

After a moment, Michael opened one eye, then the other, spotting the mob all the way on the outskirts of the pier now.

Bollocks!

"No, no, no!" he shouted, stumbling and shimmying down the rope ladder while hollering after them, "you've taken the wrong man! Wait! Wait! Come back!"

Below deck, Brendan, Julian and the other fisherman were doubled over with laughter, rolling around on the floor of the cabin.

Julian's hat had fallen off and his face was nearly purple as he gasped for air. The men high-fived, missing each other's hands and Brendan managed to crawl across the floor to the open door. "You the man Michael! You the man!" he hollered into the night. Brendan fell back into Julian's arms and they began howling again as the American found himself unable to recall the last time he'd a laugh like this, a real, side splitting bout that made his face ache. "Christ! You weren't kidding!" he finally managed, recalling the hilarity of the moment, the intense vibration of the vessel as the footsteps of a hundred desperate woman lambasted the deck above, rivaling a 6.0 earthquake. Even if he was to write about this one, no one would ever believe it, he thought.

"Here's to a lifetime supply of pints!" Julian howled victoriously.

As Brendan caught his breath, Michael suddenly appeared in the doorway to everyone's surprise and dismay. With a miserable and dejected moan he informed them, "they took Salts! Carried him off into town."

"Oh Christ!" Julian panicked, reaching for his straw hat. "Think we should go after him?" he surveyed amongst the others. "Salts is an old man! Might give him a bloody heart attack!"

Everyone but Michael busted up at the suggestion, setting off another row of hysterics.

Unable to laugh along with the others, Michael's halfhearted goodbye to the howling trio in the cabin was unheard. "Well, thanks for trying and all," he managed to whisper, sprinting away before anyone noticed the soggy tears that were streaming down his chubby cheeks.

CHAPTER FIFTEEN

Blazing torches dotted Heather Bay Beach as a local rock band played on a makeshift stage of two flatbed trailers pushed back to back. Despite the biting cold, hundreds of women in sarongs and bathing suits danced on the sand, dotting the coastline with dimpled white flesh as far as the eye could see. Plastic tables and chairs had popped up on the sand and clusters of shivering beach-goers flitted around the blazing peat moss and driftwood bonfires.

Brendan followed Julian and Sarah as a Congo line of ugly hags snaked by, a couple of them shooting hopeful glances in his direction. Averting his eyes, he quickly ducked down behind Julian's lanky frame for the remainder of the walk across the carnival grounds, where any man stupid enough to be out here was fair game, he supposed.

They came to a booth on the sidelines selling festival T-shirts and coffee mugs with silly slogans like, 'I GOT A PIECE OF TAIL AT THE MERMAID FESTIVAL' and 'I WAS MER-MADE FOR LOVING YOU.'

Sarah stopped to sift through the merchandise as Julian tapped his foot impatiently, wondering how much cash she was going to whittle out of him this time. To Julian's dread, the vendor looked the couple over, winked and handed Sarah two matching baseball caps adorned with plastic grapes, oranges and apples with the slogan, FORBIDDEN FRUIT printed on the brim.

"Oh, aren't these just precious," she fawned, trying on one of the hats before a hand mirror. The expectant look she shot at Julian prompted him to grudgingly fork over the money. Sarah snatched the straw hat from his head and replaced it with the silly cap, his cheeks turning a deep shade of red as a cluster of grapes dangled above his rolling eyes.

"It suits you," Brendan grinned, as she led him off toward the tables. Brendan started to follow, then noticed a knot of women a few yards away, pointing and whispering in his direction. He turned, picked up a fruit salad hat and shoved it on his head, hissing to the man behind the table of merchandise, "I'll take one of these too, buddy. How much?"

With matching hats adorning their heads, the trio settled into an empty table with their paper plates of greasy sausage and warm beer in plastic cups. "So," Sarah asked Brendan, "tell us about the story you're writing. Is it something along the lines of, are mermaids real?"

"Oh come on," he sighed, on the verge of being insulted by her conclusion. "Do you really think I'm actually falling for this amateur trickery? Give me a little credit."

Sorry she'd bothered to ask, her eyes cast downward.

Lowering his voice to a whisper, he told her, "Look, I'm writing a story about the truth. That's all." He couldn't bear to divulge that the new book was already slated to be a national best seller about an entire village inhabited by raving lunatics, she being one of them.

"Fair enough," she responded quietly. "So, then, what's the truth?"

Before he could answer, a woman in a cheap mermaid costume walked past the table with a large basket cradled beneath her arm. "Get you're lucky seashells!" she brayed. "Hand picked by the mermaids! Only two pounds each! They make lovely souvenirs!"

"That's your truth right there," he pointed at the mermaid with a smirk. "How could anyone argue with that?"

"Argue with it or make fun of it?" Sarah snapped, the plastic orange on her head quivering slightly above her glaring eyes. "It's called a *holiday*. Perhaps you should take one."

"Luv, please," Julian warned through clenched teeth.

Brendan leaned across the table, looking into her muddy eyes that had iced over. "I'm just writing what I see," he told her honestly. "This place is a writers dream. When you've got this much bizarre material shoved in your face, you can simply observe it and write it straight. Besides, my curiosity's been aroused."

"Among other things," she sniffed.

"And what's that supposed to mean?" he asked, knowing damn well that she was referring to Christine.

She studied his face for a moment, noticed the way he was getting sort of edgy. "I think you're in deeper than you realize."

Julian rose, stretching his lanky arms to the sky, uncomfortable with the trouble brewing between his wife and the American. "Hup hup hup! Better get some more grub before it's all gone."

Off the side of the stage the sweaty, dancing women had congealed into a massive clump of waving bodies.

Fiona stood before the camera as the band played in the background. "I've followed my nose to the annual Heather Bay beach party where things here are still in full swing. All of these ladies out here, including myself are ready for anything tonight and on the lookout for Mr. Right."

The cameraman pointed at something off to the side of the stage. Fiona spun, spotting a silhouette of a man beneath the moon directly behind her. "Get a shot of that!" she hissed.

As he turned the camera on the silhouette, Fiona quickly touched up her lipstick and was about to make a dash across the sand with her microphone in hand. Instead, she glanced behind her shoulder as the uneasy whine of seventy-five screaming women filled the air. Before the sleek television hostess could dive out of the way, a stampede of soul mate hopefuls knocked her aside, a few clawing and trampling past her body in hot pursuit of the man before the moon. "Aaaaaaaah!' she screamed, becoming lost in a throng of perfume, hair spray and elbows.

CRUNCH!

"Ooooooow! Bollocks!" she screeched.

The cameraman had somehow managed to keep the tape rolling. As the dust settled, he panned the camera down to the spot where Fiona lay, clutching her bloody, sand-encrusted nose. "Turn that off!" she bellowed.

"Oh my, Fiona," he exclaimed flipping off the power switch and kneeling down to inspect her injuries. "Your nose," he pointed uncertainly, "I think it might be broken."

"Great!" she hollered, bursting into tears. "Fucking great! Somebody get me a plastic surgeon!"

From out of the crowd, the clergyman shuffled across the beach in his long black robes, readjusting the clothespin on his nose. "Did somebody call?"

ॐ৵৵

Michael crossed the meadow, heading toward High Street. His head was hung low and he sniffled silently to himself as he trudged back to the pub, branding himself the unluckiest bastard in the world.

Female laughter trilled in the distance, breaking his sluggish stride for a moment, then he realized it had only been coming from the party down at the beach. *No thanks*, he thought resentfully, as the idea crossed his mind to pop in on the festivities. He'd made a fool of himself for the last time.

Click, click, click, click

Michael stopped dead in his tracks, whipping his head around as the footsteps that seemed to be following him came to a halt. Then he heard breathing, hot and heavy- breathing? Wiping the tears from his eyes, he squinted down the dark cobblestone street with a slight grin. Perhaps the Wolf Musk was doing its work after all.

Sniff-sniff-sniff-sniff

Suddenly, a monstrous Irish Wolfhound bounded out from a darkened shop front, whimpering desperately and barreling toward him, its tongue flapping with wild panting and foamy strings of slobber glistening from its jowls.

"Aw - Jesus!" Michael hollered, sprinting down the street in a wild panic. The dog was swift and gaining on him with each leap and bound of its long hairy legs. Michael tore through the village, screaming bloody murder as the animal picked up speed, closing the gap between them. Muscles burning as he ran, he concluded that there was only one thing to do. He slid to a sudden and screeching halt, then dove up against the door of a shopfront. All two hundred pounds of the wolfhound sped past in a blur of fur and saliva, giving him a slim chance to escape. Turning quickly and bolting the other way, he ran and ran, not stopping until he got back to the pub where he barricaded himself behind locked doors.

From the bay window in her theater-top perch, Christine peered skyward at tumultuous white clouds, their edges laced in brilliant pink and aquamarine from the shimmering Northern Lights beyond. The mother of pearl comb was soothing as she ran it through her long tresses, her slender shoulders cloaked in a wool tartan blanket. Peering into the window glass, she stared into the troubled eyes of a twenty-year-old, the smooth lids flashing back at her.

The clouds parted further, exposing a great expanse of gemstone glitter that felt as if it were radiating throughout her soul. With eyes closed, she basked beneath the illustriousness of the phenomenon, absorbing the life pulse of the twisting, gleaming ancients until she was nearly overflowing with it. Laughter and the rhythm of surf on sand tinkled through her ears like a delicate wind chime of melodic voices, beckoning her to the sea. Desperately, she wanted to find Brendan, but Charlie had phoned and made her promise to stay inside with the doors locked until he returned.

Pearl's yellow eyes were filled with concern as she watched Christine through the bars of her cage. Ruffling her feathers, the bird sang out the first line of an old melody, "No one to talk to, all by myself..."

Her racing thoughts interrupted by the parrot, Christine trailed her fingers along the cage and smiled, continuing the line in her hauntingly beautiful voice, "no one to walk with but I'm happy on the shelf. Ain't misbehavin', I'm saving my love for you."

Pearl lovingly nuzzled her beak against Christine's fingers as she leaned against the windowsill, her glance focused uneasily on the Irish Sea. The water had always been her solace, but tonight it seemed as vast and uncertain as her future. As she took a deep breath, the salty ocean air filled her lungs, eyes scanning over the tiny line of flickering torches, as if searching for some kind of signal that would justify her urgent longing to go to him. Her thoughts swirled again and confusing ideas tumbled through her mind. It seemed as if fate had brought Brendan James to this place on the Midsummer Eve for reasons beyond her understanding – and she found herself craving answers, answers that she knew would never come unless she went out there and discovered them for herself.

Christine made her decision, shaking the blanket from her shoulders. She opened the door of the cage and the old parrot scuttled out, flapping around the living room. Christine disappeared into the bathroom, turned on the shower and returned a moment later. With a wink, she nodded to the bird, slipped into her clogs and headed for the front door. "Just say I'm in the shower if anyone asks," she whispered to the wide-eyed bird, as her fingers unlatched the dead bolt.

ۍৎঌ

Brendan and the Wesley's had just finished eating seconds of the greasy meat on buns they'd bought from an overpriced outdoor barbecue stand on the beach.

The tension between Sarah and Brendan seemed to have blown over and she was busy grilling him with questions about his personal life. "So then, you kissed her? Did you look into here eyes like I said?" she asked.

Brendan looked at her with surprise, then waved off the inquiry with a grunt.

"Oh no!" Julian howled. "He's been charmed by the bloody mermaid just like every other sucker in the village!"

He swallowed the last bite of his meal. "Give me a break. She's just a girl."

"Ooh. This could get nasty," Julian teased. "You know what happens next. Right?"

Sarah leaned across the table with a wicked grin, "she lures you out into the ocean with her siren song and mangles your body on the rocks. Then, if there's anything left of your carcass, she plucks the meat from your bones with her teeth and sells it to that discount chip shop on the edge of the village."

"That's right," Julian nodded, "never buy meat from a mermaid, I always say."

"Uh, yeah. Thanks for the warning."

Charlie's desperate steeplechase had led him to the festival gathering. After searching the docks, the houseboat and every crevice and crack in between, there was no place else that Brendan James could be. Although he'd hoped to corner him in a dark alleyway, the beach would have to do if this is what it came down to. Sensing that he was here, his cold, keen eyes scanned the crowd of unfamiliar faces and then he spotted him, yes, that was he for sure. With bloodied knuckles clenched, he stalked through the sand.

The onslaught of wild, female partygoers had been dancing with one another, for lack of males willing to expose themselves to attack. The band continued playing regurgitated and off-key dance tunes for the mob that was too intoxicated to care.

Occasionally, the clouds would part and a rush of women would run off screaming after some poor sod that happened to be silhouetted against the moon. Some of the men had been captured, while others had managed to outrun them, or were clever or strong enough to slip away.

After witnessing the frightening ritual first-hand, Brendan had resorted to slumping down in his chair, adjusting the collar of his leather jacket to meet the edges of the fruit-clustered cap on his head in case they got any ideas about mauling him. Just as he was wondering why he hadn't seen Christine around yet, an eerie voice snarled from behind.

"Brendan James."

Before he could turn around, Charlie grabbed the edge of the table and flipped it upside down in a wild rage. Sarah screamed and Brendan's chair toppled over backwards in a plume of sand. As Brendan scrambled on the ground, trying to get his bearings back, he saw Charlie, looking like an evil spirit with his black coat flapping in the wind and his ghostly pale features twisted into a murderous sneer.

The crowd formed a loose circle around the sudden burst of violence. In the spirit of things, the band's drummer suddenly shifted tempo, leading the other musicians into a spirited version of <u>Blitzkrieg Bop</u> by the Ramones.

"What the hell!" Brendan hollered, his system flooding with adrenaline as he bent his knees under his body, ready to spring forward. In a flash, Charlie straddled him before he could leap, yanking his face close to his by the collar of his jacket. Adding insult to injury, he plucked a grape from Brendan's hat with his teeth, spitting it out on the sand. "Oooh!" Brendan growled with fury, "you shouldn't have done that, buddy!"

In response, Charlie slugged him in the ribs, the blow propelling Brendan backwards.

Julian pulled Sarah away from the scuffle as the unruly mob began shouting, "Fight! Fight! Fight!"

"What in the hell's the matter with you!" Brendan yelled, catching his balance with arms poised and fists raised in a classic boxing stance.

"You stay away from her!" Charlie threatened, madness burning in his eyes. "You hear me! Just stay away from Christine!" With gritted teeth, he lunged forward tackling the American down into the sand.

"Get off of me you psycho!" Brendan spat, twisting his body beneath Charlie's stronghold. Somehow he managed to dig his foot into the slippery ground just deep enough that he was able to roll over on top of Charlie. But the lean young man flipped him on his back, diving onto him again.

The two of them rolled down the beach, tumbling to the water's edge where Charlie grabbed his victim by the throat growling, "write about this in one of your horrible books you bloody freak! And stay away from my sister!"

The crowd let out a collective, "Ooooh!" upon the revelation. Brendan struggled free, landing a crushing right hook on Charlie's jaw, the blow sending him stumbling into the surf where he landed in a heap. With a wince, Brendan sprang to his feet and stood over Charlie, still reeling from the impact of the hit. "What are you! The village idiot! I hardly even know her!"

On the sidelines, Sarah shot Julian a challenging and impressive look. "Wow! Did you see that?" she gushed.

Julian cleared his throat, stepping in front of Charlie, whose stunned glare was still locked on the American.

Snorting at the absurdity of the small town mindset,. Brendan picked up his baseball cap, shaking the sand from his hair. Blood still pulsing and unconcerned about the possible consequences, he spun around and shouted, "Yeah! I'll write about it all right – asshole! In fact, I'll send you an autographed copy! How about 'kiss my hairy ass you Adam Ant wannabe!' How does that sound to you? Huh?"

Enraged by the insult and the titter of laughter it induced among the bloodthirsty bystanders, Charlie scrambled to his knees to go at him again, but found a pair of skinny, bird-like legs blocking his way. Julian stood firm now, eyes locked with the young man who'd seduced his wife. "Well if it ain't Charlie the Tuna! I've been waiting an awfully long time to get my hands on your gills!"

Charlie rubbed his jaw, squinting at the lanky, middle-aged man that was the only thing standing between himself and his target. "Yeah? And who the hell are you?" he spat, ignoring the threat.

In reply, Julian kicked a sheet of sand into his face, "I'm the man who's here to tell you that you don't mess around with my woman!"

Charlie angrily swatted the sand from his eyes and stood up with Brendan's back fixed in his loathsome gaze, "so what are you gonna do about it old man? Kick my ass with your walker?" he sneered.

A knot of angry fishermen and middle-aged men emerged from the crowd and stood behind Julian. Waving golf clubs, harpoons and canes, the snarling mob stepped forward. Charlie's eyes darted between the men and Brendan who was walking away now, the victor of the fight. "They say you shouldn't hit a man when he's down," Julian philosophized to the others. "But I say we should make an exception to that rule for this one! Eh boys?" The angry men nodded in agreement and began to close in.

Stricken with panic, Charlie attempted to talk his way out of the precarious situation while backing into the surf. "I can't help myself!" he cried with sweeping arms. "The women! They make me do it! You should see your wives when they..!" He stopped mid-sentence, clarifying his position as the livid faces inched closer. "But – but that was then! I've only done tourists and spinsters for the last three seasons!" His eyes shifted madly from one man to the next, "For Christ's sake, lads! I'm a bloody creature of seduction!"

"Then we're going to help you change your

wicked ways right now!" Julian growled, delivering a swift kick to Charlie's crotch.

In the distance, Brendan cringed and turned away as the youth crumpled over in pain, unable to watch the pitiful downfall of the legendary, Charlie the Tuna.

The men surrounded him, raising their weapons. "Let's get 'em boys!" Julian howled.

In a last ditch effort, Charlie attempted to dive into the waves, but was muscled back to shore like a wriggling mackerel by the rough, skilled hands of the fishermen who rarely, if ever, let a catch get away. He cried out with the shriek of a banshee as the flocking vultures attacked his carcass, avenging years of pent-up fury against the creature that had silently seduced their women away from them. Harsh words and balled fists were thrown, canes and golf clubs cracked as the men of Heather Bay set out to teach the hooligan a lesson in morals he'd not forget. After Charlie was subdued enough that they could carry him without too much trouble, the mob, led by Julian, carted him off in the direction of the old fishing warehouse to implement phase two of the punishment.

Feeling nauseated by the encounter, Brendan stalked away along the water's edge of the deserted cove. He flung the hat of drooping fruit into the crashing waves, wondering if it would have been better, had a herd of love-starved women carried him off into the night like they'd done to Salts the grisly fisherman.

Salts.

Despite his aching ribs, he sat down on a large boulder and began to laugh, unaware that someone was tracking his footprints in the sand.

CHAPTER SIXTEEN

He imagined the wedding. The old man on the Wurlitzer organ played the wedding march as Christine slithered down the aisle in a shimmering white mermaid tail with a bouquet of sea kelp. Her parrot flapped around the rafters of the moss-covered chapel, squawking insults at the guests and pecking an occasional ear or two. As he slipped a glittering ring of opal and pearl on her finger, he willed himself to concentrate on the sacred vows of matrimony he was undertaking, but his attention kept shifting to the clothespin on the priest's nose that was twittering and quivering. Then, SPLAT, a glob of greenish bird crap dripped down the front of his white tuxedo.

CRASH!

A wave caught Brendan's leg and he cursed, sprinting back from the icy sea spume that had doused his pants, snapping him back into present time. Stopping to catch his breath, he leaned against a large round boulder and realized that he'd walked a brisk mile while daydreaming about - his wedding? Liam's words echoed through his head, *You're in too deep.*

Having been completely absorbed with meeting the manuscript deadline, he hadn't really thought about it until now. But he'd be home in Los Angeles in a few days, home in his dark, neglected apartment in the noisy, dirty city that seemed like a shadow of something far away and long ago. There would be book signing tours and radio shows and a whirlwind of press interviews - for a while anyway. Then when the hype settled down, he'd be alone again, mapping out his next project.

Alone.

It was at that moment he realized that he didn't want to go home, didn't want to be alone anymore. What he wanted was right here - the young woman he'd discovered in this peculiar village, the girl with a couple of clamshells bobbing from her earlobes - the girl that took his breath away. But when the book was finished, he'd certainly have no business hanging around the village, particularly when the locals read what he'd written about them, what he'd written about her. He'd be more despised than Charlie the Tuna, he reflected dourly, might even be the target of another tar and feathering episode, that is, if they could manage to get the resin right this time. Regardless, he couldn't stay here and she certainly didn't fit into his world - she didn't fit anyplace but right here where he'd found her. It was inevitable. He had to leave this place. And he had to forget about Christine Hamilton. *You're in deep all right,* he thought hopelessly. *Deep shit.*

In the distance, a figure traced a set of footsteps in the sand along the jagged coastline.

Sensing eyes upon his back, Brendan turned around to look, muscles tensing with the uneasy feeling that Charlie had returned for another bout. But no one was there. He leaned back on the boulders and sighed, observing the Northern Lights through patchy white clouds, then heard the distinct sound of shoes crunching in the near distance. Springing up, he whirled around for a second time, finding his stomach fluttering, not with apprehension, but with enchantment, as her tangle of fiery hair whipped wildly in the breeze.

She jogged over to the rocks, springing easily

over mounds of shell sand. "Brendan!" she called breathlessly, stopping before him with a sudden wariness. "I just heard. He's gone insane, Charlie. I would have tried to stop him, but..." She stopped, her gaze raking over the anguish in his eyes. "Are you all right?"

He turned away from her and started climbing up the rocks. "Yeah," he said quietly. "I guess so."

She followed and tried to explain. "Look. He's just over protective of me. He really didn't mean any harm."

He jammed his foot in a crevice, lifting himself up. "Oh," he laughed cynically recalling the fury with which he was formally introduced to her brother, "he meant harm all right."

"I'm sorry," she offered genuinely, "I really don't know what else to say."

"Tell me," he began, turning to face her, "who gave him the idea that there's something going on between us?"

"I did," she said defiantly, pulling herself up after him.

Taken off guard, he stopped and sat down, raking a hand through his hair while staring at her sideways. He hadn't expected such a direct answer - that answer. "Look. I'm not going to deny the fact that I think you're an attractive young woman" he managed, clarifying, "very attractive – and very young. But it's more along the lines of an impossible fantasy, hopeless really."

Moving closer, she looked into his eyes. "Then why did you kiss me - like that?"

"Like what?" he sighed, knowing damn well like what. She was so close now he could feel her hot honeyed breath on his neck, shooting a velvet thrill down his spine.

"Like this," she breathed, running her fingers along the lines of his face, pressing her lips against his with an electric charge that he was powerless to fight off any longer. He knew it was reckless, that he might never recover from the potent dose of addictive potion that was beginning to seep beneath his skin. Helpless against the spell, his hands ran wild over her body as hers clawed with hunger into his. He drank up the intoxicating essence of her, against common sense, against the odds as all awareness of time and place slipped away, knowing now that if it went any further, he'd never be satisfied until he'd had her, not just once - but forever.

Have to stop

He pulled away as her hands desperately lured him back. "Don't," he pleaded through tortured eyes. "Don't – do this to me," he whispered, his voice strangled. With one last look, her nectar still tingling on his tongue, he wrenched himself from her grasp, unable to comprehend the dark and dangerous temptation that was tugging at his soul to stay with her forever. "Have to go," he rasped, as if he'd been hungering for her all of his life, and now that he'd had a taste of her, feared that he might starve to death without her. Stumbling down unsteadily, he began to descend the boulders, drunk with the taste of her, "have to go home now."

Turning to stop him, Christine, slid on the surface of the rocks, slick with sea spray. As she turned around to catch her balance, she twisted to the side, snagging her foot within a deep crevice. Desperate to stop him, she wrenched her ankle free causing her shoe to slip off. She turned and caught herself with hands grasping the rock. She gasped, as

Brendan climbed just below her and watched her clog fall into the sand. Before she could react, he looked up at her one last time, his eyes catching a glimpse at something that made him shrink back in horror as his feet thudded to the ground.

"Whoa!" he exclaimed in shock. Her wide, flat foot was unmistakably and hideously deformed with thin, transparent webs of skin attaching each of her long toes to the next like a miniature flipper, a larger version of the same illustrations he'd found within the walls of the church.

Searching her face for answers, the hot tears welled up in her eyes. "Oh, god," she whispered, covering her mouth.

"*The curse...*" he uttered in stunned disbelief.

Christine slid down the rocks, landing softly in the sand and spun to face him, her eyes flashing with humiliation at his utterance of the words. "How do you...!" she choked, "what do you know of the curse!"

Head still spinning, he picked up the clog from where it had fallen, his unbelieving and frightened gaze alternating between her bare foot and a single, glistening tear that streamed down her face.

Unable to bear his inquisitive eyes, the same eyes that had shifted from hungry, even tortured, to those of a gawking spectator at a circus freak show, she turned and bolted off toward the sea caves.

Frozen, he watched her edge her way through the sea foam, until her form became little more than a dark shape against the formidable cliffs. He stood now, dumfounded, still holding her shoe in his clutch. The shocking and unnerving revelation combined with the cool ocean air sinking into his heaving lungs had a swift and sobering effect.

No, he thought, turning his gaze in the direction of the caves, his head becoming clear again, *you're not going to get out of this one that easily.* And against all common sense, he went after her.

❧

Away from the merry crowds and the noise, Julian and the mob of fishermen leaned against the door of one of several, tall windowless structures situated at the far end of the docks. The bitter laughter of their voices rose and fell as they huddled together, finishing off another six-pack of bottled ale.

Julian breathed in deeply, savoring the fragrant aroma of revenge that exuded from the chimney of the old kipper smokehouse. One of the men shoveled another pile of oak chips into the underground furnace box on the concrete floor beneath the shed. As he hefted a second heap of wood forward, Julian placed his open palm before the handle of the shovel, nodding quietly, "that'll be enough, I think."

"Och!" the man disagreed shaking his bearded jowls. "It takes many hours to get the color and the flavor just so. Besides, I'm not so sure that we soaked him long enough in the brining solution." With a titter of glee he added, "never tried this with a tuna."

The rough tongues of the others burst out in a row of vicious laughter, ending abruptly as the sound of scratching fingernails clawed against the inside of the structure, followed by a dull thudding noise and another spasm of violent coughing.

The men turned expectantly to Julian, the self-elected leader of the late night prank. "Stand back lads," he warned with a wary eye, reaching to unlock the latch on the door as the others scuttled off in reverse to behold the outcome of the experiment at a safe distance. Holding their breath collectively, the door flung open, releasing a billowing cloud of greasy wood smoke into the crisp atmosphere.

Amidst rows of split herrings, skewered on metal rods and racks within, Charlie stumbled out of the smokehouse and fell to his knees, gasping and coughing, his pale skin darkened with soot, his expression glittering hatefully at his wide-eyed abductors. "Bloody – lunatics!" he managed to hiss at them between gulps of fresh air, his words inducing a chorus of guttural growling amongst the fishermen.

Charlie, being no fool, held his tongue now, not daring to divulge that, had these foolish men adored, worshipped and screwed their women to the edge of ecstasy as he had done, it would never have come to this. It was they, he thought caustically, glancing into each pair of dull, piggish eyes, that deserved to be beaten, soaked and smoked. He would have his vengeance, he vowed silently, but for now, there were far more important matters at hand – *like getting the hell out of here.*

With arms crossed, Julian circled Charlie now, inspecting him, the keen connoisseur who knew the characteristics of a properly preserved kipper when he saw one. "He may not be cured, but he's done!" he announced to the others, simultaneously kicking Charlie's ass with his bony foot, a motion that sent him tumbling face-first into the gravel outside the warehouse.

The steel butt of the pistol concealed within Charlie's waistband nudged at his ribs now as he lay belly down on the ground, the temptation to use it on the fishermen almost unbearable. But it wasn't worth the risk of wasting it. Those bullets were meant for Brendan James - and he'd see to it that they were embedded within his skull before dawn.

Peels of mischievous laughter rang out in the night as Charlie scrambled to his feet and fled from the sick madmen that had done this to him.

ᏘᎧᏘ

After furiously scrubbing off the Wolf Musk with a bottle of cleaning solution from behind the bar, Michael dried his ruddy cheeks with a cotton tea towel and slumped down before the shrine he'd erected in honor of Fiona Cross. His vision fuzzy from blubbering, he studied the photograph, the lines of her beautiful, faultless face, and then he wept for her. For how she'd given herself, given her perfect, flawless body to the unworthy likes of Brendan James, a man who cared for no one but himself - *a man too busy howling with laughter at the tragic misfortune of the fat stupid bartender that he couldn't even be bothered to say goodbye.*

In a fit fueled by rage, he lashed out violently out at the picture and candles on the counter, sending it all crashing to the floor in a heap of broken glass and splintered wood. He'd been a fool, he scowled, not just tonight, but for all of his sorry life. Who in the bloody hell did he think he was deceiving by going out there to the soul mate festival? He was an ugly man destined to live and die an ugly bachelor, alone in the pub he'd inherited from his father fifteen years ago and that was just the way of things.

Sadly, he remembered his mother, God rest her soul, and how she'd read him the fairy tale about the ugly duckling as a wee tot and how he'd longed to be beautiful, how he'd prayed for the day to come that he would transform into a graceful swan. But that day had never come, and here he sat, still an ugly old mallard, a monster that no woman could ever want. Glaring at his big hideous head in the mirror behind the bar, he was sure now that a curse had been laid across his fate, just as sure as the tears streamed down his face. His destiny, his life - it was just like Beauty and the Beast, he decided, except for the part about the girl and the castle.

A beast, he glowered, baring his teeth at the reflection in the mirror, *a snarling, snapping wild beast.* Perhaps he'd been trying too hard to become one of *them*. Perhaps he should start acting like what he truly was...

In another outburst that would have done any beast proud, he snatched down the edge of the LOVE BOAT banner on the wall and tackled it into a ball, stomping on it with his big clumsy feet.

He'd show them a beast all right.

CHAPTER SEVENTEEN

Following the treacherous path along the jagged coastline, Brendan picked his way after Christine, coming upon the wide mouth of the cave hidden between impossibly high cliffs. The moon was full and the tide high, creeping dangerously close to the low entrance where dim candlelight flickered from within.

Deeming himself certifiably insane, he made a dash between sets of crushing waves to gain access to the isolated beach hideaway, where inside, he hoped to be enlightened with a logical explanation. Clutching Christine's wooden-soled clog in his hand like some kind of a god dammed Prince Charming, he steeled his nerves, ducking into the low wide cavern.

She sat on a pile of sealskins, mindlessly trailing her fingers through the carpet of sand and pearls on the floor of the sea cave, turning to face him as he entered. He soaked in the scene for a moment, her hair blazing against a backdrop of faded paintings on the walls beneath the dim light of the anchor chandelier, her eyes flashing with resentment. It was something out of a fantasy, he thought, his head spinning between the real world and the make-believe backdrop she'd created.

She said nothing, but stared with an inhuman gaze that was both dangerous and provocative.

"I think," he began, dropping her shoe in the sand, "that you owe me an explanation."

Her eyes flicked to the shoe, then met his stare, the man who was demanding answers of her, rational answers that would fit nicely into a neat little box that he could carry home to his big city world. "I owe you nothing," she whispered, turning her back on him.

"Fine," he growled, crouching down, his breath trailing along the back of her neck. "Then I'll start. Since I've been in this village, I've seen you and your lunatic sibling swimming in the freezing sea for starters, my neighbor thinks you're eighty-year-old woman, your friend Claire professes that you're mother was a mermaid, the bartender says all of your ex-boyfriends are dead and I was hoping that you might shed some light on all of this because I'm starting to get a little bit freaked out here!"

"Seventy-nine," she whispered.

"Seventy-nine - what?" he asked, placing his fingers on her shoulder.

Slowly, she turned to face him, her pupils so dilated that the irises were nearly all black, "I'm seventy-nine years old," she uttered.

Startled by her strange eyes, he flinched, then realized it had only been the dusky light of the cave. "Yeah?" he asked with a bitter laugh, "we'll I'd like to know what brand of face cream you're using because I could make a mint peddling it in Beverly Hills."

Ignoring his sarcasm, she went on, tears beginning to brim in her eyes. "My mother, she was a hybrid like Charlie and me." She grasped his fingers, pulled him close to her face, "we inherited the long-living genes and the – rather peculiar feet." She paused, searching his face for some sign that he understood, that he believed the confession, but his expression remained blank and baffled. "I will always be like this and I will never grow old – unless…"

"Unless you fall in love with a human and the spell is broken," he finished flatly.

Holding her breath for a moment she added, "when we – fall in love, that's when the transformation will occur. When we return to a human state and begin aging normally."

"Yeah, yeah, I've heard the fairy tale," he scoffed, the walls starting to close in around him.

She nodded, slipping her foot back into the leather clog, giving him one last disturbing glimpse of her webbed toes.

He swallowed hard, pointing at the shoe, "guess I'm shit out of luck then. Must not be love." He turned away from the pained expression on her face.

"This is no fairy tale Brendan!" she shouted, rage flashing in her eyes. "What I've told you is the truth!"

In response, he laughed, a mad disbelieving laugh, then ran his hands through his hair, turning back to her incredulously. "Right. And I suppose that now you're going to ram a knife through your heart to prove to me that you'll live forever?"

Insulted, she glared at him, "I never said I was an immortal."

"Well, that's a relief. Jesus, Christine!" He rose, standing above her now with sweeping arms. "Please, don't tempt me to write about this. I'm not here to make a fool out of you."

"Is that what you think I'm after?" she spat, flinging the hair from her face. "Do you think I want to be written about? I'm telling you all of this because I thought you might understand and stop bloody writing about it!"

Brendan kicked at the sand. "Do I have 'stupid' stamped across my forehead? Do you really expect me to believe that you were born in 1925?"

She could hardly blame him, but she had to put it all on the line now, there was too much at stake. "And Charlie in 1922," she nodded defiantly, continuing, "I must leave the village soon. It's been too long and the locals are becoming suspicious of me. But I'll come back some day to a new generation and tell them that I'm the child of Christine Hamilton," she rushed, knowing that she was losing him to common logic. "That's how we've survived as long as we have."

"The curse," he said, disgusted by her ludicrous charade.

The words surged, sending a hot flash of anger that sparked in her dark eyes, "there is no curse, only lies told by ignorant old wives! Our kind have always been here, just as we are today."

"Actually, I was referring to the dead boyfriends. Is that part true?"

Saying nothing, her stare burned into him.

"Very interesting that you're not answering the question," he scowled as the room began to spin. He backed away, attempting to put some space between himself and the creature that was threatening to suck him into the fantasy world she lived in. "You may be beautiful Christine and you may have the most remarkable birth defect I've ever seen. But if you expect me to believe single a word you've said, think again."

"I've read your book *Brendan James* and I know that your next one is an expose about the village!" she accused, her voice steady and unforgiving.

He stumbled back a disbelieving step, wondering how in the hell she found out – and how long she'd known.

"You can't do this to us, now that you know."

She searched his eyes, praying that she'd somehow changed his mind, "you can't do this - to me."

He shook his head, trying to digest it all, the spell she was casting upon him that was pulling at him like a rip tide. The facts, the figures, none of it added up – couldn't add up. "Let me tell you something," he snarled, resisting the urge to shake a finger at her, "I have contracts with these people. My entire career is hanging on this one book, which happens to be the most incredible story I've ever written. So, I'm very sorry that you've been hurt and I'm sorry that this may interrupt your life, but I write it like I see it – and this book – it's not something I'm willing to walk away from."

"From what I've heard, walking away is what you're famous for," she said coldly.

Stung, he opened his mouth to respond, but the words dammed up his throat.

"Tell me," she asked, "are you planning to walk away from me? Or was I just a chapter in your book?"

"What? And join your buddies in the cemetery? Thanks, but no thanks," he growled. "Oh, and by the way? You're going to be more than a chapter, Christine," he assured her, stalking out of the cavern.

"When are you going to stop walking!" she cried after him.

Her strained voice reverberated off his back as he stepped through the sea froth on the beach and made a run for it between sets of crushing waves.

No lights were gleaming through the colored

glass panes of the Siren's Whale as Brendan approached the old pub, his head swimming with deliberations, his gut knotted with guilt. He'd never set out to hurt anybody, especially Christine, but the situation had become impossible. The locals weren't supposed to read his books – and he wasn't supposed to have fallen in love. Major rules had been broken. Things had gotten personal – and despite himself, he'd made friends, friends that he was now going to stab in the back with his pen.

He'd mulled it over on the walk back into town and found himself just as confused as when he'd seen her unearthly foot an hour ago. So what if she could speak Manx Gaelic, a language that died out in the 1920's? And just because she had fins on her toes and could take the cold like a Viking, that didn't make her anything special. Well, she could just forget about slithering down the aisle in that white mermaid tail. She was crazy was what she was, he decided, sketching out his plans to permanently remove himself from this insanity first thing in the morning.

Just as he was reflecting how deserted the village was, a lone silhouette emerged from the shadows beyond the pub and stood in the middle of the cobblestone street. Unconcerned, he kept walking - until he got close enough to make out that the shadow was draped in seaweed. Panic surged through his gut and he stopped in his tracks, recalling the terrifying encounter he'd had with the thing in the water, his alarm quickly turning to anger. Rather than backing off, he made a charge toward it, his fists already balled for a scuffle.

But the creature remained in the road, unmoving until it recognized the American. Then, in a blur, it turned to the right and scampered off into a narrow alley.

Buildings flashing by, Brendan tore after it hollering, "Yeah? You'd better run asshole because you're about to get a serious ass-kicking!" Third time's a charm, he thought lividly, slipping between Tudors in the narrow, crooked passageway. Kicking cardboard boxes and vegetable crates out of his path, he strained to see in the dark. Garbage from a heap at the end of the dead-end route wafted into his nostrils as he slowed his pace, stopping only to push his shoulder up against a couple of locked doors. "There's no escaping now!" he shouted down the length of the alley, his voice echoing off the bare brick walls. "You're trapped and the only way out is past me!" Listening intently, he made his way toward the trash where faint, ragged panting from somewhere beneath the heap broke the eerie silence. He stepped closer to a pile of plastic garbage bags and an old mattress, then saw something – a strand of seaweed. "I can hear you breathing! Get out of there!" he roared. A trickle of sweat ran down his face as he approached the rubbish. Even though whatever was in there was more afraid of him than he was of it, he felt numb with apprehension.

CRASH!

In a shower of garbage, the mattress and boxes flung forward as the creature sprung to its feet, making an attempt to run away. Brendan flinched in shock, then leaped on its back, tackling the large figure to the ground. He wrapped his arms around the slimy sea foliage, cringing at the hideous snout of the thing as it squealed like a warthog. As much as it repelled him to touch it, he raised his fist to finish it off.

The creature squeezed its eyes shut and began whimpering, "It's me! It's Michael! Brendan, please, don't hurt me!"

"Why you scum-sucking son-of-a-bitch! I ought to kill you!" he growled through bared teeth, shoving its shoulders into the ground, winding up for a punch.

Shaking with terror, Michael pulled the grotesque mask away from his face and begged, "No! Please don't!" With a nervous laugh he explained, "I-I was just trying to drum up a bit of excitement around the village!"

Brendan, who wasn't feeling quite so guilty now about betraying his 'friends', released Michael with a shove, sighing in disgust. "It was you who pulled me into the water?"

Michael gulped hard, then nodded.

Outraged, Brendan slugged him across the face.

"Ow!" he howled, clenching his head. "Bollocks, that hurt!"

"That was for making me believe you," Brendan snarled, snatching the mask from the ground. "And this," he told him shaking the grotesque rubber in his teary-eyed face, "is for me to make an even bigger fool out of you in my new book!" Rising to his feet, he looked down at Michael who was beginning to blubber. "You're pathetic," he spat.

Michael stumbled up with tears streaming down his fat jowls. "You think I don't already know that? Look at me!" he howled, flinging a strand of seaweed aside. "I'm a loser! Even the drunken ladies in me own pub won't give me a second glance!" He grasped Brendan's hand and whispered, "I just wanted a wee bit of attention is all. Is that such a terrible crime?"

Brendan noticed that Michael's eye was beginning to swell as his large body jiggled with snivels. Starting to feel sorry for the big stupid oaf, he sighed, "go on man," he nodded, "you'd better go and put some ice on that."

Michael blinked, then a grateful smile broke across his face. He embraced Brendan in a crushing bear hug that nearly knocked the wind out of him. "Aw, God, Brendan, you're a good man," he wept. "I hope we can still be mates and all."

After he'd caught his breath, Brendan reluctantly patted him on the back. "Yeah, sure."

The big man released him, his attitude unexpectedly bright and optimistic again.

As Brendan turned to trudge down the alley, Michael called after him hopefully, "by the way, did you say something about - a book you're writing?"

"Yeah," he hollered over his shoulder, "it's gonna be a best-seller - a tell-all about the psychotic inhabitants of the village - and you and your pub are all over it, buddy!"

"No shite!" he blinked, not quite believing the turn of good fortune his life had taken.

"Yeah, *no shite*," he grumbled, heading toward the Mermaid Inn, his last stop for the night. "I'll send you a copy."

"If there's anything else I can do..." Michael offered.

"Please, no," he waved. "You've already done more than enough."

⁛

CHAPTER EIGHTEEN

The Inn was unusually quiet as Brendan approached the front desk. "Hello," he called. "Anyone around?"

Claire answered from the tea room, her voice strained and annoyed, "in here!"

The cozy room was decorated with Victorian era furniture and all of the china and dishes were eclectically mismatched. She was busy placing crisp linen napkins and polished silverware on the tables with trembling hands, her eyes pink and swollen from crying. She spun around, surprised to see the American standing behind her. "Mr. James? Why aren't you down at the beach? You're going to miss all the fun," she asked forcing a smile on his behalf.

"Yeah, well I'm working," he sighed, looking her over and wondering what had her so twitterpatted. "What's your excuse?"

"Me?" she glowered, dabbing at her eyes. "I'm too old for that sort of fun. Besides, I've got tables to set up for breakfast in the morning." She noticed that he appeared to be in dour spirits as well. "Is something the matter, lad?"

"Can we talk for a few minutes?" he asked. "I'm leaving in the morning."

Claire absently set down the bundle of napkins. Something had gone wrong. Terribly wrong. "You're leaving?"

လ၁ယ

A dark figure limped toward the isolated sea cave, trudging through the rough waves that pummeled the small beach.

Inside, Christine had been painting furiously ever since Brendan left, attempting to take her mind off it all. But the only thing she'd succeeded in doing was upsetting herself even more. Paint smudged on her face and arms, she stood back to look at her work on the wall, a crude portrait of Brendan sitting at a table with a fork in hand, and on the plate before him was a dead mermaid with a huge bite taken out of her tail - a mermaid that very much resembled herself. "You arrogant son of a bitch," she growled at it, swiping away a tear.

Clothing torn and skin coated with pungent grease, Charlie staggered into the cavern beneath the flickering candle flames looking like some kind of a madman.

Christine heard the footsteps crunching in the sand and spun around in the dim light, her mouth falling open at the sight of her brother, weak, shaking and beaten. "Charlie!" she gasped, taking his soot-blackened hands in hers, searching his bloodshot eyes for an explanation. "Oh my god! What happened to you!"

He crumpled to his knees before her, his dark eyes glistening with tears. "I was only trying to talk to him," he sniveled unsteadily, flicking a resentful stare toward his sister. "But then he turned on me," he hissed darkly.

"Brendan?" she asked incredulously. "He - did this to you?"

Nodding 'yes,' he crumpled over in agony, clutching his ribs with a wince. "THIS - is what happens to us when we let them get too close!" he growled, eyes flashing black. "Has my point been made clear? Is this enough evidence for you!"

Nearly feeling his pain herself, she observed his swollen cheek and tattered coat, the greasy black sweat trickling down the side of his face, trying to conceive how Brendan could have broken him like this. "I'm so sorry," she whispered, reaching out to embrace him, but he angrily swatted her sympathetic gesture away.

Knowing she was at fault, she clamped a hand over her mouth, averting her stare from Charlie in his pitiful state.

కలుంఽ

"It's all true," Claire said. "Every word I've told you."

Brendan stared uncomfortably at the old woman across the table in the quiet tea room, her misty blue eyes boring into him with intensity. "Like it or not," she whispered, "that's the way of things."

It was exasperating, he thought, the lies, the utter madness of the fiction she was trying to pass off as fact. His eyes rolled slightly as he rubbed the stubble on his chin. "Look," he began gently, "you're a really nice lady and I like you a lot. But these statements – they'll make you look foolish in the magazine article. It'll kill your business. So, I'll ask you one last time. Do you want to reconsider your story and tell me who's really behind all of this?"

Overcome with fury, Claire slapped the arrogant American across the face and threw the porcelain teapot on the floor where it exploded into a thousand shards, causing him to jump out of his chair, his pants steaming with hot black tea.

"Jesus, Claire!" he hollered, dancing around as the scorching liquid soaked into his skin.

She rose, leaning across the table with narrowed eyes, shaking a quivering finger at him. "To hell with the business and to hell with you!" she spat. "What I told you *is the truth* and I'll bloody stand by it 'til the day I die! You saw her feet and you saw the photographs! There is no hoax Mr. James!" Her voice lowered to a threatening hiss, her eyes burned through him, "and if you write one harmful word about Christine or the village, *God help you man! God help you!*"

Stunned by Claire's conviction and scaled by the tea, he could only stare back at her with wide eyes. "You're – serious," he swallowed.

"Dead!"

ぬぐ

Within the cramped confines of the Wesley's bedroom, Sarah was decked out in a negligee trimmed in glossy black ostrich feathers. With a seductive grin on her lips, she beckoned Julian closer with an index finger, gyrating her narrow hips in his direction. Growling like a tiger for the first time in a decade, Julian cast off his bathrobe revealing the pair of red, silk boxer shorts that she'd hopelessly given him on Valentine's Day back in 1995.

Sarah squealed in anticipation as he chased her around the bed. Jumping onto the comforter, she shoved the pillows aside and ripped off her lingerie with vigor. "Oooh! Come and get me you wild beast!"

"That's right old girl!" he snarled, puffing up his chest. "Nobody messes with my woman and lives to tell about it! You saw the way I ripped the slimy bastard apart!"

Sarah gritted her teeth, "Oh, yes. Yes! You were so - so savage!"

Julian sprang to the bed, flipping Sarah on her back. Growling again, he ceremoniously clapped his hands, automatically turning off the bedside lights.

And outside on the docks, all was quiet except for the creaking and rocking of the Wesley's house-boat.

ฬฬฬ

On the fourth floor of the Mermaid Inn, Brendan hesitantly followed Claire down the narrow hall-way past guest rooms marked with brass numbers. Holding up a fat ring of keys, she unlocked a door with a crystal knob at the end of the corridor. With a flick of her eyes, she stood aside as he stepped in before her.

A stained glass lamp with camels and palm trees illuminated the small bedroom with a warm yel-low glow. Furnished with a four poster bed cov-ered in crisp white linen, the room was simple and spotless, just like the rest of the hotel. Taking Brendan by the hand, she guided him over to a col-lection of framed photographs on her dressing table.

Brendan wasn't sure if he should be feeling guilty or frightened. After her violent outburst, she'd insisted on bringing him up to her bedroom where she was either going to prove her point somehow – or gouge him in the heart with a gleaming letter opener that glinted threateningly on the window-sill. But to his relief, she handed him a black and white photograph of a young girl with a wild tangle of hair holding a baby. "Christine was five when I was born," she explained quietly. "She's watched me grow old and I've – watched her stay the same." She turned and stared out the window, her voice quavering now. "It must be heartbreaking for her. To see us turn white and wither away. To attend the funeral of an old friend - of a summer lover."

Nodding politely, he mindlessly inspected the picture. Although the young girl with the dark tresses bore a strong resemblance to Christine, it could have been anyone.

She stared at the photo over his shoulder, covering her mouth as a painful sigh escaped from her lips. "The poor thing. She still leaves flowers on their long forgotten graves."

Brendan blinked, recalling the bouquets in the cemetery, the handwritten notes in Manx Gaelic, the dead lovers Michael mentioned, the ones that Christine refused to speak of.

"What happened to them?"

"We don't know," she began setting the frame back on the dresser. "Some of them just disappeared and never came back, others were lost in accidents..." she covered her mouth, unable to go on about the string of tragedies. "She's sure it's her fault, their deaths. So she's been alone for years, refused to get involved with a man – that is - until you came along."

"And that's supposed to be a good thing?" he gawked.

Unable to come up with a response, Claire remained quiet, reaching for a yellowed photograph of a beauty with raven-hair and a handsome young man in a summer straw hat. "And this is me."

"You were very pretty," he managed, beginning to feel suffocated by the small room that reeked of rose potpourri.

"I didn't bring you here to prove that I was a

knock-out in my day. Look at the man in the picture, Mr. James," she insisted, tapping on the glass with her fingernail. "Look closely."

Although the print was cracked and grainy and the man's face shadowed by the brim of the 1940's style hat, he looked vaguely familiar.

Charlie?

By the stunned expression on Brendan's face, Claire knew that the cynical writer had recognized him. "We were lovers many years ago. I was his first."

The picture slipped in his hands, his palms beginning to sweat. "You and...? It can't be," he whispered.

Resentment flashed in her pale eyes. "Mr. James. Do you really think I've staged all this for your amusement? That I fabricated these photographs just in case you decided to pop by and question my integrity?"

He turned away. There had to be a logical explanation for this, he thought, but the odds were against it that she'd come up with such an elaborate plan on such short notice – and he had stopped stop by unexpectedly. "I don't know what to believe anymore."

"We live in a different world out here," she explained. "A place that the outsiders will never understand." She touched his arm lightly, "try to imagine that what Christine and I told you was the truth."

Torn between reality and fantasy, he glanced at the photographs again, then looked away. "I don't think..."

"That's right," she interrupted, her intention strong enough to bend his mind toward the possibility that it might be true. "Don't think, just feel. Let your heart guide you."

"I have to go," he uttered shakily, stumbling into the edge of the dresser.

Unwilling to lose him now, Claire grasped his arm, her eyes fixed on his wavering stare. "You're the one for her Brendan. I'm sure of it now. The others were only taken because they weren't you – her soul mate. But you have to let yourself imagine. Let yourself fall in love."

"I don't want anything to do with this Claire," he snapped, spooked by the fact that she nearly had him believing.

"Tonight. Follow your heart."

I don't think so lady, he thought. *Tonight I'm packing and getting the hell out of this zoo.* "Good night. Thank you for your time," he rushed, prying her fingers from his forearm before storming out of the room.

Her expression sunk as the sound of his boots thudded down the hall.

❧

Brendan stomped toward the houseboat determined to get his things packed so he could chug out on the first ferry in the morning. Liverpool, Dublin, it didn't matter anymore. He had to get the hell out of this place. If he were ever going to finish a book about these lunatics, he'd have to separate himself from them before his own emotions ruined everything – or got him killed.

With a loosely tied bathrobe cloaking his thin frame, Julian waved from the deck of his houseboat, savoring a glass of cognac. "Ah! I feel like a new man!" he said with the sly wink of a man who'd just gotten laid. "Nothing like a wee bit o' violence to get the ol' testosterone flowing, I always say."

Brendan nodded absently, fumbling through his pockets for the key. "Yeah, sure buddy," he mumbled, not bothering to look up.

Inside, he went to work furiously stuffing his clothing and personal belongings into the one small suitcase he'd arrived with.

Julian stumbled inside after him, tripping across a stack of manuscript pages that had been stacked in the middle of the floor.

Brendan glanced up at him with annoyance, hastily shuffling the sheets back into a crooked pile.

"And where are you going in such a hurry?" Julian inquired. "Skipping town on us, eh?"

Brendan threw his hands up in exasperation, deciding that he could pack the laptop in the morning. He spun to face his snooping, bothersome neighbor, "I'm leaving, is where I'm going! As far away as I can get from this fucking place!" he snarled.

"Whoa-ho-ho," Julian blinked, offering Brendan his glass of cognac and a friendly pat on the shoulder. "Here, mate. Take it easy. Just take it easy."

Waving the drink away, Brendan sunk to the dirty carpet with his back against the wall. The events of the evening, the absolute madness, the hot tea that had burned his crotch, it was all threatening to engulf the last remnants of his sanity.

"Come on then," Julian prodded, "tell me what's troubling you."

Raking a hand through unruly hair, Brendan laughed with disgust, turning his guilty eyes to meet Julian's. "You really wanna know about my problems?"

He nodded, crouching down next to him with

305

concern. "I do. We're friends now - you and me. You can tell me anything."

The derogatory sentence he'd written describing Julian Wesley came to mind now, followed by a stab of shame, *'the gangly drunk striking a strong resemblance to Nosferatu in a pair of seersucker shorts.'* And now the Nosferatu, and Brendan's only friend in the world, sat patiently, waiting for him to pour his heart out about his troubles – unaware that a wooden stake was about to be driven through his heart in the new book. Have to fix that part in the manuscript somehow, he thought, perhaps there'd be time in the final edit before the pages went to print. Some of the stuff about Sarah too...

Shit.

The whole goddamned manuscript was a vile insult to these people, to these decent human beings who'd opened their hearts and their homes to him - and he'd silently and callously slid the blade between their vertebrae as they'd slept. And to make matters worse, his obnoxious dissection of these people was the very stuff that had his editor drooling for more, the stuff that would make the book a best seller - *the stuff that would tear the very soul out of this place.* "I'm sorry," Brendan uttered without looking up. "But - what is a friend?" he asked quietly. "I mean a *real friend,*" he clarified, a trace of bitter sarcasm rising in his voice as he recalled the unpleasant and embarrassing scene with Michael in the alley.

"Can't say I know for sure," Julian admitted, turning to the American with a bashful smile, "I never really had one - that is, 'til you came along."

Julian's eager affection, like that of a golden retriever was mortifying to Brendan. He had to end

306

it, this deceitful 'friendship' once and for all. "I see," he growled. "Well, how about this? Let's just say that I discovered that one of my 'friends' was dressing up as a freaking sea creature to traumatize tourists and to stir up business around town at my expense! But can I really call him a 'friend' after he tried to drown me a couple of days ago?"

"No shite! It was Michael?" Julian guffawed, his eyes bulging wide. "In the bay? The fat bastard."

Brendan nodded and continued, "Yeah. As a matter of fact it was. And then there's Christine Hamilton, who I might mention, happens to be a raving psychotic! So if I were to say, write something less than flattering about her, would I be betraying her, or did she have it coming all along?"

Rubbing the white whiskers jutting from his chin, Julian mulled it all over with a 'humph,' but his thoughts were interrupted by a trilling voice ringing out from the houseboat next door.

"Oh Tiger! I'm ready for seconds! Grrrrrr!"

Delivering a hasty pat on Brendan's back, Julian rose to his feet, snatching up his glass of cognac. "Don't know, mate. One piece of advice though."

"What's that?" he asked cynically, his weary eyes rising to meet Julian's.

"Don't knock psychotic women," he grinned, "they make life interesting. Gotta go now."

Deflated, Brendan buried his face between his knees as the door of the houseboat shut, sniggering resentfully at the moral dilemma he'd managed to inflict upon himself. There was only one thing to do at this point, he decided.

Dragging himself up from the floor, he sat down in the chair before the computer. With the intention to write, his fingers danced just above the keyboard, but the witty, sarcastic words were nowhere to be found, jammed up somewhere between the lump in his throat and the dull beating of his heart.

Minutes passed as he sat staring blankly at the screen, contemplating the cornucopia of bizarre evidence that had been heaped onto his plate this evening. Her deformed feet, the old yellowed photographs of Charlie and Claire, the feelings of desperation he had when he wasn't near her, and knowing that he would wither away and die if he were to leave this place without her. Where were the analytical answers that would make it all okay again, that would make the questions and the thoughts and the feelings go away? he pondered hopelessly.

The startling ring of the cell phone caused him to jump. Swiping aside a stack of pages, he snatched it up, knowing that it could only be one person at this hour. "What!"

Taken aback by Brendan's hostile greeting, Jake leaned back in his leather chair with the phone pressed to his ear, "How's the writing going?"

"Don't ask," he mumbled, straightening the stack of papers he'd knocked askew.

"Look," Jake continued with jangling nerves, "I need the final chapters to keep the Editor-in-chief at bay. The ol' boy's been going ape shit ever since the pre-sales figures came in."

"What are you talking about?" If the figures were really bad he was screwed, and if the figures were decent - *he was a dead man.* "Ape shit in a good way - or ape shit in a bad way?" he gulped.

"Put like this," Jake grinned, "every major bookstore chain in the U.S. has already pre-ordered more copies than all of our titles last year combined.

Fucking staggering!"

Dead man.

"What?" he exhaled, his constricting throat threatening to cut off the blood supply to his brain.

"Congratulations. You just saved all of our asses including your own. Good job, buddy." The long distance connection crackled with static. "Brendan? You still there?" he panicked. "Say something."

Speechless, he opened his mouth to respond, but could only manage to produce a dry croaking noise.

"Brendan. I need the last chapter A.S.A.P.," he persisted. "We've got five copy editors working around the clock on the stuff you already sent in to get this thing turned around by next week." With a slight tremble he asked, "You are writing it – aren't you?"

He shook his head in disbelief, "I think I'm freaking out."

"What?" Jake sputtered. "No, no, no. You need to calm down and you need to write. Come on, man. You need to finish this book. You're almost there. Almost home."

It was at that moment he realized it. If he were to leave Heather Bay in the wee hours of the morning as planned, there would be no final chapter to the tale, no conclusion – no ending. "I'm going out to find out how this story ends, once and for all," he decided aloud, hanging up the cell phone. He stood unsteadily, threw his coat back on and disappeared into the night.

ഇരു

CHAPTER NINETEEN

High tide was closing in at the mouth of the sea cave, the thick white foam edging up to the lip of the entrance. Christine had finally coaxed Charlie outside and led him through the huge waves that pounded on the beach in great green crests. Muscles burning from guiding her disoriented and weak sibling up the slippery granite steps, she pleaded with him as they climbed another stair, "come on! We have to get you home and into bed. You're not well."

"Ohhhhhh," he moaned weakly, stealing a cunning, sideways glance at her, "I need you to care for me," he wheezed. "So much – pain."

Exhausted, the pair reached the top of the grassy knoll high above the cave where Charlie collapsed into the tangle of greens. "Can't go on," he panted. "Hurts too much."

Christine stood over him, her brow furrowed with concern. "My, god! What did he do to you? What hurts too much?"

"Everything!" he howled dramatically, suddenly clasping onto her ankles.

Peering down at him, she noticed by the moonlight that the tip of his nose was beginning to blister. With a hint of skepticism rising about his version of events, she jerked her leg out of his grasp, inspecting him a little more carefully now. "Tell me Charlie, how exactly is it that Brendan James managed to – *burn you?*" she questioned, pointing a doubting finger at the soot on his face.

Charlie stirred momentarily from another bout of writhing in the grass to gaze up at her, his overly-innocent look confirming her suspicions. "What?"

She smelled a red herring – literally. "And why do you smell like a - *bloody kipper!*" she demanded, swiping a finger across his cheek, then tasting it for herself, the distinctive flavor of burnt oak chips tingling on her tongue. "You've been at the kipper factory! Haven't you!" she spat shrewdly.

"I have not!" he protested.

"What?" she asked, poking an accusing finger at him, "did you have one of your women down there and lock yourself inside you old fool?"

"I – he made me go in there!" he lied "It was all his fault!"

"Brendan James locked you inside the smokehouse?" she challenged.

"Not – exactly," he mumbled, eyes casting away from her piercing gaze.

"Just as I figured," she said quietly.

"He might as well have!" Charlie sputtered. "He handed me over to the bloody fishermen and they carried me off! It was mortifying," he shuddered. "You can't imagine what they did to me." His body shook with a cough, his eyes raised to meet hers. "Please, I'm sick," he pleaded weakly. "I need you to care for me."

"You need a bath!" she spat. "And I can't believe that you lied about Brendan James – *you bastard!*"

The American's name stabbed in his ears. "You've got to stop thinking about him Chris!" he croaked, his eyes becoming desperate and wild, hands clawing now at the thin fabric of her blouse. "I won't lose you to him. I won't lose you to anyone!"

In his clutches, she watched the sweat trickling down his smooth forehead, felt the anxiety in his grip. "You're not going to lose me," she whispered guiltily, knowing that she was already long gone – had been since the moment Brendan had walked into her life.

But Charlie's perceptive eyes saw through her facade. "I will kill him if I have to," he threatened, the chilling confession sending a shrill pang of fear through her soul as he crushed her frail body into the hollow of his chest.

"Charlie," she winced, pushing him away, trying to steady her quavering voice, for she clearly understood that his warning was not to be taken lightly. He would kill for her, that she knew, - and he was starting to go mad. Her concern for Brendan's safety rose as she watched his eyes darken a shade. She needed to get her brother to Claire's immediately. "Come on," she prompted, kissing his cheek with a taut smile. "Let's get you into a comfortable bed at the Inn – where I can take care of you," she lied. "I'll make you an herbal draught with some nice chamomile and elderberry leaves," she coaxed, failing to mention the other ingredients that she planned to slip into his potion, something potent enough to knock him out until morning. She couldn't let Charlie run loose tonight, not like this, not with Brendan out there, unaware of the murderous vengeance that would certainly make it's way to the door of his houseboat before dawn if she didn't do something to stop it. Brendan James may have broken her heart and he may be have been an arrogant horse's ass, but he certainly didn't deserve to die for it.

"You've got to stop thinking about him," he whispered, wrapping his arms around her so tightly she feared she might suffocate.

"I can't!" she finally burst, lashing out at her brother. "I can't forget about him!"

With a swift motion, he caught her wrist, pulling her down to him face to face. "Then we must leave this place tonight – or I'll kill him Christine! I swear I'll do it."

"Well, he doesn't want me anyway! So therefore you can't kill him!" she cried, swinging her free arm to hit him. But he caught her fist and gripped it in his, eyes black and soulless. "Oh, yes I can – and I will, that is a promise. He isn't worth an eternity," he hissed. "Only in his death can you live."

A picture of Ned, a long-forgotten summer lover ran through her mind now, a lover who had died at sea in a mysterious accident after his boat had capsized in calm waters. Although his body was recovered and there had been no signs of foul play, she'd always suspected Charlie in the back of her mind. Now she was sure of it.

"I hate you!" she sobbed, throwing a weak punch at his chest, still entangled in his arms. Rather than fighting back, he took the hits with patience, nuzzling his face within her tangle of glistening hair as she cried.

Someday, he knew, she would thank him.

The cool night air was bracing against Brendan's face as he jogged down the isolated pier toward the looming green theater in the distance. Out of breath, he opened the back door of the building and bounded up two flights of stairs, not stopping until he stood before the door of her rooftop apartment.

Heart pounding with anticipation, he rapped

against the wood. Not knowing what would happen after he crossed the threshold of this place terrified him, but he didn't care anymore. Nothing mattered now but discovering what was to become of his life, of her life – and how it was all going to come together. He knocked again, this time more urgently. "Christine!" he shouted hoarsely.

"I'm in the shower," he heard from behind the door. "Come inside."

Gingerly he tried the knob and to his surprise it turned. In the unfamiliar apartment filled with eclectic furnishings, he stepped across the floor, unsure of her intentions. He cleared his throat, "Christine?"

"In here," she called beyond the sound of trickling water. He stepped closer to the bathroom from which steam was billowing up from beneath the slightly open door. Did she actually want him to go inside? he wondered.

"Look," he began, shuffling uncomfortably just outside the bathroom. "We need to talk – about what happened earlier. It's just that…"

"In the shower!" she shouted.

"I – I know," he stammered, pressing his ear against the door. "I'll just wait out here, er – until you're finished."

"I'm in the shower."

"You – do you want me to come in?" he asked uncertainly, his mind running wild with the possibility that he might be making love to her within moments – if she'd have him, the very thought driving him wild. When she didn't respond, he pushed the door open a bit further with the toe of his boot, entering the steamy room. "Hi," he said, seating himself on the edge of the white-tiled counter, knowing that at any moment she was going to step out from behind the curtain. Mentally, he braced himself for her strange feet again, silently vowing that he wouldn't flinch this time. "Um, I'm going to be honest with you," he began, "something that I'm not very good at."

But before he could get out the words that he so desperately needed to say, a pair of glowing yellow eyes peered down from the top of the shower rod and hissed, "wanker!"

Startled by the glowering parrot, he jumped backwards, hitting his head on the oval shaped mirror above the sink, knocking it down and sending a tray of perfume bottles and toothbrushes scattering across the slick surface of the floor.

Pearl, frightened by the sudden motion began flapping around the small room wildly, squawking at the top of her lungs.

Swiping at the old bird, he managed to catch a tail feather as she flew off into the living room. Turning back in exasperation, he flung open the shower curtain, saw the stream of water spraying out against the wall, and realized that the parrot had been messing with his head. "Come back here you miserable excuse for a pet!" he hollered, shaking the single feather in his hand.

Now perched on the coat rack among a black hat and a couple of light sweaters, Pearl blinked back at Brendan as he stormed out of the bathroom after her. Noticing that he'd left the front door open and the bird was now inching her way toward it, he slowed his pace to avoid spooking the parrot outside. "Nice birdie," he growled through clenched teeth. "Yeah, come here you pretty birdie so I can wring your stinking mangy neck."

Pearl scuttled a few inches closer to the door as

he closed the gap between them. The feathers on the back of her head stood on end now and she glanced at the hallway.

"Don't even think about it," he warned caustically. "I've got enough problems already."

In response, the bird sang a line of an old song to him, "*I do love to be beside the sea-side*," and flapped out the door as he dove after her.

"Shit!" he cursed, scrambling to his feet.

The parrot had flown out an open window the end of the corridor and disappeared in the fog. "You stupid bird!" he called out into the dark night sky, sure that he heard it spit out another faint and far away "*wanker!*"

ৎত্ৰ্থ

Weary from the long walk to the beach, Brendan trudged through pebbly sand, watching the band as they scrambled to pack up the generator and electrical equipment. Another set of monstrous waves rolled in where the stage had been an hour earlier, greedily sucking up a mouthful of plastic chairs. Jumping back to avoid stepping in a trail of thick sea froth, he scanned the rocks concealing the cave. High tide on the island was formidable, he determined, watching as the plastic furniture was swallowed by the black and restless ocean.

"Can't – go – on…"

Brendan spun around the second he heard the ragged voice behind him. It was Salts, the old fisherman that the horny mob of spinsters had carried off and he was staggering across the sand like a hunted animal.

"Jesus!" Brendan gawked, staring at the bare-footed old geezer outfitted in little more than a pair of tattered boxer shorts and a beaten fishing cap that sat askew on his balding head. The fixed grin of a madman was plastered across his face, his skin stained with red and pink blotches of lipstick making him look like a leper.

"Run!" Salts wheezed, hobbling toward town. "Run for your bloody life, lad!"

Whirling around, Brendan expected to see a mob of women sniffing out the trail of footprints Salts had left behind, but he appeared to have escaped his captors undetected.

"Right," he nodded with a shudder as the old man lurched away, realizing that Julian's warnings about the women were to be taken literally. A dash of fear spiked through his gut, but he proceeded toward the cave anyway, unsure of what he was going to do next.

ೲ∾ೞ

On the count of three, just go. This is insane. What in the hell am I doing?

Clenching his fists in frustration, Brendan tried to muster up the balls - or the stupidity to slide down the side of the boulder and cross the beach to the opening of the isolated sea cave. He covered his ears as a deafening wave exploded across the sand below, inching toward the mouth of dimly lit hollow. She couldn't possibly still be in there, he rationalized, but the glow of flickering candlelight was just enough to make him wonder. No, he decided, turning back to face the village. He'd go back to the theater and wait on the steps until she came home.

If she came home.

What if she's fallen asleep? he asked himself, staring at the yellow luminescence on the side of the cave walls, noticing that the sand was damp right up to the edge of the cavern entrance. Just as he'd nearly talked himself out of it, he unmistakably heard her voice in the near vicinity.

"I hate you! Why did you have to come back here!"

Scanning the skies to ensure that the AWOL parrot wasn't playing tricks on him again, he knew that she was inside the cave and she could see him from wherever she was.

"No!" he hollered, shimmying down the side of the rocks, unable to leave her there. "Just stay where you are! I'm coming to get you out of there!"

Branding himself certifiably insane, he held his breath, counting down the seconds as another bone-crushing wave cascaded across the beach, then curled back in on itself.

Now!

Thudding to his knees in the slick sand, he hauled ass across the slushy ground, reaching the cave a split second before another set pulverized the beach in a blinding explosion of sea spume. He dove into the entrance as the powerful force sucked greedily at his ankles, dragging him back. Brendan managed to dig his fingers into the sand, pulling against it with his arms until he was miraculously released and free within the damp cavern. Allowing himself a victorious sigh, he closed his eyes for a moment, then cursed after realizing that it was going to be next to impossible to get back out again. With a mere eleven seconds between waves, then having to climb back up the rocks to safety, it had not only been a foolishly thought out plan, but a potentially deadly one. Willing himself to stay calm, he half expected to find Christine beaming back at him, her brave rescuer as he opened his eyes. But there he stood now, his expression falling as he peered around the dimly lit cavern and discovered that she wasn't even in there. And to add insult to injury, he saw the wet painting on the cave wall of himself devouring the lovely mermaid, the unflattering depiction doing little to improve his mood after he'd just risked his own life on her behalf. At the very least, she could have been in there for him to rescue, he thought miserably.

SMASH!

An immense surge of water exploded through the entrance of the cave, jarring him from behind and flattening him forward on his face. As he struggled to grasp onto something, anything, the salty spray snuffed out the dim candlelight flickering from the anchor chandelier above. With the breath knocked out of him, and surrounded by suffocating darkness, he felt the icy fingers of the water lifting and sucking his body backwards to a watery grave. Clawing and powerless against the extraordinary force, he was dragged along like a goldfish being sucked down a toilet bowl, tumbling and howling as the surf carried him off. "HELP!" he managed to scream out, seemingly to nobody, before another huge swell enveloped his body. As he battled against the freezing black water, it wasn't the unfinished book that he thought of now. It was that he was never going to see Christine again - and the fact that he was well on his way to join the other schmucks in the graveyard who'd fallen for her.

High above the cave on a knoll of tangled grass,

Christine glared at Charlie through red-rimmed eyes. At first she'd thought she was imagining things when she'd heard Brendan's voice, but she'd just heard it again and it sounded as if it was coming from the beach a hundred feet below.

Charlie, exhausted from struggling with her hadn't heard the faint cries and lay now with his arm loosely curled around her waist. Slowly, she lifted her head, craning her neck to see beyond the edge of the bluff.

Past the lighthouse, the rocks, and in the midst of the tumultuous swells, something small and far away was flailing in the choppy waters. She inhaled, suddenly bolting out from her brother's greedy hold. "Brendan!"

Cat like, Charlie instantly spotted the tiny figure and was on her again, whirling her around with a rough grip on her wrist.

"Hang on!" she hollered at Brendan over the edge of the cliff, her strained voice drowned out by the crashing waves.

Pulling herself out of Charlie's grasp, she made a dash toward the granite steps as he removed the cold steel weapon from his waistband.

"I wouldn't do that if I were you," he warned lethally, the end of his gun now trailing on Brendan's tiny head bobbing in the water. "I told you I'd kill him, Christine. Did you think that I was bluffing?"

She spun around, saw the ugly cold gun and swallowed hard. "You'll never be able to hit him at this range. Just put the gun away Charlie," she challenged, trying to buy herself a little time.

"Oh, I don't know about that. I'm a good shot," he reminded her, his finger tightening on the trigger.

"I'll never speak to you again if you fire that thing!" she spat, returning to his side as he followed Brendan with the barrel, ignoring her threat. Feeling a surge of panic well up from within, she knew that if she didn't act quickly, he would shoot him dead, for after seventy years of experience handling a gun, Charlie was an expert marksman. She moved forward to the edge of the cliff, blocking his aim with her chest. "I'll jump!" she warned, her entire body trembling, her heels inching toward the craggy edges. "I swear I'll do it Charlie if you don't drop the gun!"

The cloud cover parted, revealing a glittering slice of ethereal colored lights in the velvet sky as long tresses whipped wildly around her tear-streaked face.

"You'll be mangled on the rocks if you miss," he spat. "Now move aside!"

She stood her ground, the loose rocks beneath her feet tumbled over the bluff into the sea below. "I won't let him drown – and I won't stand by and watch you murder him Charlie! He's all I want! Can't you see that?"

By the fixed glare in her eyes, he knew that she wasn't lying. Not willing to risk losing her, he slowly lowered the pistol to his side, taking her delicate hand in his. "You mustn't go after him! The transformation will occur!"

"He'll drown!" she cried.

"And you will perish!" he reminded her. "I beg of you Christine! Don't condemn me to an eternity alone – or yourself to the life of a mortal!" he exploded, his fingers trembling with restrained fury. "This isn't what you want!"

In response, she wrenched her hands out of

his grasp, her expression defiant.

He whispered the one phrase he knew would pull her soul back to his, whispered it in the old language that would bind them together for all of time, "*tra ta'an ghrian ersooyl, cha vod ooilley ny cianleyn ayns y siehll jannoo soilshey yn laa...*"

"When the sun is gone," she gulped, "all the candles in the world cannot make daylight..."

"Come to me now," he beckoned.

With words caught in her throat, the ancient proverb had reached her heart and she wavered for a moment.

"Think about what you're about to sacrifice" he breathed vaporously, "a life of eternal beauty and wonder, to see the world three-hundred years from now, to absorb the knowledge of mankind - to live forever. It is a gift – Christine - and it is a curse. But we will keep searching for others of our kind. They are out there somewhere, I promise you. Don't throw our future away."

Torn between her brother's words and the man she loved, she glanced slightly at the sea then back at Charlie, knowing that she had to make the most important decision of her life right now. Illuminated by moonlight, tears spilled onto her cheeks as she stared into his dark eyes. "I want to live, Charlie," she uttered.

Smiling with gratitude that she'd made the right decision, he nodded. He was truly sorry for the loss she would have to endure, but it was for the best, and in time, she would grow to understand that. With sweeping arms, he reached forward to embrace his beloved. But just as their fingertips were about to touch, he noticed the look in her eyes, a haunted and empty hunger that he had known once, a very long time ago.

"But more than that - *I want to love,*" she whispered diving backwards over the edge of the cliffs.

"Noooooooo!" he screamed as her body sunk into the great void of blackness below.

As her figure cascaded toward the water and the rocks, the Northern Lights flared up with the blinding luminescence of all the stars in the heavens, bathing her form in a haze of effulgent glimmer, so brilliant that Charlie was knocked back to the ground, shielding his eyes from the blinding glare.

Twisting and turning in what seemed like an endless sea of energy, the scorching force felt as if it was searing her soul, stripping the very core of her being, the being that had been alive for nearly a century without ever having fallen in love. About to hit the water, she forced herself to pivot into a horizontal position and succeeded just seconds before plunging into the blackness.

The sea was freezing and rough, a new and unfamiliar phenomenon that she'd never imagined could be so painful. Gone was her tolerance for the cold, and the powerful strength to weather the waves. She could only think of her mother now, understanding how she had been taken by the sea.

Kicking toward the surface, she pleaded silently with the spirits that it wouldn't end like this - and she thought of Brendan flailing in the cove – praying that she wasn't too late to save him.

With a final bolt, the glowing energy that had enveloped her body shot through her torso in a single streak of white lightning, then dissipated into the ocean floor, leaving her alone in a sea of darkness.

She crashed to the top, gulping in breath after breath of cool air while spinning around in the choppy murk searching for some sign of him.

Muscles burning with pain, Brendan fought against the emerald crests, flailing wildly to keep himself afloat. Numb with cold, he'd witnessed the spectacular light show – and had felt the water vibrating with electricity as it hit the ocean floor, an event that had spooked him even more than the fact that he might not live to write about it.

Awestruck, Liam O'Leary had been watching the cove through a spyglass from his usual stone perch just above the lighthouse and had seen the brilliant lights that lit up the sky like the Chinese New Year. And he'd seen Christine jump from the cliffs, still not quite believing that he'd possibly witnessed an actual transformation. Not having a telephone in the cottage and being too distant from the fishing boat, he hobbled off toward the lighthouse tower as fast as his rickety legs would carry him.

Brendan emitted another cry, his throat raw and limbs weak from fighting off a fate he refused to accept. He gasped for air, for life itself, turning to look back at the fuzzy twinkling lights of the village he'd betrayed and thought that perhaps this was the way it was meant to end. Vision blurred from the stinging salt water, something beautiful suddenly filled his eyes - a woman in the water, her figure silhouetted beneath the glowing light of the moon. "Christine!" he called out impossibly as another great swell engulfed him.

She'd heard his voice and remained silent,

listening for another cry from the great vastness of water. And then a beacon of light swung across the bay, illuminating the pair for a moment, now just meters away from each other. She saw him out there - saw the haunted look of a dead man looming in his eyes. With his eerie gaze fixed on her beautiful face, he failed to shield his eyes from the beam of light as it swung across the water, the blast of white-hot brilliance, blinding him for a moment. Unable to see anything but large white spots, the turbulent current grabbed at his ankles, threatening to suck him under. He squinted, but his vision wasn't returning fast enough. He could hear her hollering now, but wasn't able to find her again. Spinning around in circles and dizzy from the motion, he was still unable to make out his surroundings. The outline of the lighthouse tower seemed to wave and bend as a wave of nausea rose in his gut. He opened his eyes again, spitting out a mouthful of salt water.

৵৽

Liam O'Leary was wheezing as he reached the top steps of the lighthouse. Quickly, he fished a key from his pocket and unlocked the door to the control room.

Although the lighthouse had been automated for over fifty years, requiring only weekly maintenance, Liam was the only man on the island who knew how to operate it manually in case of an emergency. The old man hunched over the control panel, flipping off the main switch. The beacon of bright light snapped off and the heavy machinery groaned to a halt. With a strenuous shove, he swung the giant spotlight to face the center of the cove and activated the main switch causing the beacon to hang steady, illuminating Christine. Liam signaled to her, flashing the light on and off, but Brendan had sunk beneath the surface before she could spot him.

Christine followed the movement of the beam where it stopped and stood still. And trusting the lighthouse operator, she dove behind a swell, plunging into the depths where she went to work groping around in the murk.

The powerful light spilled across the ocean floor, and with his vision returning now, Brendan could now make out the rocky bottom, littered with thousands of oysters. As the pain ached in his lungs, he realized that his own life had become one worth living, now that he'd found someone, someone who made him *feel*. He prayed that he would survive this. He vowed to change his ways – well, yeah, he thought. *I'll tone it down a bit,* he bargained.

And then she appeared before him, a fan of shocking red hair like fingers of coral. With his lungs burning, he blinked, sure that he saw her lower half encased in the silvery tail of a siren, his ears ringing with faint melodic singing, so ethereal he assumed that he must have drowned. But the hands tugging on his shoulders were real. He opened his eyes and saw her floating beside him, her form human once again. With an urgent glance, she pointed upward, taking his hand in hers and together, they moved toward the surface, swimming hard against the current toward the main beach.

Fatigued, the pair leaned on each other as they trudged through the surf, collapsing from exhaustion in the sand. The Northern Lights had faded to a mere remnant of gossamer in the sky, barely visible to the naked eye. Brendan turned his head slightly to face the woman by his side, stroking the slick hair away from her forehead. For several minutes, they lay in the sand panting, neither speaking a word.

"Did you see..." she finally began.

"A wise old woman once told me that it's more important to feel than it is to think," he said between ragged breaths, staring up at the sky.

Christine nodded, as a tear rolled down her cheek. "And you believed her?"

"I tried not to," he admitted wearily. "It's almost enough to make a guy like me 'stop walking' as you put it."

Her gaze uneasily shifted toward the black water of the cove. "Almost?"

"You have to leave the village. Right?"

She stared at him with unsettled green eyes. "Actually, I don't have to go anywhere..."

"But the locals..."

Tilting his chin up to face her, she ran her fingertips across his cheek. "The curse – it only lasts until we fall in love."

Awestruck, he was still for a moment, his mind trying to absorb everything that happened. "And you're willing to - sacrifice that?"

With a slight grin, she pointed down, his bleary eyes following her gaze. Gone were the hideous webs and scales on her feet. A set of perfectly normal toes wiggled back at him, evidence that the transformation had been made. Astonished, he stared back at her with wonderment.

"Just like a fairy tale," she whispered, "except for the happy ending part."

"What do you mean?" he questioned curiously, narrowing his eyes.

"Well," she smiled indicating the beach and the people that were starting to gather along the shore to discuss the disturbance with the Northern Lights, "this is no way to end a story."

Pressing a finger over her lips, he kissed her tenderly, not ever wanting to let her go. As they parted, her eyes searched his face. "You know, this could actually work out," he grinned, "I've always been attracted to older women. Did I ever tell you that?"

In the lighthouse tower, Liam O'Leary set down his spyglass that was trained on the couple. He smiled to himself, pleased with the outcome and reset the automation function of the light. "Send that one to your publisher, lad!" he tittered gleefully. Rising to his feet, he quietly blew out his oil lantern and locked up for the night.

From the grassy bluff above the caves, Charlie lay helplessly on his back, squeezing his eyes shut as the last ghostly glimmer of light dissipated from the dark sky, knowing now that Christine had transformed into a mortal. Alone and weeping, he cursed at the heavens, then turned his back on the ocean and ran away into the night.

൰ঌ

Pale, bluish moonlight spilt a silvery gleam over the dome of glass on the top floor of the Mermaid Theater where the quiet voices of two rose and fell from within.

Inside Christine's flat, the couple, stumbled across the floor through dim light, carelessly peeling off layers of wet garments between searing kisses as he carried her into the bedroom. A twinge of guilt stabbed at him as they passed by the empty bird-cage. "I –uh accidentally lost your parrot," he panted, tugging her blouse off.

"I don't care," she breathed, helping him out of his jeans.

The suspended boat bed rocked gently as he laid her down, soaking up the magical vision as she basked naked beneath a thousand hanging strands of glittering glass and pearls that caught the moon-light in a kaleidoscope of dancing colors. Her skin was fresh cream and ivory velvet, her hair thick and wet with the dampness of the sea, ropes of copper swirling around her perfect and flawless form. He stood before her now, nude and vulnerable, his entire body aching with desire. Trailing her fingers down his chest, she pulled him close and nipped at his lips, his mouth upon hers with mad and throb-bing hunger. Falling closer until he was on top of her, their slick flesh fused together with a surge of electricity. He wanted to savor her - and consume her all at the same time, so thoroughly, so completely that he feared there would be nothing left.

Nearly blind with need, she arched her back, ready to swallow him whole. If he were to have her now, he knew he'd never be the same again, for this woman, this phenomenon, was something beyond everything he had never dreamed of. "You sure you're not mad about the parrot thing?" he rushed.

"Shut up about the bird and make love to me," she whispered, her feverish fingers digging at his hips, guiding him deeper and deeper into her flesh into the secret place where he fell completely and totally beneath her intoxicating spell.

"Aw, god," he groaned, plunging into her body.

Limbs entwined, the pulsing waves of pleasure increased to maddening heights with every searing spike of indulgence. In the fevered dance, they rode upon swell after swell discovering each other, flesh and soul, entangled as one, each hopelessly lost in a sea of ecstasy - both knowing that they'd crossed the boundary beyond the point of return as bodies wound around one another like a Celtic knot, the dance picked up velocity, becoming frenzied and urgent, promising to release the torturous desires that had dammed up within them for all of their lives. Unable to hold it back any longer, he cried out with writhing pleasure, she shuddering violently with the unearthly climax, leaving them both exhausted and whole.

Entwined on a pile of blankets, Brendan wrapped his arms around her silky skin, lazily opening his eyes as cool moonlight flooded through the filmy curtains. "Am I dreaming?" he wondered aloud, gazing into her fathomless eyes.

"No," she smiled, curling into the hollow of his chest. "You really are in bed with an eighty-year-old mermaid."

"Oh, no," he teased. "You're not the vicious type are you? The kind that lures unsuspecting men into the sea and then rips them apart for kicks?"

With a mischievous grin, she curled a finger at him and smiled. "Come here and I'll show you."

Groaning with pleasure, he felt a second wind coming on.

In the wee hours of the night, Charlie found himself standing before the door of Claire's room on the top floor of the Mermaid Inn. Disoriented and delirious, he couldn't quite recall how he'd gotten there or how long he'd been roaming the streets.

The knock startled Claire from her restless slumber. Figuring it was one of the guests, she quickly threw on her white cotton robe and unlatched the door, aghast to find Charlie standing there, his eyes swollen with heartache, his clothes tattered and torn. She inhaled sharply at the sight of him as he stepped across the threshold of her bedroom. Without speaking a word, she embraced him in her arms, a gesture so pure and loving that it set him weeping again like a child. Eyes glistening with tears, he managed to smile at her as she closed the bedroom door.

CHAPTER TWENTY

As the gleaming light if dawn rose over the village, hazy sunlight spilled across the fields of heather and craggy shores, turning the early morning fog into pink tufts of candyfloss.

On this day, some would awaken to find themselves in the arms of soul mates, while others would arise with hangovers – or worse.

In his rumpled and still damp clothing from the night before, Brendan stood in the stairwell of Christine's building, promising himself that this would be the last time that he kissed her. "Christine," he panted breathlessly, growing intoxicated with the honeyed taste of her lips, "I really need to go now."

"Can't you just stay a little longer?" she teased, sliding slender fingers beneath the edge of his shirt, sending a spike of electricity down his spine.

As much as he regretted leaving her now, there wasn't any other option. "I really can't. I promised my editor..." he began, his voice trailing off for a moment. "Look, let's meet at the beach a little later. Around three. We have some things to talk about. Gotta go."

With that, he pulled away, his tall frame disappearing into the swirling pink fog that cloaked the pier. Standing in the doorway, she sighed miserably, realizing she'd just made the greatest mistake of her life.

Claire stood by the window in her room next to the rumpled, unmade bed. A white sheet was wrapped around her shoulders and her cheeks had a youthful glow to them. Her eyes followed Charlie as he walked down the front path away from the Inn - where he'd spent the night in her bed. Looking up, he spotted her in the window, and blew her a kiss.

Pulling the curtain shut, she stood and faced her wilted reflection in the vanity mirror. "Ah, the first one is always the best," she grinned. "He'll be back again old mum. Someday..."

ॐ

By ten o'clock that morning, Brendan was still hunched over the laptop computer in the kitchenette, adding the finishing touches to the manuscript. He'd worked straight through the morning, his weary eyes now scanning over the last page of the book, his hands beginning to tremble with anticipation. *God, it was brilliant*, he thought, beholding the last paragraph in his gaze before sending the document off to New York by e-mail.

ॐ

Christine's sheer white halter dress billowed in the breeze as she stood before the granite mermaid monument in the village's cemetery. Removing a clog from her foot, she placed her bare foot in the soft ground below the statue, leaving an imprint of her human foot in the mud. With stormy green eyes, she blinked back the tears and set a bouquet of lavender at the base, then ran away.

༄ ༺

Michael Blake was sweeping up the shattered shrine paraphernalia from the floor of The Siren's Whale when the front door opened. Charlie walked inside, his eyes concealed by a pair of sunglasses to hide the black eye and scrapes he'd earned the night before.

"Jesus man! Look what the cat dragged in!" Michael gawked, setting the broom and dustpan aside. "You up for a pint this early?"

"No," he said quietly. "I stopped in to say goodbye."

"Lucky you," Michael huffed with envy. "Wish I was going somewhere."

"No luck last night?" Charlie inquired, sliding into a stool.

"Och!" he snorted miserably. "Even if I had a bloody horseshoe up me nose and four leafed clovers shooting out of me arse, I still wouldn't have any luck man. The girls hate me."

With a slight smile, Charlie reached into his coat and removed a small, worn leather book. "Here," he said, handing it to Michael. "I brought you something. A little parting gift."

"What's this?" he asked, inspecting the cover.

"I want you to have it," Charlie told him. "I know it all by heart. It's what I use when I, you know, with the women. Just take it."

"No shite?!" Michael gushed.

Charlie spun around on the bar stool, rose and moved toward the door without turning back. "See you around, my friend."

"Yeah mate! Cheers!" Astonished, he watched Charlie the Tuna disappear into the sunlight that streaked through the door of the pub, then eagerly flipped through the handwritten pages of the small volume, unable to imagine what this was all about. As he squinted to make out the scrawled words, his expression turned sour the moment he realized what he was looking at. "You've got to be having me on," he scowled. "Bloody *poetry*?"

With a dejected sigh, he heaved his bulk into a chair and dramatically read a verse of the poem Lorelei aloud.

> 'High yonder in wondrous seeming,
> reclines a mermaid fair.
> Her golden jewels are gleaming,
> and she combs her golden hair.
> A comb of gold is she plying,
> and warbles a wondrous song,
> that a thrilling melody sighing,
> floats like a spell along.'

"Mmmmm. Please," said a female voice. "Go on. Its - spellbinding."

Looking up in surprise, Michael saw a silhouette draped across the doorway of the pub, her slender, curvaceous figure outlined in the morning sunshine. Astonished, he squinted to make out her face, but the orange light was glaring back in his eyes. Gravitating toward him, the woman's high heels clicked across the wooden floor. And as the door closed behind her, Michael realized this wasn't just any woman – this was the woman of his bloody dreams.

Fiona Cross lifted her tortoise shell sunglasses, being careful not to disturb the thick white bandages on her nose, and shot a dazzling smile his way.

A huge, bashful grin spread across Michael's face as he returned to his place in the book. "Now where was I? Ah, yes, here we are..."

With an uncorked bottle of champagne standing by on the edge of his desk, Jake Hogan snatched up the last chapter of <u>Misadventures and Merfolk</u>, twittering with delight as he settled into his chair to read the conclusion of what was sure to be the next national best-seller.

With the laptop case slung over one shoulder and his carry-on duffel bag over the other, Brendan quietly let himself through the gate of the Mermaid Inn and turned onto the cobblestones of High Street. In his black leather jacket, he blended in among the tourists, most of them frantically flocking to the ferryboat station that had reopened just yesterday after the arrival of a brand new fifty-passenger vessel.

With the crush of chattering guests checking out of the hotel, Claire hadn't noticed Brendan when he'd slipped inside the lobby and dropped the key to her houseboat behind the counter in a small, unmarked envelope.

Checking his watch now, he figured he had enough time for some quick browsing around the shops. He adjusted the strap of his heavy luggage, containing everything he'd arrived on the island with, and set off down the street.

From a mile out at sea, the sails of Charlie's teak yacht billowed in the breeze as he maneuvered the craft away from the shoreline of Heather Bay. With his webbed feet planted firmly on the rough surface of the deck, he turned the wooden wheel toward the open sea without looking back. And as the boat disappeared into the orange glare of the sun, skimming effortlessly across the water, the name painted across the back of the boat glimmered in the sunlight,
Claire.

ɕɕ⤫ɕ

Christine's heart was heavy with anxiety as she sat shivering on the rocky beach, her knees curled up under a wool tartan blanket. Her eyes darted across the dismal landscape, searching for some sign of him. It was ten minutes past three o'clock and she feared that her suspicions were about to be confirmed. After Claire's urgent phone call about the houseboat key he'd returned this morning, Christine's hopes and dreams had sunk right out the bottom. So in honor of the occasion, the final goodbye, she'd brought something for him, a small bouquet of lavender with a note, identical the ones she always left in the cemetery for her long dead lovers. If he were going to leave now, after everything they'd weathered, after the most exhilarating and pure lovemaking she'd ever experienced - *after all she'd sacrificed for him,* she was going to make damn sure that Brendan James would never forget her face when he stepped on that ferry back to Dublin. That is, if he had the knackers to show up and face her one last time.

Ten minutes passed and then he appeared, his

tall lanky frame sauntering across the sand toward her, his boots crunching across the pebbles - with his luggage in tow.

"Nice of you to come," she said quietly without looking up. "The flowers," she indicated with her chin, "I brought them for you."

Curiously, Brendan picked up the bouquet, inspected it, then set it back down in the sand. "Interesting choice," he said, crouching down beside her. "But I'm not dead yet."

"Yet," she mimicked under her breath. Her eyes flicked up to meet his for a brief moment, then returned to the sand. And what in the hell was he grinning about? she thought bitterly.

"I brought you something too," he offered, removing a small boutique shopping bag from the inside of his coat. "Here."

Confused, she snatched the parcel from his hands, felt the weight, and couldn't imagine what he was up to. Were break-up gifts customary in Los Angeles? she wondered.

When she didn't immediately open the package, he took it away from her and removed the paper himself. Wrapped in tissue, he unrolled a pair of delicate white sandals, the leather straps studded with glittering rhinestones.

Uncertain of his intentions, she stared at the pair of shoes that he'd chosen for her. "Now that you've got feet," he began, sliding the sandals over her toes, "and now that I've, as you put it, *stopped walking*, I thought that these would be appropriate."

Taken aback by the beautiful shoes glistening on her feet, she turned to meet his gaze as he buckled the tiny strap around her ankle. Her eyes shifted to his luggage. "But I thought you were..."

Taking her face in his hands, he whispered gently, "when the sun has gone out, all the candles in the world cannot make daylight." His insides melted as he watched the tears forming in her wide green eyes. "Besides, I can't live in Claire's houseboat forever."

"So, you're staying – here? In the village," she sniffled.

"Yeah. Is that bad news or something?" he teased, wiping a teardrop from her cheek.

"But – your book," she breathed.

"Yeah, the book," he sighed, settling down on the sand next to her. "We definitely need to talk about that."

Before she could ask him how in the bloody hell he was going to handle the situation, his cell phone rang. He waved a hand to silence her, then answered it to her great annoyance. "Jake, what's up buddy? You get my e-mail?"

Blood throbbing in his head, Jake Hogan gripped the phone in his hand so tightly that his knuckles turned white. "Brendan! What in the hell is this shit you sent me!" he exploded. "This is not the time for practical jokes! We're down to the wire on the deadline and you've sent me this fucking fairy crap fiction!"

Holding the phone away from his ear, Brendan stood and walked toward the ocean a few paces. "It's the truth Jake," he whispered. "Every word."

Jake shook the stack of manuscript pages he'd just read, flinging them across the office in a flutter of white confetti. "I want the goddamn last chapter rewritten! Do you hear what I'm saying! You've got less that twenty-four hours to make this happen or we're talking breach of contract! Think about that!"

Brendan turned back to Christine as Jake's voice sputtered out another string of vile curses.

And he thought about it.

"Sometimes you've just got to see it to believe it," Brendan laughed into the receiver, hurling his cell phone into the ocean.

Shrugging his shoulders he turned to Christine with a grin.

Aghast at his behavior, she rose to her feet, unsteady in the awkward heeled sandals. "You!" she accused with a finger pointed at his face. "You actually - sent them the book!? You wrote about what happened last night!"

"Yeah," he confessed, pulling her close to him. "Every damn detail."

"What!"

"And no one's ever gonna believe it," he laughed.

"You bastard," she whispered, the corners of her lips cracking into a smile. "You brilliant, *stupid bastard*," she howled, tossing her head back with laughter.

"Thank you very much," he bowed.

Taking her face in his hands, he pressed his mouth against hers and they sunk down to the outspread tartan blanket, kissing each other for what seemed like - an eternity.

හ☾ඏ

EPILOGUE

ONE YEAR LATER:

Brendan and Christine strolled down High Street together, with arms entwined, each wearing a gleaming band of gold on the ring finger. Christine's hair hung loose around her radiant face, as she tugged at the sleeve of Brendan's tweed sport coat upon approaching Merfolk Books. Setting his large wicker shopping basket down, the couple stared at the front display window where a cardboard cutout of his face peered back at them, positioned before a monstrous stack of, <u>Misadventures & Merfolk</u>, a novel by Brendan James, and a number-one New York Times best-seller.

Brendan grinned as the jolly shop proprietor waved cheerfully in their direction. "How's your next book shaping up Brendan?" she hollered.

"Almost finished," he smiled proudly. "Almost finished."

"And hello Mrs. James!" she waved to Christine. "Have a lovely afternoon you two."

"We will," Christine grinned, squeezing Brendan's hand in hers. "We will."

From far off, above the rooftops of the village, a whoosh of feathers rustled by and Brendan could have sworn he heard a far off voice squawking out, "wanker!"

₭ੲ

Kelly Reno lives in Los Angeles, California. She is the author of 10 previous books.